Éilís Ní Dhuibhne was born in Dublin. She was educated at University College Dublin and has a BA in English and a PhD in Irish Folklore. She worked for many years as a librarian and archivist in the National Library of Ireland and has taught Creative Writing at Trinity College Dublin, University College Dublin, and Boston College, as well as the Irish Writers' Centre, The Faber Academy, and other institutions. The author of more than thirty books, including a memoir, six collections of short stories, several novels, children's books, plays and many scholarly articles and literary reviews, her work includes *The Dancers Dancing, Little Red and Other Stories, Fox, Swallow, Scarecrow* and *Twelve Thousand Days*. She has been the recipient of many literary awards, among them the Stewart Parker Prize for Drama, the Butler Award for Prose, three Bisto awards for her children's books, several Oireachtas awards for novels in Irish, the PEN Award for Outstanding contribution to Irish Literature, and a Hennessy Hall of Fame Award. Her novel, *The Dancers Dancing* (Blackstaff, 1999; new edition 2007), was shortlisted for the Orange Prize for Fiction and her memoir *Twelve Thousand Days* was shortlisted for the Michel Déon Prize for Non-Fiction. One of Ireland's most important short story writers, Ní Dhuibhne's stories have appeared in many anthologies and have been widely translated. She is a member of Aosdána, an ambassador for the Irish Writers' Centre and President of the Folklore of Ireland Society.

Selected
Stories

ÉILÍS NÍ DHUIBHNE

·THE·
BLACK
·STAFF·
PRESS

First published in 2023 by Blackstaff Press
an imprint of Colourpoint Creative Ltd
Colourpoint House
Jubilee Business Park
21 Jubilee Road
Newtownards BT23 4YH

With the assistance of the Arts Council of Northern Ireland

Printed by Clays Ltd, Elcograf S.p.A.

A CIP catalogue record for this book is available from the British Library

PB ISBN 978 1 78073 369 2
EPUB ISBN 978 1 78073 370 8

www.blackstaffpress.com

To all my wonderful editors,
especially Patsy Horton

Contents

Foreword

'It is precarious and delicate, our dull and ordinary happiness.'
                                                    'The Banana Boat'

This collection of fourteen stories represents more than four decades of Éilís Ní Dhuibhne's published work, from her early stories 'The Postmen's Strike' and 'Blood and Water' which appeared in the Attic Press collection *Blood and Water* (1988), to 'Little Red', the title story of her collection *Little Red and Other Stories* (2020), published by her long-term publishing partner, Blackstaff Press. Readers returning to Ní Dhuibhne's writing will remember the delight of first encountering her stories, with their incisiveness and wry humour, and discovering her keen eye for the incongruous and the familiar made strange. To those of you meeting her work for the first time, a special welcome; many pleasures are in store from this master storyteller and skilled author of that apparently, and deceptively, simple literary form, the short story.

Throughout her long and varied writing career, Éilís Ní Dhuibhne's work shows the influence of her earliest profession as folklorist. Recalling her travels to rural and urban areas as collector of stories, she has remarked on the particular fragility of the oral story and folk tale, observing, 'It is a complex work of art that is carried in the human memory by the human voice, received by human ears.' Reflecting on what might be the best or most apt metaphor for these 'migratory stories', she concludes that 'they are most like lights … All good stories are flashes of light, stars of knowledge.'[1] In many of the short stories featured here, older tales provide perceptible guiding lights – for example, the European fairy tale of Little Red Riding Hood, the medieval tale of Chaucer's Wife of Bath, a German folk ballad of a young man's heartbreak, or the Scottish and Irish stories of the Big Bodach. These are tales to be retold and reimagined, preserved and adapted, repeated and remade. To quote again from Ní Dhuibhne on storytelling, 'I counterpoint my own stories set in the now, with oral stories, set in the past, or, more accurately, set in the never never or the always always.'[2]

Early stories such as 'Blood and Water' and 'The Flowering' are fine examples of Ní Dhuibhne's interest in the complexity of heredity and descent, where she reveals the difficult and sometimes painful consequences of our genealogical searches. As the narrator of 'Blood and Water' experiences in the story's close, 'I find the facts running away

1 Éilís Ní Dhuibhne, 'Stories Like the Light of Stars' (2011), quoted in Giovanna Tallone, '"Stories Like the Light of Stars": Folklore and Narrative Strategies in the Fiction of Éilís Ní Dhuibhne', *Estudios Irlandeses: Journal of Irish Studies* [Online], 12.2 (2017): 154–166, 156.
2 Éilís Ní Dhuibhne, 'Negotiating the Boundaries. An interview with Éilís Ní Dhuibhne', interviewed by Christine St Peter, *The Canadian Journal of Irish Studies*. 32. 1 (Spring 2006): 68–75, 70.

from me, like sticks escaping downstream on the current' (p.14). This story unfolds by means of a child's sharp eye for family history – 'Greetings over, we would troop into the house, under a low portal apparently designed for a smaller race of people' (p.3) – and continues through the potent adolescent attitudes of embarrassment and repulsion. This teen disgust is memorably caused by discovering 'a big splodge of a dirty, yellow substance, unlike anything I had encountered' (p.6). Later as an adult she realises, with the benefit of a course in ethnology, that 'the stuff was only butter daubed on the wall after every churning for luck' (p.6); but this revelation doesn't succeed in removing that early disgust nor in absolving the lingering shame: 'And more often than that, much more often, I feel in my mind a splodge of something that won't let any knowledge sink in. A block of some terrible substance, soft and thick and opaque. Like butter.' (p.14).

The author's own experience as a child raised in Dublin, who spent summers with relatives in the Gaeltacht (Irish-speaking region) in Donegal, and who spoke both Irish and English at home, deeply informs these ancestral stories. Many of her stories' central characters occupy a liminal position, on the threshold between worlds. The girl in 'Blood and Water' – a character who reappears in Ní Dhuibhne's 1999 novel, *The Dancers Dancing*, as the protagonist, Orla – remembers her time in the Gaeltacht thus: 'On the one hand, I was the child of a native, almost a native myself in fact. On the other hand, I was a "scholar" – one of the kids from Dublin who descended on Ballytra in July, like a shower of fireworks, acting as if they owned the place, more or less shunning the native population' (p.11).

Another instance of such liminality appears in the character of Lennie from 'The Flowering': 'In her own lifetime – she is in her thirties, neither young nor old – real life has entered the museum and turned into history' (p.37). The source of this story comes from Elizabeth Boyle's history *The Irish Flowerers* published by the Ulster Folk Museum in 1971. Lennie's discovery – or is it invention? – of the life of her ancestor Sally Rua is absorbing and disturbing. We read of how a woman's creativity, in this case Sally Rua's love of crochet, leads her 'to go mad'. What Lennie finds is 'enough to drive you crazy. Archaeology, history, folklore. Linguistics, genealogy. They tell you about society, not about individuals. It takes literature to do that' (p.39). And what place can be occupied by the oral tradition of past ancestors? Lennie's first response is not encouraging: 'What oral tradition? It went away, with their language, when the schools started. Slowly they are becoming articulate in the new language. Slowly they are finding a new tradition. They are inventing a new tradition. Transform, adapt, or disappear' (p.39). Survival and creativity prove crucially interlinked. In an interview with social anthropologist Helena Wulff, Ní Dhuibhne underscores her aim in this story 'to convey an urgent message that women writers who have found fulfilment in writing should be given every opportunity to write. If their inner drive to write is thwarted, their lives will be thwarted also.'[3] Commenting on 'The Flowering' as a literary classic, Gerardine Meaney has observed that it is one 'that will be in the anthologies (if they still do them) a few centuries hence.'

Histories, or more precisely her stories, of migration are powerfully retold in 'Gweedore Girl' and 'The Pale Gold of

---

3 Helena Wulff, '"Ethnograficition": Irish Relations in the Writing of Éilís Ní Dhuibhne', in Rebecca Pelan (ed.), *Éilís Ní Dhuibhne: Perspectives* (Galway: Arlen House, 2009), p.254. See also Helena Wulff, *Rhythms of Writing: An Anthropology of Irish Literature* (London: Bloomsbury, 2017).

Alaska'. In her new situation as a domestic servant in Derry, the girl from Gweedore feels 'completely lost and very tiny, like a little spider or a fly. But I was still myself. I was myself, only smaller' (p.71). The emigrant fate of Sophie, moving from Donegal to New York and Philadelphia to the gold fields of Missoula, Montana and the Klondike, represents one of Ní Dhuibhne's most poignant chronicles. The love affair between an Irishwoman and North Wind, a Native American man, is briefly and heartrendingly told, as in this short passage, with its subtle echoes of the Irish ballad 'Dónal Óg': 'She could no longer weigh up one choice against another and see, quickly, which was the best. North Wind had skewed her power to do that, had taken away her ability to distinguish black from white, silver from gold, bad from good, good from better' (p.150). While Irish is the language used with her husband Ned, Sophie learns from North Wind a new vocabulary: 'The names of the months. The month of the melting snow. The month of the greening grass. The month of the rutting stag. He told her about the animals in the mountains: the great brown bears, the thin mountain lions' (p.147).

Very often, the emotional power of Ní Dhuibhne's writing comes from the gap between the matter-of-fact tone of what is said and the depths of what is hinted beneath. The closing lines of 'The Pale Gold of Alaska' offer a good example: 'It was generally thought, among the Irishmen, pious or secular, sensible or wild, who were hitting gold with Ned, that Sophie's ordeal in Missoula at the hands of the Indians had affected her brain, and that she was not quite right in the head' (p.157). A later story, 'The Coast of Wales', has too many instances to name, as demonstrated by this one short illustration: 'There's something new to learn every time I come here' (p.298); and another longer one, 'I used to hate the sight of a hearse. My heart would sink if I met one on the road. But I no longer fear them now that I've met death face to face, tried to shoo it away, and lost the battle. Now I can cast a cold eye on every hearse that passes by, because I've driven behind yours' (p.305). Such technique is usefully summarised by Raymond Carver, himself a great practitioner of the short story: 'What creates tension in a piece of fiction is partly the way the concrete words are linked together to make up the visible action of the story. But it's also the things that are left out, that are implied, the landscape just under the smooth (but sometimes broken and unsettled) surface of things.'[4]

Carver has also noted the value of a feeling of threat or sense of menace in a short story; as he pithily wrote, 'For one thing, it's good for the circulation.'[5] The creation of tension, suspense or a sense of threat is certainly one of Ní Dhuibhne's narrative achievements, characterising stories from the dystopian 'The Postmen's Strike' to the dating adventures in 'Little Red'. This is all the more impressive given that her stories often begin with deceptively ordinary or everyday settings or events. 'The Banana Boat' is a heart-stopping story which starts with the mundane details of any family holiday, succinctly rendered: 'One thing was clear: this would be one of our last holidays as a family. Next year they would probably refuse to come with us … Veteran of family holidays, I just switch off my ears and concentrate on the road' (p.160). Before the story finishes, 'two ends to the story of my day and the story of my life' (p.176) are contemplated (a metafictional nod to Mary Lavin who, along with Canadian writer Alice Munro, is referenced in

---

4 Raymond Carver, 'On Writing', *Fires: Essays, Poems, Stories* (New York: Vintage Books, 1989), p.26.
5 Ibid., p.26.

the story; both have been formative influences). By its end, both narrator and reader have imagined the unimaginable in terms of tragedy and loss.

How the everyday can change, forever, is rendered by Ní Dhuibhne in lines of quiet precision:

> One moment a family is cocooned in the happiness, or whatever, of normal life. The next it is elsewhere, in another land or another ocean. It happens in a few moments.
>
> Those are the few moments I am in, the liminal time between ordinariness and tragedy (also of an ordinary kind; to others it will be so, ordinary and instantly forgettable. While for me it will be the tragedy – the raw edge of the unimaginably terrible. Parents never get over it. I have seen it. I have heard it. I know it) …
>
> It is precarious and delicate, our dull and ordinary happiness, seeming sturdy as a well-built house but as fluttering and light as a butterfly on a waving clump of clover. As ephemeral as that; as beautiful and priceless. (p.178, p.181)

'The art of the glimpse' is William Trevor's well-known summary of the short story, a phrase recorded in a 1989 interview conducted by the *Paris Review*. In that conversation, Trevor attributed the strength of the short story to 'what it leaves out just as much as what it puts in, if not more'.[6] Another much-cited observation about the Irish short story was offered by Frank O'Connor who suggested that the short story captures 'at its most characteristic, something we do not often find in the novel – an intense

---

6 William Trevor, 'The Art of Fiction no. 108', interviewed by Mira Stout, *Paris Review*, vol. 31, issue 110 (Spring 1989), 119-151, 135-6.

awareness of human loneliness.'[7] Responding to this, in her introduction to the *Granta Book of the Irish Short Story*, Anne Enright has written: 'Are all short stories, Russian, French, American and Irish, in fact about loneliness? I am not sure … Connection and the lack of it are one of the great themes of the short story, but social factors change… the most I have ever managed to say about the short story is that it is about change.'[8]

That seemingly simple word, 'change', is especially accurate as an insight into Ní Dhuibhne's preoccupations as a short-story writer, such as the changes resulting from emigration, or ageing, or simply from falling in love – which, as the narrator of 'Bikes I Have Lost' reminds us, is 'not like learning to ride a bicycle. It's more like falling off one' (p.282). Some result from historical catastrophe: the sinking of the *Estonia* ferry in September 1994, en route from Tallinn to Stockholm, with the loss of 852 lives is the subject of the story 'Estonia'. In her most recent stories, the life-altering subject of bereavement comes to the fore, with the emotional landscape of loss and grief finely evoked in the stories 'The Coast of Wales', and 'New Zealand Flax'. Yet the subject of loss is central to many earlier stories also, including the two long stories 'The Moon Shines Clear, the Horseman's Here' and 'Bikes I Have Lost' (both from Ní Dhuibhne's 2012 collection, *The Shelter of Neighbours*).

'The Coast of Wales', first published in the *Long Gaze Back* anthology, edited by Sinéad Gleeson, and written in the aftermath of the death of Bo Almqvist – the Swedish folklorist and husband of Éilís – in November 2013 is a

7 Frank O'Connor, *The Lonely Voice: A Study of the Short Story* (London: Macmillan, 1963), p.19.
8 Anne Enright (ed.), *The Granta Book of the Irish Short Story* (London: Granta, 2011), p.xv.

masterpiece in quiet emotion, devastatingly rendered. (Her later memoir, *Twelve Thousand Days*, published by Blackstaff Press in 2018, recounts the history of their thirty-year relationship from its beginning to its shocking end.) The stories in this collection provide many 'flashes of light' into bereavement; ones further illuminated through wryly rendered insights. In 'The Coast of Wales', there's always 'something new to learn' in a Dublin graveyard, by a widow, 'to use that word all widows I have met – they're all over the place – can't stand' (p.298, p.302). In 'New Zealand Flax', the grief-tinged lines between dream and reality, between imagination and 'the real thing', are so blurred that recollecting the past and reliving it as the present become one:

> 'Make the most of the time you have left. It will be over soon enough. There's plenty of work to do.' He winks. 'You can do mine, if you don't want to do your own.'
> 'Yes,' she says. 'I will.'
> He always gives good advice. (p.319)

If the short story is 'an arrow in flight towards its target' (p.195) – a line from Mary Lavin recalled by Francie Briody, a character in Ní Dhuibhne's wickedly funny 'Literary Lunch' – then reader beware! In 'The Postmen's Strike', she minutely and hilariously imagines a New Ireland, and with some palpable hits: Irish, in this alternative future, is feared as 'a pagan language, with anarchic undertones in every aspiration. It's been unofficially banned since 1984' (p.23). In this future, 'Irish researchers are now the experts on Ireland, incredible though this may seem' with alarming results (p.24): 'Everything must be said and written in Hiberno-English. That is the law' (p.27). The title character of another history-defying fable, The Wife of Bath, now a bar maid in Limpley Stoke, provides the narrator with a feisty update, including her dislike of the 'husband mad' Jane Austen, before dissolving into paper (p.57, p.65). Even Ní Dhuibhne's short lines can make you laugh out loud. These are some personal favourites: the dating exploits of Fiona in 'Little Red', which include meeting men 'in the 63–72 dating age group' who tick 'maybe in the future' beside the little pram symbol (p.326); or the description of Alan, the chairman in 'A Literary Lunch': 'People who liked him said he was charismatic' (p.183).

To finish, one more quotation from Raymond Carver illuminates the artistry of these stories: 'It's possible, in a poem or a short story, to write about commonplace things and objects using commonplace but precise language, and to endow those things – a chair, a window curtain, a fork, a stone, a woman's earring – with immense, even startling power. It is possible to write a line of seemingly innocuous dialogue and have it send a chill along the reader's spine.'[9] Ní Dhuibhne's skills as a writer can transform a 'splodge of butter', a coat made of sealskin, a two-wheeler bicycle, Christmas coloured lights going on 'in the deep dark winter valley' (p.235), or the 'flower-studded ditches' of her beloved West Kerry: 'purple selfheal, blue sheep's bit, everywhere the brilliant yellow of dandelion and buttercup' (p.158). Infused by her training as a collector of folklore, many of her lines of dialogue have a spine-chilling power. These are just some illustrations, that range from a child's terror and adolescent regret to an older woman's terrified excitement:

---

9 Carver, 'On Writing', p.24.

'"We don't like to use the strap, Helen," she said' (p.267); '"He was in an accident," she said. "Just a few days ago. It was in the paper."' (p.292); 'You're probably wondering how I got your address? ... A little bit of detective work' (pp.330–1). Other lines from her stories are, thankfully, heart-delighting: 'Emily closed her eyes and listened to her heart being happy' (p.112).

For my own ending here, and before the stories begin, I return to Éilis Ní Dhuibhne's comments on 'migratory stories':

> All good stories are flashes of light, stars of knowledge. They are the light in the eyes of a storyteller and of those who love stories, the creative spirit that does not go out as long as people want to be entertained and know how to entertain themselves by weaving words and memories and ideas into interesting patterns.[10]

The concluding episode in 'The Moon Shines Clear, the Horseman's Here' shows these words in practice, in the exchange of stories between Muriel and Polly. Muriel is the mother of a dead boy, Paddy; Polly is his childhood bus-mate, his girlfriend and the mother of Paddy's son, Conor, of whose existence Muriel learns for the first time. Thirty years ago Paddy died by drowning but the local story of his death is 'made up, a sham. Fiction' (p.237), a tale composed by the owner of the boat to protect his culpable son. In Muriel's telling and retelling of his death, Paddy has been 'transmogrified into a hero: a brave, strongly drawn character in a story that she has half-remembered, half-invented' (p.237). In contrast, Polly's

---

10 Ní Dhuibhne, 'Stories Like the Lights of Stars', 156.

story of Paddy is 'a fresh story, it is the first time she has told it to anyone, and so her tale is not polished, not as well paced, not as neatly composed as Muriel's' (p.237). Even in beginning, Polly has to decide how and where to start: 'She decides, or memory decides, or Muriel, or the pressures of the moment, the pressure to relate, the pressure to sympathise, the pressure to attract compassion, the pressure to confess, the pressure to create, what to leave in, what to exclude' (pp.237–8). But she does tell her story, and she finishes it. Muriel serves as 'the perfect audience' and 'the story is shaped by her listening as much as by Polly's telling: Paddy's story belongs to the two of them' (p.238). When the story ends,

> Muriel and Polly sit in silence. The coloured lights on the fuchsia bush twinkle against the black sea and the black mountain and the black sky. They sit in silence. They let the story settle. And for minutes it is as if he is here again, on this earth. Alive, seventeen. He is not on the pier or in the park or on the mountainside but on the bus. He is sitting on the bus, silently staring out the window, motionless as a seagull on a rock, lost in a boy's dream. (p.238)

Finally and fittingly, it is worth noting that Ní Dhuibhne is a master composer of story endings. In the words of Joyce Carol Oates, when a short story ends, 'the attentive reader understands why'.[11] Many of the conclusions to these stories are puzzling and, in some instances, we are given a choice of endings, to make our own. The final lines of the last story 'Little Red' offer a magnificent case in point:

---

11 Joyce Carol Oates (ed.), *The Oxford Book of American Short Stories* (Oxford: Oxford University Press, 2013), 5.

What was the point? Where was the story? Who had put such ideas into Ellie's head? That's what Fiona thought. It is not a proper story. No tension. No fear. No loss. No relief.

The key thing is missing.

But Ellie had nodded, apparently perfectly satisfied with what she had heard. (p.337)

I warmly recommend leisurely readings, and rereadings, of these perfect and properly improper stories; may the reading journey bring you to others of her writings, and warm congratulations to Blackstaff Press on this very satisfying collection.

Margaret Kelleher
Professor of Anglo-Irish Literature and Drama,
University College Dublin

Introduction

My first short story, 'Green Fuse', was published by that great figure in Irish literary history, David Marcus, in 'New Irish Writing' in the *Irish Press* in 1974. It was hardly a story at all, rather a description of one day in the life of a lovelorn teenager. (Somebody, complimenting my mother on the publication, said, 'I liked Éilís's essay in the paper,' to my huge annoyance. *Essay?* But, he had a point). I am grateful to David Marcus for publishing it and continuing to take more stories from me over the next ten years or so – a decade during which I was figuring out how to shape raw material drawn from memory, experience, or imagination – often, from a combination of these – into a narrative that cohered into a proper *story*. I think the last one David Marcus published for me in the newspaper was 'Blood and Water', in 1983, the story with which this selection opens. At that point, I felt I was finding my voice, or one of them, and had learnt a few tricks of the trade.

Since 1974, I have written around eighty short stories (a respectable oeuvre, one might think – although Chekhov, who died aged forty-four, wrote about five hundred!). It wasn't easy to select fourteen, but with a lot of help from Patsy Horton, my editor at Blackstaff Press for the past twenty-odd years, the task was managed. We bore some practical issues in mind – some stories tend to get anthologised regularly, so we left those out. Otherwise, it was a matter of going through the collections and picking out the ones I liked best or thought most representative. If Patsy agreed, they got in.

Mainly the arrangement is chronological, in order of publication. An exception is 'Blood and Water', which we placed ahead of the earlier 'The Postmen's Strike' (1979), included really as an example of a youthful satirical voice not entirely dormant, as some later tales, for example, 'A Literary Lunch', indicate. 'Blood and Water' is more representative of the style of story I began to write from the 1980s. During that decade I came across Alice Munro's work for the first time – by accident; she was not well known in Ireland then. I was stunned by her skill in dealing with some of the sort of material I wanted to write about then: childhood memories, women's lives. I had tried writing about Donegal before, but my stories (discarded) emerged as dated, clichéd. Alice Munro, in stories like 'Chaddeleys and Flemings', demonstrated a way of writing about the past that was not *of the past*, but reads as an honest contemporary voice.

From then on, I paid much more attention to the way I shaped a story and read more systematically as a writer (which in no way detracts from ordinary reading pleasure). From Chekhov, one can learn description and character; from Joyce, the trick of the epiphany; from Katherine Mansfield, the power of light and shade – of what is often called 'luminosity'; from McGahern, good dialogue. But from Alice Munro one can learn all these things, and more, especially how to handle complex time structures, how to make a large spacious story that is as full of meaning and effect and suggestions as a novel.

Another important influence on my writing was my discovery of cultural feminism in the 1980s. Possibly because of my positive experience with David Marcus, and because I belonged to the first generation of Irishwomen who expected to have careers even if they married and had children, I had not understood that women had suffered marginalisation in the literary world, as in all other spheres. I hadn't grasped this fact, even though I had read hardly any work by women as a student of English literature in university. My feminist enlightenment inspired and energised me. I began to focus on women's experiences, in contemporary Ireland and in the past. In 'The Flowering', I imagine the situation of a young woman with an artistic gift, whom circumstances frustrate and prevent from doing the work she loves. It is based on a historical story, but also expressed the frustration and desperation I sometimes felt in my thirties: I wanted to write (and actually I did, goodness knows how), while at the same time holding down a full-time job and being a mother and wife.

The concept of 'herstory' was one that appealed to me – and stories like 'Gweedore Girl' and 'The Pale Gold of Alaska' are tales in which I imagined a history for my female ancestors, about whom I knew so little in fact, apart from their names, sometimes, and where they lived: Donegal. Place matters to me in my writing, and I see that a number of the selected stories are located in Donegal, specifically around Glenvar on Lough Swilly, where my father came from, a place that meant a great deal to me when I was growing up. That lovely part of Ireland was definitely the locus of the mysterious, the beautiful, the poetic for me when I was a child and teenager, even though, or perhaps because, I lived in an old suburb of Dublin. It was my first inspiration.

In my collections, there are stories that I like better than others. They are not always other people's top picks. On the whole I like stories that, to me, feel rounded; that have a subtext – I think this is what people mean when they say 'Leave space for the reader.' I like to give the reader a little work, some food for thought. And I like stories that have something approaching 'luminosity' – that lift the veil over facts to throw light on a deeper truth.

Obviously, few writers sit down at the desk saying, 'Today I'm going to lift the veil over reality to reveal a deeper truth.' Or, 'Today I am going to compose a well-shaped story.' People sometimes ask me, and other writers, 'Where do you get your ideas from?' Often, I forget. Stories are everywhere, though, all around us. They happen every day, everywhere. I think I feel the urge to write a story when something I encounter resonates with some feeling or thought buried inside me. It is that conjunction that generates the spark, and if I grab it before it fades, I get the story. 'Gweedore Girl', I remember, was inspired by a photograph in the Lawrence Collection in the National Library, where I used to work. The photo, of a girl of seventeen or eighteen standing outside a cottage with a bag on her shoulder, was actually entitled 'Gweedore Girl', which I found both poignant and patronising. Who was this girl? Where was she going? The inspiration for 'Pale Gold of Alaska' was a reference in Micí Mac Gabhann's book, *Rotha Mór an tSaoil*, to a woman who sank into depression after being kidnapped briefly by a Native American. 'New Zealand Flax', 'The Coast of Wales' and 'Bikes I Have Lost' had their origins in real events. Life is a good source for stories:

you can change it, add and subtract events – it never comes with exactly the right shape – but in general I believe that stories that are deep and meaningful express feelings and emotional experiences which are, or were, the writer's own. This applies to the most fantastical and inventive fictions as well as to the realistic. That, I guess, is 'the deeper truth' one lifts the veil from. I am looking for what lies under the surface, for some sort of truth about life. That's what I am seeking, first, for myself, and then for my readers.

I have been very lucky with my editors. The very first story I ever submitted for publication was published, and from then on my luck has held (even if I have never made much money, at least not directly, from writing). When I approached Attic Press with my first collection, Mary Paul Keane said, 'We were hoping you would come to us,', and published the book within three or four months. Anne Tannahill invited me to send a manuscript to Blackstaff in the late 1980s, and I have benefited from her wonderful editorial judgement, and that of her successor, Patsy Horton, and their team of amazing editors, Hilary Bell, Michelle Griffin, and others. Caoilfhionn Nic Pháidin, who published all my Irish language books with Cois Life, was equally brilliant as a wise editor, and a pleasure to work with, as are her successors in Cló Iar-Chonnacht.

My husband, Bo Almqvist, seldom read my work but was totally supportive of it – helping me by giving me time and space, always, from the word go. I took this for granted, but realise now that I was lucky to have a husband who was also a writer (of scholarly work) and who had complete unquestioning respect for other writers. Such support should not be underestimated in the life of a writer.

Blood and Water

I have an aunt who is not the full shilling. 'The Mad Aunt' was how my sister and I referred to her when we were children. But that was just a euphemism designed to shelter us from the truth that we couldn't stomach: she was intellectually challenged. Very mildly so. More of a slow learner, perhaps. She survived very successfully as a lone farmwoman, letting land, keeping a cow and a few hens and ducks, listening to the local gossip from the neighbours who were kind enough to drop in regularly. Her house was a popular place for callers, and perhaps that was part of the secret of her survival. She did not participate in the neighbours' conversation to any extent, however. She was articulate only on a very concrete level and all abstract topics were beyond her.

Had she been born in the fifties or sixties, my aunt would have been scientifically labelled, given special treatment at a special school, taught special skills and eventually employed in a special workshop to carry out a special job, certainly a duller job than the one she actually did.

Luckily for her, she was born in 1925 and had been reared as a normal child. Her family had failed to recognise that she was different from other children and they had not sought medical attention. She had merely been considered 'delicate'. The term 'intellectually challenged' would have been meaningless in those days, anyway, in the part of Donegal where she and my mother originated, where Irish was the common, but not the only, language. As she grew up, it must have been silently conceded that she was a bit odd. But people seemed to have no difficulty in suppressing this fact, and they judged my aunt by the standards which they applied to humanity at large: sometimes lenient and sometimes not.

She lived in a farmhouse in Ballytra on Inishowen, and we visited her once a year. Our annual holiday was spent under her roof, and had it not been for the lodging she provided, we could not have afforded to get away at all. But we never considered this side of things. On the first Saturday of August we would set out, laden with clothes packed into cardboard boxes, and enough groceries from the cheap city shops and street markets to see us through the fortnight. The journey north lasted almost twelve hours, travelling in our ancient, battered cars: a Morris Eight and a Ford Anglia are two of the models I can remember from a long series of fourth-hand crocks. Occasionally they broke down en route and we spent long hours in nauseating garages: sometimes I stood around with my father while the mechanic tinkered away; at other times I went walking down country lanes or along the wide melancholy streets of small market towns. Apart from these hitches, the trips were delightful odysseys through various flavours of Ireland: the dusty rich flatlands outside Dublin; the drumlins of Monaghan, hinting of secrets and better things to come; the luxuriant slopes, rushing rivers and expensive villas of Tyrone; and finally, the ultimate reward – the furze and heather, the dog roses and fuchsia of Donegal.

Donegal was different in those days, different from what it is now and different then from the urban areas of the east of Ireland. It was rural in a thoroughly elemental way. People were old-fashioned in their dress and manners, even in their physiques: weather-beaten faces were highlighted by black or grey suits, shiny with age; broad hips stretched the cotton of navy-blue, flower-sprigged overalls, the countrywoman's uniform long eschewed by her city sisters. They lived in thatched cottages or spare grey farmhouses. At that time there was only one bungalow in the parish where my aunt lived, an area that is now peppered with them. All these things accentuated the rusticity of the place, its strangeness, its uniqueness.

My aunt's house was of the slated, two-storey variety, and it stood surrounded by a seemingly arbitrary selection of outhouses in a large yard known as 'the street'. We usually turned into the street at nine o'clock at night. My aunt would be leaning over the half-door waiting for us. Even though she was a bit deaf, she would have heard the car chugging along the dirt lane while it was still a few hundred yards away: it was always that kind of car. She would rush out as soon as the car appeared and stand twisting her hands shyly until we tumbled out. Then she would walk over to us slowly and shake hands carefully with each of us in turn. Care, formality, slowness: these were her characteristic traits.

Greetings over, we would troop into the house, under a low portal apparently designed for a smaller race of people. Then we would sit in front of the hot fire, and my mother would talk in a loud, cheery voice, telling my aunt the news from Dublin and asking her about the local gossip. More often than not my aunt would try to reply. After five minutes or so, she would indicate, a trifle resentfully, that she had expected us earlier, that she had been listening for the sound of the car for over two days. And my mother, at this early stage of the holiday still in a diplomatic mood, would explain patiently, slowly, loudly, that no, we had been due today. We always came on the first Saturday, didn't we? John only got off on the Friday, sure. But somehow my mother would never have thought of writing to let her know when we were coming. It was not because my aunt was illiterate that she didn't write – one of the neighbours would have read a letter out to her. It had more to do with a strange convention firmly adhered to by my parents of never writing to anyone about anything except one subject. Death.

While this courteous ritual of fireside conversation was being acted out by my parents, my sister and I would sit silently on our hardbacked chairs, fidgeting and looking at the familiar objects in the room: the Sacred Heart, the Little Flower, the calendar from Bell's of Buncrana depicting a blond, laughing child. We answered promptly and monosyllabically the few questions my aunt put to us, always about school. Subdued by the many boredoms of the day, we tolerated this one additional boredom.

After a long time my mother would get up, stretch, and prepare a meal of rashers and sausages bought from Russell's of Camden Street. To this my aunt would add a few provisions she had laid in for us: eggs, butter she had churned herself, and enormous golden balls of soda bread, which she baked in a pot oven. I refused to eat this bread. I found the taste repellent and I didn't think my aunt washed her hands properly. But my sister always ate it when we were

4

on holiday and I used to tease her about it, trying to force her to see my point of view. She never did.

After tea, although it was usually late, we would run outside and play. We would visit each of the outhouses in turn, hoping to see an owl in the barn – we never did – and then we'd run across the road to a stream which flowed behind the back garden. There was a stone bridge over the stream, and on our first night we invariably played the same game: we threw sticks into the stream at one side of the bridge and then ran as fast as we could to the other side in order to catch them as they sailed out. This activity, undertaken at night in the shadow of the black hills had a magical effect: it plummeted me headlong into the atmosphere of the holidays. At that stream on that first night, feelings of happiness and freedom seemed to suddenly emerge from some hidden part of me like the sticks emerging from underneath the bridge, and it counteracted the faint claustrophobia, the nervousness that I always had initially in my aunt's house.

Refreshed and elated, we would go to bed in unlit upstairs rooms. These bedrooms were panelled in wood that had once been white but was now faded to the colour of butter and they had windows less than two feet square that had to be propped up with a stick if they were to remain open. All the windows were small – my mother told us it was because at one time there had been a tax on glass. I wondered: the doors were tiny too.

When I woke up in the morning, I would lie and count the boards on the ceiling and then the knots on the boards until a clattering of footsteps on the uncarpeted stairs and a banging about of pots and pans would announce that my mother was up and that breakfast would soon be ready. I would run downstairs to the scullery, which served as a bathroom, and wash. The basin stood on a deal table and the water was in a white enamel bucket on the dresser. A piece of soap was stuck to a saucer which sat on the windowsill in front of the table. As I washed, I was able to look through the window at the elm tree outside and the purple hill beyond. In a way it was pleasant, but on the whole, it worried me. It was so public. There was a constant danger that someone would barge in and find me there, half-dressed, scrubbing my armpits.

The scullery worried me for another reason. On its wall just beside the dresser, was a big splodge of a dirty, yellow substance unlike anything I had ever encountered. I took it to be some sort of fungus – God knows why since the house was spotlessly clean. This thing so repelled me that I never even dared ask what it was and simply tried to avoid looking at it when I was in its vicinity, either washing or carrying a bucket of water back from the well, or doing anything else. Years later when I was taking a course in anthropology at the university, I realised that the stuff was only butter daubed on the wall after every churning for luck. But to me it symbolised something quite the opposite of good fortune: some unspeakable horror.

After dressing breakfast – rashers and sausages again, cooked by my mother over the fire. She did all the cooking while we were on holiday. For that fortnight my aunt, normally a skilful frier of rashers and baker of bread, abandoned domestic responsibility and behaved like a child. She fiddled about in the hen house, she fed the cat or, like my father, she simply sat and stared out the window while my mother did the work. After two or three days of this my mother would grow resentful and begin to mutter, gently but persistently, 'It's no holiday! I'm being taken advantage of.' And my sister and I would nod and agree somewhat half-heartedly, since our share of the housework was not heavy. My sister did the table-setting and dried the dishes; I was in charge of fetching water from the well, which was considered a privileged task and much more fun than the other jobs. In fact it was far from being romantic and was not even faintly amusing after the first couple of times. Water is surprisingly heavy, and we seemed to use an awful lot of it. The blue-rimmed, blue-white enamel bucket had to be filled about a dozen times a day.

My sister and I spent most mornings at the beach, undressing in the seclusion of a dilapidated boathouse. Boats were no longer kept there, and it had a stale, sour smell, as if animals, or even humans, had used it as a lavatory and it had never been cleaned up. Even though the beach was always deserted, we liked to undress in private, going to great lengths with towels to conceal our bodies from one another, until we emerged from the yawning door of the building and ran down the golden granite slip into the sea.

Lough Swilly. 'Also known as the Lake of Shadows,' my sister often informed me; that was the sort of fact she liked. 'One of only two fjords in Ireland,' she would occasionally add. Its being a fjord meant nothing to me, and as for shadows, I was quite unaware of them. What I remember most about that water was its crystal clarity. From a slight distance it looked greenish, but if you looked at it from my aunt's house on a fine day, it was a brilliant turquoise colour like a huge jewel set in the hills. And when you were bathing in that water, it was as clear as glass. I would swim along with my face just below the lapping surface, and I would open my eyes and look straight down to the sandy floor and see the occasional starfish, the tiny scuttling crabs, the shoals of minnows scudding from place to place, guided by some mysterious mob instinct. I stayed in for ages, even on the coldest days, even when rain was swirling in soft curtains around the rocks. It had a definite benign quality, that water. And I always emerged from it feeling cleansed in both body and soul. When I remember it now, I can understand why rivers are sometimes believed to be holy. Lough Swilly was, for me, a blessed water.

The afternoons were spent *en famille*, going on trips in the car to visit distant wonders, Portsalon or the Downings. And the evenings were spent 'raking' – dropping in on our friends, drinking tea, playing with them. This pattern would continue for the entire holiday with two exceptions: on one Sunday we would go on a pilgrimage to Doon Well, and on one weekday we would go shopping in Derry, thirty miles away.

Doon Well was my aunt's treat. It was the one occasion, apart from Mass, on which she accompanied us on a drive, even though we all knew she would have liked to come with us every day. But the only outing she insisted upon was Doon Well. She would begin to drop gentle hints about it soon after we arrived: 'The Gallaghers were at Doon Well last week. Not a great crowd at it.' Then on the chosen Sunday she didn't change her clothes after Mass, but instead donned a special elegant apron and performed the morning tasks in a particular and ladylike way: tiptoeing into the byre, fluttering at the hens. We set out at two o'clock and she sat with my sister and me in the back of the car. My sense of mortification at being seen in public with my aunt was mixed with another shame, caused by ostentatious religious practices. I couldn't bear processions, missions, concelebrated Masses: display. At heart I was Protestant, and indeed it would have suited me, in more ways than one, to belong to that faith. But I

8

didn't. So I was going to Doon Well with my aunt and my pious parents and my embarrassed sister.

You could spot the well from quite a distance: it was dressed. In rags. A large collection of sticks to which brightly coloured scraps of cloth were tied advertised its presence and lent it a somewhat flippant, pagan air. But it was not flippant, it was all very serious. As soon as we got out of the car we had to remove our shoes. The pain! Not of going barefoot on the stony ground, but of having to witness feet – adult feet, our parents' and our aunt's feet – so shamelessly revealed to the world. Their feet were ugly: big and yellow, horny with corns and ingrown toenails, twisted and tortured by years of wearing ill-fitting boots, or no boots at all. To crown it all, both my mother and aunt had varicose veins, purple knots bulging hideously through yellow skin. As humiliated as anyone could be, and as we were meant to be no doubt, we had to circle the well three times, reciting the Rosary aloud. And then my mother said a long litany to Colmcille, and we had to listen and respond, in a thousand agonies of shame, 'Pray for us.' The only bearable part of the expedition came after this when we bought souvenirs at a stall with a brightly striped awning that would have looked more at home in Bray or Bundoran than here. We stood and scrutinised the wares on display: beads, statuettes, medals, snowstorms. Reverting to our consumer role, we – do I mean I? I assume my sister thought the same about it all – felt almost content for a few minutes, and we always selected the same souvenirs: snowstorms. I have one still; it has a peeling blue backdrop with figures of elves and mushrooms under the glass, and painted in black letters on its wooden base, 'I have prayed for you at Doon Well'. I bought that as a present for my best friend but when I returned to Dublin

I hadn't the courage to give it to her, so it stayed in my bedroom for years until I went to study in Germany and then I brought it with me. Not as a souvenir of Doon Well, but of something.

We went to Derry without my aunt. We shopped and were always treated to a lunch of sausages and beans in Woolworths. I loved this trip to Derry: it was the highlight of the holiday.

At the end of the fortnight we would shake hands with my aunt in the street and say goodbye. On these occasions her face would grow long and sad, and just as we climbed into the car she would begin to cry quietly to herself. My mother would say, 'Sure we won't feel it now till Christmas. And then the summer will be here in no time at all!' And this would make everything much more poignant for all of us. I would squirm on the seat, and although I often wanted to cry myself – not because I was leaving my aunt, but because I didn't want to forsake the countryside and the stream and the clean, clear water – I laid aside my own unhappiness and diverted all my energy into despising my aunt for breaking yet another taboo: grown-ups do not cry.

My sister was more understanding. She'd laugh kindly as we turned out of the street into the lane. 'Poor old Annie.' But I couldn't laugh, I couldn't forgive her. For crying, for being herself, for not being the full shilling.

There was one simple reason for my intolerance, so simple that I understood it myself even when I was only eight or nine years old: I resembled my aunt physically. 'You're the image of your Aunt Annie,' people in the valley would beam at me as soon as I met them. Now I know, looking at photos of her and looking in the mirror, that this was not such a very bad thing. She had a reasonable enough face, but I could not see this when I was a child, much less when a teenager. All I knew then was that she looked wrong. For one thing, she had straight unpermed hair, cut short across the nape of her neck, unlike the hair of any woman I knew (but quite like mine as it is today). For another, she had thick, unplucked eyebrows and no lipstick or powder, not even on Sundays, not even for Doon Well, although at that time it was unacceptable to be unmade-up, and outrageous to have straight hair and wear laced shoes. Even in a place which was decidedly old-fashioned, she looked uniquely outmoded, almost freakish. So when people said to me, 'God, aren't you the image of your auntie,' I would cringe and wrinkle up in horror. Unable to change my own face and unable to see that it resembled hers in the slightest. And how does a ten-year-old face resemble one that is fifty? I grew to hate my physique and I transferred that hatred, easily and inevitably, to my aunt.

When I was eleven and almost finished with family holidays, I visited Ballytra alone, not to stay with my aunt but to attend a Gaeltacht college which had just been established there. I decided not to stay with any of my relatives. I wanted to steer clear of all unnecessary contact with my past, so I lived with a family I had never met before. Even though I loved its rigorous, jolly ambiance, the college posed problems for me. On the one hand, I was the child of a native, almost a native myself in fact. On the other hand, I was a 'scholar' – one of the kids from Dublin who descended on Ballytra in July, like a shower of fireworks, acting as if they owned the place, more or less shunning the native population. Even if I'd wanted to, it would have been difficult for me to steer a median course between my scholar role and my other one as a cousin of the little natives who had been my playmates in former years but were now too shabby, too rustic, too outlandish, to tempt me at all.

In the event, I made no effort to play to both factions: I ignored my relations entirely and threw myself into the more appealing life of the scholar. They seemed neither to notice nor to care, no doubt just as bound by their own snobberies and conventions as I was by mine.

When the weather was suitable, that is when it did not rain heavily, afternoons were spent on the beach, the same beach where my sister and I had played. Those who wanted to swim walked there in a long straggling crocodile from the village. I loved to swim and never missed an opportunity to go to the sea. The snag about this was that it meant passing by my aunt's house, which was on the road down to the lough: we had to pass through her street to get there. For the first week she didn't bother me, probably assuming that I would drop in soon. But even though my mother had warned me to pay an early visit and had given me a headscarf as a present, I procrastinated. So after a week had gone by, she began to lie in wait for me: she sat on a stone seat in front of the door, looking at me dolefully as I passed. And I would give a casual little nod, as I did to everyone I met, and walk on.

One afternoon the teacher who supervised the group was walking beside me and some of my friends, much to my pride and embarrassment.

When we came to the street, my aunt called out softly, 'Mary, Mary.'

I nodded and continued on my way.

The teacher gave me a funny look. 'Is she talking to you, Mary?' he said. 'Does she want to talk to you?'

'I don't know her,' I said, melting in shame. 'Who is she?'

'Annie,' said the teacher. 'That's Annie Bonner.'

He didn't let on to know anything more about it, but I bet he did: everyone who had spent more than a day in

Ballytra knew everything there was to know about the place. Everyone, that is, who wasn't as egocentric as the scholars.

My aunt is still alive, but I haven't seen her in years. I never go to Inishowen now. I don't like it since it became modernised and littered with bungalows; instead I go to Barcelona with my husband, who is a native Catalonian. He teaches Spanish part-time and runs a school for Spanish students in the summer. I help him in the tedious search to find accommodation for them all, and really, we don't have much time for holidays.

My aunt is not altogether well. She had a heart attack just before Christmas and had to have a major operation at the Donegal Regional. I meant to pay her a visit but never got round to it. Then just before she was discharged, I heard she was going home for Christmas. Home? To her own empty house on the lane down to the lough? I was horrified. God knows why, I've seen people in direr straits. But something gave. I phoned my mother and angrily demanded why she wouldn't have her, just for a few weeks. But my mother is getting on; she has gout and can hardly walk herself. So I said, 'All right, she can come here.' But Julio was unenthusiastic. Christmas is the only time of year he manages to relax: in January the bookings start, the planning, the endless meetings, the telephone calls. Besides, we were expecting his sister Montserrat, who is tiny and dark and lively as a sparrow; the children adore her. In the end my sister, who is unmarried and a lecturer in Latin at Trinity, went to stay in Ballytra for a few weeks until my aunt was better. She has very flexible holidays, my sister, and no real ties.

I was relieved, after all, not to have Aunt Annie in my

home. What would my prim suburban neighbours have thought? How would Julio, who has rather aristocratic blood, have coped? You see, I am still ashamed of my aunt, still ashamed of myself. Perhaps I do resemble her. And not just facially – maybe there is some mental likeness too. My wide education, my brilliant husband, my posh accent, are they just attempts at camouflage? Am I really all that bright? Sometimes as I sit and read in my glass-fronted bungalow, looking out over the glassy sheet of the Irish Sea, trying to learn something – the grammar of a foreign language, the names of Hittite gods, something like that – I find the facts running away from me, like sticks escaping downstream on the current. And more often than that, much more often, I feel in my mind a splodge of something that won't let any knowledge sink in. A block of some terrible substance, soft and thick and opaque. Like butter.

The Postmen's Strike

Matilda stretched, jumped out of bed, and walked over to the window. The sun danced in irregular lines on the grass. A bird sang in the single tree. Spring had come to Denmark at last.

Matilda put on the coffee and went into the shower. She turned the water on as strongly as possible, and used more bubble bath than was necessary. She wanted to smell extra-sweet, on the first day of spring. When she came out of the bathroom, trailing a large purple towel, she was humming a little tune. She had learned it in Ireland long ago, from the *Walton's* show on Saturday afternoon. 'Deep in Canadian woods we met' was the first and the only line she knew. She hummed for the last three lines of each verse, but at the beginning of each she sang, 'Deep in Canadian woods we met'. These words had always fascinated Matilda. They had the power to conjure up two different pictures in her imagination. The first was of a member of the Canadian Mounted Police colliding with an exiled Irish rebel in the middle of a huge pine forest – perhaps Seán Ó Duibhir an

Gleanna, who liked that sort of background. The second picture was also of a Canadian Mounted Policeman, and also set in a pine forest, but this time he ran into an Irish milkmaid. What else could those words possibly mean? Matilda danced around the floor, humming, drying, and wondering. While thus occupied, she heard a thud from the hall. The post. You can tell a lot about a person from the way they react to the sound of the postman. Matilda always reacted in the same way: she dropped everything and flew to the mat. It was as if she were afraid he would come back and take the letters away again if she didn't pick them up one second after they arrived. In fact she had never experimented to see. No letter had ever lain on Matilda's mat for more than one second after it had been dropped there. The four times she had been away from her flat on holiday during the past ten years were periods when no post had come anyhow. There were many such interludes in Matilda's life. She had a few friends in Europe and America who sent a card or a letter now and then, but for the most part her post consisted of official correspondence. Even this afforded Matilda, who was of a cheerful disposition and easily pleased, some pleasure.

Today, one envelope lay on the mat. It bore a strange stamp, and the postmark read 'Ireland'. Matilda stared at it in astonishment. She had not had a letter from Ireland in nine and a half years. Immediately after she had left that country, ten years before, she had enjoyed a regular correspondence with her parents, siblings, husband, and literate child. But six months later, the postal workers in Ireland had gone on strike. Telecommunications also became affected, and soon it was apparent that other strikes, such as airline and shipping, were on. Nobody left

16

the country and nobody from outside could visit it. Not that many tried: as soon as the Bord Fáilte campaigns died down, most people, including Irish emigrants, seemed to forget that the place existed. After two years, Matilda noticed that the European maps no longer marked the position of her native country. The EEC stopped referring to Ireland as a member, and Greece reigned uncontested in the slot reserved for the country that receives most and contributes least. After the official disappearance of Ireland, Matilda rarely thought of it, except when a snatch of an old song or a St Patrick's Day meeting of the Copenhagen Irish Society recalled it suddenly to mind.

She stood in the hall, shivering with apprehension and cold, since the towel had slipped down her back and it was chilly for the time of year. She opened the envelope. The single sheet was handwritten. The hand was faintly familiar, but the address and signature were not.

Ailesbury Palace,
Ballsbridge.
22 March 1990.

My old jewel,

Hoping this finds you as it leaves me and the care? That is, well. The boys are doing fine. Things is now come to pass in Ireland where we can write letters again. The strike is over, thanks be to _____. It was a terrible nuisance. Funny we managed all the same. The post office workers have got ten per cent. Not what they were after but it's better than nothing. Aer Lingus are back too, from this Friday. People are saying the planes are not safe, because foreigners think they're UFOs. But personally I think that's just old guff. So I'll be in Copenhagen next Wednesday, if all goes well. It'll be marvellous to have you home, all the same. I was never much of a hand at the old cooking.

Your own shegouhska
Rashers

P.S. I resigned from my job in the Department of External Affairs and am now employed as a Public Poet.

Rashers! It must be Michael, using a new name. Matilda went into the living room and sank into her good armchair. Michael! He sounded crazy. Ireland, too, probably had gone to the dogs. Left on its own, of course, what could you expect?

Matilda took a mouthful of coffee, and then suddenly choked on it at the thought of Michael against the backdrop of the new Copenhagen Airport. 'Deep in Canadian Woods We Met'! Wednesday. She began to calculate rapidly. Was it possible to change address, job, even town of residence, before Wednesday? The answer came effortlessly: no. There was not a hope of it. If there were, would it be worth it? The answer came slowly. Well, maybe, probably, and considering what Michael had been like ten years ago when he had not been called Rashers and had a respectable job as a Third Sec., yes. Then again, it might be interesting, and certainly it would be amusing, to find out what exactly had been going on in the Old Sod, as the Copenhagen Irish Society president called it, during the long period of isolation. And, despite what Rashers clearly imagined, there was no obligation to return. A word with Matilda's lawyer would set him straight on that point, if necessary. Probably there was no such thing as divorce in Ireland as yet, but ten years' separation was grounds for something. Even if it had been her fault originally, since it was she who had insisted on coming to Copenhagen to teach Old Irish, when she really ought to have stayed at home and looked after her husband and family. Still, in a way that had been a mutual decision: they both had known her career was being frustrated by Michael's: he was to be posted to the worst mission in the world, newly opened in Uganda, a year after Matilda's trip to Copenhagen. Matilda had promised to join him without protest, if she only had one year of freedom in which to develop her own interests. She would never get the chance to teach Old Irish in Uganda.

Matilda went to the sideboard and took out a bar of chocolate. She kept it there for visitors. Alcohol was practically unobtainable in Denmark: citizens were rationed to one litre of spirits per year. Feeling guilty about putting on weight, Matilda sat in the armchair and gnawed off chunks of the delicious stuff. She speculated idly about her use of chocolate as a release in moments of stress and indecision: probably it would be useless as an aid to relaxation if it were not a taboo-food.

Wednesday morning. 11 a.m., Kastrup Airport. Matilda wore a white raincoat and a dark-green scarf. Her body exuded the light foliate perfume without which she felt positively naked. People glanced at her appreciatively: she cut an elegant figure, etched against the nondescript but expensive background of the Arrivals Hall.

She waited patiently: the Dublin flight had been delayed forty minutes, owing to take-off difficulties. Some things do not change, thought Matilda, lighting a cigarette and restraining an impulse to tap her small leather-shod foot against the hard floor. A middle-aged man with a head like a boiled egg came and asked her for a match. She offered him her lighter, unsmilingly. He thanked her with indelicate warmth, and stood two steps away, smoking a fat cigar. Matilda then began to tap her toe, just loud enough to be audible to him.

Finally, the flight arrived. Matilda felt nervous. She lit another cigarette and sat down on a seat placed a short distance from the gate from which Michael would eventually emerge. Would they recognise one another? What would he look like now? What had he looked like ten years ago? A number of images were stored in the back of her mind: Michael in shorts going to play badminton; Michael going to work in blue jeans and a white shirt and tie; Michael going to bed in striped pyjamas. She had no clear picture of Michael's face. Well, it didn't matter, it would look different now anyhow. And she, she must have changed. Years of living in Copenhagen had turned her into a slim, elegant creature, quite unlike the dumpy motherly figure she had been when last in Dublin. He wouldn't know her! How would he react? How would she react? Would she shiver? Take fright and run off or be unaccountably happy in an indescribably sweet and lovely way?

People began to file through the gate in dribs and drabs until eventually there he stood, quite unmistakably. He was carrying a small suitcase and a briefcase, and, Matilda noted approvingly, a plastic bag which, she hoped, contained a tiny supply of whiskey and some cigarettes. His eyes had not changed one bit: they were wide and brown, and they darted curiously about. It was they that gave him away. Otherwise he bore no resemblance to the old Michael. He had shaved his beard and moustache. His sallow skin glistened with health and aftershave. He had become conservative in his dress, to an extent which was truly remarkable: without looking exactly like a dandy of the turn of the century, he successfully conveyed the impression of being ideologically sympathetic with say, Oscar Wilde or Jack London. His whole appearance, in short, thought Matilda, as she approached him with a carefully confident gait, had nothing in common with that of the old Michael except its slight absurdity.

He recognised Matilda as soon as he caught sight of her.

'Darling, is it really you?' he asked. His accent had an Anglo-Irish tinge, very odd when one considered the definite Hiberno-Irish flavour of his letter. He did not sound the 'r' in darling, and the 'ea' in really he pronounced as 'ay'.

'Yes, Michael. Or, should I call you "Rashers"?'

Matilda had difficulty in letting go of the last word without an accompanying giggle. But, for the second time in an hour, she suppressed a natural urge, and choked instead.

'No, no, no. Not at all, not at all. Purely a professional title. Only a nom-de-plume. Merely for amusement. Rather a catchy little appellation, isn't it, my dear?'

Michael chuckled. Matilda's cover girl face preserved its 'normal' pose of bland dignity. She allowed her long, grey eyes to express neither alarm nor amusement: it was too early in the day to take any definite line of action. The new Michael might be an eccentric genius, or he might be an idiot (like the old Michael). She should not make up her mind on a moment's acquaintance.

'I can see that it might be effective in certain types of business.'

'I am not a pork butcher, you know!' Michael laughed.

Matilda's mouth formed itself into a smile. She would not make up her mind on two moments' acquaintance either. But ...

'How long do you plan to stay?' she asked casually, guiding him in the direction of the bar.

'Mm. Two weeks is as long as I can manage, I'm afraid. Very busy at the moment, you know, in Ireland. We are frankly up to our eyes.'

His tone suggested that Ireland was his personal office.

'You must tell me all about it. About Ireland, that is. I … we … know nothing. I hardly know where to begin.'

'There's a lot I want to find out about, too, kittens!'

Matilda blenched. She couldn't prevent it. It made her feel sick to hear him use the pet name he had invented, according to himself, when they were both little more than twenty. Michael had not learned a sense of discretion during the ten years of absence, whatever else he had learned.

'Yes. Would you like to have a drink here? Or shall we hurry home?'

'Oh, we could have a small one, I think!'

Wondering if he knew that it would have to be a small strawberry yoghurt or a lemon juice, Matilda led him into the bar and called the waiter.

'Drinking laws have become rather tight here in the past while,' she explained to Michael. She felt she had one up on him: for some reason she was proud to live in a country with such a superior moral law.

'That's fine with me. I've been in the Pioneers for the past seven years.'

'You still have the Pioneers?' Matilda injected the question with no more than a dash of polite curiosity.

'Pioneers, Legion of Mary, Vincent de Paul; you name it, it's been revived and is flourishing in the New Ireland.'

Matilda recrossed her legs. The artificial air of the bar was making her feel itchy.

'Do you all speak Irish?'

'Bless your dear heart, no. Nobody speaks Irish. Nobody even knows Irish. It is a pagan language, with anarchic undertones in every aspiration. It's been unofficially banned since 1984.'

Michael spoke with an authoritative air which Matilda found at least as irritating as the unnatural oxygen which the Danish airline forced its customers to breathe, on land as well as in the air.

'I still teach Old Irish here.'

'How extraordinary!'

She was accustomed to defending herself against this sort of opinion.

'No more extraordinary than teaching Latin.'

'It is much more extraordinary than teaching Latin, and you know it.'

'Oh, the Romans and all that! We approach it from a socio-linguistic point of view. Nothing more. No value judgements are allowed.'

Matilda did not particularly wish to get involved in a tedious academic quibble with her ex-husband, or husband, or whatever he was. But academic quibbling was preferable to 'kittens' conversation.

'How can you approach it from a socio-linguistic point of view, when nothing is known about the society that spoke it, or how they spoke, or whether they spoke?'

Matilda could have explained that she was adept at approaching 'it' from whatever point of view fashion dictated. For one prolonged period, when the Christian Democrats had been in power, she had approached it from a rigidly fascist viewpoint. Her essay, 'Maeve: an Irish precursor of Thatcher' had won her no small fame in Copenhagen's intellectual circles at that time. Later, when the Christian Democrats were replaced by the Socialists

(Left) – owing to a new rise in the cost of petrol and the simultaneous, although unconnected, leaking of a reactor in a nuclear power station outside Aarhus, which threatened all animal life within a radius of ten miles with extinction – she had been advised to change her approach: she revised her textbooks, and taught her student(s) to interpret all Old Irish literature as an expression of repressed communist ideals on the part of the ancient Gael.

'We know exactly what the society was like and we know exactly how they spoke. You are naturally out of touch with modern research on Ireland. If you care to read my latest work, "Marxist Dialectic in the Book of the Dun Cow", you will be brought up to date.'

Michael's eyes flashed.

'I am completely up to date, thank you. Irish researchers are now the experts on Ireland, incredible though this may seem. And we have discovered through years of patient scholarship that there was no Book of the Dun Cow. Or no Old Irish or Middle Irish and even no Book of Kells. And no High Crosses or Round Towers or Saints or Scholars, or Scribes or Bards or Harpists or Harps. Or Penal Days or Mass Rocks or Famines or Tally Sticks. Or 1798 or 1916. Or anything commonly masquerading under the title of Irish History. We have rewritten it.'

This trenchantly-delivered manifesto did not disturb Matilda in the least. She had seen histories rewritten time and again during her ten years at the University of Copenhagen.

'Indeed?' she asked, although she was not desperately interested.

'Yes. We have discovered that the Irish are simply an offshoot of the English. There were no Irish people as such before the island was settled by the English in the sixteenth century. We are all the direct descendants of the English nobility of the Renaissance period.'

'Indeed?' asked Matilda again, taking a draught of yoghurt and hoping the answer would not be too long.

'Yes, indeed, to be sure, and really and truly. And as true as I'm sitting here. We are the English as the English were before they got ruined by industrialisation and that awful coal dust. We are the English who ruled the waves and invented the spinning jenny.'

'But not the English who span with it?'

'No, definitely not. Damned trade unionists. Social Welfare sheep.'

Matilda laughed one of her sympathetic laughs at Michael. Relaxing in his chair, his loose bow tie flopping out over his grey jacket, his fingernails long and clean, he was not altogether unattractive.

'Perhaps we ought to move along now? The traffic tends to get heavy after one. The great going-home, you know.'

'Certainly. Delighted. I can't wait to see your home, need I tell you? I have wondered so often how you lived, here, alone!'

Matilda wished she had a Danish husband and three children, just to show him how silly his way of thinking was.

'It has been some time, hasn't it?'

She glided along in front of him, her silk blouse swishing against the lining of her coat. She was aware of the effect she was making, on Michael and on the other onlookers ranged around the yoghurt bar. Her satisfaction with that caused her to experience a rush of self-confidence. She felt sure she would solve this Irish question without serious difficulty.

*

Michael was charmed by Matilda's flat.

'It is perfectly charming,' he kept murmuring to himself, as he examined the vague but safe water-colours and the natural colourless furniture.

Matilda tried to recall their old house in Dublin. She remembered it as being reasonably habitable. But if Michael's reaction to her very modest apartment was genuine, what could his own home be like?

'You still live on Firhouse Green?'

She knew he did not.

'No, no. We moved a few years ago. In to Ballsbridge. I've got a state house, of course. A man in my position ...'

'Of course.' Matilda took four glasses from the sideboard. And, on second thoughts, a half-consumed bar of chocolate.

'It used to be the German embassy. Our house. When we broke off diplomatic relations with the world, we had to do something with the embassies.'

'So you distributed them among public officials?'

'We distributed them amongst ourselves. Ex-diplomats. But, yes, in a manner of speaking, you are right. Because we all became public officials, of one kind or another. Except for those who were incapable of it, owing to physical or mental deficiencies.'

Matilda poured two glasses of milk.

'And you are now a ... Public Poet, didn't you say?'

'Yes, indeed. I am Chief Poet of the New Ireland. We have tried to make use of the natural talents of our people. Every five years, every man, woman and child, and household pet, in the New Ireland, undergoes a test to determine his or her or its natural aptitudes. According to the results of these tests, state employment is allocated to the various individuals.'

'So all employment is nationalised?'

26

'Oh, yes.' Michael raised his glass to his mouth and sipped some milk. He went blue in the face.

'Pasteurised?' he spluttered.

'I suppose so.'

'*Plorsoon!*' He wiped his mouth with a red handkerchief.

Matilda did not enquire into the meaning of the term, and its etymology she would rather work out for herself.

'What sort of work do people mainly do?'

'Many people are food-providers. They plant potatoes and milk cows. The entire Central Plain, which now includes a substantial portion of Ulster, is one vast dairy and potato land. The coastal zones are inhabited by proper people. As it happens, many have a natural aptitude for poetics. They work for me. They lie in the dark and compose epic ballads in Hiberno-English, which we hope to export to the United States as soon as we open our doors to the international market once more. Other people, quite a lot, have a natural aptitude for nothing except talking. They sit around peat-fires all day and all night, talking their heads off. They are not productive but they are happy.'

'What language do you speak?'

'Hiberno-English. Everything must be said and written in Hiberno-English. That is the law.' Michael raised his eyebrows so that his forehead wrinkled up like a prune, and said confidentially, 'I must say, it's a hell of a relief to be able to take a break from the damned language. I have no natural aptitude for it myself: it has been uphill work.'

Matilda scrutinised him closely, and summed him up. He had changed completely. His voice was different. He spoke without that hesitation-which-was-not-quite-a-stammer which had hallmarked his oral expression in earlier days. Then, he had always seemed to be apologising for what he said, although that was so innocuous that his small, usually captive audience found it spent most of the time asking silently 'Why?' Matilda, his most faithful listener, frequently found at the end of one of his boring monologues on radical politics or the oil crisis that she had not absorbed one word of sense, so busy had her psychoanalytic faculties been during the course of the awful experience. The new Michael, alias Rashers, Public Poet in Chief of the New Ireland, was anything but apologetic. Sitting opposite Matilda, on the most comfortable chair in the room, which he had selected for himself, he stared her straight in the eye. His words rang out. He impressed her with his self-assurance, which she feared might be stronger even than her own. The old Michael had been in a continuous state of dither. The new Michael knew what he was about. It was as if he had required a setting as strange and irrational as himself in order to flower. The New Ireland had been created by the likes of Michael for the likes of Michael: the world, including Matilda, might find it hard to fathom, but ...

'There you are,' said Matilda.

'Yes,' said Michael, without a trace of that hesitation-which-was-not-quite-a-stammer, and added, with a sardonic smile, 'but I forgot one small detail. It emerged, under examination, that a small proportion of Irishmen showed an extraordinarily high ability in the field of science and technology. These people were all Christian Brothers. They were assigned the task of scientific research in the cause of the New Ireland, and have developed a new type of nuclear power, more efficient and stronger than any which has so far been evolved in any part of the world.'

Matilda decided not to be negative and ask how they knew this, and he went on: 'The I-Bomb was perfected two weeks ago. We have chosen this moment to release

Europe, Africa, Asia and America from the isolation they have been suffering for so long, owing to the ten-year strike by the postmen, Aer Lingus, Sealink and Irish Continental. The world has been exposed to the dangers of insularity for long enough. "No world is an island", as the Deputy-Chief Poet said in an address to the Department of Poets and Telepathists three weeks ago. The world is about to be introduced to the new master-race. Future generations will thank us for saving humanity from itself.'

In the course of this proclamation, Michael had poured himself a generous glass of whiskey, into one of the small tumblers which Matilda had suggestively placed on the table. Matilda eyed the whiskey greedily.

'Do you think I might have a little?' she asked. She wanted to celebrate the fact that she had caught a glimpse of a tiny spark of light. At the end of a long murky corridor there glowed a neon sign which possibly conveyed the message: New Michael equals Old Michael.

'Yes, of course. How clumsy of me not to have offered. How unforgivable. I ought to be shot. I ought to be hanged, drawn and quartered.'

Matilda poured herself a drink and groped along the dark corridor towards enlightenment.

'Do you have capital punishment in the New Ireland?'

'Yes, yes, bless your heart, yes. Capital punishment and almost every kind of punishment you can think of. People are being punished right, left and centre. Especially left and centre. For the slightest offence.'

'Such as …?' she said, with her poker-faced voice.

'Protesting against the true regime. Trying to escape. Trying to write books of a revolutionary nature. In Irish. Or Anglo-English. Or Hiberno-French. Attempting to assassinate the Theeshock, or his band of guards, or members of the real government, with home-made pikes. It hasn't been easy, I can tell you, building up the New Ireland. So many people had been contaminated by the old ideas, the old way of life. Their minds could not be reformed to fit into the New Ireland. We had to develop a means of getting rid of them.'

The neon light shone brilliantly at the end of the corridor. Besides spelling out the obvious message, its light revealed a dark, indeterminate spot in Michael's intellect. Another prod or two and the precise nature of that spot would be known to Matilda.

'So you, that is, the New Ireland, plan a take-over of the world?'

'The epitaph of Emmet at last will be written
When the rest of the world at our feet is lying smitten.'

'You wrote that?' Matilda took out her pocket handkerchief and grinned into it.

The spot was as soft as forest moss.

'When emotion swells up in an Irishman's heart
To talk in rhymed couplets he feels he must start.'

'You mean you do it all the time, when you're feeling a bit hot under the collar?'

'"Hot under the collar" is hardly the phrase
I would have chosen to describe the ways
A master of poesie feels when he's pressed
By ignorant foreigners from east or from west
To explain the New Ireland in verse or in rhyme
Or in anything else that suggests the sublime.'

Michael was beginning to perspire.

'No, of course not. It was a very silly choice of expression. Kindly accept my apologies. I think the custom is positively charming.'

Relaxed at last, Matilda could allow herself to become contaminated by Michael's way of talking. She could well understand how the tendency to be verbose could grow on a person: gushing was fun!

'That's quite all right,' said Michael, hurt, and mopping his brow.

'Are you going to inform the People of Denmark of your plans?'

'When people first hear it they will not be charmed.
I come all alone and I come all unarmed.
The moment for breaking the great new secret,
In my honest opinion, is not just quite yet.
When the moment is ripe, I will tell the world all
By means of a personal telephone call.
The judicious use of our new Irish phones
Ensures quick transmission without broken bones.'

'When will the moment be ripe?' Matilda used her Spanish-Inquisition tone.

'Well ... it's ... the problem is, that quite frankly, the moment is ripe. But ...' Michael's cloak of authority was slipping rapidly from his shoulders.

'But ...' Matilda used the unpunctuated, open-ended 'but'.

'But we have been forced by a new strike by the telephonists and postmen to postpone the ripe moment until a settlement is reached.'

Matilda smiled openly.

'And ...'

'And ... who knows? You ... remember ... the ... last ... time?'

He spoke in the Old Michael's voice, with that hesitation-which-was-not-quite-a-stammer impregnating every syllable.

'I remember, naturally. But surely the New Ireland can deal with a problem like that?'

'Well it ... it ... is hard ... to ... explain ... exactly. But ... somehow ... it ... seems ... impossible ... We ... cannot ... do ... a ... thing ... about ... it.'

'Why did you come here, then?'

'Well ... I ... decided to seize ... the opportunity ... to ... visit you ... and ... take ... you back to the ... the New Ireland.'

'You mean, Aer Lingus is liable to go on strike again soon?'

'It ... could ... happen ... today ... or tomorrow. The post office came out ... after ... two ... days. Aer ... Lingus ... has ... lasted ... a ... week. That ... I ... can ... tell ... you ... is ... a ... bit ... of ... a ... stretch.'

'Come on,' said Matilda, her mind acting swiftly. She pulled on her raincoat, her dark-green scarf, and dabbed her ears with the foliate perfume without which she felt positively naked, in one second flat. She pulled Michael out of his chair and propelled him towards the door, grabbing his briefcase and suitcase in transit. But not his plastic bag.

'Where are we going?'

'To the airport.'

'Now?'

'We can't take any chances, can we? You want to go back to the New Ireland, don't you?' Michael's expressive brown eyes suggested that he was not quite sure what his answer to the question would be. But he didn't get a chance to utter it. Before he could say 'Jack Robinson' he found himself fastened securely into a first-class seat on the evening flight to Dublin. It was only two seats behind the one that he had sat in on the way over that morning. Matilda was sitting next to him now, however, so he did not feel unhappy. They were going home to the New Ireland, together. They would build a new life there, with the two teenage children and the dog, in the old German Embassy on Ailesbury Road. With any luck, the strikes would all restart in a day or two. They would return to the good old New Life. Michael would lord it over the apprentice poets and journey poets and master poets, in the Department of Poets and Telepathy. What a vision!

He turned to Matilda, in a burst of confidentiality: 'Oh what a life we will have, my Matilda, Me and you and the dog and the childer!'

'Yes, darling, I can hardly wait,' said Matilda. She was only half-listening to Michael. Her eyes were riveted to the right hand of the second-in-command air hostess, who had promised … The second-in-command air hostess raised her right hand a fraction of an inch and waved the third finger gently.

'Excuse me for one minute, darling. I've got to go to the *mná*.' Matilda patted Michael's arm affectionately, and walked down the aisle towards the toilets. But instead of turning to the right, she turned to the left, and climbed out through the emergency exit, on to the runway. Two seconds later, the engines of the plane began to rev up. Within minutes the old boneshaker was mounting into the air above Kastrup. Matilda had a moment of sentimentality as she watched it hover unsteadily above the airport, looking like a farmyard fowl among all the slim streamlined jets. The moment did not last for long, however. As she revved up her own little engine and pulled out of the airport carpark, her feeling was one of unadulterated relief.

The Flowering

Lennie has a dream, a commonplace, even a vulgar dream, and one which she knows is unlikely to be realised. She wants to discover her roots. Not just names and dates from parish registers or census returns. Those she can find easily enough, insofar as they exist at all. What she desires is a real, a true, discovery. An unearthing of homes, a peeling off of clothes and trappings, a revelation of minds, an excavation of hearts.

Why she wants this she does not know, or knows only very vaguely. It is partly a general curiosity about the past of her family, and more particularly a thirst for self-knowledge. Why does she look this way? Like some things and not others? Why does she do some things and not others? If she knew which traits she has inherited from whom, which are independent qualities, surely she would be a better judge of what she is herself, or of what she can become? When she begins to ask these questions she becomes excited, initially, then dizzy. The litany of queries is self-propagating. It enjoys a frenzied beanstalk growth but reaches no satisfactory conclusions. And the more it expands, the more convinced is Lennie that the answers are important. The promise, or rather the hope, of solutions, glows like a lantern in the bottle-green, the black cave of her mind, where Plato's shadows sometimes hover but more often do not make an appearance at all. Drunk on questions, she begins to believe that there is one answer, a true all-encompassing resolution which will flood that dim region with brilliant light for once and for all, illuminating all personal conundrums. Of course when Lennie sobers up, she knows that such an answer is impossible. The only thing she has learned about the truth – she believes in its existence; that is her one act of faith – is that it is many-faceted. This is as true of the past as it is of the present and the future. Knowledge of ancestors would not tell her all she needed to know in order to see herself, or anything, clearly. But it would provide a clue or two.

Clues. There are a few. Place, in particular, looks promising. The same location for hundreds of years, if popular belief holds any veracity – the documents suggest that it does. Wavesend. Low hills swoop, black and purple and bright moss-green, into darker-green fields. Yellow ragweed and cow parsley decorate them. Royal red fuchsia, pink dog roses, meadowsweet and foxgloves flounce in the ditches that line the muddy lane leading down to the shore. Leonine haunches of sand roll into the golden water of the lough. Golden lough, turquoise lough, indigo lough, jade lough. Black lough, lake of shadows. The shadows are the clouds, always scudding across the high opalescent sky. The terns, the oystercatchers, the gulls swoop into those and their own shadows after shadows of herrings, shoals of shadowy mackerel. Shadows on the other side of the shadowy looking glass of the water.

The house of stone, two storeys high, with undersized door and narrow windows squinting in the grey walls. Cross-eyed, short-sighted house, peering at the byre across 'the street'. A cobbled path brings people limping there to milk the cows, or if they are women – and usually they are, since cows are women's work – go to the toilet. The milk bounces into wooden buckets, the other flows through a neat square hole into the green, stinking pond. The midden. A ridiculous word which always made Lennie laugh. Piddle, middie, midden. Riddle.

Inside, dark is relieved by bright-painted furniture. The blue dresser displaying floral tea-bowls, willow patterned platters, huge jugs with red roses floating in pinky-blue clouds on their bellies – the jugs came free, full of raspberry jam; that's why there are so many of them. A special clock, known as an American clock, with a brass pendulum and a sunray crown. Red bins for corn and layers mash.

The stuff of folk museums. Lennie gets it from textbooks (*Irish Folk Ways*) and from exhibition catalogues, as well as from her own memory. The exhibited model and the actual house overlap so much that it is difficult to distinguish one from the other now. In her own lifetime – she is in her thirties, neither young nor old – real life has entered the museum and turned into history. A real language has crept into the sound archives of linguistic departments and folklore institutions, and it has faded away from people's tongues. In one or two generations. In *her* generation. It has been a time of endings. Of deaths, great and small. But this she finds interesting rather than painful. She was, after all, an observer of life in Wavesend, someone who bad already moved on to other ways of living and speaking before she came to know it and its ways, before she grew to realise their importance. She was never really part of the Wavesend way of life and so she was not confounded or offended by its embalming and burial while some of its organs still lived on, weakly flapping like the limbs of an executed man. Saddened she was, but not bewildered.

Other clues to her past are folk-museum stuff, school history stuff, too. The Famine. Seaweed and barnacles and herrings for dinner. A bowl of yellow meal given to a traveller caused her immediate death. Ate the meal and dropped dead on the hot kitchen floor, Glory be to God; she hadn't eaten in a month, the stomach couldn't take it. Lennie's ancestors had yellow meal, and seaweed, and barnacles, so they survived, or some of them survived. What does that tell her about them? The litany goes on. Oh Mother Most Astute! Oh Mother Most Hungry! Oh Mother Most Merciful! Oh Mother Most Cruel! Give us our gruel! The Lennies turned, became Protestant, and later turned back again. Some of them went to America and later came back again.

Wolfe Tone passed by the house on his way to France. Drugged. Red Hugh passed by the house on his way to Dublin. Drunk. Lennie's great-great-great- grandmother saw the ship and waved.

The Great War. Artillery practice on the shores of the Lough. The sound of cannon reverberates across the night-still waters. Boom. Men stir in their heavy sleep. Boom. An infant shrieks. In the fragile shelter of daylight, soldiers visit the house to buy milk and eggs. So, were they friendly? Did they chat? Did someone fall in love with one of them? They gave Lennie's father a ride in a car. His first car ride. That's the sum total of it. It must have been exciting, Daddy! It was. It was.

A personal experience tale: when Daddy was seven he fell off a bike, a man's big bike that he had been riding with his legs under instead of over the crossbar. Ten months in a Derry hospital followed the experience. The wound on his leg would not heal. Home, with the abscess, to live or die. Philoctetes. Folk belief: the miracle cure. A holy stone from the holy well, the well of St Patrick, was taken by his grandmother. You shouldn't take stones from shrines or ancient sites of worship, from open-air museums, but people did not know that then. She took it home without a by your leave and placed it on the wounded spot, and the next day she returned it to its ancient site. The wound healed. He always limped but he was healed by whatever was in that stone.

And what was it like, in hospital for ten months all alone? Not a single visit for the little seven-year-old boy. Not a single visit. He forgets. He doesn't remember it at all. Perhaps he cannot afford to remember.

It's enough to drive you crazy. Archaeology, history, folklore. Linguistics, genealogy. They tell you about society, not about individuals. It takes literature to do that. And since the Lennies couldn't write until Lennie's grandparents went to school, and not very much after that, there isn't any literature. Not now anyway. The oral tradition. What oral tradition? It went away, with their language, when the schools started. Slowly they are becoming articulate in the new language. Slowly they are finding a new tradition. They are inventing a new tradition. Transform, adapt, or disappear.

But look, there she is, hunkered over the black stool in the bottle-green dimness of that cavernous byre, her long hair cloaking her visage and her long, adroit hands squeezing the hot teats. There she is! Sally Rua. Lennie's great-aunt. A tall girl, with adder-green eyes and a mole on her chin and two moles on the sole of her right foot. Gentle on the whole, sometimes acerbic and brusque. People who dislike her – women, mostly, because she is the sort of reserved woman many men unaccountably gravitate towards – say she is a snake. When her hair is wound up behind her long white neck, the simile is accurate enough, although boys who love her compare her, more conventionally, to a swan.

She lived in that house in Wavesend, slept in the bedroom with the window that has to be propped open with a stick and the green wardrobe with cream borders that her own father made for her. In the mornings she went to school in the low, white cottage beside the church. The rest of the day she was engaged in all the busy activities of the home. Baking and boiling, feeding and milking. Teasing and carding and spinning and weaving and knitting and sewing and washing and ironing. And making sups of tea for the endless stream of callers. Rakers, they called them, those who shortened the day and the night and stole the working time. A hundred thousand welcomes to you. Just wait till I finish this skein.

When Sally Rua was thirteen, a lady from Monaghan, a Miss Burns, came to Wavesend to open a lacemaking school there. The Congested Districts Board had sent her, and her brief was to teach twelve likely girls a craft which would help them supplement their family income. The craft was crochet. The people of Wavesend, and Miss Burns too, called it 'flowering'. Twelve girls, including Sally Rua, assembled in a room in the real teacher's house, which had been kindly lent to Miss Burns. There she began to teach them the rudiments of her craft.

Miss Burns was thirty-six, pretty and mellow, not mad and volatile like Miss Gallagher, the real teacher who was lending them her room. She wore snow-white, high-necked blouses with a dark-blue or a dark-green skirt, and her hair was fair. Leafy brown, fastened to the nape of her neck in a loose bun. Her face was imperfect. There were hairs on her upper lip, quite a little moustache, and Sally Rua thought that this softened her, made her gentler and more pleasant than she might otherwise have been; more cheerful, more enthusiastic about her work of teaching country girls to crochet.

The atmosphere in the chilly room where they worked around a big table was light-hearted. An atmosphere of well-aired orderliness, appropriate to the task in hand. It had less to do with the embroidery, or even with Miss Burns, Sally Rua thought, than with the fact that boys were absent. This resulted in a loss of excitement, of the difficult but not unappealing tension which tautened the air in the ordinary classroom, so that no matter what anyone was doing, they were vigilant, aware that extraordinary things were going on all the time under the apparently predictable surface of lessons and timetables. Here in the single-sex embroidery class there was none of that; only peace and concentration.

The first thing they learned to crochet was a rose. Sally Rua had sewed the clinching stitch and severed her thread by the end of the first day, although most of the other girls spent a week completing the project. By then, Sally Rua could do daisies, grapes, and shamrocks, and had produced a border of the latter for a linen handkerchief. She worked on her embroidery at home as well as at the school, gaining extra light at night by placing a glass jug of water beside the candle, a trick Miss Burns taught them on the first day. (She had also told them that a good place to store the embroidery, to keep it clean, was under the pillow, unless they happened to have a box or a tin. Nobody had.)

'You've already learned all I'm supposed to teach you!' said Miss Burns at the end of the week, smiling kindly but with some nervousness at Sally Rua. She had encountered star pupils before and was not afraid of them, but there was always the problem of what to teach next, and the suspicion that they already knew more than the teacher. 'You could stop coming here, if you liked. You can already earn money.'

Sally Rua did not want to stop coming. Her primary education was over now – the flowering was by way of finishing school. The prospect of spending her mornings sitting outside the house at home, working alone in the early light, and being called upon to do a thousand and one chores, was not immediately appealing. She'd be doing it soon enough anyhow.

'Maybe you can show me how to do that?' She pointed at a large piece of work lying on the table. It was a half-finished picture of a swan on a lake. Miss Burns had drawn the picture on a piece of paper and pinned some net to it. Now she was outlining the shape of the swan with stitches.

'That?' Miss Burns was confused. 'You won't be able to do that. I mean, you won't be able to get rid of it. The Board wants handkerchiefs, not this type of thing.'

'What is it called?'

It was Carrickmacross lace: appliqué. Miss Burns, who came from Carrickmacross, or near it, was doing a piece for her sister who was getting married in a few months' time. The 'picture' was to form the centrepiece of a white tablecloth for the sister's new dining room.

Sally Rua offered to finish it for her, if she showed her what to do, and after some deliberation Miss Burns agreed to this, although it was not strictly ethical. However, Sally Rua continued to do her roses and daisies, and was earning twice as much money as any of the other girls already, so the aims of the Congested District Board were not being thwarted. And Miss Burns was finding the swan tedious.

It was slow work. Sally Rua spent over a week completing the stitching, which looked anaemic and almost invisible against the background of its own colour. Then the paper behind was cut away. And the scene came miraculously to life, etched into the transparent net with a strong white line.

'It's like a picture drawn on ice,' said Sally Rua. In the centre of the hills behind Wavesend, which were called, romantically but graphically, the Hills of the Swan, was a lake, the habitat of several of those birds. Every winter it froze over: the climate was colder in those days than it is now in Donegal. The children of Wavesend climbed the hills in order to slide, and Sally Rua had often done that herself, and had seen crude pictures drawn on the glossy surface with the blades of skates. Once, she had seen something else: a swan, or rather the skeleton of a swan, frozen to the ice, picked clean by stronger, luckier birds.

Miss Burns gave Sally Rua cloth and net to do a second piece of appliqué. She allowed her to make her own pattern, and suggested a few herself: doves, stags, flowers. Sally Rua drew some foxgloves and fuchsias, in a surround of roses, and this was approved of. It was a complicated pattern to work but she managed to do it. Miss Burns said she would send the piece to a shop in Dublin that sold such embroidery, and gave Sally Rua more material. This time, she did a hare leaping over a low stone wall. There were clouds in the background and a gibbous moon.

'It's beautiful,' said Miss Burns. 'But I'm not sure ... it's very unusual.'

'I've often seen that,' said Sally Rua, who had never seen a stag or a dove and had already done the flowers. 'It's not unusual.'

'Well,' said Miss Burns, 'we'll see.'

The shop in Dublin wrote back three weeks later, Miss Burns's last week, and said that they liked the appliqué and were going to send it to New York, where it would be on exhibition at the Irish Stand at a great fair, the World's Fair. They enclosed a guinea for Sally Rua, from which Miss Burns deducted 9p for the material she had supplied.

'You should buy some more net and cambric with some of that money,' Miss Burns advised. 'The address of the shop in Dublin is Brown Thomas and Company, Grafton Street. Do another piece of that Carrickmacross and send it to them. You are doing it better than they can do it in the convents.' And she added, because she was a kind and an honest woman, 'You can flower better than me now, too, you know. You should be the teacher, not I.'

Sally Rua, who had known she was better than Miss Burns on her first day's flowering, took her teacher's advice. She walked seven miles to Rathmullan, the nearest town to Wavesend, and bought some yards of net and cambric. She created appliquéd pictures of seagulls swimming on the waves of the lough, of an oystercatcher flying through the great arch at Portsalon, and of the tub-shaped coracles from which her father and brothers fished. Each of these pictures was despatched to Brown Thomas's, and for each of them she was paid ten and sixpence, half of what had been paid for the first, and, it seemed to her, inferior piece. She heard no more about that or about how it had been received at the World's Fair.

The time required to do the appliqué work was extensive, and in fact it did not pay as well as the ordinary flowering. Sally Rua continued to do a lot of that, although she did not particularly enjoy it. However, she could turn out a few dozen roses or daisies a week, and that was what the merchant who called to the school in Wavesend every Friday afternoon wanted. For every flower she received 4p. The money formed a useful contribution to the family economy, and so the aim of the Congested District Board was fulfilled. and Sally Rua's life settled into a pattern that she found rewarding: flowering and housework by day, appliquéing (and some other forms of entertainment) by night. She was happier than she had ever been before.

It did not last. By September, Miss Burns had left Wavesend and the lacemaking school had stopped. In March of the following year, six pictures later, Sally Rua's father and two brothers were drowned while fishing on the lough during a storm. When the wake and funeral were over and the first grieving past, the practical implications of the disaster were outlined to Sally Rua by her mother. She could no longer afford to live on the farm at Wavesend unless her daughters went out and earned a living (the only son, Denis, was married). The flowering would not be enough. Sally Rua would have to get a real job, one that would support her fully and leave some money over for her mother.

She went to work as a maid in a house in Rathmullan, the house of the doctor, Doctor Lynch. She was the lucky one; Mary Kate and Janey, her sisters, had to go to the Lagan to work as hired girls for farmers. Sally Rua's polish, and her reputation as a skilled needleworker, ensured that she had the better fate. The house in Rathmullan was a square stone block on a low slope overlooking the roofs of the town. It was called 'The Rookery', because it was close to a wood where thousands of crows nested. Sally Rua's room was in the attic, of course, at the back of the house, above the farmyard and with a view of the trees and the crows, which she would have been happier without. It was a small, cold room, but she had little time to spend in it. Her days were long, hectic rounds of domestic and farm routines. The Lynches kept other staff, but not enough, and there was always something to be done.

At first, Sally Rua was not unhappy. Mrs Lynch was a reasonable woman who wanted her servants to be contented, if for no other reason than she would get more out of them in that way. She spoke Irish to them, since she knew they preferred it, and to her children, because really she felt more at home in that language herself, even though the doctor, from Letterkenny, wished English to be the language of his household. That did not matter: he was not often at home, and never in the kitchen where Sally Rua spent most of the time when she was not in the byre or the dairy. When she described her life in Rathmullan to her mother, whom she visited once a month, she painted a picture of a calm, contented existence.

This description began to change after about three months. Sally Rua, speaking in a voice which had become low and monotone and should itself have been a warning to her mother, said she was anxious. Her mother, legs parted to catch the heat of the flames, looked at her – anxiously – shook her head and did not pursue the matter. Sally Rua, lying that night on her high bed in Rathmullan, watching the shadows of the giant oak trees gloom across the floor, wept. She told herself she was stupid. She told herself she was sad. She told herself she was miserable, lonely.

What she was missing was the house at Wavesend, her sisters, her friends. Her mother. Homesick she was. She had been homesick from day one. But there was more to it than that. What really made her cry with misery and frustration was the way she was missing her work. Her real work. The flowering.

She had hoped, at first, that there would be some need for that here. That Mrs Lynch would ask her to make some antimacassars for her big armchairs and sofa, which could badly do with them, or runners for the dressing tables and sideboard. After about six weeks she realised that such requests would not be forthcoming. There was plenty of needlework to be done in the Lynch household, all right, but it took the form of mending sheets and underwear and nightgowns, rather than of anything elaborate. Sally Rua was expected to spend every night working at the linen closet and wardrobe of Mrs Lynch and her daughters. She had been employed chiefly for her skills in this line; the other work she spent twelve hours a day doing was simply thrown in as a little extra.

There was, of course, no possibility of doing embroidery in her own room during her spare time, simply because she had no spare time. Every minute in the Lynch household that was not spent sleeping or eating had to be devoted to Lynch work. The only free time she had was one Sunday a month, the Sunday she spent visiting her mother. She did a bit of flowering while she was at home, occasionally. But a few hours a month were insufficient. There was never time to get even one flower finished, never mind a whole picture.

Sally Rua became more and more miserable. She also became more and more cross. She snapped at the other maids and at the lads in the yard, and even at Emma and Louise, the daughters of the house. Gradually her personality was transformed and she became renowned for her bad temper as she had once been renowned for her skill at the flowering. She became so crotchety that sometimes on her day off she did not go to Wavesend at all, but wandered around Rathmullan, staring at the ruined abbey, at the boats moving across the shadowy lough to Buncrana, and at the seagulls wheeling over it. She stared at the crows who built their nests in the high, scrawny oaks that surrounded the Lynch's house.

Once, on a winter's evening, when the moon was a full white circle behind the skeletal trees, she saw a hare on the fence that divided the garden from the bog. Its coat of fur was brown and gold and yellow and purple, streaked with odd white patches. It had a small white bun of a tail. Never had she seen a hare at such close quarters. She was so near that she could see its tawny eyes gazing at her, and its split, trembling lip.

For minutes she stared, and all the time the hare stayed as still as the fence it sat on. Then something happened. A twig fell, a scrap of cloud shadowed the moon. And at that same moment, the hare and Sally Rua moved. She bent, picked up a stone, and flung it hard at the hare's white tail. Before she had stooped to the ground, before she had touched the stone, the hare was gone, bounding over the moonlit turf at a hundred miles an hour.

A few days later, Sally Rua screamed at Mrs Lynch. Mrs Lynch had simply asked her to make a white dress for Louise's Confirmation and had suggested that she do a little embroidery on the cuffs and collar. It was the first time such a request had been made. Daisies, she suggested, might be appropriate. Sally Rua had taken the material, a couple of yards of white silk, and thrown it into the fire. She watched it going up in flames without a word or a cry, and then, as Mrs Lynch, having got over her shock, began to remonstrate, she picked up all the cushions and tablecloths and textiles that were lying about the room (the drawing room) and pitched them on the fire as well. At this point she began to scream. This helped Mrs Lynch to regain her presence of mind, and she ran for help to the kitchen. John, the hired man, and Bridget, the cook, caught Sally Rua and pinned her down to the sofa, while someone was sent for the doctor. There was a certain gratification in imprisoning Sally Rua in this way; it was a slight revenge for all the abuse she had heaped on them over the past months.

There was no psychiatric hospital in Letterkenny then, as there is now. But there was a poor house, with a wing for those of unsound mind, and that is where Sally Rua went. Later it became a psychiatric hospital and she experienced that too, for two decades before her death. She reached the age of seventy-six, and was completely mad for most of her life.

Sally Rua. She went mad because she could not do the work she loved, because she could not do her flowering. That can happen. You can love some kind of work so much that you go crazy if you simply cannot manage to do it at all. Outer or inner constraints could be the cause. Sally Rua had only outer ones. She was so good at flowering, she was such a genius at it, that she never had any inner problems. That was the good news, as far as she was concerned.

Sally Rua. Lennie's ancestor. Of course, none of that is true. It is a yarn, spun out of thin air. Not quite out of thin air: Lennie read about a woman like Sally Rua. She had read, in a history of embroidery in Ireland, about a woman who had gone mad because she could not afford to keep up the flowering, which she loved, and had to go into service in a town house in the north of Ireland. The bare bones of a story. How much of that, even, is true? She might have gone mad anyway. She might have been congenitally conditioned to craziness. Or the madness might have had some other cause, quite unconnected with embroidery. The son of the house might have raped her. Or the father. Or

49

the grandfather or the hired man. People go mad for lots of reasons, but not often for the reason that they haven't got the time to do embroidery.

Still and all. The woman who wrote the history of embroidery, an excellent, an impassioned book, the name of which would be cited if this were a work of scholarship and not a story, believed that that was the cause of the tragedy. And Lennie believes it. Because she wants to. She also wants to adopt that woman, that woman who was not, in history, called Sally Rua, but some other, less interesting name (Sally Rua really was the name of Lennie's great-grandmother, but what she knows about her is very slight), as her ancestor. Because she does not see much difference between history and fiction, between painting and embroidery, between either of them and literature. Or scholarship. Or building houses. The energies inspiring all of these endeavours cannot be so separate, after all. The essential skills of learning to manipulate the raw material, to transform it into something orderly and expressive, to make it, if not better or more beautiful, different from what it was originally and more itself, apply equally to all of these exercises. Exercises that Lennie likes to perform. Painting and writing, embroidering and scholarship. If she likes these things, someone back there in Wavesend must have liked them too. And if someone back there in Wavesend did not, if there was no Sally Rua, at all, at all, where does that leave Lennie?

The Wife of Bath

We're in the Roman baths at Bath. Well, not actually in them, most of us, because we take heed of the sign at the edge of the pool letting us know that the water is not fit for drinking or bathing in, because it hasn't been treated. It's oilskin-green, the water, and steaming in the winter air. All around are antique pillars, beige and terracotta, comfortable and crumbly as fresh digestive biscuits. All around are tourists, French and Swedish and Japanese, emitting small polite sounds, pretty perfumes. Discreet dismay. Controlled disapproval. Of Johnny.

He's on the first step, stooping to test the water with his grubby paw. He's on the second step, splashing. He's on the third, where the water is reasonably deep, and where he therefore thinks it opportune to paddle. His small face is concentrated and stern.

Disgust, plain as Medusa's moon face which is graven on a rock at the side of the bath, is painted on the Gorgon visages emerging from the furry collars of their winter raincoats, peering from beneath their felt, astrakhan, squirrel, fox, hair hats.

It's turned Jim to stone. And no wonder.

So it is I who pull Johnny out. And no wonder.

'Johnny!' I don't shout, I whisper. It's not a church but you feel that sound is sacrilegious here, it's all so ancient, so nice. Bath seems so frightfully bloody nice.

'Johnny, how could you!'

He looks nonplussed, uncomprehending, and indeed the question is rhetorical. Why wouldn't he? Put his feet in a pool of deliciously hot water? The water is not two thousand years old, after all. It's a few minutes old, young and mischievous; it springs boiling and bubbling, full of its own power, full of its own salts, full of its own bubble bath for all I know, from the ground. In other less refined parts of the world, where the crust of the earth is thinner and younger than in England, people swim in this kind of thing, they use it as a public jacuzzi, they wash their clothes in it. Besides, Johnny always does what he feels like doing: plays the piano in a bar, if it happens to contain a piano, swings out of velvet curtains, rushes on to the altars of cathedrals, shouting and singing, effervescent as a fountain, frisky as a lamb. Why wouldn't he paddle in a pool?

He's not even dripping wet. It's just his feet, which happen to be encased in rubber wellington boots. It's as if he knew and had prepared in advance. But this can hardly be the case. It's just one of those miraculous fortuities, sometimes used as proof of God's existence, like the increased proportion of male births following great political catastrophes. How terrible, to have been a mother in 1947, when the world was apparently full of little naughty boys, hardly a girl in sight, if you believe the statistics.

'How could you!'

The Gorgons have released Jim. He's now disgorging

emotions of some sort. What sort? Shame, anger, pain, hatred, fear? They are not positive, that's all one knows, springing up, sulphurous, hellish, splashing out haphazardly over me and Johnny, whom he tends to regard as a unit, like splutters from a kettle, sparks from a firecracker. Sulphur sulphur everywhere and not a drop to drink.

'Johnny, how could you!'

Drink the oilskin filth. God, he'll be sick after this or we're all monkey's uncles. Untreated hot water, two thousand years old, two million years old. How could he!

I met her in a pub. The Hop Pole Inn, it's called. It's in Limpley Stoke, five miles from the centre of the town. She was fat, of course, but that sort of fat which is fertile and attractive, not the morbid, sad kind. Pleasantly plump, people used to say, in the old days before beauty became synonymous with skinniness. She'd a denim skirt, tight and certainly short for someone with such thick thighs, red tights, a red sweater, the long loose kind that's fashionable now and always among students, but not so much among forty-year-olds. Only hers was not all that loose; it left not too much to the imagination. Her hair was dyed blonde, sticking out around her head in yellow spikes from under a navy-blue bandana type of thing. She was drinking a pint, at the bar.

And what was I doing? I was alone, pussyfooting across the threshold, cat creeping into the inn, cavilling, apologising. To whom? There was nobody there; it must have been to myself. But then, I had a dim suspicion that something or somebody was missing, that I'd mislaid a thought or a time or a person, but I was damned if I could remember what. I'm getting so absent-minded! Yes, I eat half a banana a day for the potassium, which is great for the memory, preventing or staving off senility in most, but not, apparently, in me. What those bananas do for me is they make me fat.

'Yes, love?' she turned to me, and I realised she was the barmaid, after all, though on the wrong side of the bar.

'A pint of bitter,' I said.

What do you mean, you don't drink pints and you don't drink bitter? As a matter of fact, you don't really know what bitter is, except in the north of Germany where it's definitely something else, and plural, and if it were that or them you would most certainly not order it.

She heaved herself off the stool and went in behind the counter, drawing a pint of oaky liquid in a few seconds. So efficient, so quick, so much less a pain in the ass than the beer I'm used to.

'On holiday then?'

'Yes,' I said, after a pause. And then, remembering Johnny, I added, 'What's a holiday?'

She answered nonchalantly, 'Search me. I've never had one, as such. Pilgrimages, voyages, yes. Holidays, no. But anyway, welcome to beside Bath.' And she came back outside. 'What's your name?'

'Oh!' I paused again. 'Maureen,' I said. 'I think.'

It was the first name that came into my head. It's the first name that always comes into my head, because, when I was three, the girl who lived in the house next door and was five and tall as a tree and lovely, was called Maureen. She had long hair, brown in colour, and ate nothing except celery. All this I knew. But not my own name.

'I'm Alisoun.'

'Hello, Dame Alisoun.'

'They call me ...'

'I know, I know.' And I did. 'Tell me, have you always kept a pub?'

'No, of course not. I didn't need to, in the old days. Merry England. I had a husband to support me then.'

'One husband?'

'Five, ten, a hundred. What does it matter? They don't support me any more. So I run a pub: don't own it, naturally. I'm just the manageress.'

'It should suit you! You've the personality for the job, I'd guess.'

'Oh, sure! Jolly, matronly type, that's me. I can do it as well as the next, but the fact is, it doesn't suit me at all. What I fancy is ambling around on a stout mare, going on trip abroad or at home. Having a chat.'

'You can have chats here though, can't you?'

'In between the washing up, I can. I used to leave all that side of it to Bert. But poor old Bert, he ...'

'Kicked the can.'

'Yes. Poor old Bert!'

'You should get a dishwasher.'

'I have already. Just like a husband, it is. Does all the easy things and leaves the messy ones for me.'

Hm. 'Tell me,' I settled myself comfortably in my seat, which was a deep tweed cushion. 'Tell me about Jankyn. What happened in the end, to him and you?'

'I'd nearly forgotten about him. It's such a while ago.'

'He was a student.'

'A clerk, he was, of Oxenforde. Is that the one you mean? You know him?'

'Sort of. He's written a lot about the Church Fathers.'

'Yeah, he was a great one for the books, old Jankyn. Or young Jankyn, I should say. Cor, he was half my age, even then. But nice hair he'd got. I fell for his hair and put up with the books for the sake of that.'

'I thought you fell for his legs.'

'Oh, them too, them too! Men's legs, my word! I haven't seen legs like those in three hundred year or so ... at least it feels that long. They're out of fashion. Such a pity.'

'I can't agree, I must say.' And I considered legs, white, black-haired, skinny, and white, black-haired. Grey-white like flour and water paste.

'They weren't the same, the legs I knew. Oh no, not at all. You know men's legs now, how they're thin and all? It's from covering 'em up all the time. if men had their legs out, like we do, they'd be a lot fatter, they would. They used to be much fatter.'

'Even his?'

'His weren't so much fat as shapely. That's what I liked about 'em, actually, as he walked up the aisle.'

I could see the legs then, golden brown, covered with fine hair that the sun danced on, the way sun dances on drops of water, on little summer waves. The legs walked along an aisle, disembodied.

'Was that in the abbey?'

That was it. On the altar, Johnny, fat round legs in blue jeans, screaming: 'I just want to touch it, touch it, touch it! Let me touch it!'

'Naw, it weren't in the abbey, at least not that one you're talking about, beside the Pump Room and all. Lor, no, I wouldn't have been seen dead in that neighbourhood, even then. There weren't no Pump Room then, of course, not that prissy place they have now. No baths, no abbey, nothing like that. Just a nice little tavern and a few washerwomen, very civilised really. I can't stand that place now.'

'It's a bit Jane Austeny.'

'You can say that again. One woman I never could take,

Jane Austen. Silly bitch. Man-crazy.'

'She seems less interested in them than you were, in all fairness,' said I.

'Well, maybe I should have said she was husband mad. The only thing in life was husbands, as far as she was concerned, and she never even got one.'

'Weren't you obsessed with husbands yourself.'

'I was more interested in getting rid of them. Because I had them, one two three four five, once I caught a fish alive. I knew what they were like. Not Jane. It was all pie in the sky as far as she was concerned.'

'At least she did write and analyse the situation a bit.'

There is somewhere a pen rusty, an inkwell dry, a quire of paper lying unopened in a drawer. Did I read of it, did I see it, is it mine? Or some other woman's? Or every woman's?

'So bloody what? Jankyn wrote. Whenever he wasn't reading, he was writing. That was the trouble with him!'

'Remember what you said: if women wrote stories, they'd write such wicked things of men.'

'I would.'

'I would too.'

We laughed together. Her mouth opened in a huge guffaw, the kind women who have made it, who no longer give a straw, who are themselves alone, have. Some are born with it, some acquire it. A rare trait either way.

'Are you married?' she asked.

'Oh yes, I believe so.'

'It's better in the long run, really. It's an experience.'

'It's difficult for me. I'm a feminist.'

'Well, I don't see what that has to do with the price of eggs. I am too, always was, not like Jane Austen.'

'Oh, I don't know if you were, really. I think there are those who'd dispute that.'

'Bloody fools they are.'

'You depended on men rather a lot. I mean, one husband is more than enough for most feminists. But five? God, Elizabeth Taylor is hardly a feminist ... you're more like her.'

'Like hell I am!' She uncrossed her ample legs and stood, feet apart, on the floor. 'I had no choice, you see, that's the difference. What could I have been? I couldn't read or write, like Jankyn. I couldn't star in the movies. I couldn't, really, at that time, manage a public house. Fact is, I couldn't do anything except part my legs on a horse or in bed. And I did that to the best of my ability.'

'You were good at embroidery, I believe.'

She gave me a crafty look.

'Yes, I was. But I did it for pleasure, pure pleasure. It was my art, embroidery, I passeth 'em of Ypres and of Ghent, but I didn't bloody want to wear out my eyesight doing it and selling it for half nothing to ignoramuses who couldn't tell the difference between guipure and appliqué. Do you know anything about needlework?'

'Well ...' No. Not needlework. The point in, the point out, dragging and pulling endless threads. To make, not create. I think I must be different. I am impatient, I want to make new things. To weave perhaps? Weave what? Am I a weaver? Maureen the weaver. Is that who I am?

'The main thing about embroidery, all embroidery, is that it's a great craft and it's always undervalued. I needn't tell you why.'

'No.'

'So, who'd try to kill themselves embroidering? Marriage was easier, in the end, and much more lucrative. Let's be honest. Let's call a spade a spade.'

'Jane Austen did. And Jankyn.'

'Jankyn thought he was smarter than me. But he got his comeuppance, as you know. I got everything back, finally, and he was glad to give it to me. And I got rid of him, too.'

'How?'

That was always easy. They all went, you know, on crusades or whatever, you know; that was how I got shut of them as a rule. But Jankyn, he actually died of jealousy.'

'Really? Isn't that rather unusual? I don't mean to be offensive ...'

'Not of me. One of the drawbacks of the academic life. Another clerk at Oxford got a promotion Jankyn thought he deserved. Because of contacts, you know, the olde storye. Poor Jankyn. He was learned but not very wise, and he couldn't take it. He went mad and then he died.'

'But you married again.'

'Time and time again.'

'That's what I can't understand, really. You knew what it was like. It had always been full of problems. You didn't need the money or anything, but you kept on marrying. Why on earth?'

'Well, I like sex, that was one reason. The main reason ... and the Next, the Next always seems the best. Jankyn walking down the aisle, young with good legs, fair hair ... you know what I mean?'

'Yes.'

Yes. Polygamy is the strongest instinct. Especially in women.

Next is Best.

*

'Like another pint?'

I had another pint. My head was misted over, steaming. From the fog shadows emerged and then went right back again. A golden legged man, for whom I felt huge surges of desire for seconds, until he vanished. And other men for whom I felt no desire, except to know their names.

'And then, there's the battlefield aspect. For the sex war. In the Middle Ages, my prime, so to speak, it was the only sparring ground. Different now. Women vote and belong to trade unions and women's groups and political parties. They can fight with men in all kinds of arenas. But then there was just the one old place. Bed.'

'You think it's all still about maistrye.'

'Oh yes, of course. It was in my day, my olde daye, I mean, and it still is. The difference is that in the Middle Ages I had to get it within marriage ... you don't think those damn pilgrims would have listened to me if I hadn't been married?'

'They listened to the prioresse.'

'Married to Christ. Jesus, I couldn't have stood that. I need to use my instrument, as I've pointed out more than once before.'

'We used to gloss over that bit in class.'

She looked puzzled but not very, and she wasn't the sort of woman to be thrown by a misunderstanding.

'What I mean is, I couldn't have controlled anything outside of marriage, but inside, I had some power.' She tossed her yellow head and thrust out her red breast.

'Really? My impression was that Jankyn, the one you cared about, the only one, gave you a rough time.'

'He did.' Her eyes took on a dreamy look, as she stared through a mullioned window at a dim view of the Avon.

'Hardly feminist, to put up with that!'

'No. But it was worth it. I mean, I loved him.'

'Love hadn't been invented really.'

'It had, as a matter of fact, but it hadn't got to Bath. Didn't matter though. I fancied him. He did things for me. In our bed he was so fresh and gay!'

Our bed is wide and covered with a brown candlewick counterpane. The sheets are white, ironed, fresh. We gaze upon five windows, giving a view of the Hop Pole Inn. We lie in bed from six in the evening, when it gets dark, to six in the morning, when it is light. Jim reads his books: there are ten in his weekend bag, and hardly anything else. Johnny watches television. He has a bath, plays with Lego, draws pictures.

'What's that, Johnny?'

'It's a dirty nappy and wee wee pie.'

'Oh my, it's very good!'

Johnny smiles his angelic smile.

'Would you like to go to bed, Johnny?'

'Nooohh!' he screams, and I hope the hotel manager will not run up to find out what's the matter. Jim lifts his head to scowl at both of us and when the blood-curdling screech fades, bows it once more to the seductive page.

'Were you not a bit of a masochist?'

'Yes. I was a bit of a masochist. I have to admit it ... for a while. And he was a bloody sadist ... it all turned us on, let's face it ... for a while. In the end, I got over it, him, everything. I got what I wanted from him.'

'Maistrye?'

'Yes.'

'It's all so futile!'

'Futile?'

'All that fighting and shouting and scheming. Just to better some no-good little clerk.'

'He was my husband. It was my life.'

'But what a waste of energy! Wouldn't it be better to use it doing other things?'

'Like what?'

'Fighting for women's rights. Educating yourself. Writing books, like Jane Austen.'

'I hate Jane Austen. I hate all that Pump and Assembly Rooms lot ... prim and proper, butter wouldn't melt in my mouth types. They're rotten through and through, much more masochistic than I ever was.'

'But at least she did something ... you didn't do anything. You didn't even exist, for heaven's sake: you are just a figment of some man's imagination, and he chose to make you a nymphomaniac, a woman exploiting men, a shrew ... and see, just look how you've ended up!'

She pouted. 'See how you've ended up!' she said angrily. 'Look at you! Tied to a husband who doesn't talk to you, who spends his holidays with his nose in a book and has affairs with his secretary the rest of the time, while you spend your life battling with that little brat!'

'Johnny's not a brat.'

'He is. Everybody knows that.'

'What can I do?' She looked at me knowingly.

'There's not much. But they do grow up.'

In the dining room we eat breakfast in a corner, secluded, as far as possible, from the other guests. Jim hides behind a newspaper, his hands emerging from time to time to prong a piece of bacon or egg, or snatch a slice of toast from the rack in the middle of the table. Johnny grabs handfuls of cereal, eats a bit, flings the rest on the floor. He crawls under the table and across the room, under the cloth of another table. He pinches an elderly lady on the thigh. She screams and Johnny doubles up with laughter.

'Take him away!' Jim growls. I get up and take him away.

'I'm sorry, Mum,' Johnny says, in his most penitent tones. 'I didn't know I was doing anything wrong. Can I watch TV now?'

As we walk up the shallow red stairs to our room, a frog jumps out of Johnny's pocket and scuttles up ahead of us, fortunately taking a wrong turn on the landing. I pretend I haven't seen him.

'Did you have children?' I asked her suddenly. 'There's lots of stuff about reproduction and so on as an excuse for all the hopping in and out of bed, but there's no mention of kids. I bet you never had one in your life!' I felt triumphant. I'd got her now.

'I'd fifteen,' she said idly. 'How many have you?'

'Him.'

'Just him. All the fuss about that little whelp. I had fifteen, but I never saw them from the day of their birth until they were old enough to behave themselves like decent human beings, and not for long then either. If there's one thing I can't stand, it's children.'

'Didn't it harm them, never seeing you?'

'I would have harmed them much more if they had.'

'And what became of them all?'

'Oh, I forget ... the usual things, I suppose. Millers,

summoners, friars, pardoners, franklins, that sort of thing.'

'You never kept up contact with them?'

'They never kept in touch with me! Children never do, didn't you know?'

'Mm. I ring my mother once a month.'

'Oh, well, I was so mobile. It's only recently that I've come back here, to settle down. I was a roving spirit before then. I've been a wild rover for many a year and now I'm serving up whiskey and beer.'

'You were in Jerusalem, I remember.'

'Oh, I'd love to go back! There and everywhere else.'

'I've always thought travel was so liberating.'

'Let's go on a weekend break to Bath. It's so good to get off this island, even for a few days!'

'With Johnny?' Jim's tone was sceptical.

'It'll be fine.'

'Very well, whatever you wish.'

We churned across the sea to Fishguard, we drove two hundred miles on the M4, we got lost in Limpley Stoke.

'At Limpley Stoke my heart was broke!' Johnny chanted in the back of the car.

'Can't you get him to stop? He's driving me demented.' Jim had been driving around the narrow steep lanes for more than an hour.

'Shut up, Johnny, shut up, please shut up!'

'Feel like a swim?'

'Yes, I always feel like a swim.' I lighten.

'Let's go then ... I can't swim, but I like to bathe.'

'I'll teach you. It's easy as cheese,' I said.

We got up on her broad-backed mare and ambled at a smart pace into the centre of Bath. The crowds were there, the sweet-smelling well-dressed hordes, milling into the museum, queuing up to drink tea in the Pump Room, nodding and smiling, bowing and scraping. I thought I saw Catherine Morland there, I thought I saw Isabella, and a chill descended, momentarily; a deathly fear of doing wrong, putting a foot wrong, not minding my Ps and Qs.

'Pints and Quarts!' yelled the Wife of Bath. 'We're in!'

And we dived, dove, jumped, into the hot natural baths, the crowds cooed oohed aahed and disappeared and I struck out across the pool. Oh, how I love to swim. It dissolves me, it absolves me, it frees my heart and my mind and my soul; above all my soul it frees.

'Alisoun, Alisoun, do not droun!'

'I'm dissolving,' she said, 'I am.' And she was. Bits of her were melting away, as if she were made of baked sugar or something that couldn't last in water.

'Get out, good wife, before you're gone!' I cried. 'Get out.'

'No no, I can't, it's too lovely! Look, you're dissolving too, you soon won't exist, and you did once, not like me. I was just one man's invention. I'm made of parchment. I can't last in water. But you, you're real, and you're going too. It's something in this water … Look at the way it bubbles … You better get out, get out while you have a chance!'

'Does it matter?'

'Does it matter? Does it matter? Does it matter?' The question echoed around the ancient crumbling edifice, bounced off the walls, resounded delightfully in my ear, like some lovely symphony of heavenly sounds. Aquae Sulis: it lapped over me, over her, the Wife of Bath, and we melted away, feet, legs, bottoms, tummies, breasts, one by one.

'Look, you're three-quarters gone!'

Suddenly Jim and Johnny flashed across my line of vision. Then I had a momentary realisation of who I was, what I was, of the privileges and duties that I should bear. But they were all disappearing. There was no weight in the pack any more. I could see only Johnny and Jim as a whirl of limbs, golden, gliding, in the warm stream rising from the warm water, the water which lifted the gravity from every mortal thing, which bore away everything with liquid ease, as I melted, laughing, into the sacred spring.

Gweedore Girl

Mrs McCallum asked, 'Can you cook?'

I said, 'Yes.' This was not the whole truth.

'What can you cook?'

I thought for a moment before answering. 'Most things.'

She looked me in the eye and I knew she did not believe me. 'Most things?'

'Eggs. Porridge, potatoes. I can fry,' I said. 'Bake bread. I can churn.'

'It will not be necessary to do that,' she said, and closed her notebook. It had a dark red cover and later I found out that it was her accounts, listing every penny spent, which she showed to Mr McCallum on Fridays after tea.

I got the situation as a general. I was to have twelve pounds a year, plus board and lodgings. Supply my own uniform. When she asked, I said, yes, I had my own uniform, new. It was not new and it was not a uniform. I had an old cotton dress, blue-and-white striped, which I'd got in the pawn in Falcarragh for three shillings. It was tight around the chest and short in the skirt, but the colour was fresh and suited me. My three aprons I made myself from flour sacks. I washed them ten times and bleached them in the sun until they seemed white as snow. Then I sewed them, finishing them off with frills. I thought they were beautiful, until I saw Mrs McCallum's apron, bought from the shop. It looked like a white lily. Nothing you make at home is as good as the thing you buy in the shop.

My mother said, 'I don't know why young girls are so mad to get married.'

'You did,' I said. She married my father when she was eighteen. (He was thirty-six then, but it was not a made match. I know that much.)

'You'd be wiser off staying single and bettering yourself. You'd have a good life, away from this place.'

I thought she was telling me this because she knew, or suspected, that nobody would want to marry me – the reason being that I am not pretty enough. My mother is small and stout, with a thick bolster of a bosom and brown bulging cow's eyes. She was the best-looking girl in the parish. I know this because she has told me so herself – more than once. She does not use the word that means 'pretty' or 'nice' to describe her youthful good looks, but a word that sounds more like 'elegant' or 'gallant'. When she says that word I see her as a girl made of polished, golden wood, like the curved leg of a fine sideboard, and not a woman made of soft, hot, smelly stuff.

'I was the best-looking girl in the parish,' she says, sighing, looking wearily at me. She is always weary. There are so many of us to look after.

We all look different – some of us like her, some of us like my father, some of us like both of them, some of us like neither. I am more like my father, big made and jet-haired. My eyes are blue and I've a mouthful of slab teeth, horse's teeth.

'Your father looks like a bull,' my mother says sometimes. 'And you take after him.' She hasn't got a lot of time for my father or his side of the family, which is a cut below her own.

My mother says: 'Moya Devanney had great go in her.' Moya Devanney is her first cousin. She went to Derry and worked there for thirty years and they thought the world of her. When her missus died she left her the house and a thousand pounds. 'She'd great go in her and she did well for herself.'

We own our own farm, ten acres, and we own a boat and a seine net. Also twenty hens and ten ducks. Geese before Christmas. We sell the eggs to Hughie the Shop or exchange them for tea and sugar. Only at Easter do we eat eggs ourselves, and on Shrove Tuesday we use some for pancakes.

In the winter my mother sits by the fire and knits socks. The man from Falcarragh comes every Friday to collect them. Tuppence a sock. I helped her knit before I came here but I didn't enjoy that much – the hairy wool scratching my skin, the endless, dull stitching in the half-dark kitchen.

I am allowed an egg for breakfast. I have my breakfast in the kitchen, when Mister and Missus have finished theirs in the dining room and when he has gone to work. I like best being alone for breakfast but often she is in with me, heating milk for the child and telling me all I should do and how I should do it.

69

She is very small. I am like a giant beside her. She likes this, that I make her look even smaller than she is. My mother liked it too. Small women are usually very proud of being small, I have often noticed – as if being small means that they are very clever and good babies, who normally could not be expected to do a single thing for themselves. 'And the size of her!' my father would say proudly when my mother had given a hand with the hay, or baked a big stack of scones for a *meitheal* – something as ordinary and easy as buttermilk scones, that size had no bearing on one way or the other. And she'd smile, as full of herself as a bonny boychild after a bowl of poundies, all thirteen stone of her, wee pet!

That's what himself calls the missus. Sometimes I am beside her in the kitchen when he comes in in the evenings. And over he comes and kisses her and says, 'My wee wee wee pet.' Three wees, like the three wee piggies. And gives me a look as if to say, You big ould heifer, you. And this even though the missus is expecting and has a huge tummy on her like a turnip. But all that does is make the rest of her look tinier. And to be honest, the rest of her is very slight and thin, not swollen up at all. I believe she's delicate, although they'd never let on.

She wears nice clothes – a dark-blue skirt and a frilly blouse, snow-white, starched (by me), a fresh blouse every second day. She sits in the kitchen and chats. 'Don't you miss your family?'

'Sometimes.'

'How many brothers and sisters have you?'

When I tell her – twelve – she gasps and smiles.

'Are they all still at home?'

They are. I'm the eldest.

'It must be strange for you, living in the city.'

'It's different.'

It is different. Every single thing about it is different, so that when I first came to Derry, first got off the train, first came into the McCallums' house, different from any house I had ever been in, I felt completely lost and very tiny, like a little spider or a fly. But I was still myself. I was myself, only smaller. That is the thing that I have found out. And after a few days I began to grow back to being my big self again, and the strange things all around me shrank back to being their own size.

'It's exciting,' I added. 'But you get used to it.'

'Exciting?' She could be as nice as you like when she was interested in something.

'Yes. It is all so different and that makes it exciting.'

'Maybe it is like going to a foreign country, where people speak a different language, and wear different clothes, and where everything looks strange?'

That's it to a tee. It was just like that. Foreign. Foreign language, foreign clothes, foreign place. But, you know, I don't think she knew what she was saying. When she said 'like a foreign country' she was laughing; she meant it was not, of course, really a foreign country. That's where she's wrong. She didn't seem to know at all that at home we speak a different language and that the houses are different and even the people look different. If she knew this, she thought it was unimportant, that they were differences that didn't count. She had never been to Gweedore. Or, maybe, anywhere.

'Have you been to a foreign country?' I asked.

'Och no. We go to Portrush on our holidays. That's it.' She wanted to go to France. Her friend had been there last year, staying in Paris. And she wanted to go to London. That's what she meant by foreign. 'No harm in dreaming,' she said. 'I'll never see further than Portrush. Or Dublin, if I'm lucky.'

I wondered what Portrush was like. She tried to tell me. There is the sea and a beach and a place for men to bathe and women to bathe. There is a promenade and a lot of hotels, and brass bands playing along the seafront in special stands, like merry-go-rounds. (What is a stand? What is a merry-go-round?) And people on holiday, walking about. There are children making sandcastles and old men paddling. Sometimes I thought it sounded like Derry, sometimes like Gweedore. Sometimes I just could not picture it at all. I hoped she'd say, You'll see it yourself when we go in the summer, but she never did. It was January when I started with them, and I thought she would be having the baby at maybe Easter, if not sooner. Maybe they would not go to Portrush at all.

I had to do everything in the house. Clean everything, scrub everything, cook everything, wash everything, and also mind the baby. Missus did nothing, really. Nothing worth mentioning. She was too small, too delicate, too tired. At first I was tired too, very tired. I felt homesick because I was so tired. I would lie on my bed, when I finally got there at about eleven o'clock, and cry from tiredness. It was, I thought, as if I had come into a lovely place, a place like the Eastern world, the shining kingdoms I knew about from old stories, but had to work so hard there that the magic world turned into a nightmare.

After a while I became accustomed to the work and managed it better. And I must say that from the start I loved the house. It astonished me. The storytellers never described the insides of the castles and palaces the princes and princesses lived in at the end of the tale. They just said they were full of good things to eat and drink, and fine golden goblets and cups of silver. But they must have had other things in them. Lace cloths, silver vases of carnations, brass bowls with green plants growing in them, cabinets full of white china painted with roses. Mirrors, curly-legged tables and chairs. They must have had beds covered in silk sheets or snowy linen trimmed with crochet. Mrs McCallum's house was so cluttered up with such things that I felt I would never get to know them, and I could hardly imagine that she had ever had the time or the strength, let alone the money, to get them all.

But I did get to know them, soon, because I had to dust them all three times a week. I got to know them intimately, the china shepherdesses, the green cat on one side of the fireplace and the white dog on the other, the silver cruets, like baskets lined with blue glass, the twisted candlesticks. First it seemed like a treasure cave, or a shop crammed with things, confused, unknowable. And I was moving around, wondering. And then I knew them, every one. Liked some. I liked the shepherd, who was pale-pink and blue, and had a harmless smiling face and a wavy crest of yellow hair, not like any boy or girl I have ever seen. Hated some. The green cat, which was the colour of York cabbage, crinkled like that, with a wild, angry snarl. Why would anybody like a thing the like of that?

Mrs McCallum did. 'I love my green cat,' she said when I once criticised it. 'It is so artistic.'

Artistic. A new word for me. Like arthritis. The cat was like gangrene, arthritis, bitter cabbage, and I thought that is what artistic meant, except it was good, like France. Flat, plain 'France'. It reminded me of bedsprings, springy steel things. I did not like the sound of it much but it sounded much better than 'artistic'.

*

73

She went out a lot, the missus, even in the state she was in. I realised that is how she came by so much stuff – she went to the shops every day and bought. Sometimes she showed me the things. A blue shiny plate. A new silver instrument for beating eggs. More often she got clothes for herself or for the child. Ribbons, stockings. Also hats, jackets, dresses, nightgowns.

'He'll murder me if he finds out,' she said.

What could I say? I did not think he would murder her. I did think he would be cross. She showed him her red book on Fridays and they shut themselves into the room, locking the door, all important. She was nervous – for good reason – and he bossy and stiff like a sergeant major, even though normally they were not like this to each other. It was as if they both decided to become different people, on Fridays. And they did this because they liked it. I could see it when they came out, they kept glancing at each other, their eyes looking teasing and dangerous. And they went straight up the stairs afterwards, always.

She did the real shopping too, and that was her excuse for being out all the time. She called every day to the baker's, the dairy; several days a week to the butcher's, the greengrocer's, the grocer's. She only sent me to the shops when she was so tired she could not get outside the door, or when it was raining very heavily, or when she had forgotten something. Mostly she left me with the baby and the house while she was out.

I did not get to the shops but I met the delivery boys who carried the things she had bought to the house in the baskets of their bicycles, or under their arms. The baker's boy and the milkman, the grocer's lad and the butcher's. They came and banged on the window of the kitchen and left their parcel on the sill. All except the butcher's boy. He came to the door, knocked, handed over his brown parcel stained with blood. If he left it outside the cat would have got it.

The butcher's boy was Elliot and he came of a Tuesday, Wednesday, Thursday and Saturday. Mondays we ate cold meat left over from Sunday and on Fridays, fish, since they were, like me, Catholic, although they looked Protestant. Elliot looked Protestant too, like all the other boys. He wore a brown jacket with patches everywhere and a big peaked cap covering his head and his eyes. The only different thing was that he always had a white shirt. You could see the snowy collar sticking out over the jacket.

He was full of cheek. 'There you are, wee pet,' he said on the first day, and ran off.

'How is my wee fairy today?' he said on the second day.

'Cheek of you,' I said, or something like that. 'None of your lip.' I'd learned some of these expressions from school and from Mrs McCallum. 'Cheek of you calling me wee pet and me old enough to be your mother.'

I thought he would say something like, And big enough to be my father – in Gweedore, boys teased me about my height. But he said, 'You don't look it', in a serious and nice voice.

All of a sudden I felt like crying. I did not know what had come over me. 'Go away out of that,' I said. 'Haven't you a job to do? Like meself.'

In the morning I get up at six and light the range and bring them tea in bed. When I go into the bedroom Missus is awake, lying against the white bolster with her fair curly hair frizzed out against it, some of it falling down over her shoulders. Her dress is lying on the chair beside the bed and her clothes, her white underclothes, are sometimes on the chair and sometimes on the floor, so that I have to pick them up as soon as I've left down the tray on her knees. He is asleep beside her. All I see are his big brown whiskers sticking out over the edge of the quilt, wiry and thick, funny beside her soft fair face and her soft white nightdress. The room smells of them and of bedrooms, that thick, skinful, shameful smell. As soon as I open the door I get it and then I am walking through their smell as if it were a soup. The smell of their sleeping bodies, lavender water, soap, the smell of their chamber pot under the bed (I would have to empty it later, carrying it, covered by a bit of newspaper, out to the lavatory down the back). The child is with them in his cradle near the bed and always cries when I walk in.

I leave the tray and get out as quickly as I can from the room. As I go out, I know she is stretching out for the baby and his eyes are opening and looking at me. He was just pretending to be asleep. There is always a difference between people who pretend to be asleep and people who really are. Maybe it is that people who are asleep can't pretend anything, and you can see that on them. They look so foolish, often, their faces doing things they wouldn't let them do if they could help it.

'Any chance of a cup of tea?' he said.

'The missus doesn't let me give tea to people.' She hadn't said that. But it was just because it never occurred to her that I would. She had said in the interview, 'No followers', and Mister had glanced at her and smiled, as if to say, We don't have to worry about that.

'She's not here,' he said. 'I just seen her down in the Diamond.'

This was after I had been with them about three weeks. It was the beginning of February.

He came in and sat at the table while I wet the tea. When I had my back turned to him he took off his cap, and when I turned around I saw his hair for the first time. It was a big fair bush, curly gold, standing out in a crest around his head. I had never seen such hair on a boy before and could not take my eyes off it.

He took bread and butter and dipped it in the sugar bowl. 'She'll be raging,' I said, 'if she finds out.'

'You're allowed to eat,' he said. 'What time do you get up in the morning? When do you go to bed?'

My bedroom is a room at the back of the kitchen, cosy and warm in winter, at least. It used to be a storeroom and there are shelves along one wall still, containing broken crockery, old basins and jugs and chipped potties, that she doesn't want to throw out yet, but can't use. There is no window, so I have to leave the door open or light the candle to see anything. A bed, a chair. On the wall is a little mirror without a frame. It has brown freckles all down one side, but if I light the candle, I can see myself all right. I can see myself but I can't do my hair or anything at the same time, because there is nowhere to put down the candle.

Nevertheless, I spend a long time looking at my face in the mirror, because at home we hadn't one and I do not really know what I look like. Now I still don't know. That is, I know, but I do not know if I am pretty or not. The face in the freckled mirror looks nice to me. The cheeks are pink, the eyes are blue, the mouth is red, the hair is black and curly. It is not a bit like Mrs McCallum's face, of course, and maybe there are all kinds of things I do not see, in the dark, and because I am trying to make it out to be better than it is. How can you know these things? Maybe I look nice to myself, and to everyone else, ugly.

Before Elliot comes, I go up to her room if she is out and do my hair in the mirror on her dressing table. After a while I use her brush with the silver back, and I dab a bit of her lavender water behind my ears, and a little of her powder on my nose, which is shiny because I am so hot from all the work.

He asked me if I had a half-day.

Wednesday. I get off after the lunch, and I'm allowed off until nine at night. What do I do with the time? I walk around. I walk around and look in all the shops. I walk around the walls and look at the river. I walk by the harbour and look at the boats. Walk and look is what I do. I love that.

He could meet me at six. I'd like to go to a show? There is a music hall on the Strand, but the show is not over until half past ten. Then we'll just go for a walk.

Since this is what I do all the time I am pleased enough.

It is better walking with him than walking alone. People don't stare at me when I am with him, looking me up and down, as if they despised me or as if they liked me. When I am with him they just glance at us and look away again quickly, or else stare at him. It is better, because he talks to me and makes jokes, and because he knows the place inside out, tells me who lives in what house, tells me stories about every place we see.

What sort of stories? Stories about women who were murdered and chopped up into small pieces and served up in pastry for dinner. Stories about the devil appearing at card games and about ghosts who come back to repay money they owed to usurers or to landlords. A story about a bailiff who was cursed by a widow and taken off by the devil in his bag. The bailiff had met a man who turned out to be the devil. The devil said he was walking around, planning to take whatever would be offered to him from the whole heart on that day. A woman cursed her pig for digging up her potatoes, saying, 'The devil take you!' And the bailiff said, 'Take that pig now!' 'I will not,' said the devil, 'because she did not offer it from the heart.' Then they see a mother chasing her son across the road. 'The devil take you!' she says. But the devil will not take him, because the wish was not sincerely meant. Then they come to the house where the bailiff is going to issue an eviction notice to an old widow. She comes out and begs him for mercy. But he won't give her any. 'The devil take you!' she says. And the devil takes the bailiff off to hell because the widow's wish came from the heart.

Elliot laughed a lot at this story, which I did not think so very funny. A lot of his stories were about money, or bailiffs.

He had other stories, though, some concerning himself.

He found a baby in a bag on the Strabane Road once when he was a little boy. 'I was walking along collecting blackberries,' he said, 'and I saw this bag with two legs sticking out of it. I thought it was a wee cat or a dog or a doll maybe. And I went over and took off the bag and it was a little baby. No clothes on her or nothing.' 'What did you do?' I asked. 'Went to the police,' he said.

He asked me questions as well. Not questions like Mrs McCallum's how-many-brothers-and-sisters-have-you-don't-you-miss-them? He really wanted to know things. He wanted to know how many of us slept in the same bed and what sort of cover we had on the bed, and how many cups and saucers we had. He asked if I could swim or if I went fishing on the shore or in the burn. He wanted to know how many new dresses I had had in my whole life and what sort of dress I would buy if I had all the money in the world. He wanted to know what my mother looked like and my father, and what I got to eat at the McCallums', and what Mrs McCallum wore in bed, and how many pairs of shoes she had, and what he worked at, and how many pairs of shoes he had, and how many shirts, and did I iron them? Everything? The tails and all?

I wanted to know everything about him, too, but I did not ask questions. Why, I don't know. Maybe because so much of the time went talking about me, about Gweedore and about the McCallums. I didn't know there was so much to say, but now I found out there was. My life turned into a big, long story that went on and on and I kept finding new things in it that I hadn't ever thought about. He even asked me about my dreams, so that when I was finished talking about things that had really happened, there was all that stuff that happened when I was asleep to tell him as well.

He wasn't backward about talking about himself either and I found out things. He lived with his mother who was a widow, his father had been a driver, driving a horse and cart for a coal merchant, and now his mother worked at the shirt factory. He had only one sister and she was also at the shirt factory. Her name was Victoria. She was a card, he said, and he told me a lot of things about her, about the funny things she said and did.

Being with him was like being in an egg, I thought. The two of us in one shell. When I was not with him I thought about all kinds of things – I was worried about what Mrs McCallum thought of me, I wondered how they were getting on at home, I thought that maybe I would not have a job next year, and also that I would still be in this job and that I could not stand it. Worries and ideas. But when I was with Elliot it was as if all that stuff was not in the world. It was as if the world stopped moving, and there was only one whole thing, me and Elliot, one whole, bright, perfect egg, with the light shining on it.

Missus had the new baby in March. There was a midwife in and a nurse for a week, but the bulk of the nursing and the work fell on me. I have seen many babies being born and I knew that this birth was not difficult. A short confinement and a healthy baby. She made the most of it, however, her being so little and delicate and all.

'She is so fragile,' she said. The baby was a girl, tiny, only five pounds, but of course that was because Missus is tiny herself. I told her this but she ignored it. She wanted the baby to be delicate. 'Isn't she tiny, a tiny little doll? Her head is like an eggshell! I am afraid she will snap under my fingers if I am not careful.'

She would not feed her herself, her breasts were small and anyway she wouldn't want to. A woman like that. Too much trouble for her. She'd sooner let me do the work and lie there reading books from the library that he brought home for her. I was up to my eyes boiling bottles and boiling milk and nursing the baby as well, and there was the other wean to mind, the wee fellow, with his wee nose out of joint because of the new arrival. His mammy paid little attention to him now that she had her new pet, a wee girl. For a month she stayed in bed playing with her – Molly, she started calling her. I was up and down the stairs a hundred times a day.

'You are a treasure,' Mr McCallum said.

We were alone together a lot of the time now. The whole house was through-other thanks to wee Molly. Sometimes he ate his dinner in the kitchen to help me out a bit. More often he ate it from the tray with herself up in the bedroom, which did not help me at all, just made matters worse. Up and down with the soup, up and down with the dinner, up and down with the sweet, up and down with the cup of tea. I was getting thin.

He patted my shoulder. He patted my head. He patted my bottom. Nothing more. And I didn't mind him much.

He was bigger than me, which was nice for a change (Elliot was barely the same size, and a good bit thinner). And I felt I knew him so well. Knew his shirts and his underclothes, his socks. I knew his thick sleeping smell, his sleeping whiskers. I made his food for him and threw out what he did not eat in the pig's bucket. I knew the smell of his piss. He was as known to me now, really, as my own brothers or sisters. Better known, in fact, than most of them.

I got used to it and I started to wait for it, to tell the truth. The feel of his big hand on me. I missed it if he forgot, but he didn't usually. He'd just rub me, wherever, just once, and then we'd go on with whatever we were doing as if this hadn't happened. It meant we looked each other in the eye in the morning, amused. I wasn't afraid of him at all.

He rubbed my breasts, standing beside me, asking me to put down a bigger fire than usual, his mother and father were calling to see Molly. My body leaped to life when he did that and I wished he would go on. I had to catch my breath. But he just said, 'They'll come at seven o'clock just after tea. Please see to it, there's a good girl. And we will have some biscuits and cocoa at about ten.'

'Very well, sir,' I said.

*

Elliot rubbed me, too. My legs, my breasts, down there, between and inside. A sin, I supposed, but I never bothered much about sins one way or the other, and I liked it quite a lot, especially if I did not think about it while we were doing it. And I loved to kiss him. We kissed all the time. After the first month or so we didn't walk around much any more. The evenings were getting longer and we went outside the city to the banks of the river, or to fields, and we sat and kissed, or lay in the grass and kissed, rubbing our bodies hard together. I knew that to do anything else, any of the tame, calm things we did at the beginning, would have been a waste of our short time together: the time we had now was meant for lying in the grass and kissing, for that alone, and there was never enough time, for kissing Elliot, for feeling his body, hot and sweet and pounding, press into mine. I always left him with huge reluctance, unable to believe that I could continue to exist away from his arms and his mouth.

When I came home from these evenings I was dishevelled, with my stockings torn as often as not, and inside I felt strange. Ripped. I was with him, wrapped up in him in every way, and then I was ripped away from him, so that I felt torn like an apple that has been broken in two. I'd want to cry and even scream for a while. I could not bear being without him – even though I knew that tomorrow I might see him again and in a week I would lie in the grass with him again, and taste his mouth and his skin, and draw his heat and his strength into me. Knowing it all did not lessen the pain a bit.

That was strange. But even stranger was the fact that gradually my own world would come back around me, would close over me like skin growing over a scratch on my arm. Elliot would fade away, and the house and the babies and the shepherd on the mantelpiece would swim around me once more and take over. Her yellow hair that I combed for her sometimes. His big hand on me.

For a day or two after Wednesday I hated the hand, Mr McCallum's hand. I put up with it. I had to. But it made me angry and disgusted. And the funny thing was, after Wednesdays he was worse. He never missed Wednesday night, although I was not home until nine o'clock. He'd be there waiting for me. As if he knew. Well, he did know – not that I was with Elliot, but that I was with some boy. I don't know how. Maybe people can smell it off you? And that annoyed him and made him touch me not once, on Wednesdays, but three or four times. Made me wish I could lock the door of my room, but I could not.

Easter is when people get married.

Elliot came to me the week before Palm Sunday. It was not a Wednesday. I no longer saw him every Wednesday because on some Wednesdays he had to work, or to be with his mother. Also the McCallums sometimes asked me to work on Wednesdays now, to mind Molly.

This was a Tuesday. He called around with the meat, and came in for tea. She was in bed. I was worried that she would hear anyway, and come down, as she sometimes did, in her wrapper, but I had not seen him in ten days and I let him in.

'Little Biddy.' This was his name for me. 'We could get married.'

I hadn't expected that. I had thought about it and I wanted to marry him but I did not think he would ask me yet.

'Glory be to God,' I said.

'You want to, don't you?'

'Yes.'

'I think we should. You are fond of me?'

'Yes. You know that.' I was more fond of him than I ever had been of any other human being. It is amazing how fond I was of him. Fonder than of my mother and father and twelve brothers and sisters put together, or of the McCallums or the babies, or my pal at home, Sava. It is astonishing that you can be that fond of somebody you haven't even known for long. It is not sensible. Still, that is how it was with me, I might as well be honest.

'Well then.'

'My situation ...'

'You are not their slave. Maybe you can stay on for a while anyway. You don't have to tell them.'

'No? Wouldn't I live with you? Where?'

'You could live with me and my mother. Or you could go on living here. It would mean we could ... Biddy, I don't want to wait.'

He meant, stick it in. That's what he was saying to me. We had not done that. I hadn't let him because I know what happens next. And we had such a nice time not doing it anyway, pressing hard together. I thought that would be enough for him since it was for me. For me it was all I thought I could get. That is what I thought then.

'Well ... when would we?' I said.

'Palm Sunday.'

'But that is next Sunday!'

'Yes. I know someone who will marry us then, and I can get a licence quickly.'

'Is it a priest?'

Elliot was a Catholic, he told me when I asked him. But

I thought you could not get married on Palm Sunday if you were a Catholic. I felt a shiver running down my back. Someone walked on my grave.

'Yes, yes, a priest.'

'All right then,' I said. I was so fond of him, I could not imagine not marrying him sometime anyway. I knew perfectly well that it was the only right thing and the only possible thing in the world. On the other hand, I could not imagine marrying him now. So suddenly. I thought all that would take a long time and that lots of people would know about it and be part of it. 'I will go on living here for a while until we find our own place.'

'You're a treasure,' he said. He had not said that before. 'But there is one thing. I need a pound to buy the licence now, and I will need a pound for the wedding on Sunday. Can you give me the pound?'

I didn't like parting with one of my pounds. I only had three altogether. But I gave it to him. I knew he gave most of his money to his mother.

On Wednesdays when I was not with Elliot I stayed at home with the baby, or else walked around, as I used to do before I had started courting him. For that is what it was, courting, although I had not called it that earlier. I had not called it anything. I didn't need to, since nobody knew about it apart from the two of us and when we were together we were like one person. It is only when there is another that you need to put names on things.

The city was familiar to me now, and the shops and everything less surprising and smaller than they had seemed when I first came. I felt somehow impatient with them, tired of them, fed up with them. They had seemed so glittering and grand and now I had no interest whatsoever in them. Dusty, they seemed, full of useless gimcracks, stupid clothes that cost more money than I would ever have. When I was on the street I found myself thinking of home, home in Gweedore, and of the shore, and of the burn. I wished I could be at home for a day or two and see my friends, and see the chickens and the ducks, and talk the way we talk there, and see the cats. The children, my brothers and my sisters. I missed them now, whereas before, I had not thought about them much. I missed my father. He would be turning the field near the house, putting in the seed potatoes and the cabbages. I thought of the clay, brown and thick and wet and stony and smelling of the dead and the living – the Gweedore clay.

I took to going down to the harbour and looking at the boats. It is not, of course, like the harbour at home. There are a lot more boats, big ones and small, and more going on, in Derry. I thought the seagulls and the waves would remind me of home, but they didn't. They were the same, really, as the seagulls and waves at home, but they didn't remind me of them. The waves broke against the wall, plop plop plop. The seagulls wheeled and screamed. But to me they were all flat, like pictures in a paper or a book.

Something was being built at one end of the harbour. Later I found out what it was – a factory for curing fish. I liked to stop there and look at the muddy building site. Men swarming all over it, men in dirty old clothes carrying big stones, bags of mortar, hammering and sawing and breaking up the ground with huge axes. In McCallums' I had only seen Mr McCallum and the delivery boys, the postman, sometimes the men in the shops. They were pale men with white soft hands, men that were indoors most of the time. Not like my father or the men at home.

Now I saw where the other kind of men were. They were at the harbour. They were on the boats and they were on the building sites. Their bodies were different from Elliot's and Mr McCallum's. They were wider, broader, stockier. Stronger. They had red skin, leathery, and their hands had thick fingers. They were always covered in clay or mortar or dust and they smelled of that sort of thing. They smelled of clay and of work, not of themselves. Like my father. Those men were part of their work and part of the earth, like animals, I suppose. Real animals. Elliot and Mr McCallum were like women, like the pussycat, soft, sleepy. Well looked after.

Aye. Still, watching the men at the harbour, I would think how superior Elliot was, with his white face, his long, fine hands, his mop of angel hair. I would think how strange it was, that I, a Gweedore girl, would fall in love with and marry such a boy as Elliot.

On Palm Sunday he called for me at four o'clock. Where were they? I don't recall. I think they were out visiting, for once, themselves and the older child. I had the baby with me, in the cradle, and we were together in the kitchen. I had a new dress, because he had asked me to be fine for the wedding. The dress was lilac and white, with a lilac sash. I'd done up my hair with a matching ribbon. Over it all I had a new white apron, just to fox Mrs McCallum.

'You look lovely,' he said when he saw me. I had the kitchen neat as a pin. My big, lovely kitchen.

'Thank you.'

He was wearing his Sunday clothes. He also looked lovely. But he always did. He was the most beautiful boy I ever saw.

'Something terrible has happened. Sit down there, will you?' His mother was being thrown out of her house. She couldn't pay the rent because she'd been sick during the spring and had fallen behind. 'I had to give her the pound to fend off the bailiffs,' he said. 'There was nothing I could do. But we can get married next week. That is all it means. I'll need another pound, though.'

'It's my last pound,' I said, as I gave it to him. I'd spent fifteen shillings on the dress and the apron and things. I was crying as I said this, because of the pound and because I was so disappointed.

'I'm so sorry, my dear darling. But what could I do? I really couldn't do anything else. It is only another week and you'll like it better on Easter Sunday anyway.'

'Who are the witnesses?' I hadn't even thought of this before.

'Two butties of mine. Douglas Hamilton from the shop and his girl. Victoria will be there, too, and my mother.'

'Is she better?'

'What?'

'Your mother.'

'She's a bit better. She might be able to come, or she might not. But she knows about it.'

'I never met her.'

'You'll meet her next Sunday. Or would you like to meet her before that? I could take you home on Wednesday?'

'Yes. I think I'd like that. I think I should see her before the wedding, don't you?'

'If you want to. Grand. I'll call for you on Wednesday then, at about four o'clock.'

'Don't call for me. I'll meet you somewhere. Say somewhere.'

'I'm going to be so busy on Wednesday. But all right.

I'll meet you under the clock at Austin's the draper's on Wednesday.'

'At four o'clock.'

'Four o'clock. I've got to run now. Bridget' – he took my head in his hands, he kissed me on each cheek and then, quickly, on the lips – 'I love you very much.'

He'd never said it before. I believed him. I still believe him.

You know how this story ends.

I was under the clock on Wednesday from four o'clock until six. Staring at the sky. It was a strange sky, with streaky clouds and fluffy clouds mixed together, and sharp blue patches with white streaks racing across them. I watched the fluffy clouds turn black and the streaky clouds race across, across, across, for two hours, and the seagulls wheel and the starlings flock and chatter on the shiny gutters.

Then I went home, all dressed up in my finery. I knew his address but I thought I'd wait until he came for me. I still thought he'd come for me.

By Sunday, Easter Sunday, he had not come, not even with the meat. Another boy left it on the windowsill, liver, dripping blood. When I asked him where Elliot was, he said he hadn't a notion.

On Sunday I went to his house, leaving the baby alone. This was at five o'clock, the time we were supposed to get married at. It was on Ross Street. Fifty-three Ross Street, a little two-storey house with no garden.

A girl about my own age answered. She was much smaller than me and had fair hair.

'Victoria?'

'I'm not Victoria.'

'Is Elliot there?'

'What do you want with him?'

'I'm a friend of his.'

'Well, I'm his wife.'

I screamed and shouted and pushed into the house. Into their sitting room.

'Go home,' he said when he saw me. He did not use my name, then, or ever again. He looked weary, as if I were a bold wean that had to be humoured. 'Go home. Just go home.'

'But you're supposed to be marrying me,' I said.

'I got married last week. To Louise.'

'You asked me.'

'Leave this house. You are trespassing.'

'And you took my money. You took my two pounds on me.'

'If you don't get out, I will call the police.'

'Two pounds. You owe me two pounds.' I shouted about the two pounds. There were lots of things to shout about but that is what I latched on to, the thing that mattered least to me.

'If you were a man, I'd knock you down.'

'I'm not a man. I'm a girl.'

'You're as big and awkward as any man, any old ape of a Paddy digging his way through the muck.'

He put his arm around Louise. She was as small as Mrs McCallum, although not, really, as pretty. To tell the truth, she was like me, a smaller version of me, if the reflection in my foxy mirror is anything to go by. He did not press her tightly to him, but handled her lightly, as if she were fragile and easily damaged.

I had to go away. I had to go home without my two pounds and without Elliot.

91

*

I reported him to the police for taking my two pounds, and promising to marry me, and threatening to strike me if I were a man.

It was Mr McCallum who told me to do that.

When I came home he was waiting. They were wondering where on earth I'd gone, leaving the baby alone and unattended. I hadn't even thought of what I would tell them if I'd been off getting married, much less what I would tell them if I'd been off not getting married. And I felt so confused. I felt I was not in the world at all, that the world had turned into a new place that I did not recognise, where nothing was where it should be or what it should be. If the baby had jumped out of the cradle and bitten me, I would not have been surprised.

Mr McCallum put his arms around me and patted me on the bum.

'Sue him,' he said, 'for breach of promise, dear little Biddiebums.'

He led me into my room and put me on the bed. And licked me. He was full as an egg and could do no harm but he did rather a lot that I could have done without. I didn't care. I didn't have the strength to do anything about him, and I don't know what I could have done anyway. I felt that I was all heart. I could see my heart like a big cow heart, the kind they have in the butcher's, red and livery and covered in a lacy veil of white dripping, and I could see it throbbing, I could feel it throbbing, big and ugly and bloody and torn, inside its veil, inside me. It felt as if it would burst out through my ribs, as if I were filled up with it. And sometimes I felt empty as well, as if I had been tipped upside down and poured out. Either way, I didn't care what happened to me and I let him slobber all over me from top to toe and then fall asleep at the end of my bed.

The next day I was dismissed by him, for having been away from the house without permission when I was supposed to be minding the baby.

I met Elliot in court. He looked better than ever, in a starched white shirt and a black jacket, and when the judge found against him, he nodded curtly and left the courtroom without looking at me. In case it would do some good, maybe. As much as I wanted my two pounds, I wanted him to look at me and to say my name. Bridget.

I dreamed of him that night, and on many other nights.

I dreamed I was to meet him in a town by the sea, not Derry or Gweedore or anywhere I know. One of the places that I go to when I dream. This is a flat place with sand dunes and a lot of rushes. In this particular dream it was near Derry.

I was in this place with Elliot and I knew that Louise was not far away. I arranged to meet him in the sand dunes, near a house that stands there.

When I came to the sand dunes a woman approached me and asked me to walk with her to the corner of the road. The woman was not any woman I know but she was very tall and she looked like someone I knew. My mother maybe, or some woman I see often but do not talk to.

I did not want to miss Elliot and I knew if I was not there that he would not wait for me. But I did not want to disoblige this woman. I decided I would try to do both things.

I walked halfway down the road with the woman. Then I said, 'Is this far enough?'

'No,' she said. 'It's not far enough. You must come the whole way with me.'

But I didn't.

The next thing Elliot appeared, with Mr McCallum. Elliot signalled to me, with a knowing, sly face, his head down in his collar, that he could not talk to me now, and Mr McCallum looked at me and then looked away, as if he did not know me.

I looked at the woman. She was lying on the ground. I picked her up. She had turned into a piece of paper. She was a large cut-out doll, drawn in heavy black ink, with an old ugly face like a witch. She was folded in two on the ground and I opened her up and spread her out and read her.

Elliot was gone and I had to run after him, as in all my dreams about him, knowing I could not catch him again that night, but that I would meet him, some other night, in some other dream.

They wrote about me in the paper:

GWEEDORE GIRL DECEIVED AND RUINED.

That was not right. I was deceived, but not ruined (by which they meant up the pole).

I had got my two pounds back, and had another job by then, not as a general, but in a shop, which was much better. I lived in a room over the shop with four other girls who worked in it, and was free much more than I had been with the McCallums. I'd even got a new boy – a carpenter from the yard down by the docks, with black hair and thick hands, twinkling eyes. His name is Seamus and he is a good boy, kind, and funnier than Elliot, and earning much more money. I know I can marry him any time I want to.

It is amazing that I know that Seamus is good and kind and honest and will never mistreat me; also I will never love him. Or maybe that is not amazing at all. Maybe those two knowings are the same, two different knowings in the same shell, or one and the same knowing, bright as an egg with the sun dancing on it.

Estonia

Lunchtime, the best time of the day, is over. Emily has spent it as she often does, walking the streets, not altogether aimlessly but permitting herself to digress every step of the way. First, she window-shopped in Grafton Street, going into one shop and examining three racks of evening dresses: still black velvet; stiff, noisy taffeta. She is not going to a ball, she does not require a frock, but as she stroked the cloth, she remembered dances she had attended and dresses she had worn. Life can be measured in skirts of satin, as well as in years of work, as well as in examinations passed and books read, or husbands married or children offered to the world. (Emily tends to philosophise while she shops. Maybe that's why she likes lunchtime so much.) After the dresses, she bought an egg mayonnaise sandwich at a takeaway and ate it in Stephen's Green, sitting on the grass on the bank of the olive duck pond, surrounded by hundreds of other lunchers. It is still possible to sit out in late September. The temperature is nineteen degrees. Low yellow sun bathes everything that is not golden already in syrupy light. When

Emily was a child and still believed in heaven, her picture of it – a high, pinnacled golden gate, shut – was coloured in this precise tone of sunlight.

'Wasn't it terrible, the disaster in Sweden?' Her colleague, Frances, meets her at the door of the office where they both work.

Emily is a librarian. She spends her day cataloguing books, sitting at a computer from nine to five with a box of fragrant volumes at her feet.

'What disaster?'

'I just heard it on the news at one. A ferry sank last night in the Baltic.'

'Oh!'

'They don't know how many people are lost. Hundreds, though. It's the biggest disaster since the war, in Sweden.'

Frances speaks urgently, with the mixture of excitement and thrilled incomprehension which people cushioned in safety feel for distant calamities. But she has a special reason for telling Emily this news, news which will cause only the faintest ripple of interest among Irish people in general. Emily's husband is Swedish, or half Swedish, and he is in Sweden at the moment at a football match.

The news does not cause Emily any personal alarm. She knows he could not be on any ferry since he is fully occupied with the match. It is being played in Stockholm, and when it is over he will fly to Umeå to visit his mother for two days, killing two birds with one stone. Emily glances at her watch. Tuesday. Today is his last day in Stockholm. Tonight he'll take the plane and fly north. She knows he has not drowned. Neither has his mother. It is too bad about the others, whoever they are, but Emily is not going to feel more than a vague, intangible, ineffective dismay on their behalf – more of a disappointment in being reminded that this is a world where accidents can happen than a grief for the suffering or destruction of people who are, dead or alive, strangers.

Much more real to her, in fact, is her own irritation that lunchtime is over. Altruism is not one of her gifts.

She sits down at her computer and pulls a book from the box at her feet: the one unpredictable factor in her working life is what the box will contain. She enhances this small pleasure by treating the selection as a lucky dip. Closing her eyes, she feels covers and weights, surfaces, thicknesses. It's not entirely a game of chance: you can tell, with your fingertips, the difference between a literary novel and a blockbuster, a collection of poems and a scientific treatise, a children's book and an official report. She is, after all, mildly depressed today, so she chooses what she likes best – a volume, hard and solid, with a gloss that caresses the skin, smart sharp corners. As she hoists it aloft its scent assails her: the seductive perfume of a smart new novel. And here it is, seduction, *The Seduction of Morality* by Tom Murphy: shining as a sixpence, adorned by a tenderly brushed portrait of a little girl in a flowing white dress, with sheaves of promising auburn hair braided over her shoulder. The novel, Emily notices, glancing inside, is set in the 1940s. Did girls look like that then? Did they ever look like that? She'd love to read the book and find out what's inside. But that is not what she's paid to do. Her task is cataloguing. In this case, all she needs to do is key in the cataloguing data, which some other librarian, in some other library (the British) has decided already.

The *Estonia* was making the crossing from Tallinn to Stockholm. A storm blew up when she had been at sea for a few hours, but nobody felt concerned. At midnight a loud rumbling sound was heard by those in the cabins above the car deck, and people in the cabins below the car deck noticed water dripping through the ceiling. Twenty minutes later the Estonia was at the bottom of the sea. More than eight hundred passengers were still in it. Others floated on the surface of the water, in life jackets or on rafts. Many of them were dead, too.

By five o'clock Emily has catalogued twenty-five books, an acceptable rather than a remarkable number: she can do fifty if she rises to the challenge of her task and puts her mind to it, and one of her colleagues can achieve that every day. But Emily's mind wanders; she spends time thumbing through the pages, or talking. A larger part of her time than she would care to admit is devoted to daydreaming.

When she started working here, books were catalogued on slips of paper, which were passed on to typists. The work could not have been described as exciting, but in those days it did demand a certain, limited, intellectual effort: cataloguers made decisions as they went along. They examined the contents of the books, they discussed subject headings with colleagues. Now most of that is done for them when the book is being published. All they have to do is copy information from the back of the title page and co-ordinate it with the computer system in operation in their library. Occasionally problems occur: old books; books published by tiny publishers who do not know the rules; pamphlets. If it were not for these items which escape the technological net, Emily's job could be done by a robot.

In the old days staff working with books had other privileges. They were allowed to borrow the books and read them, for instance. Now that is not permitted: it would breach security regulations seriously. This loss bothers a few people, like Emily and her friend Frances. But most of them don't seem to mind very much – the most efficient librarians, Emily has long suspected, seldom read books.

Lars is not a librarian but a sports journalist. You see him on television, on the sidelines of a football stadium or on the bank of a swimming pool, interviewing managers, footballers, swimmers who have just won, or just lost, the eight-hundred-metre freestyle. Often, he simply sits in the studio reporting on the events of the day. On television he adopts the anxious, urgent voice of most reporters. His face, however, as befits a sports reporter, remains good-humoured and benign, belying the desperation of his tone.

'You always sound as if you'd run a race yourself,' Emily nagged, in the early days of his career. 'Does it have to be so unrelaxed?'

She'd tried to make him change his style completely, in more ways than one – to stop wearing a jacket and tie, for instance, and have a jumper instead. Is there some rule which says that no man on television can ever wear a jumper? Or, say, a colourful, checked shirt? He laughed, but he hadn't changed his outfit or his voice and at this stage she didn't care. She had stopped watching television. Even news programmes, which had been her favourite, she had dropped from her schedule. It was as if her interest in what is going on in the world, the disasters of the world, had changed from being minor to being non-existent. The news seemed to seldom intersect with her life. And it seemed more and more like one of those games people play at parties, where one starts some story and others tack bits on to it. The inspiration is arbitrary, the plot is seldom strong. The ending, in particular, invariably fails dismally.

Emily met Lars when they were students together, studying third year English and Latin. Instead of concentrating on work for their finals, they concentrated on one another, for a whole year of green, sublime, fraught passion. At the end of the year, Emily graduated with mediocre results. Lars failed altogether. He didn't care – his real love was running, or hurdling, to be specific. He managed to get a part-time job in a leisure centre, and hurdled competitively for a few years. When he was twenty-two, three things happened: he ran for Ireland in the European Games (coming third in his event); he got a job as a sports reporter with a newspaper. And he married Emily.

Or, it would be truer to say, she married him.

She had already got the job in the library then. It wasn't anything she had planned, but simply an opportunity that had arisen. 'You might as well do it,' her parents had said. 'You might as well take it,' Lars had also said. It was not as if there was a great deal of choice. There was then, as ever, it seemed to Emily, a jobs crisis. The attitude in the air around Emily, in her home, in college among her friends, was that jobs were so scarce as to be like gold dust. Any job at all, no matter how unsuitable, was better than none.

Emily felt lucky. She was without career ambition. A job she considered to be simply an adjunct to reality, not a major component thereof. Many girls she knew then worked in department stores, in restaurants. They became secretaries. These were girls with good degrees, some with postgraduate degrees. They were a carefree lot, mostly beautiful, mostly convinced that their destiny was to be taken care of by a husband. This was in the 1970s, a time when you might have expected more ambition in young women. Emily had one ambition: to marry Lars.

101

She felt if she were married, all the other problems of her life would fade into insignificance. Being married to Lars would compensate for its shortcomings. It would liberate her. Roads, green and juicy with promise, rainbow-ended, would open before her.

But after they married, it seemed that whatever choices she had had earlier began to vanish altogether. Lars's job was on temporary contract, from the beginning and always. Emily's cheque was needed to pay the bills, to make sure the roof would be over their heads, to secure the children's education. Lars became successful, but never successful enough to bolster up Emily's need for security, which perhaps was impossible to bolster. Perhaps she did have a deep famine-fear inside her, which nothing could appease.

So she worked, she raised the children as best she could. She stayed in the same job, doing the same things, year after year. The cheque was regular, and swollen by increments until it became significant, almost an end in itself. For many years, dreaming of alternatives and complaining about the reality were her hobbies. Eventually she realised she couldn't change and no longer wanted to: she clung to her secure, familiar work as a drowning man clings to a straw.

And she became, in her spare time, a poet. Whatever qualities she repressed as she worked during the day found an outlet in the words she wrote at home, late at night. 'Found an outlet' is not the right phrase. The poems erupted, like volcanic dreams, full of strange, exotic images, narratives whose relation to her days was as tenuous and slender as the link between the black and silver world of fairy tales and the grey world of farm labourers, as the link between the haunting notes of southern spirituals and the bleak monotony of days on the plantation. Her poems were so strange that at first they were unpublishable. But, schooled to perseverance, she continued. Anyway, she had no choice. She wrote as she dreamed, relentlessly, spontaneously.

There were practical advantages to this habit. As a hobby, poetry was flexible and versatile. She could write on scraps of paper as she travelled to work, or during lunch break, or even at her desk when nobody was looking. She could write in her head, in her blood, in her heart. In her sleep. And she did – it was as necessary as breathing to her, if not as easy.

Her luck turned. She found publishers; she won attention. By now, her children at college, she is established as a minor Irish woman poet – that is how she would place herself, being as sensitive as anyone else to the literary hierarchies and fashions, if asked to make a public pronouncement. Secretly she knows, like every poet, that there is no hierarchy in literature as far as the writer is concerned. Writing is art; writing is work. The artist simply does the work – simply, with total concentration, makes the thing itself, the thing in hand. And then it is finished, for better or worse, and goes away to find its own place and context, its own judges, in another world, the world of the reader. The writer goes back to the empty page and stays there. The work is its own highest reward. Of course, Emily, like everyone, hopes there will be others, and usually there are.

There is a price to pay. She has made no progress in other aspects of her life. She is still at the lowest level in her job, where she is likely to remain – in any case, there have been no promotions in fifteen years. Once married women began to stay on at work, all promotions stopped. It has nothing to do with discrimination against women, it's just a coincidence. If anyone suggests otherwise, the management laughs and says they are prejudiced and hysterical.

Estonia became independent a few years ago, around the time of *glasnost* and *perestroika*. Before that, if you were a person like Emily in Estonia, you would have slaved all day in a paper factory. You would have shared a one-room flat with another family, and a toilet on a landing with fifty people. You would have spent your spare time queuing for bread and soap.

In those days if you offended the regime in the slightest way, you would be punished. Lars had heard of a woman, a university professor, who had had an illegitimate child. She had the baby smuggled out of the country to Sweden. When the authorities discovered this, many years after the baby had grown up, this woman was dismissed from her job at the university. She was stripped of her degrees and removed from her apartment. She was sent to work at a jam factory. Somebody in Sweden had told Lars about this woman, or he had read it in a newspaper. In fact, hardly anyone visited Estonia in those days: you needed a visa to get in; you needed a visa to get out.

All has changed. Estonia, and the other Baltic nations, Latvia and Lithuania, have become the darlings of Scandinavia. So Lars says. There is always a bunch of Estonians and Latvians at any event, at any inter-Nordic gathering. They are eager to discover the way of life of their Baltic brethren. They are busy trying to get their countries off the ground again, after many years of suffering and stagnation. The Estonians Lars meets are always very friendly and very poor. They are a mixture of naivety and cunning, as they try to learn the ways of European life.

Scandinavians love to visit Estonia. Tallinn, the capital, is old and picturesque, and the way of life still impoverished enough to be fascinating to well-off Swedes and Danes. Besides, many commodities are cheap – alcohol, caviar, handcrafted goods. Swedes go to Tallinn on shopping trips and bring back food and drink. The *Estonia* was one of the huge ferries which plied the Baltic, from Tallinn to Stockholm, Stockholm to Tallinn, carrying a dual cargo of container trucks and tourist shoppers. It offered an attractive package: a round trip, one night in a hotel, breakfast and dinner on board the ferry, for eleven hundred Swedish kronur, or about a hundred pounds, all in. There was a disco, a cinema, and three bars on the ship. When it began to list, many people were dancing or drinking. Many more were asleep.

Emily could now survive without her job. She could give it up and concentrate on being herself, on being a poet. The children are almost grown up. Lars is still on contracts, but he is so successful that the chances of his ever being without work are practically nil. Emily could write a novel. She could even do nothing. Just nothing. That is the idea that attracts her most of all, after twenty-five years of trucking in and out of town on the bus, day in day out, after twenty-five years of being what history decided she should be: a working mother.

But something prevents her. The older she becomes, the more reluctant she is to give up anything. The library has changed in many respects since she started to work in it, many of them for the better. It is warmer, it is more comfortable, it is more humane than in the old days. And it has become so familiar to her that she needs it. It has become so familiar that she, who had once hated the place, loves it.

So she stays put.

She is doing well at her poetry, anyway. She has published four volumes. It's not enough to make her a household name. It's not enough to earn her much money. But as a quiet writer, she enjoys quiet success, and participates in the literary life of Ireland, at one of its levels – not the most exalted, but not the lowest, either. She is invited to give readings and workshops. She is asked to book launches and parties, to which she goes, and to conferences, residencies, seminars abroad, to which she often cannot go, because of the job. Still, her life feels active and full. As compensation for career mistakes, her choice of pastime was good – better, probably, than golf or drink. Poetry consoles her in more ways than one, as it has consoled people in hospitals and in labour camps and in death camps. And she is in none of these things, but in a large, rich, gracious library.

She was in Oslo six weeks ago at a gathering of writers. She had given a reading and a talk on Irish women poets, and listened to other people, from all over Europe, doing the same kind of thing. In the evenings there were receptions and parties, and dinners at restaurants in the centre of town.

There were no other Irish people at the conference, so Emily attached herself to the Scandinavians, with whom she felt an affinity, because of Lars, and whose language she could speak, also because of Lars.

Olaf she met on the second night at a reception in the city hall. A woman from Helsinki introduced her to him just before the speeches began. He had laughing eyes and looked as if he were permanently on the verge of a fit of the giggles. He giggled all the time, as the Lord Mayor, who was hosting the event, spoke. Well, the Lord Mayor would make anyone laugh. He was a huge rotund man, with a round face, a red beard, little glasses. He looked like a troll. He looked like Santa Claus.

The Lord Mayor joked about the traditional enemy, the Swede, who thought Norwegians were stupid, and he told a joke about how many Norwegians it takes to fix a light bulb. But then he said that even though the Norwegians could not fix a light bulb, they could write, and they could compose music, and they could paint. He mentioned Ibsen, and Grieg, and Munch. How many Swedish artists have achieved such international recognition? he asked.

'Why does he keep going on about the Swedes?' Olaf whispered. 'There are Danes at this party, too!'

There are some advantages to having been a downtrodden, colonised country, the Lord Mayor went on. It is countries like that which produce the best artists.

'And the best oil,' said Olaf. 'They even make Volvos now in Oslo, not in Gothenburg. Did you know that? Maybe Gothenburg's cultural renaissance is about to take off!'

Olaf was a Gothenburger, with a lilting accent not unlike that of the Norwegians. He was boyish-looking, with very well-defined features and curly brown hair. His clothes hung loosely, easily on him. A sort of linen jacket. A T-shirt.

He fetched Emily a glass of wine – not her first, her third – and talked to her about his wife and children. 'I have three,' he said. 'I love children, I really love them.'

He laughed when he said this, as he laughed all the time, but his tone changed to one of apologetic confession. So Emily knew what he said was not a boast, but a truth. And she could see that he would love his children, any children, and that they would love him. She could see him playing football, hide-and-seek, she could see him tumbling around the floor. She could see his children racing to meet him when he came home from work or when he came home from conferences – because he did not work, not like Emily. He was full-time.

'Oh, you are so successful?' Emily asked.

You could never tell with writers from other countries. You could not distinguish between the successful and the maybes and the ones who would be very lucky to get a review, the way you could at home, where everyone in the literary community could place everyone else in the pecking order as soon as they heard their name.

'I do many odd jobs. I grow vegetables, I pick berries. I fish. And I am poor – poorer than you, probably.'

'That must be awful. For you and your kids.'

'It's not awful. It's fun. I love it. We are happy.'

It's different for you, Emily privately defended herself, as she always did when faced with braver, more committed people. It's different in Sweden, where the state will look after the children if you don't. That means you can take risks that I couldn't.

'I make things,' Olaf was saying.

'Oh? Things?'

He made furniture. As well as writing children's books, he designed chairs and tables. He showed her photographs of the chairs: chairs with three legs, chairs with wheels. 'They've even won prizes!' he said. 'Booby prizes, for the chair nobody can sit on!'

His books had won prizes, too. She saw them in the stall at the conference – books with oddly dressed, strange children grinning on the covers, and stickers saying 'Little Nobel 1995'. Maybe he was not so poor after all?

This suspicion did not put her off him, although she worried about it for half an hour or so. But she walked with him in the park that surrounded the city hall, and along the wide main street. She went with him to Holmenbro, where the ski slopes were, and climbed a tower which gave them a view over several miles of Norway. She walked with him in the woods.

From the first moment she had felt attracted to him. She had felt a strong physical sensation, such as a man might feel, she thought, but which was quite strange to her. The emotional attraction was far from strange, and she warned herself to be careful. She was forty-five. Her hair was bleached, her thighs looked like cold porridge. The flesh on her upper arms dropped like the chin of a cod when she stretched. It is women like you, she told herself, who are the worst. Old fools.

Olaf was fond of her, that was clear. But men could be fond of her as a friend, not as anything else, and she would not know the difference. Her antennae were not attuned to sexual messages, as those of more experienced women can be – at least, that's what novelists suggest. She maintained a dignified friendliness. It was easy for her to ignore the stirrings in her body – she was used to ignoring everything that stirred inside her.

Olaf was not. In the woods near Holmenbro, at two o'clock in the afternoon, on the last day, he spread his jacket under a tree and they sat down. Then, he removed first her clothes and then his.

'Someone will come along and see us!' Emily, on seeing his body, thought about being caught. She'd longed to kiss him for the whole week and now she had to think of the risk, not of the kiss.

'It doesn't matter,' said Olaf, kissing one of her nipples. 'They'll go away again, fast enough!'

'But ...'

'You're not afraid, are you? You want this?'

'Yes,' said Emily.

His body was hot and silky, twining around hers. He was good-humoured, laughing, but not boyish in his lovemaking. Rather, he was joyfully serious, lightly competent – a poet, a children's writer, a craftsman, what would you expect? He was golden, he fitted her like a glove. We are like gods, she thought, the leaves fondling her back, his body, a boat sailing through her. I am a nymph in the forest. I am a dryad. I am a lynx. I am forty-five.

Somebody actually *loves* me.

What happened was this. The ship's vizor was damaged – the door on the bow which opens to let traffic in. There is another in the stern to let it out. Emily has often used these ferries, called ro-ro ferries, herself, on the way to France or Wales. You drive on, park, drive off. It's so simple. There is one compartment for all the cars and buses and trucks and, in the case of Swedish ferries, trains. This takes up a floor of the vessel. Nobody calls it a ship. You do not even think you are on a ship when you are on one of these ferries. It is more like a town, or a shopping centre. You need never see water once you come aboard.

The vizor was damaged. In the storm it became more damaged and some water leaked in. Then it broke and a lot of water swept in. When the floor of the car deck was covered by one foot of water the big trucks began to slide. They slid to one side of the ship. The ship turned over. It was as simple as that. Once the listing had begun nothing could stop it. 'Listing ten, listing twenty. We're sinking!' This was the last message the *Estonia* sent out. It was received by the *Mariella*, which was sailing not far off.

*

Olaf owns a mobile phone.

'I never knew a poet who owned a mobile phone!' Emily teased him.

They spent the whole afternoon and night making love, first in the forest and then in the hotel. They missed the closing ceremony of the conference.

'I'm not just a poet, I write children's books!' he said. 'We need mobile phones, to ring up children.'

'Sure.'

'I ring mine all the time. I'm going to ring them now!'

'Do you think it's a good idea?'

They were sitting in the middle of his bed, naked, drinking wine.

'You ring yours too! What's the code for Ireland?'

'00 353 ...'

She was saying hello Lydia before she could stop him.

When Emily goes home she sees Lars is on television, reporting on the ferry disaster on the six o'clock news. Although a ferry disaster is not a sporting feature, the television station asked him to cover the story for them, since he is there anyway. The disaster is not a big story in Ireland but it is worth covering directly if it does not cost too much.

Soon after the newscast the phone rings. It is Lars. He asks her to join him in Sweden for a few days, if she can get off. He is getting extra money, and her fare would be paid for by some sports outfit or other that he had worked for. She could come for a long weekend.

She says yes, it's a long time since she's been to Sweden, and she'd like to go, for more reasons than one. She knows she will not see Olaf if she visits Lars and his mother, and in a way, she doesn't want to. But she thinks it would do her good to be in his country for a few days.

When she left Oslo she thought about him for a few weeks and then stopped thinking about him. She knew she would never see him again and it is not easy to remain loyal to the memory of a man you will never see again. She had thought he would telephone but he did not. Until yesterday. He rang her at work.

'Hello, it's me, Olaf,' he said.

What is it like, hearing the voice of a man, a man you were in love with recently, on the phone in your office? The objects in the room, the telephones, the boxes of books, shifted themselves and settled comfortably in the yellow September light. Emily closed her eyes and listened to her heart being happy.

'I said I would phone.'

'How are you? Are you well?'

'Yes. I am well. Everything is fine. I am missing you.'

'Yes.'

'You know? It is good to be with my wife and children again. But ...' He giggled. It did not sound as good on the phone as close up, but it was still infectious. 'Are you alone?'

'No.'

'Your colleagues are listening?'

'Yes.'

'Maybe I'll ring you later.'

'Ring me at home. You've got my number at home?'

'It will be all right?'

'Yes.'

'OK. About 11 p.m. You know I love you.'

'Yes.'

'It is all right. We do not have to do anything about it. We do not have to do anything about anything any more. I have found that out, now that I am old.'

'We can talk about that later.'

'Goodbye, then.'

She catalogued about sixty books that afternoon. Frances noticed, but said nothing.

How would he phone at eleven? Maybe he would go to some secret place. The bathroom. She envisaged him beside a pile of logs, in an open-sided shed, with the stars glinting icily above him. His ear glued to the phone, his eyes laughing. She saw the forest stacked darkly behind him.

He did not phone at eleven and she was not surprised. It hadn't been possible, because of the family. Or he had forgotten. She did not doubt his intentions. She did not doubt his love. It was genuine, like the promise to call. Genuine, but leading nowhere.

There was no time to give the alarm. Most people on the ferry hardly realised what was happening. Only the very alert made it to the deck, and only the very bravest managed the ninety-foot leap into the sea.

The sea was raging and ice-cold, but there were life jackets and rafts. Up-and-down rafts, the reports called them, Lars said. *Op och ner flottar.* Overturned, they meant. Thrown out upside down, or overturned by the waves. Some of the survivors sat on the bottom of overturned rafts for five or six or ten hours. Only a hundred and thirty of the thousand passengers did survive. Lots of people who found a raft died anyway, of cold. And being rescued, when rescue at last came, was not so easy. A helicopter can take one person at a time. That person has to grab a rope, and tie himself to it, while standing on an overturned raft in the raging sea, before he can be hoisted to safety.

Most of the survivors were men, between the ages of twenty and thirty. You had to be young, strong, fit, and courageous. As well as lucky.

She flies on the complicated flight journey from Dublin to Manchester, from Manchester to Copenhagen, and from Copenhagen to Stockholm. From Stockholm she will fly with Lars to Umeå, to visit his mother.

There is a wait of two hours at Copenhagen. She walks around the airport, which is big and elegant, with many restaurants and shops proffering temptation to the traveller – shoes, fine casual clothes, gold and amber jewels. Perfumes, hair decorations. Smoked eels and pickled herrings and cheeses. She loves looking at these luxurious goods, but buys nothing. Everything is outrageously expensive and she and Lars decided, a year or two ago, to resist airport shopping.

She wonders if she might by some astonishing coincidence meet Olaf at the airport. Perhaps he could be on his way to another conference today? By some miracle he could have been in Copenhagen, promoting one of the Danish translations of his books? She laughs at herself for being foolish. Why should he be here? Miracles like that do not occur. Still, she looks at all men who are slim, and dressed in loose, easy clothes, who have dark curly hair. What surprises her is that so many men fit the description.

At the newsagent's she gets a copy of *Dagens Nyheter* and goes to sit in the waiting area for the Stockholm plane. It is a hushed, silent area, where a handful of well-dressed people wait on the clear blue seats. At this airport there is none of the bustle or haste you feel in London or New

York. Instead there is opulence, space, good taste. There is a warm nurturing sense of security. That is the main sensation of Scandinavia, as far as Emily is concerned. A sense of security.

Olaf Andreason, Författare, Göteborg (52)

The newspaper is full of information about the ferry disaster: photographs and theories about why it happened and stories from survivors. In the middle is a centrepiece, listing the names of the drowned.

He had not looked fifty-two. Maybe it is not him. There are so many Andreasons in Sweden, there could be another writer of the same name. It does not say 'children's writer', even. It would say children's writer, if it were Olaf. And she talked to him that day. Wouldn't he have said, 'I'm in Estonia actually'? Or, 'I'm just getting the ferry. I've been to Estonia, shopping'?

Olaf Andreason, Författare, Göteborg (52)
Marit Andreason, Bibliotekarie, Göteborg (52)

His wife. His wife was Marit, he had told her that. Marit, and a librarian.

Lars is waiting for her at the Swedish airport. He hardly ever meets her at airports but this time, of course, he has to. There he is, in his new blue raincoat, standing at the end of a long blue corridor. When she sees him her heart warms up, to her great surprise. She feels a gush of love for him, a gush of calm, wifely love. The smile which breaks out on her face is uncontrollable, delighted. She runs to Lars and hugs him unrestrainedly, holding him in her arms for minutes.

'I can't breathe!' he laughs. 'Are you all right? What's the matter?'

'I missed you,' says Emily, closing her eyes. 'I love you.'

The papers are full of the story of Sara and Kent.

They had met as they clambered up the sides of the ferry, trying to reach the deck. They promised one another that they'd meet in Stockholm and eat a celebratory dinner, when they reached it. And then they jumped the ninety feet into the sea.

In the water they met again, bobbing about in their life jackets. All night they sat on a raft together, talking and telling jokes, hugging one another for warmth. Other people on the raft had complained. Two died. Sara and Kent kept their spirits up.

Sara was a large, plump, lovely girl of twenty. Kent was a little older.

'We didn't panic,' he said. It was Kent who told their story first, to the TV men. 'We decided to stay calm and keep our sense of humour. And we held on to one another for warmth.'

The Pale Gold of Alaska

Soon after her eighteenth birthday, Sophie went to America with her sister Sheila. They embarked at the port of Londonderry, and sailed as steerage passengers on a White Star liner called *Maid of Erin* to Philadelphia. The idea was that they would join their older sister, Winnie, who had provided the money for their fares, as soon as they arrived. They were planning to get jobs as housemaids. Winnie, who was twelve years older than Sophie and eight years older than Sheila, had friends in Germantown where she had been working for six years. She would be able to fix them up in good situations without difficulty.

The plan was scuppered before the *Maid of Erin* was a hundred miles west of the Irish coast. North of Bloody Foreland, on the very night of embarkation, a storm blew up, whipping the sea into raging mountains and fathomless valleys: dark, terrifying – above all nauseating. Sheila, whose body was thick as a ploughman's, succumbed to seasickness, while delicate Sophie by some miracle remained unscathed. The ship was full of moaning, tortured people;

117

it was sour with the smell of vomit, and jagged with the howls of bewildered children. Although the storm abated after a few hours, and for the rest of the voyage the ship glided over a buttermilk ocean between silvery blue skies, the illness lasted nearly as long in Sheila's case. She was not an easy patient, being both demanding and self-pitying. As often as Sophie could, she abandoned her sister and sought solitude on the deck.

There, on her second day at sea, she met a weaver called Ned Burns, one of the few passengers besides herself who had escaped sickness. Lighting his pipe in the shelter of his palm, he had spotted her over the ridge of his broad weaver's hand as she strolled slowly along the narrow gangway; he had smiled and asked her for the time of day. (A quarter past three – they were allowed to walk on the deck between three and four o'clock every afternoon.) By the time Sheila had got her sea legs, Ned had shown Sophie how to elude the stewards and walk on deck whenever she felt like it. And by then it was too late to nip the relationship in the bud. Before the *Maid of Erin* had reached its destination, Ned had asked Sophie to marry him.

He was four years older than her, a tall, fair-skinned, curly-haired man, with a boyish face and a thin mouth, which in his case succeeded in looking vulnerable rather than mean. His manner was quiet, and this, coupled with the lips and his surprised-looking eyes, conveyed the impression that he was lacking in self-confidence, or weak. But he was neither of these things, as Sophie discovered very soon after meeting him. His eyes did not evade, but stared steadily into hers, as if pleading with her – for what she was unsure, but she believed she could give it to him, whatever it might be. Also, although he was not talkative in company, when alone with Sophie he had plenty to say, unlike any man or boy she had ever known before. What he said was often very amusing, usually in an acerbic way; he was always willing to be unkind or even cruel if that served his wit. He came from a village in south County Derry.

'Sure they're all like that in Derry,' Sheila had said, when Sophie had offered Ned's sense of humour as an excuse for her engagement to him. Why she had to offer excuses she did not know. But his good looks, his apparently trustworthy personality, would not seem sufficient motivation to Sheila. Probably nothing would.

'Well,' Sophie said as firmly as she could, 'I've said yes.'

'You'd never have got away with this sort of carry-on at home.'

Sheila began to cry. Tears of frustration or annoyance, or jealousy or anger, rolled down her face, which was a round potato face, pocked with bumps and shadowy mistakes, not at all like Sophie's. Sophie's face reminded people of a glass of new milk, or a spray of thyme, or other things of that kind, redolent of nature at its most beguiling and benign.

'It's ridiculous, getting married at your age.'

It seemed no more ridiculous to Sophie than going to work as a maid in the house of a complete stranger in a foreign country. She said this, somewhat tactlessly, shouting it over the noise of the engines, which accompanied them all the time on board, a constant roar like that of an infuriated bull. They were watching the New York skyline as they conducted this final, decisive conversation. Night had fallen and some of the buildings of the city were lit, creating spots and pools of light, scattered haphazardly on an inky background like saffron-coloured flowers, flaming orange lilies in the sky.

Sheila paused before replying, to stare at the skyline and

to allow her mind to flirt with the exoticism of her present situation.

Soon she would be in America.

'America'. It was a word she had carried in her head for a long time. A word, a dream and a hope, shining in her eyes, encouraging her heart.

But it was not something her mind could encompass, now that the moment of landing was drawing so close. America. The word becoming land and lights and buildings in front of her eyes. Too abruptly it had appeared, in the end, after all the voyaging and imagining. She felt as if she had awoken suddenly from a vivid dream. She tried, briefly, to cling to it before it vanished completely, before reality rushed in and blotted out the picture she had carried in her head for most of her life. But she was not the sort to linger unnecessarily in the confusing borderlands of consciousness.

Turning her back on the land of the free she gave herself to the sisterly spat. 'At least you'd get paid for it by a complete stranger,' she snapped. The dream was gone already. Petty details rushed into her head to replace what had borne her across the Atlantic on waves of nausea. Now all she could imagine was the lonely time ahead, the interviews with strange, foreign rich women, women who might well be impatient and unkind; the days full of new, bewildering work. The shine was dulled, the hope inverted, all the sport drained out of the future by this new turn of events. Loneliness loomed, instead of promise. Everything, even her own body, seemed terrifying. The realisation of her homeliness hit her like a punch in the belly; no man would ever make an impulsive proposal to her. Probably no man would propose to her at all, even after long and careful consideration. No widower or fat old bachelor, no country bumpkin that better women would take. She would live out her days in the kitchen of a stranger's house, slaving until she died, alone in this new hostile continent.

They were met in Philadelphia by their sister Winnie, who had jobs lined up and waiting for the two of them, for Sheila and Sophie. She was not pleased when she found out that Sophie's plans had changed. Now Sophie was not interested in working as a maid. She was going to be a married woman; she was going to live in a rented room with Ned.

'And how will you pay back your passage, may I ask?' Winnie twisted her long mouth and raised her thick black eyebrows.

'Never you fear, you'll get your money back,' Ned retorted. 'Sophie will be making more dollars than the pair of yez.'

How? wondered Sophie.

She would be working in a textile mill, that was how. It was not the future she had foreseen for herself when she had agreed to marry Ned. But it would be her destiny for a while, all the same.

Sophie and Ned got married almost immediately in St Patrick's Chapel. Sheila and Winnie, as well as several neighbours from their home in Donegal, came to the wedding, and afterwards to a saloon owned by somebody from home. Lynch's was the name of the establishment. Ned drank quite a lot, the day of his wedding, but Sophie, Winnie and Sheila did not drink a thing. There was nothing available in Lynch's Saloon that wasn't alcoholic. They had never touched a drop of any kind of alcoholic drink in Ireland, and they were not about to start now.

Afterwards Ned and Sophie went to live in a room they would share with two cousins of Ned's at the back of a row house in Moyamensing. The men worked in the cloth mills at Southwark where Ned and Sophie had been taken on. Ned drove a loom and she worked in the finishing room, where a machine rolled the interminable lengths of cloth on to giant spools, ready to go out to the shops. Her job was to check the cloth for broken threads, stains, bits of fluff, to remove what could be removed, and to stop the machine if the cloth needed to be cut. She had to keep her eyes on the cloth as it rolled through on the machine, never stopping, all the time. White, black, blue, grey, were the colours that came through, mainly. Occasionally red, green, yellow – the cloth was dyed every colour under the sun, with strong aniline dyes, brilliant colours she had never seen before. (Where she came from, cloth was blackish-brown, cream, or a rust colour obtained from lichens that grew on the rocks.) Sophie liked the colours. She continued to like them all the time she worked in the factory, even when her back was breaking and her eyes were itchy and red from looking at glaring colours for twelve hours at a stretch.

Ned called her *Síoda na mBó*, which means something like 'silken cow', when they were in the alcove that contained their bed, and which was concealed from the main part of the room by an old cream-coloured woollen blanket with faded blue stripes at one end, the end that touched the floor. They had to speak in soft voices there, so the cousins in their bed out in the room would not hear. 'Silky cow, silky little frisky heifer,' he whispered in her ear as they snuggled under the blankets in their corner – it was April, still quite cold, especially inside the damp old house. He pulled her blouse off and buried his face in her breasts. 'Silk blouse, silk skin, silk breast,' he whispered. She stroked his curls, which were not silky at all, but wiry and dry, completely different from her own smooth hair. She half listened to him, pleased at his compliments, if that is what they were.

At the same time she got used to them. Soon it was as if they hardly applied to her at all, as if they were just words he said, the way women in Donegal say prayers. The same words over and over again, uttered in a sleepy singsong voice, uttered so often that the speakers do not even know what they are saying.

Maybe that was how Ned had learned to repeat himself, to chant an incantation over and over again? He liked to pray. Before he got into bed he knelt on the floor and buried his head in his hands, chanted five decades of the Rosary. Sophie had to join in although she had always found the Rosary dull and slightly repulsive. She did not like the sight of broad bottoms sticking out in the air above the bowed heads of their owners, the embarrassingly intimate smell of praying people, the monotonous sad sleepiness of their voices as they repeated the pious, superior words over and over and over and over again. Hail Mary full of grace. Fifty times a night. Holy Mary Mother of God. Pray for us sinners. Until she was half-dead from boredom.

Followed, maybe, by silken blouse, silken skin. Silken sinner. Not fifty times. Just as often as he felt like it.

Sophie, accustomed anyway to the admiration of men, took his laudatory litanies as her due. Kisses and words of admiration were what she mainly got from Ned, in bed, and that was not so different from what she had always received from other men, in the street and at dances, outside the chapel on Sunday – admiration, expressed or tacit, but reliable and regular as the Rosary.

Soon, however, she began to learn that there were limits to Ned's admiration.

Ned wanted her to be neat, well-turned-out, pretty. Also he wanted her to work well and be popular at the mill. But it was important that none of this be taken too far. She should be a credit to him, but only up to a point. At first Sophie did not understand what was expected of her. She did not know that she could easily, without knowing it, step out of the field of Ned's admiration and into another area where he would despise her.

For a few months after they were married, he encouraged her, in every way, to do what she was good at: being attractive and sociable, working well. She made friends in the neighbourhood; she worked as conscientiously as she could; and, with her own money, she bought a new outfit for the summer in one of the big stores in town.

She wore this outfit, a tight black skirt, a white high-necked blouse, a small black and red hat, to Mass the first Sunday after buying it. As usual, it was clear to Sophie and to Ned that many people looked at her with pleasure. Kathleen Gallagher, a middle-aged woman who lived around the corner from them, said, 'That girl is the belle of Philadelphia', and her husband, Dan, nodded and said, 'Some folks have all the luck.' Ned stared at Sophie with his wide blue eyes and said nothing whatsoever. On Sunday evenings they usually went for a walk together with her sisters, but that evening he said he was going to Lynch's.

'Can I come with you?' she asked.

'You wouldn't want to spoil your expensive rig-out,' he said. It was said in a voice she had not heard before, a dry, jealous voice, full of censure. He ate some bread and continued, in a gentler tone, 'Women don't come to Lynch's, anyway. You didn't like it at our wedding.' So now he was joking again. That was something he could do: move from complaining to joking in a few sentences. It was as if he had to complain, express his annoyance or anger or whatever it was that Sophie's success aroused in him, but that he regretted it almost before the words were out of his mouth.

After that, he took to going to the saloon every Sunday night. Sophie continued the custom of meeting Winnie and Sheila, on her own instead of with Ned. In a way it was easier like that and the sisters, who did not seem to like Ned much, certainly preferred it.

'Nothing stirring?' Winnie asked in September, when Sophie had been married for six months. Sophie was still slender and girlish. She had taken to doing her hair in a new style, pinning it up and letting some fair, wispy curls fall down over her forehead and around her small ears, neat as oyster shells. She tossed her head, dislodging a few more wisps, and did not answer the question.

'You'll have to get out of that factory soon,' Sheila said, with some satisfaction. She had become a parlour maid for an old couple in Germantown, and her life was considerably easier and more luxurious than Sophie's. 'You should get a baby for yourself and then Ned would have to find you a proper place to live.'

Two young men whistled after the sisters, saving Sophie the trouble of thinking of a response. Sheila raised her eyebrows disapprovingly at Winnie. Two old maids already, thought Sophie. That is what they were. Buxom, with their dense hair pinned to the backs of their heads in hard black balls, her sisters looked like women whose fate was sealed. Sealed by themselves: they lived in a city that was full of men, men from all over Ireland and Germany and Poland and Italy and other countries, looking desperately for women. But Sheila and Winnie never met any of them, any man at all, it seemed, except for old fellows who did the gardening or worked in the kitchen in their prim-and-proper houses. Men who were as old-maidish as themselves.

They had shut themselves away from the world of men, the world Sophie inhabited. And by now they were afraid of them. If a young man whistled, they assumed the next thing was that he would do something unspeakable to them: the thing Sophie did several nights a week with Ned, the thing they could not – it seemed to her – even imagine. They equated that with being strangled or stabbed to death. Pleasure for Sheila and Winnie, Sophie thought, was having a cream waffle and a strong cup of tea in some rich woman's kitchen, their substantial bottoms positioned to catch the heat of the fire. Beyond that their desires did not seem to stretch. Could this be true?

The young men had been whistling at Sophie, of course, it was assumed by all. Sophie was wearing her Sunday rig-out, her belle-of-Philadelphia hat on top of her distracting hairstyle. She walked daintily, proud of herself, happy to flaunt her fine clothes when Ned was not around to put a damper on her tendency to show off.

Not that it was a question of clothes, or demeanour. Men whistled at her all the time, even when she was wearing her old, patched factory dress. If Ned was not with her, they whistled. Maybe they whistled at all young women? Maybe it was the custom of the town?

'She's time enough,' Sheila responded on Sophie's behalf. 'Sure she's only a child herself.'

'People will be talking all the same,' Winnie said.

This was the sort of thing Sophie had to put up with. She was so used to listening to her sisters complaining about her that she hardly even heard it. She knew why she was not expecting, but was pleased with the situation. Time enough for all that. Walking along the dry, summer street under the shade trees, dressed in a snow-white blouse, seeing the crowds of people, was all she wanted. She did not want a baby to expand her waistline and limit her freedom. How could she have a baby in that room, anyhow, with nothing but a curtain dividing her bed from the two cousins?

The cousins were both in love with her. Sophie had known this might happen from the minute she heard about the arrangement from Ned, and she knew it would happen the minute she saw the cousins: they were Ned's age, but genuinely shy and awkward, unlike him. One of them had a girlfriend, a little girl with a sharp, pointed face who had come from Tipperary and who was not very good-humoured. She seemed to spend half her time not talking to the cousin, punishing him for various misdemeanours. He accepted this as normal. Chief among his many flaws was that he was in no hurry to get married. Sophie knew that in the end he would have to capitulate. He would marry this girl – her name was Agnes – whom he did not love, who was not beautiful, and who did not seem to like him very much. He would have to, if he did not find a replacement for her. At least he would know what his wife was like before the wedding.

In the meantime he permitted himself the marginal amusement of being in love with Sophie. The mixed pleasure of this experience was enhanced, and even more confused, by the fact that his brother was also in love with her, and of course by the secret, silent nature of the emotion. It was never mentioned, by anyone. But anyone could sense it in the room, in the looks that the brothers gave to Sophie, lingering tender looks at her back, shy yearning looks at her face, amused looks or desperate looks at one another. It was obvious to Sophie, and she thought it must be so to everybody. She did not take it too seriously. Men and boys had been in love with her before and had said nothing about it. As long as you said nothing you didn't need to do anything. It never seemed to do them much harm. They did not die of unrequited love, not at all. They got over it, they went away or they became involved with some other woman. In a way she thought they might enjoy it, this secret, silent passion. It gave them something to think about when they were working – digging fields or footing turf, or standing all day at the huge loom, pushing the heavy shuttle to and fro, to and fro.

The rooming arrangement gave rise to plenty of comment in the factory and in the saloon, some of it ribald. People were careful not to pass remarks in Ned's hearing. He had already got a reputation for being belligerent.

But inevitably he heard something. A reference to Sophie's good looks, followed by a reference to Sophie's band of admirers, followed by a reference to Sophie's husbands. 'Sure she's got three husbands to look after her' was the comment. 'That should do her, with her blondie curls and her black hat' was what was said. It was considerably less offensive than remarks that had been going the rounds for months behind Ned's back.

But it turned out that Ned had not had the slightest suspicion of the emotion that filled the high, dark room. He had not even suspected that the arrangement would look odd, or scandalous, to neighbours. So innocent, or so wilfully blind, was he.

Sophie was to blame for the unfortunate state of affairs, in his opinion. He stopped talking to her. The same punishment that the girl from Tipperary gave to his cousin.

This went on for a week. It went into a second week. It seemed he would never open his mouth again. She could see he had it in him, was the sort of man who could close up inside his shell and never emerge again. Reluctantly, and with some trepidation, she asked him what was going on.

He found it hard to speak. But he did.

He told her she gave herself airs. 'What are you but a factory girl?' he said. 'You're making a fool of yourself, dressing up in fine rags and feathers.' He looked her up and down. 'It's not as if you're all that good-looking.' Then he laughed. So that last bit was a joke, not a criticism. He was back to being his normal fault-finding, joking self.

Not quite.

He led her to the alcove and did not bother drawing the curtain, even though it was broad daylight and the cousins might walk in at any moment. He pulled off all her clothes, the first time he had ever done this. She stood, naked, in the sunlight which fell in a narrow dusty bar across the wooden floor. Then he raised his hand and hit her.

She had never understood the expression 'he saw stars' before. Now she saw them, a galaxy flashing brilliantly in her head. She sat down on the bed, her face numb. He hit her again. Her nose bled a little. She did not scream or say anything. But she began to punch him – on the face, on the chest. Her hands pummelled him, hard, but it was like hitting a stone.

'Stop,' he cried. 'Stop.'

She didn't stop. Her hands flailed out, raining blows on him. He didn't reciprocate them and soon he started to laugh.

Sophie continued to hit him. But after a while she started to laugh too, although she did not know what she was laughing at. They both became infected with giggles, and rolled on the bed, unable to stop laughing.

Then he made love to her, and it was the first time the lovemaking worked, for Sophie. But afterwards he pulled away.

'I'm sorry,' he said, his voice so dry she could hardly hear.

She pulled a blanket around herself. He found her nightgown and threw it to her, drew on his own clothes and dropped to his knees at the side of the bed.

Soon after this, before winter set in, Ned suggested they move. Not to a new room, but to a new place. The west. Montana. There was copper mining going on there, silver and gold mining as well, and more money to be made than in the factories of the east. Also, more fresh air and more space for living. He and Sophie would have a house of their own immediately, instead of having to save in the building society and wait for years, as would happen in Philadelphia. Their pale skins would get pink and healthy; their lungs would breathe freely.

Sophie was unsure. Now that she knew Ned better, going off with him alone, into the wilderness as it were, seemed more dangerous than it had when she had first met him. She knew he would not harm her seriously – the beating had not been repeated, yet, and anyway it was not a beating in the usual sense, the sense in which that word was used in Ireland, and Philadelphia. She heard women shouting and screaming sometimes, on Sunday nights, she saw black eyes and bruises, sad shamed faces, which were not to be commented upon. She did not think that Ned would do that to her again – he was not a drunkard, he was not the sort of man who loses his temper and lets fly. Maybe she could handle him, his attitude which was after all a simple enough matter, of jealousy. She knew she must not go too far. She must not expect too much praise, for anything, from anyone, and above all she must not reveal to him if she got it. That was all that was required, really, to keep him happy. He loved her because she was beautiful, and clever, and sensible, and neat. But she must never carry any of these desirable attributes to what he considered to be excess. That was all. It should be easy enough. She would have to do that anyway, even if she stayed in Philadelphia. She would have to do that as long as she stayed with Ned.

There was the matter of leaving her sisters, and her friends. But she had made friends easily in the factory. There was no reason to suppose that she would not make new ones in Montana. Leaving her job would not be a sacrifice. It was enjoyable to work with other people – ready-made friends, in their scores – but the hours were too long. Having Sunday free no longer seemed like enough when you worked for eleven hours every other day. In Montana, she would not have to have a job. Ned would make enough money for the two of them, or more of them if necessary. She would be a real wife, and mother she hoped, at home in her own house, doing whatever she liked, while he was off in the mines digging for silver, for money, for the two of them.

They travelled to Butte by train, a journey of three days. Sophie sat alone on a wooden seat in a third-class carriage, as a concession to her femininity. Ned went in the luggage van, in the coal van, in the cattle truck, as necessity obliged, thus saving the price of one fare. It was the way the Irish did things. Any man would have considered it madness to waste money on a railway ticket. Tickets for transatlantic ships had to be bought. Stowing away on board ship was too risky. But once you landed in America, you never paid for travel again if you could possibly help it. 'The land of the free,' Ned said, climbing on to the roof of the guard's van.

Missoula, where they ended up, was a town of dirt streets and low wooden buildings. A boardwalk, constructed from two planks laid side by side, provided a footpath. High pine trees grew everywhere, on lots between the houses, on the side of the street. There were general stores, hardware stores, draperies. Several saloons, a hotel. Also three churches, Catholic, Presbyterian and Anglican, the Catholic being the biggest.

The mines were to the north of the town, and Sophie and Ned went there, to a smaller village higher in the Rockies, called Greenough. Ned staked out about a half-acre of land just outside the village, close to a settlement of people who had converged on this place from half the countries in Europe. He did not sign for the land – it wasn't necessary to do that, according to some Irishmen who lived there. First come first served. Didn't it belong to somebody? Sophie asked, surprised. They laughed and pointed to the high, rugged silver peaks behind them. *Na Fir Dearga.* The red men. They've moved up the mountains. It belongs to us now.

Ned's land was on the edge of a forest, mainly fir and pine. Sophie walked into it between the tall, bare trunks of the fir trees. The sun came slanting through them in thin gold lines and the trunks stretched like telegraph poles towards the sky. The passages between them were like the aisle of the big church in Philadelphia.

Not for long. Ned, with help from two of the other Irishmen, chopped down dozens of the tall trees, a lot more than he needed. With some of the logs thus gained he built a cabin, and the rest they stockpiled for firewood. The cabin consisted of two big rooms plus a porch (this was Ned's personal addition, his poetic touch). He furnished the rooms with a bed, a table, two chairs. The fire was an open fire, on a stone hearth at one side of the kitchen. Later they would get a stove, and other luxuries.

Ned started work in the silver mines as soon as he had finished the cabin; he apprenticed himself to an experienced miner, who would pay him well while teaching him the miner's trade. Ned worked deep in the earth, all day and sometimes long into the night. Sophie was left alone in the cabin for very long periods. She had never in her life spent so much time on her own. In fact she had never spent any time alone – her parents' house in Ireland was always full of people. Then all there had been was the ship, and the room in Philadelphia.

She got to know some of the other women in the hamlet. There were very few of them – most of the men who came to the mines were single. During the day, the village was inhabited only by these few women and their children. There was no school for the children, so their noise was to be heard all day as they played around the cabins, or ran in and out of the forest.

There was work to be done. Getting food, preparing it. They ate meat mostly: venison and wild mutton. There were elk, goats, and sheep in the mountains – also bears and mountain lions. Ned learned how to set traps; he hunted when he had free time, bagging easily what they needed. She had to skin animals, peeling the pelts from their cold bodies with a sharp knife. Then they had to be butchered, hacked into pieces, dried or cooked over the fire. Flour they could buy in Greenough, and transport on a cart to the cabin. She had a big sack in the corner of the room, and every day she baked loaves of bread. In the summer, berries grew richly on the floor of the forest. She gathered perfumed raspberries, bloody blueberries, honey-coloured huckleberries, bitter cranberries. She made three varieties of jam, spending hours tending the pots of viciously bubbling, stickily smelling, viscous messes, watching the chemical colour change: she poured berries of pink or yellow or green or blue from her bowl into the pot. But by the time they

133

were boiled and set they were all a dark, carmine red.

When they had been a few months in the area they bought a cow. Then there was milking to do all summer, morning and evening, the hot flank of the beast on her cheek, the teats tough and testing between her fingers, the heavy odour of the cow dung, cow body, churning through her body night and morning, morning and night. Churning once a week in a barrel made by Ned. Come butter come butter come butter come, the rhythmical turning of the handle like a fast violent reel, her back breaking with the effort of it, her complexion pink as a hot summer rose, her wrist thickening. Butter in golden pats lined up on the table. A neighbour, a Swedish woman, taught her how to sour the milk and make a thick, creamy liquid which tasted sweet and sour at once, which enhanced the flavour of huckleberries, even of bread. She showed her how to make cheese.

Sophie loved the cabin. It was different from the house in Donegal, which she had found stuffy and crowded, and from the room in the city. The wooden walls emitted a pungent, resinous smell. The fire burned wood all the time, adding to the spicy atmosphere. On the walls, she hung animal skins: a thick brown bear skin which they had got for a few dollars in Greenough, beaver skins, a rough buffalo skin. On the floor were deer skins, red and silver, snowy white. She loved the various textures of the furs – the fine silky deer skins, the thick shag of the bear like scutch grass, the dense velvet of the beaver. The shapes of the skins too she liked; they were like flat maps of animals. Alone in the cabin she felt the company of the creatures who had once inhabited the skins.

In September, before winter came, Ned bought her a coat made of sealskin which someone who had come down the river from Canada sold him for a few dollars. The sealskin was thick but flat, silvery grey and silvery white, shimmering like ice or seawater, gleaming like the animal from which it had come. When she wrapped herself in it, she felt she was a different person. She did not feel human at all, but part of the huge animal world which surrounded her now on all sides, which was with her inside and outside her cabin. She felt like the animals she did not see but heard in the depth of the night, barking or screaming in the forest and the mountain.

Outside her cabin, close to her front door, was the forest. The high, dark-green trees, secreting a world of animals, of berries, of strangely shaped fungal growths, some of which they learned to eat, fascinated her. Behind the forest the great mountains loomed, purple or silver, golden or flame-coloured, black or stone, depending on the light. Never had she lived among such high mountains, so close to a vast forest. A clear sweet river – they called it a creek – ran at the end of their clearing, forming a border between it and the forest. In this creek she washed her clothes. In this creek she washed herself, when Ned was away and nobody was looking.

They were not always alone. On Sundays, there was Mass in the morning, and then the saloon. The mores of Philadelphia did not apply here. Women went to the saloon as well as men. They even drank alcohol. Stout was the drink, or whiskey, both from Ireland, with Irish names on the labels. Tullamore Dew. Black Bush. Also a light beer which the Germans liked.

Sophie took to drinking port wine. She sat at a table with a woman called Kathleen Sullivan, drinking this and chatting. The men drank whiskey and played cards. Twenty-one, forty-four, poker. One man had a fiddle. He held it straight under his chin, the way they do in Donegal, and played Irish tunes. Jigs and reels. Old slow songs that brought tears to Sophie's eyes, although she did not know why. Not because they reminded her of home. She was glad to be here, glad to be away. It was much better than Ireland.

There were not enough women.

Men stared at her constantly, even when Ned was present. He didn't like it, but did nothing about it, attributing it to the shortage of women rather than to any intrinsic worth of Sophie's. She was careful to maintain her distance with all of them, which was easy enough. They were rough diamonds, not the kind who knew how to talk to a woman. Except on Sundays, when the whiskey and music softened them, their minds were focused on one thing only: money.

Ned was preoccupied with money as well. He spent so much of his time underground, in the dark cold earth, chipping away at the rocks for silver. His pay was good, but he experienced danger for it, as well as backbreaking work. None of the silver he retrieved was his: it belonged to the owner of the mine, who paid him by the hour. He began to work longer and longer hours, greedy for the dollars which were mounting up, slowly, in a bag he kept under the bed in the cabin.

Burglary was a threat.

Anyone was a potential robber. Everyone knew who was earning, who was likely to have money stashed away, who used the bank. Your best friend might rob you. In this community, assembled of people from all over Europe, none of whom intended to stay there permanently, nobody was entirely trustworthy. But you had to hope for the best, trust some sort of moral bond or sense of interdependence that would prevent your workmate or neighbour from breaking into your house and relieving you of every penny you'd got.

You could not hope for that as far as the Indians were concerned.

Sophie was warned to stay indoors as much as possible, both to keep an eye on the house and to protect herself from being snatched away by one of the red men who sometimes roamed around Greenough, looking curiously at the people who had so recently relieved them of their territory. Some of these men were known in the town. They sold skins to the store, they bought whiskey at Clancy's. None of them worked in the mine, however. 'How do they live?' Sophie asked. 'Them fellas?' said Ned. 'Hunting. Fishing. They grow maize.' They used to grow maize in the valley at the foot of the Bitterroot Hills, on the plains. They would settle in a place and cultivate the rough, dry land until it yielded the maize, beans, and the peyote they used as a medicine and a drug. Their women knew how to make the roughest land fertile. But as soon as they succeeded in transforming scrubland to fertile soil, the army moved them on. Now they were pushed into the hills, higher even than the silver mines. They were often starving: the women came down to Greenough carrying their babies in baskets strapped to their backs, and scavenged in the bins for leftovers, scraps of meat or bread the miners had thrown out. 'They'd eat anything,' Mrs Sullivan said disdainfully. 'They're not like us. They have no sense of cleanliness. Ugh.' All the women in Greenough hated the Indians.

One day, Sophie walked up from the river carrying a bucket of ice. It was November. The ground was covered with snow and the air was so cold that it seemed to freeze in her nostrils as she breathed. At the mine, the men had to melt the seams with fires and blowtorches before they could begin to dig.

Sophie had to put ice in a pot on the fire to get water.

From the eaves of the cabin, hunks of venison and mutton, legs and shoulders, hung, coated with white ice crystals. Whole rabbits, half a deer. Trapping was easy in the winter. And you could take all the meat you could get. There was no danger of it going off, so you could kill more than you needed. All you had to do was skin it and hang it outside the house in the cold, to freeze. When Sophie needed some, she brought it inside and let it thaw out before cooking it.

She was wearing her sealskin coat, which almost kept her warm and which had a huge hood. The hood gave her blinkered vision: she could only see what was in front of her eyes: the river, the spiky trees weighted with snow, the path back to the cabin.

She went into the cabin and put the bucket on the floor, near the fire. She stretched her numb hands to the flames, to thaw the fingers before taking off her coat.

A cold hand, heavy as a falling tree, clamped her mouth.

Another hand gripped her stomach.

So this was it.

What she felt was – nothing. Not fright, not terror. Nothing. It was as if every smidgen of herself, even her capacity to be afraid, had vanished.

Not for long.

She had heard stories. Terrible stories. They seeped into her consciousness. What they would do to you. First, all the men of the tribe would rape you. Then you might undergo unspeakable tortures. Not so unspeakable that every child in Greenough did not know what they were – that Sophie did not know what they were. Hadn't Mrs Sullivan regaled her with accounts, whispered over a glass in the saloon, as part of the Sunday night entertainment. Stories to make your hair stand on end. Burnings, in the worst places. Cuts at the most female, intimate parts of you. Finally you would be scalped – after your death if you were lucky.

Now the burden of stories flooded Sophie's head. A deluge of imaginings annihilated her, blacked her out.

When she came to, she was lying on her own bed. The Indian was standing beside her. He had a mug of water in his hand. He handed it to her and she drank a few drops of the ice-cold liquid.

He smiled.

Sophie did not return the smile. But she felt less afraid now. Instead she felt limp and helpless, as if her body had been squeezed in a mangle and all the feeling had been wrung out of it. Or as if her mind and her eyes were outside her body, hovering somewhere over her head like a dragonfly staring down at herself. It was not an unpleasant sensation.

'I need some meat,' he said. His English was slow and all his words were spoken with exactly the same emphasis, like a row of stiff pegs on a clothesline. In this his English was not so different from the English of most people in Greenough. Sophie and Ned spoke Irish usually when they were alone, or among other Irish people. Almost all the settlers had some language that was their own – German or Swedish or Icelandic or French – and their English was for use with outsiders. So what language did the Blackfeet speak? That he could speak at all, like other human beings, was a surprise for Sophie. The women who scavenged on the rubbish heaps of Greenough were as silent as trees.

'Take it,' said Sophie, not looking at him.

'Goodbye,' he said.

That was all. He left the cabin, unhooking a side of deer from the eaves outside. Then he walked away. She got up and watched him from the little window as he moved into the forest, disappearing from her view more quickly than he should have. Maybe, she thought, he was not real. Maybe he was some sort of ghost.

Kathleen – that is, Mrs Sullivan – complained that her children were driving her mad.

'Don't they play in the snow?' Sophie asked. She had been married for two years. The idea of children increasingly embarrassed her. Even looking at them embarrassed her. She did not envy Kathleen her brood, not at all. But she was always conscious that envy was the emotion Kathleen, and everyone else, attributed to her. Poor little Mrs Burns. Childless, God help her.

'They play in the snow. They slide on the lake. They ski down the slopes on those wooden yokes their father made for them. But it's dark most of the time and they have to be inside.'

'Why isn't there a school for them?'

'There's nobody to teach a school here,' Kathleen said.

'I could teach them to read and write,' Sophie said. 'If I had some books I could.'

Kathleen thought it was a good idea.

Ned did not agree. 'You can hardly read or write yourself,' he said.

What about the letter she wrote every month to her sister? What about the local newspaper she read aloud to him once a week? What about that?

'It's one thing being able to write a letter to your sister and another teaching children to write or to read.'

What would he know about it? Ned Burns, who'd been brought up in the bad end of County Derry, who'd seldom darkened the door of any school.

'Teachers go to school till they're eighteen years of age. Then they have to be apprenticed to a master teacher for six years. That's how long it takes to be a teacher.'

His scorn was so immense that she believed he must be right. But Kathleen was sceptical. 'Apprenticed for six years? I never heard tell of that,' she said. 'Anyway, what odds? You know more than the children anyhow,' she said. 'And more than most of us.' She did not say 'more than Ned' but that's what she meant. Ned could read a bit, and sign his name. But he could not read a newspaper. He couldn't be bothered, the small print hurt his eyes. And he had never written a letter.

'I suppose they get some sort of training,' Sophie said.

'We're not going to get a trained teacher out here in the back of nowhere,' said Kathleen. 'There aren't many like you here, either.'

'What do you mean?' Sophie was not being entirely disingenuous.

'A girl like you. A fine-looking girl who can read and write. Nobody knows what you're doing here.'

'I'm here because I'm married to Ned,' Sophie protested.

'Aye,' Kathleen said, looking curiously at her. 'Well ...'

'I'm fine,' Sophie said. 'I like it here.'

'Well, that's grand,' Kathleen said. 'But you could spare a thought for the children.'

'If you can't have a child of your own, I don't think you should interfere with other people's,' was Ned's rejoinder to that. 'You think you're so clever but ...' He did not finish the sentence.

The sun shone on the snow, and it was warm in front of the cabin. Light scattered across the trees. Sophie was inside, writing a letter to her sister. She told her about the attempt to teach, and, in a watered-down way, about Ned's reaction. Then she tore up that letter and started another one which made no reference to the incident. Sheila would probably agree with Ned. Or else she would use the information as ammunition against the marriage.

A knock on the door.

The Blackfoot again.

'What do you want?'

'Flour, please,' he said.

'I haven't got much,' she said, thinking, that's the trouble. You give in once and then they keep coming back. All beggars were the same.

'We have none,' he said.

'All right,' she said. 'But this is the last time.'

He handed her a small basket made of bark. She went to her flour sack and scooped two scoops of the crunchy yellow flour into the basket. When she turned, he had come into the kitchen and closed the door behind him.

'It is so cold,' he said, by way of explanation.

'Do you go to other cabins? Like this?'

He shook his head and smiled at her.

She smiled as well.

Then it started to happen. What should not have been possible, with a man like this, a man who was not real, who was a sort of animal. Blackfeet. Red men. Savages. She felt her heart change inside her. It changed so that she could feel it, she could feel her whole mind and body and soul begin to change, to ignite, and she felt this change as her heart tossing around inside her like a lump of butter in a churn and her muscles shivering. His brown eyes stared at her, as if he knew what was happening to her. But he couldn't have.

'Here is your flour,' she said, handing it to him and speaking in a cold, neutral voice. 'You'd better go now.'

'Thank you,' he said.

She wondered, later, where he had learned his English. Just hanging around the town? Or in some other way? There was nobody she could ask. She had no business talking to someone like him at all. The correct thing for a woman to do, when confronted by an Indian, was to scream her head off and run as fast as she could away from him. If Ned knew this had happened, he would probably strangle her.

She still read the paper. She read it on Saturday nights after she had come home from the store, when Ned was bathing his feet in a tub of hot water. His toes were almost frozen off sometimes, with the cold of the mine.

'Gold discovered in Yukon,' she read. 'Gold has been discovered in the Klondike region of the Yukon Territory in northern Canada. Already hundreds of eager prospectors have arrived in Dawson City, with a view to bettering themselves. The seams, which have been found close to the junction of the Klondike and Yukon rivers, are said to be exceptionally rich …'

'Gold,' Ned said. 'Gold is better than silver.'

'The Klondike must be an awful place,' Sophie said. 'Up there in the north. Haven't you heard of fools' gold?'

'You're such a fool you wouldn't know the difference between gold and silver,' he said. And he laughed.

But she did not laugh this time, and let him go to the saloon on his own. When he came home he was very drunk. She pretended to be asleep. But he woke her up to tell her that several men from the village were planning to set off for the Yukon as soon as the ice melted. They hadn't needed to read about the gold in the paper. Already, somehow, word had reached Butte that there was more gold up there than had ever been found in the whole of North America before. 'It's for the taking,' he said. Sophie knew it could not be so simple, but nodded and pretended to agree.

Blackfoot looked about twenty years of age to Sophie, who was now twenty-two herself. His image was in her mind most of the time as she went about her tasks or lay in bed before falling asleep. (Ned seldom kissed her, or caressed her, any more. He was too tired, most of the time, after the work at the mine. When he came home at night all he did was eat his dinner, say the Rosary, and flop into bed.) It was a disturbing image, and she tried to dislodge it from her head, but couldn't. His tall, strong body clad in its beaver skins. His bronze face with its pools of dark eyes, its polished cheekbones. His hair fell to his shoulders, thick and opaque, unlike any hair she had seen. She felt her fingers itch to touch it just to find out what it felt like.

If he had not been able to speak English this would not have happened to her, she thought. Or if she had not been able to speak English, but only the Irish she had spoken at home, and still spoke with Ned. If he had only spoken his savage's language, and she her own, she would have kept away from him.

By now, four years after Ned had started his apprenticeship to the silver miner, he had learned all there was to know about the trade. He could locate a mine, he could drill and blast. He could identify different kinds of minerals. He could evaluate them.

'The value of silver has dropped,' he told Sophie. 'It's gone from eighty cents an ounce to forty cents.'

At first, Sophie did not understand how this had happened.

'President Jackson did it,' Ned said, neutrally. 'He devalued silver.'

How could a man, even if he were the president, have enough power to change something like the value of silver? Apparently that is just what he had been able to do, by simply ordering it to be so. It sounded to Sophie like the wedding feast at Cana.

'Gold is the thing,' Ned said. 'We'll never get anywhere if we don't mine that.'

Then it struck Sophie that gold could change its value too. It struck her that it had no value. 'Why is gold valuable?' is what she asked.

'What?' Ned was incredulous.

'Can't its value change? If President Jackson changes his mind?'

Ned didn't appear to think so. Anyway he didn't give her an answer. His mind was made up. Already he had planned every inch of his journey, from Missoula to the Klondike. He would take a paddle steamer most of the way. Then he would walk from the Yukon fork to Dawson City. That was where the best gold was: clear, bright yellow, the most valuable kind.

'Why? It's nice to look at, but it's of no use.'

'Of course it's of use,' he said.

'What use is it?' Sophie persisted, as her mind wrapped itself around this idea. What use is silver? More use than gold. Silver knives and forks, silver cups and bowls. They last and last. They shine and can be shone up again, clean and bright as water.

'It's use,' he said. 'Don't be stupid. There's so much you don't understand.'

'I suppose so,' Sophie said. But she wondered. Gold. Why did they want it so much?

'Because it looks like the sun,' North Wind said.

'That's probably it,' said Sophie, although she wondered. Did it have some properties she was unaware of? Could it cure some pain? Could it endure for ever, like – perhaps – a man's lineage?

North Wind. That was his name, Englished, but for a long time Sophie could not say it. It sounded so silly.

'What does Sophie mean?' he asked.

'It doesn't mean anything,' Sophie said. 'Names don't have a meaning.' He looked sceptical and as she said this she wondered if it was true. Edward. How could a sound like 'Edward' mean anything? It was not a proper word, just a name.

North Wind came to the cabin again and again, as the winter turned to spring. Ned had moved away, not to the Yukon, but higher into the mountains behind Greenough, the Bitterroot Mountains, where he was digging for gold.

'Do your people use it?' she asked North Wind.

'No,' he said. 'We use instead beads made from shells. Wampum.'

'The same thing!' said Sophie.

No, it was not the same thing. The shells lay everywhere, on the shoreline of the lake. On beaches at the foot of the high cliffs that fall into the Blackfoot river. The Indians did not blow up the mountains in order to get them. The earth gave them the shells, for nothing.

He came to the cabin for meat and bread. They both

146

knew that was why he was coming. It was for no other reason. To him she looked old and pale. Paleskin, and she was very pale, even now, with her fair hair, her white peaky skin. Even her eyes were colourless, by comparison with his. Black hair, bronze skin, dark brown eyes. He was the colour of a dark forest animal, a fox, a bear, while she looked like an urban aberration.

He told her things. The names of the months. The month of the melting snow. The month of the greening grass. The month of the rutting stag. He told her about the animals in the mountains: the great brown bears, the thin mountain lions. One had come and taken a child away from the camp where he lived with his tribe before the snow melted. The lions were short of food – and he blamed this, like almost every misfortune, on the white settlers. He told her about the Great Spirit that inhabits the whole earth, that owns the forest, the mountains, the plains, the waters, the animals.

The Great Spirit sounded to Sophie like God. But she did not say this to the Blackfoot, who would have scorned her. He thought everything about the white settlers was stupid.

'Our land is more valuable than your dollars,' he said. 'It will last for ever. It belongs to the Great Spirit and white men cannot buy it, although they think they can. If they cut down the forest and blow up the mountain, the Great Spirit will punish them.'

But he did not know how the Great Spirit would go about this. In fact, most of the punishment going seemed to be meted out not to the white men, but to the Blackfeet. They were half-starved on their cold encampment. Several of them had died during the winter – the miners had taken the lion's share of the game on offer from the Great Spirit, apparently.

'You have more guns,' was the explanation he had for this. Guns, dynamite, steam engines: the Great Spirit was no match for these weapons.

Ned found gold. He came down from the mine and showed it to Sophie: nuggets of rich, dark, solid gold. He said fifteen decades of the Rosary in thanksgiving. Sophie's knees were worn out by the time he'd finished. Then he drank half a bottle of whiskey and tried to make love to her, but fell asleep before he could.

One of his colleagues took the nuggets to Butte to sell them.

'Our fortune is made!' said Ned.

Sophie had been excited when she held the rough, heavy lumps of gold in her hand. They glittered like the water in the lake when the sun shone on it in the middle of summer, sparkling it with a million diamonds. It was like holding that sparkle of sunshine in your hands. The darkness of the gold reminded her of the dark eyes and dark skin of the Blackfoot. Indian gold.

But she was not so sure about the fortune. 'What will we do then?' she asked uncertainly.

'Go somewhere,' said Ned. 'Out of this hellhole. Back east. Back to Ireland.'

When she walked in the forest she did not see the Great Spirit. But she heard the trees talking to her. She watched the light seeping through the high roof of the fir needles as she moved along the aisles. She watched the rich green and carmine carpet of berries sprouting around her toes.

Wrapped in her sealskin, she felt she was a seal. She felt she was a tree.

Naked, bathing in the deep dark pool of the creek, she

felt she was a fish. A slippery salmon, fat and juicy, its skin the same colour as the shingle on the banks of the river.

North Wind came to the cabin while Ned was there, during the week of waiting for his fortune to be brought back from Butte. North Wind knocked on the door and Ned answered it. When he saw the Indian standing there, dressed at this time – it was the month of the long sun – in very little, he hit him on the jaw. Then he turned and picked up his rifle. By the time he had got back to the door, North Wind had vanished.

'Fucking bastard,' said Ned. He was so angry that for a while he did not think to ask what North Wind was doing there. But later he remembered. Had Indians ever come to the cabin before? No, said Sophie, wondering if this lie were wise or foolish. No. Sometimes the women come, searching in the bins.

'Shoot them if they come here,' said Ned. His voice grew tender. 'You shouldn't be here on your own.'

'I'm used to it now,' said Sophie, as nonchalantly as she could.

'At least you won't have to be alone here again,' he said.

But the news from Butte was bad. The gold was not valuable. It was too dark.

'What?' Sophie could not believe this. 'It's still gold, isn't it?'

'It's gold. But it's gold that's no more valuable that silver.'

So it was true, Sophie thought. Gold was not always precious. Some of it was and some of it wasn't. Maybe it was not precious if you could find it too near home, if you came upon it too easily? Was that it? Or was it that someone decided, some powerful man sitting in Washington, that some kinds of gold were important and some were not?

'No no.' Ned would not hear of it. 'That's not why. It's the colour that's wrong. It's too dark. It's redskin gold.'

Too dark. Only the white light blond gold of the snowy Arctic would be good enough for America. The gold of the Klondike.

'I'll stay here,' Sophie said, when Ned announced that he would go there, as drawn to it as the bees to clover. Once you started on this road there was no turning back.

'You can't,' he said. 'It's too dangerous.'

'More dangerous than the Klondike?'

It seemed that her life had become a balancing act as she moved from east to west, choosing the lesser of two evils all the time. Ned was better than Sheila and housework in Philadelphia. Being alone in a cabin in Montana was better than working in a factory in Philadelphia. Now going to the Klondike with Ned was supposed to be better than staying in the cabin here. But her judgement was faltering. She could no longer weigh up one choice against another and see, quickly, which was the best. North Wind had skewed her power to do that, had taken away her ability to distinguish black from white, silver from gold, bad from good, good from better.

'There isn't enough money. You can't stay here.'

'If I taught the children, they'd give me food and fuel,' Sophie protested weakly, but knowing as she said the words that they were true. She could stay here on her own and survive.

'Don't be silly,' he said firmly. 'You can't teach anyone.'

'What if the gold in the Klondike also turns out to be the wrong kind?'

150

'It's the right kind. And I'm going to get it,' he said. In spite of his experiences, Ned had not changed. He was still always convinced that he knew exactly the right thing to do, the right way to go.

When Ned had been on Granite Mountain, mining the dark and useless gold, this had happened. North Wind had come to the cabin when Sophie was washing clothes. She washed them, during the summer, in the creek, rubbing the hard soap on them and scrubbing them on her washboard. She liked to watch the suds dancing off downstream in the sunlight.

'You should not do that.' North Wind was suddenly there beside her. You never heard him coming.

'Why?' She smiled up at him.

'It poisons the water,' he said.

Of course. That was what she would never think of. 'It's just a tiny bit of soap.' She watched the white, lovely suds.

'Yes,' he said. 'But if all the white women do it, it is a lot of soap. Then, no fish.' He helped her fill a tub with water. Then he helped her wash.

'Do you do this at the camp?'

He laughed. 'No,' he said. 'Never.'

'Have you a wife?' she asked suddenly, out of the blue. Did they have wives? Not in the sense that she was Ned's wife. Not in the sense of a priest and Mass and signing your name in a book. A real marriage.

He did not answer.

She touched him then. He was kneeling at her big wooden tub, splashing some shirt around in the soapy water. She touched his slippery hand under the surface of the water. He took out both their hands and pulled her

151

towards him, kissing her. He led her into the forest and laid her on the soft old needles. First, he dealt with her nipples, kissing them until she twitched with desire. Then he turned her on her stomach, so that the pungent needles tickled her skin, teased her belly and her thighs. He slid into her from behind. This time what she felt was not the twittering of birds, but an overwhelming delight which encompassed every inch of her body, back and front and in and out, which seemed to wrap her and him and the forest and the sky together. America. Gold. Heaven.

Ned had to go to Missoula to get some supplies for the journey.

Soon after he was gone, North Wind came in.

They made love on her bed.

'We are going away,' she said afterwards, the languor the lovemaking had given her body blunting the pain of what she was saying.

'Why?' He looked curious rather than dismayed.

'Ned wants to go to the Klondike, north of here.'

'I know where it is,' he said, patiently.

'Sorry. Well, you know why we're going then.'

'Gold fever.'

'Yes.'

'You will get rich.' He laughed. 'There's plenty of gold up there.'

'I will die, maybe.' She realised this was true.

'You will be all right in your sealskin coat. You will be at home.'

'I am at home here.' She realised this was true too. She had been here for five years. Ireland was a dim, unpleasant memory. When her mind moved to the Klondike, she saw endless snow. The snow was beautiful but even here she had learned what an enemy it could be, how imprisoning, how threatening of starvation and isolation. And here the snow lasted for about five or six months. Half the time the earth was green. There was hot, very hot, sun. The water in the stream ran warm, so that bathing in it was like bathing in a tub. Up there, the snow would last for much longer. Maybe it never melted? There would be no food apart from meat and fish.

'We move all the time.' North Wind had been on the move since the moment he was born – the year of Little Bighorn. He had moved farther and farther away from home, if home was the sowing fields, the winter hunting grounds. He had moved to the badlands.

'Yes. But we don't have to. We were doing well here.'

North Wind shrugged.

'He wants gold because he does not have a child,' she said.

'If he had a child he would need gold for another reason,' North Wind said.

'How many children have you?' she asked him, blushing suddenly and feeling weak.

'None,' he said. 'I have no wife.'

Her heart leaped. 'Why not?' she asked, smiling.

'I am young. Twenty-two.'

She had assumed they would mate as soon as they could, like cats or dogs. Everything she assumed about the Indians was turning out to be wrong.

'Would you like to be my wife?' he asked.

'I'm Ned's wife,' she said.

'Among the Blackfeet, if you get tired of one husband you can take another.'

'I'm a Catholic,' Sophie said. 'I couldn't do that.'

'If I kidnapped you, you would have no choice!' He laughed and gently pushed her down again, stroking her so that she laughed for joy.

They were ready to go. The mining tools were packed in one backpack, and food in another. All the clothes were in a lighter pack, which Sophie would have to carry. The cabin was ready to be closed up and abandoned. Somebody might come and take it over while they were gone. No arrangement was made, one way or the other.

'We might come back here,' said Sophie.

'Aye, surely,' said Ned.

He went to Clancy's to have one for the road, the night before they were to set off for the steampaddle at Missoula.

When North Wind came, he was not alone, but accompanied by four other men. He did that to make it look like an authentic raid. He could see the headline in the newspaper: REDSKINS CAPTURE WHITE WOMAN. It would absolve Sophie from blame, at the risk of starting a war, but it was so easy to give rise to a war that the risk hardly counted. A battle could start over a stolen sheep just as easily, or a frightened child. In addition, it would help to assimilate Sophie to the tribe. Abduction of a white woman they would understand.

The men were painted, black and red and blue stripes on their faces and bodies. One of them wore a war bonnet and the other three had feathers sticking out of their loose black hair. They carried machetes.

Sophie hardly recognised North Wind. She knew his voice, but apart from that he did not at all resemble the man she had got to know, taken to bed with her. He looked like a redskin. He looked like a savage.

She did what white women did in these circumstances. As he carried her away on his horse – a mangy, underfed nag – she screamed loudly.

He clapped his hand over her mouth.

Already Kathleen Sullivan and all the little Sullivans were out. They were also screaming, at the tops of their voices, in their Kerry–Montana accents.

The Blackfeet did not know what to do with her.

'I'm happy now,' she said to North Wind. They were on the move again, moving to somewhere new where the Greenough gang would not find them.

But before they could dismantle the tepees and get out, Ned and Mick Sullivan, Mossie Fitzgerald and Miley Gallagher, Fritz Zumpfe and Jon Johannsen, and several others, converged on the camp. They carried shotguns, pikes, shovels, axes, anything they had available.

'Fucking savages.' Ned's voice was heard above the others. 'I'll rip them apart. Fuckers.'

Nobody was hurt.

A miracle.

The Blackfeet had run away, all of them. They were packed and ready to go anyway as Ned and his friends came upon them.

'Brave braves!' Ned said sarcastically. 'As soon as they sniff a real man, off they run.'

Sophie looked at him, neutrally.

'I'd like to strip their skin off and roast them skinless,'

Ned said. 'Did they do you any harm?'

She did not answer.

'The poor wee woman's not right after it. No wonder,' said Miley Gallagher. 'Give her time. She'll tell you what happened when she's had time to let it all sink in.'

'Aye,' Ned said.

They went to the Klondike three days later.

Sophie had a baby, up there in the north, sometime the following spring. The baby was fine, a small light-skinned boy with black straight hair, not like Ned's or Sophie's. They called him Teddy. People often said to Ned, 'He's the image of you.'

Sophie loved her child. She fed him with her own milk, she wrapped him in furs, she sang to him and told him stories about Ireland, about the mountains, about the creek that ran sweetly outside her cabin in Montana.

Before Christmas, Ned hit gold – the pale gold of Alaska, which was the most valuable kind. His joy was boundless. 'By summer we'll be rich enough to go back home. We'll buy a good big farm in Derry and live like gentry.'

After Christmas the baby caught a cold. For two days the sound of his small cough racked the cabin and then, unable to get his breath, he died.

After that, the black sickness descended on Sophie, immured in her cold cabin in a land of ice. It descended on her mind and her heart like a blanket of black frost, blotting out every song and every flower that grew there, snuffing her flame.

Nothing ignited it again.

Ned prayed for her, night after night, in long litanies of supplication to his beloved Virgin. Mother Most Merciful,

Mother Most Pure, Mother Most Renowned, pray for her.

After a while Sophie, who had not been one for praying before, began to join him in his prayers. Morning Star, Help of the Sick, Comfort of the Afflicted. Pray for Us. She recited them not only in the evenings, kneeling at the rough wooden chairs in the cabin before bedtime, but all day long. Mother of God, Star of the Sea. She walked around the shanty town, wrapped in her sealskin coat, chanting these incantations, without cease. To the litany she added an epithet of her own. North Wind, North Wind, North Wind. Nobody noticed that it broke the rhythm of the song, or that it was in any other way extraneous. Nobody would have commented if they had.

It was generally thought, among the Irishmen, pious or secular, sensible or wild, who were hitting gold with Ned, that Sophie's ordeal in Missoula at the hands of the Indians had affected her brain, and that she was not quite right in the head.

The Banana Boat

We'd been on holiday for a week, in a summer cottage in west Kerry. The weather had been glorious. Every day the sun shone, blessing the landscape. I had been sunbathing on golden strands, swimming in clear blue water with views on each side of moss-green hills rolling into the ocean, or walking along lanes lined with flower-studded ditches – purple selfheal, blue sheep's bit, everywhere the brilliant yellow of dandelion and buttercup. The typical outdoor sound had been the buzzing of bees. It had been a honeyed landscape and a honeyed holiday.

Our two teenage boys had not been enjoying it much, however. John was sixteen now, and Ruan fourteen. John was only happy when on the golf course. He would play thirty-six holes, on his own, staying away from morning until dinner time, coming home pale and exhausted under his tan. He refused to play with Ruan, claiming that his game was not good enough. Ruan denied this but in fact he had other fish to fry: computer games. All day he would spend close to the television set, controlling a hand-held pad and watching cartoon figures jerk around the screen to the sound of a monotonous tune. We had a constant struggle to get him away from the games, to encourage him to spend some time outdoors. The struggle dominated the holiday. He did not want to go for a walk, he did not want to go for a swim. We, of course, had bought the machine that seemed to control his life, but we blamed him for his addiction. How could we have foreseen that it would lead to this?

One thing was clear: this would be one of our last holidays as a family. Next year they would probably refuse to come with us.

After a week the weather forecast promised a break. We would have a showery day. Usually when the RTÉ meteorologists forecast a showery day it meant heavy rain where we were, out on the southernmost tip of the Dingle Peninsula. Mists were always rolling in from the Atlantic, hitting the hills of our parish and falling on us as rain, even when the rest of the country enjoyed sunshine or at least sunny spells. I suggested we go on an outing to Tralee, where the weather is often better than it is out here and where there is a big swimming centre, with pools and slides and all kinds of amusements. The response was not exactly enthusiastic, but eventually both boys agreed to come.

The weather forecast was wrong: next day dawned bright and sunny, just the kind of day we had grown used to. The swallows were fluttering around, chirping, high above the meadow in front of our house, and the island lay in a pale-blue sea like a basking whale, complacent and enormous.

'It's a good day for golf,' John said sleepily, turning in his untidy bed. 'Do we have to go?'

Yes. We have to go.

John insisted that he wouldn't go for a swim. I thought he might change his mind when we got to Tralee, and packed his swimming togs along with everyone else's. We piled into the car, lightly dressed, and set off, me driving as usual. At some stage in the past ten years this had become normal, although when I had married I did not know how to drive and Niall did.

There is bickering in the back of the car. John continues to insist that he won't go for a swim, and Ruan retaliates by saying that he won't go if John doesn't.

'OK OK!' I say, since there is nothing else to say. But this begs the question of why we are going to Tralee at all.

'We can go to the heritage centre,' I say. 'You haven't been there, Ruan, have you?'

'I hate heritage centres,' he says.

'It's got a little train that takes you on a trip through history,' I continue. 'Tralee through the ages.'

'For fuck's sake, he's fourteen years old,' says John.

'Must you use that word?' Niall sighs deeply and switches on the radio.

Veteran of family holidays, I just switch off my ears and concentrate on the road.

I love driving along the narrow roads, with the fuchsia branches dripping onto the sides of the car. There is a lovely, lustrous light falling on everything – hazy blue hills across Ventry Bay, olive green hills closer. It is so beautiful, in this sunshine, that you could hardly believe it was real. It surprises me, in a way, that the boys seem so uninfluenced by the surroundings. But as far as one could tell, nature has absolutely no effect on their moods. If anything, it annoys them. They don't seem to see scenery in the way I do. So what are they seeing, as they stare out the windows, scowling?

160

*

'Did you turn off the oven?' Niall asks.

'Yes,' I say confidently. But of course how can I be sure? 'I think so anyway.'

Why should he ask? I remember then that two years ago we left the house – the same house – and came back two hours later to find the kitchen filled with thick black smoke and the oven on the point of bursting into flames. We managed to put it out and since then a new cooker has been installed.

'I don't think it would matter anyway,' I say. 'This one wouldn't go on fire even if it were left on. That old oven was filthy and covered with grease. Plus it always overheated – the thermostat didn't work.'

I believe this and I have absolutely no reason to suspect that I have left on the cooker or the oven. I'd been washing up – we have an optimistically planned washing-up roster and today is my day – and had been close to the oven for long after we'd finished cooking Ruan's breakfast fry. Still, the question makes me uneasy. And it opens up uneasinesses that are never far from my mind.

The holiday has been working fairly well, so far, but nevertheless I have often been assailed by worries. Niall believes this happens because I am a compulsive worrier, but I believe it happens because there is plenty to worry about. I worry about my job, back in Dublin. I worry about what is going on in my absence, things I have forgotten to do, things I have done – this always happens on holidays, especially on holidays in Ireland where there is not enough going on to blot out the memories of work. The details of the worries vary from time to time but the anxiety remains the same. I worry about money, pensions, the future. I worry about my elderly mother. I worry about Niall, who is also elderly, or getting there, older than me. That he could become ill, that he could die, is always an idea conducive to a good old worry.

Sometimes I think that this must be the root of all the worries and is the reason why I cannot be quite at peace. We are having a wonderful life together, just as we are having a wonderful holiday (when we forget that the boys are hating every minute of it). But I am somehow conscious of the threat of mortality putting an end to it all. Death hovers somewhere around, lurking in the corners like the mists that are always somewhere out there on the Atlantic, sweeping towards us on the wind. Maybe it is because of this that I am always afraid that the rug of my joy can be pulled from under me, that the whole delicate edifice of my domestic happiness will suddenly disappear. The structure of our secure, contented life seems to be held together by some magical charm. But I worry that at any moment that charm may lose its subtle, intangible power.

Maybe that is it. Or maybe it's much simpler. That I'm premenstrual, or premenopausal. I'm never quite sure if my worries are rational, or simply the result of some physical imbalance. Mind, body, reality: worries are thoughts but they are not like plain, unemotional thoughts. Emotional thoughts, they can have their origins in various places, or in more than one simultaneously. Stop worrying, men say. Niall says. The boys even say this. Nothing is going to happen. Everything is going to be all right. They do not believe in God, but they believe in the steadfastness of the spell that protects ordinary lives, whereas I believe in nothing. Or perhaps it is not that, but that as males they are naturally brave, naturally carefree, naturally insouciant. 'You have nothing to fear but fear itself' is one of Niall's mantras. 'The coward dies a thousand times, the brave man once' is another. These sayings always encourage me for a while, and then they lose their power.

Niall wants to buy a table for the bedroom, so that he or I can sit there, at the window, and write, while the children watch television in the living room. As we drive down from the Connor Pass, I suggest that we turn off at Castlegregory, where there is a furniture store. Once, years ago, we bought a little suite of Dutch furniture there, big chunky wooden armchairs with wide squat armrests, covered with dull purple velvet. The memory of that suite of furniture does not attract me to the store, but I know that Niall will jump at the chance to visit it. I guess that his desire for the worktable will outweigh even his innate dislike of digression and changes of plan. And I'm right.

'What a good idea,' he says cheerfully, smiling across the gearbox.

'What?' snaps Ruan from the back of the car, more alert than one might imagine. 'We're turning off at Castlegregory?'

'Maybe we could go for a swim there later?' I suggest wildly. 'We could rent out boats and things at that water sports centre.'

'But I don't want to rent out boats and things,' says Ruan, not unpredictably.

'Me neither!' John chimes in automatically. At this stage his grumpiness has become lukewarm. His dismay at the way the day is developing is so immense that even his normal supply of negative energy has diminished.

A certain amount of half-hearted, uninformed complaining about the articles for hire at Castlegregory water sports centre goes on in the back seat, as we drive along the flat road between small fields and gardens overflowing with flowers: nasturtiums, geraniums, roses, tumbling abundantly over lawns and fences, a horticultural counterpoint to the abundant wildflowers of the landscape. Before I have actually turned off the main road for the village of Castlegregory, however, Ruan has performed one of those miraculous U-turns of which he is still capable, at fourteen. He has decided that he might like to go for a swim at Castlegregory. Probably he remembers previous swims during previous summers – the water around here, in the flat sandy stretches of the Maharees, tends to be considerably warmer than on the other, more rugged side of the peninsula. Maybe that is what has caused his change of mind, or maybe it is something else that he has remembered, or spotted on the roadside. One never knows but is grateful for even the slightest co-operation.

The village of Castlegregory is pretty in the way of Dingle, with pastel stuccoed houses and plenty of windowboxes on its three narrow winding streets. But the hordes of tourists who swarm up and down the streets of Dingle are lacking here. Two women wearing shorts and T-shirts, bronzed to the colour of toffee, stroll along the footpath dangling plastic bags of shopping. Otherwise the village seems as deserted as an off-beat Italian hill village at midday. You might assume, if you did not know otherwise, that the natives were all taking a siesta or a long leisurely lunch, and that come four o'clock the village would buzz with life.

We see a pub, painted pink, with a lot of geraniums dangling outside and a sign saying 'Seafood. Pub Grub'. It's called the Natterjack Inn. Inside, it is pleasantly furnished with pine and súgán, and the menu looks right. Like the village, the pub is deserted.

We sit in a large conservatory, open on two sides to let plenty of air in, and furnished in a higgledy-piggledy way with old wooden tables, benches, some comfortable straw-seated súgán chairs. There are flowers and potted plants dotted around it in an odd assortment of tubs and skillets and pots. In one corner is a pool table. The boys' eyes light up when they see it. They get some coins. The balls crash out. They are happy for a while.

There are crab claws on the menu and Niall and I order them, while for the boys there are chicken nuggets and chips. I get a glass of white wine and Niall a beer. We sit and sip these drinks, the sun shining through the Perspex roof. We talk about the natterjack toad. The barman tells us that yes, Castlegregory is one of its few remaining habitats in Ireland. If you walk down the lane opposite the pub until you come to a lake, you can hear the toads and even see them sometimes, at eleven o'clock at night. The barman has often done this. We wonder if it is worth coming back at eleven o'clock some evening just to hear the croaking of an endangered toad. As I sip the wine and feel extraordinarily happy, I think that it probably is. But I do not make a plan, knowing I might be forced to stick to it if I do. Even in my mildly inebriated state, I am not optimistic enough to hope that John and Ruan will put the natterjack toad high on their list of holiday priorities.

When the crabs come, they are great: the biggest crab claws we have ever seen. They taste quite good too. Not perfect, but, given the sunshine, the flowers, the happy chatter of the boys, the wine, I am more willing than usual to pretend that they are perfect. For the price, which is low, it is a fantastically good lunch. We sit and munch and sip, and I feel that this is what a holiday should be: a family enjoying lunch in a sunny conservatory, with a colony of natterjack toads within walking distance and the wine cool and good.

At night, Niall and I go for walks sometimes, just to escape from the noise of the television, which tends to fill the house. Last night we walked down to the graveyard, which was cleaned up by some youth employment scheme a year ago. We recalled that when we had last been in it, the long grass had been treated with some weedkiller, which had turned it straw-coloured and had created an eerie effect: long drooping hay draped over stones and walls and everything, like a surrealist vision of Golgotha. Morbid grass.

This year, all that is gone. The grass has grown back, and already it is long – apparently the employment scheme does not extend to ongoing maintenance. The old sign outside warning that the ground is uneven and that the graveyard contains ruins is still there. We went inside and looked at the first, most elaborate grave, which is that of Tomás Ó Criomthain, the Islandman. 'Ní bheidh ár leithéidí arís ann', his most-quoted sentence, is engraved on the headstone, which stands sturdy and tall against the backdrop of the island where he lived, whose inhabitants he was referring to: 'Our like will not be found again'. In the quiet of the graveyard the words regain some of their meaning, which have been diluted by overuse outside (you hear this saying everywhere, you read it on T-shirts in Dingle; if there is one sentence every Irish speaker knows, it is this one). There in the graveyard, however, I accept the truth of what he said, looking at the other, older, more poignant graves. Seán Ó Dálaigh Os. Died 1944. He was a writer who used

166

the pseudonym Common Noun. His son was Niall's best friend in the parish. We often went out on Sunday nights with him and his wife, Peig. Both of them are now dead. Almost all the natives of this parish are dead, although not in these graves. The valley is full of houses, but mainly they are summer houses, populated by people like us from Dublin or Cork, from Germany or America. The houses are busy for a few weeks, a few months, of the year. The rest of the time, empty. There must be more empty houses in this valley than anywhere else in Ireland – and still the sign 'SITE FOR SALE' is ubiquitous; still the builders are busy making new white houses, the well-drillers steadily boring into the rock for water.

The graveyard has been improved. You can walk through all of it now, which you usen't be able to do. We passed the Islandman's grave, and Common Noun's, and turned the corner at the back – it is a tiny graveyard, containing only about thirty stones. Down at the back, the ground is uneven, and pocked with holes. I looked into one of these – morbidly, wondering if indeed I would see what one might expect to see. And yes, I did. There were some sticks that might have been bones. I stepped back and got a better view. Then I saw the skull, framed by a V-shaped bit of stone – not stone, wood, the V-shape being the surviving bit of coffin. Everything else had rotted away, apart from a little cowl to shelter the head. Even most of the bones of this skeleton's body seemed to have disintegrated, or to have mingled with the dust that once covered him or her – there was no headstone, so we didn't find out who it was.

Close to this grave is the grave of Bríde Liath, with its sad, sentimental lines: *'Is anseo a luíonn Bríde Liath, an cailín is gleoite agus is deise a mhair riamh ar an saol seo'* – 'Here lies the most beautiful, virtuous girl that ever walked the path

167

of life'. A Famine victim. There is a story about her, burying her three little children and then her husband, one after the other. Then dying herself, of starvation.

After lunch, Niall and I leave the boys playing pool and walk to the furniture store. It is farther away than we think, since previously we have driven there. We get a good look at the village of Castlegregory and wonder again at its beauty and its neglect by the tourist industry, which is capricious, unjust, and in a way not very intelligent – unless it is that everyone wants to be where the crowd is, which could well be the case. When we eventually reach the shop, a sign informs us that it is closed on Wednesdays. Today is a Wednesday.

We decided, more or less by a mutual consent possible thanks to the pleasures of the Natterjack Inn, that we wouldn't bother going to Tralee, but simply have a swim here and then go home. We drove out to the beach, one of the flat, sandy beaches of this area, backed by dunes and caravan parks. It always seems very light-hearted and gay to me, and indeed it is the sort of place where families with small children come for a beach holiday: the sky is wide and blue, cotton clouds floating around airily over the pale-green rushes and marram grass and clipped grass of the caravan parks, and places to park the car.

'It's nice, isn't it?' I ask.

'Yes, if it weren't for that strange building down on the beach,' says Niall. 'What on earth is it?'

That's where we're going. It's the water sports centre. It's not a building, it's a collection of paddle boats and surfboards, water bicycles and banana boats, canoes and bodyboards – all the sort of thing that makes my heart sing, maybe because I longed for such playthings during a childhood of summer holidays but only read about them in children's books. These things look attractive to me, and to Ruan and John, but I suppose if you did not know what they were, they would constitute a blot on the landscape and look like some sort of exceptionally offensive fish farm.

We park and go down to the beach. The tide is in and there is only a narrow stretch of sand, with plenty of people already sitting on it – plenty by Irish standards, that is, where having the whole beach to yourself is not unusual. We find a place close to the rocks and settle in. John says, 'I might go for a swim later.' Niall reads the newspaper. Ruan puts on his togs – which this year consists of shorts and a T-shirt and looks exactly the same as what he wears all the time anyway – and says, 'Give me some money. I want to rent out a surf bike.'

I am delighted that he is interested enough to do this. I give him a few pounds and he runs off. I am pleased that he is old enough to take care himself of the transaction involved – he can make the enquiries, do the hiring, go off surfing. All I have to do is provide the cash and take it easy.

I put on my own swimsuit, and think about getting in. John doesn't change his clothes, but sits and stares moodily out to sea. A so-called banana boat is taking half a dozen children on a ride. They sit astride a longish banana-shaped tube, and are pulled by a motorboat which goes increasingly fast. When the boat makes a sudden turn, all the children fall off the banana into the water; we can hear their screams of joy or whatever, their laughs as they scramble out of the water and try to regain their seats on the banana.

Where is Ruan?

'There he is!' I say. The part of the beach where the windsurfing and water biking goes on is separated from the part where we are by a string of buoys and a sign saying 'NO PLEASURE CRAFT BEYOND THIS POINT'. It is not too far away, but much too far to distinguish an individual's face or even clothing. There are a lot of pleasure craft bobbing around there – thirty or forty at least, it seems, several with children on them, peddling or paddling or surfing. I am pretty sure I can distinguish Ruan, however. I can tell the shape of his body, or perhaps it is the way he holds himself: rather stiffly and determinedly, his back straight and his head down. He is making a beeline for the horizon, which also figures – he probably thinks he is a bit old, at fourteen, to mingle with the smaller children who cycle up and down by the shoreline. Actually, the bay curves out in a semicircle so that even as you go out to sea the shoreline is not too far away – I discovered this when Ruan did the same thing, i.e. went out too far, a year or two ago. I ran along that semicircle shouting at him to come back in. I feel he is old enough now to take care of himself. Anyway, there are lots of paddle boats and surfers around where he is. After a while he turns and makes back for the shore and then he goes out again towards the mouth of the bay, and back again.

I sunbathe for a while and then, having observed an older man (older than me, I mean) swimming with obvious pleasure, I go down to the sea. There is a fringe of brown seaweed on the edge of the tide, and I realise that there is no hope of getting John to come in. That brown fringe will deter him, if nothing else does. He is unafraid to die, but he is squeamish about squelchy substances. I wade through the soft obnoxious stuff, thinking, as I always do when I walk in seaweed, of a working holiday I spent on the Frisian

Islands when I was a student. They are situated in a shallow, sandy zone (Erskine Childers wrote his novel *The Riddle of the Sands* about that area – I think I should try and read that novel sometime) and people walk on the flats in their bare feet for the sake of their health. *Wattlaufen*, the activity was called – something like that. The theory is that the oils or the vitamins from the seaweed sink into the soles of your feet and do you good. I suppose the seaweed baths at Ballybunion – which I experienced last year – are based on the same idea. Anyway these reflections take me through the brown mess which certainly looks rather unattractive, and into the clear greenish water.

It feels colder than I remember it, not any warmer than the sea at Ventry or Smerwick, where I have been swimming recently. Maybe this is related somehow to the tide. But it is not painfully cold, and this is the test for me now. If my feet don't ache from the cold, I know the water temperature is reasonable. I plunge in immediately, and start swimming. It still surprises me that I am doing this. All my life I have been one of those swimmers who waits for a long time, walking around and paddling the water with my hands, before getting down to it. I was like this as a child and continued until now, when I am forty-five. I remember being amazed at John who, when he still went for swims, ran in and started swimming straight away, not making even a break between his run down the beach and his first strokes in the water. In fact I can see him running down this beach and doing just that, as I sat on the towel at the rocks where I can see him now, reading the newspaper.

Niall seems to have fallen asleep. He is hardly visible because he is wearing green trousers and a beige and brown shirt. Camouflage. They are his favourite colours. He always blends in easily with nature, and there he is now, no more obtrusive than a clump of grass or a bramble bush. John in his turquoise shirt is easier to spot.

I get accustomed to the water very quickly and as usual I have a wonderful swim. The broad bay is rimmed with mountains – greeny lilac mountains, Binn Os Gaoith, Cathair Chon Roí, the Sliabh Mis range. I remember a poet telling some story about Mis at a conference I attended earlier in the year. Mis, some goddess or poetess, some mythical creature, lived in those mountains. I couldn't remember the story. I didn't like the name Mis, either. It sounded sneaky, and perhaps sexual, it sounded like an Irish word for some soft, secret enclave of the female body. Soft seaweed.

The water is clear as glass. I swim along, looking through the water ripples at the rippled sand beneath. Ripple, lap, plash, paddle. Back and forth I go, looking up occasionally at the rim of mountains, at the umbrella of blue and white sky, looking in at my husband and son on the beach, looking over to Ruan, still peddling furiously in and out, in and out, peddling away all the anger of the holiday and his teenagerhood. I stay in for about a quarter of an hour or twenty minutes, then plod through the seaweed and back to the towels. I spread one out and lie down to dry in the sun. Some women have taken the next spot. I can hear them talking as I lie there. What I catch is the end of a recipe, cooked recently for some party or celebration.

'I did a bake,' the voice says. 'You know, courgettes and peppers and everything with breadcrumbs and cheese on top.'

'Mm, sounds lovely,' another voice says.

I wonder what they had with it.

The conversation fragments. 'That green top you had on looks lovely on you,' I hear. There is some discussion as to which green top is meant. 'I went home and watched a video for three hours last night, until three o'clock in the morning.' I wonder where. Was it one of those caravans back up behind the beach? Or a rented house? Or a summer house, like ours? 'That fellow from ER was in it.' George Clooney? John Carter, my favourite, young and noble-looking, standoffish?

There is a summer house on the coast visible from the window of our summer house. Even now if I stretch a little I can see it. Grey walls with a touch of blue – the woodwork, a lovely faded blue, the blue of the summer house in the garden in *A Passage to India*. A slated roof, sloping in four slopes over the house, rather than the usual two back and front. Hip-roofed, that is the term. It is a beautifully proportioned house, perching, as it seems, right on the edge of the coast, with nothing behind it but the sound and the hunk of the island. There are no other houses on that side of the road. You can't get planning permission to build there. But the bungalow – it is always called 'the bungalow', as the island is always called 'the island' – was built before that rule came in, perhaps before there was any such thing as planning legislation. It was the first summer house in the valley, which is now chock-a-block with them. Built in the twenties or the thirties, it is a reminder of more gracious times.

But although it looks perfect from a distance of about half a mile, the bungalow is really a ruin. The roof is beginning to cave in, every window is broken. Nobody has stayed in it for forty years.

Once it rang with laughter. Or quarrels. Or songs. Niall remembers visiting there in the fifties on his first trip to the valley. He remembers a little girl – she now lives in America, and owns her own summer house in this valley – reciting 'The Owl and the Pussycat' in the middle of the kitchen. He remembers helping a local farmer to tie straw on to the seat of a chair, helping him to pull the rope taut. He thinks the house was beautiful inside, simple and rustic, with lots of books. It belonged to a professor of Irish and Greek, and his family and extended family spent long summers there long ago.

It is the oldest summer house. But it did not survive beyond a single generation – a long generation, it is true. Is this the fate of summer houses? People build their own, bring their children, come faithfully to their house for forty or fifty years – ours is already thirty years old. And what then?

The people of Long Island or Martha's Vineyard, of the Frisian Islands, of the Swedish archipelagos, could probably tell us. They have had a summer-house culture for hundreds of years. But I don't know. There is only one old summer house in our valley, and there it stands, a gracious ruin.

I look over at the pleasure boat enclosure. We've been here for about an hour. It's half past four. Niall stirs and asks if we will go home soon.

I look over at the boats. At first I can't see Ruan. Then I catch sight of him. He is moving out again. He seems to be cycling faster than previously and soon he is going out farther than he went before as well. He passes the last of the big paddle boats, and is out among the wind surfers. Then he passes them. He is beyond the mouth of the bay, well past the curve of the beach. He is out, alone in the sea, on his surf bike, still moving quite quickly.

'Look at him, he's heading for Tralee!' I say, a bit anxiously. I can see Fenit far away, miles across the water.

'Stupid eejit,' says John.

'Do you think he's all right?' I ask Niall.

Niall can't see him at all.

'Of course he's all right,' he says. 'But it's time he came back. I want to go home.'

I keep my eye on Ruan – on what I think is Ruan. He gets smaller and smaller. Then he disappears – the banana boat is moored out there, about a kilometre out, a speck from here, and he seems to be behind that.

I give in to my anxiety and run to the lifeguard who is sitting in front of a hut close by.

'I think my child has got carried out to sea,' I shout at him.

He seems unalarmed. But he asks me if I see him and I show him what I think is Ruan – a far-off speck in the bay. It could be just an empty boat, or a lifebuoy, or any of the many objects that are bobbing about on the water. He looks through his binoculars and says, 'He's on the banana boat. You should go to Johnnie over there' – he indicates the sports centre hut – 'and ask him to do something. He could send out a boat.'

I run along the beach, passing the families sunning themselves, making sandcastles, picnicking. When I get to Johnnie's I am quite alarmed. But the woman there is calm.

'There's a strong offshore,' she says.

I am impressed by the professional abbreviation.

'Don't worry. The boat has already gone out to pick him up. There's a few of them out there. The offshore takes them out on days like this but we keep an eye on them.'

I see a small orange dinghy out at the banana boat. It takes a long time to do whatever it is doing – utterly invisible from where I am. But I feel relieved. Everything is being taken care of.

'What's his name?' the girl asks – she is a cheerful, competent-looking young woman with a kind face, and a mobile phone.

'Ruan,' I say. She repeats it and then asks someone on the phone if the boy in the boat is called Ruan.

'He's not?' I hear her saying.

I feel real fear then.

'What does he look like?' she asks me.

I tell her. Blond. Blue eyes. Smallish. As I say these things, I realise how useless they are as a description. The description could apply to almost every boy on this beach. What should I say? Nose a little flat and broad, like mine only smaller? Mischievous grin – no that wouldn't do. They all have that and he probably isn't grinning mischievously now anyway. Crooked teeth – I should get him to an orthodontist very soon. If ...

I realise right now that there are two ends to the story, two ends to the story of my day and the story of my life. I think of Mary Lavin's story about the widow's son, which I have recently seen told dramatically and well by a professional storyteller. In one version, Packy is killed as he collides with a startled hen as he cycles home from school with the good news that he has won a scholarship (the equivalent of the lottery for bright children in those days. I remembered, even as I stood on the sunny beach wondering if my child were ... all right, the day I got my own results from that scholarship exam). In the second version of the story, Packy is not killed, but the hen is. Packy's mother nags him so much about the killing of that hen, which was her prize hen, or perhaps it was a prize cockerel, that he leaves home in anger and disgust a few weeks later and is never heard of again. The message of the story is that the loss you suffer through no fault of your own is much easier to bear than the one you bring about by your own actions.

But it's going to be more ambiguous than that.

I should perhaps have come over here with Ruan, booked his bike, warned him not to go out too far. I thought he was wise enough, at fourteen, to take care of himself. But I had misjudged him. I had misjudged the situation – the offshore wind, the vigilance of the water sports centre. I had misjudged everything.

'Where do you think he is?' the woman asks the man on the phone. I can see him nowhere. I think he is the boy on the banana boat, the boy who is now in the rescue boat. That is the boy I had my eye on, the stiff-backed, determined body that I think is my own body replicated, and also Niall's body. But if he is not Ruan, as they say, I have no idea where Ruan is. He could already be far out at sea. He could be at the bottom of the sea.

She talks to a young man who has suddenly appeared beside us. 'Tell him to find Ruan,' she is telling him urgently.

I am not shaking, I am suspended in a sort of jelly. The water is full of happy children and fathers (mostly it has to be said) paddling around, laughing and having a good time. The beach is golden, with its holidaymakers, its bronzed boys and girls, its bikini-clad mothers passing on recipes for vegetable bake, its toddlers making sandcastles. Normal life. And I am part of it still, but only just. I am on the edge of a cliff. In a minute I could tumble off and fall into another kind of life altogether. A life of pain and tragedy. Loss and mourning. Funeral arrangements. If ... The long aftermath of life without Ruan. Unimaginable.

It happens. On Friday a girl was drowned in a swimming pool in France. An Irish girl I mean. Aged fourteen.

Yesterday a man was drowned in Bray, near where we live in Dublin. On our beach in Dublin.

Peig Sayers lost several sons to the sea. Everyone on the island did. A commonplace tragedy then, not so commonplace now but it happens. It happens all the time.

One moment a family is cocooned in the happiness, or whatever, of normal life. The next it is elsewhere, in another land or another ocean. It happens in a few moments.

Those are the few moments I am in, the liminal time between ordinariness and tragedy (also of an ordinary kind; to others it will be so, ordinary and instantly forgettable. While for me it will be the tragedy – the raw edge of the unimaginably terrible. Parents never get over it. I have seen it. I have heard it. I know it).

'So who have you in the boat?' The young man is on the mobile phone. 'Well ask him, John. Ask him for Christ's sake. Ruan. Ruan. Ask him to tell you his name.'

There is a pause. In that pause I see in my mind's eye the small, stiff, determined figure making his way to the banana boat. In that second.

'His name is Ruan,' the young man exclaims. 'You gobshite, John!'

The young man turns to me. 'You're all right. He's in the boat. You should have called him some ordinary name like John or Michael for Christ's sake!'

I laugh and make a joke. I touch the young man's arm in gratitude (he doesn't like this; we are both practically naked but I hardly care).

I wait for a long time. What seems like a long time. Fifteen, twenty minutes, before the rescue boat comes to the shore. Ruan scrambles out, pale and cold-looking, and swims in the last bit of the way over the fringe of brown seaweed to the beach, which is stony down here and now looks sharp and sordid to me, with its rows of plastic machines, its pleasurecraft.

There is another story on my mind as I drive home. 'Miles City, Montana'. Alice Munro. A story about a near-drowning. The narrator's daughter Meg has a close shave in a swimming pool. She is rescued because her mother has an intuition as she walks towards a concession stand (what is a concession stand? some sort of kiosk, I suppose) to get cool drinks.

'*Where are the children?*' flashes through her mind. Back she runs, just in time. Is it intuition or just a mother's natural, normal anxiety? I think the point of the story is that a child who is looked after in the normal way, by parents who are protective, and normally anxious, tends to be safe and survive, while a child who is neglected ... There is another, remembered boy in the tale, a boy who drowns. I could remember the description of his retrieved body, grotesque, with green weed in his nostrils. Usually in Kerry, bodies are not retrieved, but perhaps that is not the case right here, Tralee Bay. It's more sheltered than the broad rough heartless ocean that stretches in front of our house, that beats eternally against the rocky shores of our parish. It's about that, as well as about the power of a mother's intuition.

I had no intuition. Just anxiety. I saw him. I saw him moving faster. I saw him being swept out. I admired him too, for getting off the bike and on to the banana boat, which was moored and big. The banana boat was exactly the right thing to head for. Of course I knew it was him, I recognised the way he carried his body. I recognised the way he cycled on a water cycle, as you know someone's way of walking. That's not intuition. It's familiarity. A mother's familiarity – Niall and John apparently did not recognise this at all. I knew it was Ruan, on the banana boat, in the rescue boat. Even as I was terrified to death, even when the friendly young woman's voice revealed alarm and said Ruan was not in the boat, but some other boy, I had a suspicion, in a deeply rational part of my mind, that the distant speck had the familiar shape of Ruan. The bits of the jigsaw that I had seen told me it was so.

He would have been saved anyway. The boat was on the way out before I reported the thing to the water sports centre. He was never in real danger.

That's what he said himself. In fact he insisted he was in no danger at all, that he had deliberately cycled out to the banana boat because he wanted to sit on it, that he could easily have cycled back. So why did he come back in the rescue boat? He had two answers to this. One was that the man in the boat offered him a lift. The other was that his 'go was up' (the bike was rented for an hour) and that the man wanted it back.

So maybe the man in the boat was a good psychologist? He was casual about the whole trauma, making little of it, to protect the macho feelings of the teenage boy. To protect his own feelings, as a businessman and owner of a water sports centre, competing with a strong offshore wind.

Ruan refused to talk at all about his experience and was unusually cross and angry as we drove home.

Along the flat sunny roads of the plain, up to the alpine drama of the Connor Pass, down again to Dingle, and home. Home.

As we went along by Ventry Bay, I remembered the day we had found the kitchen full of smoke. Accidents. We could go back now and the house could be burnt to the ground, if I had in fact left the oven on – and I could have. I am increasingly absent-minded. I thought it unlikely that this would be the case. Just as I had known it was Ruan when the girl said, 'He's not?', I knew that speck on the banana boat was a speck I recognised. Ruan. I felt that we still belonged to the lucky section of humanity that does not fall over the edge, usually. We still belonged to the charmed circle that may get an occasional premonition of disaster but does not actually experience it head-on.

And sure enough, as we turn into the long grass of our field it's clear that the oven was not left on. The house is still standing at the end of its field, waiting for us to open the door and sleep there.

We are still safe. Alive and safe. We still belong to real life, the life that is uneventful, the life that does not get described in newspapers or even, now that the days of literary realism are coming to an end, in books. The protected ordinary uneventful life, which is the basis of civilisation and happiness and everything that is good: the desirable life. We still belong to the part of life that is protected from danger, by its own caution, by its own love, by its own rules, by its own belief in its own invulnerability. Usually.

But how reliable is that 'usually'? In a minute it can be swept away, on a freak wave, on an offshore wind, by a fast car or a momentary lapse of concentration. It is precarious and delicate, our dull and ordinary happiness, seeming sturdy as a well-built house but as fluttering and light as a butterfly on a waving clump of clover. As ephemeral as that; as beautiful and priceless.

Ruan's close shave happened on 16 July 1999. I thought

about the event and wrote these thoughts down late that night and then fell asleep beside my husband in the wood-panelled bedroom we have shared, on holidays, for twenty years. In Fairfield, New Jersey, John Kennedy Junior, his wife and her sister were just taking off into the sunset in their Piper Saratoga II HP, on their way to a family wedding in Martha's Vineyard – the famous holiday resort five thousand miles from Dingle on the opposite shore of the Atlantic. An aviation expert, Mr Serge Roche, some days later described the Piper Saratoga as 'reliable'. By then, the newspapers were full of speculation about what had happened, and why John Kennedy Junior, his wife and her sister were at the bottom of the ocean.

A Literary Lunch

The board was gathering in a bistro on the banks of the Liffey.

'We deserve a decent lunch!' Alan, the chairman, declared cheerfully. He was a cheerful man. His eyes were kind and encouraged those around him to feel secure. People who liked him said he was charismatic.

The board was happy. Their tedious meeting was over and the bistro was much more expensive than the hotel to which Alan usually brought them, with its alarming starched tablecloths and fantails of melon. He was giving them a treat because it was a Saturday. They had sacrificed a whole three hours of the weekend for the good of the organisation they served. The reputation of the bistro, which was called Gabriel's, was excellent and anyone could tell from its understated style that the food would be good, and the wine, too, even before they looked at the menu – John Dory, oysters, fried herrings, sausage and mash. Truffles. A menu listing truffles just under sausage and mash promises much. We can cook and we are ironic as well, it proclaims.

Put your elbows on the table, have a good time.

Emphasising the unpretentiously luxurious tone of Gabriel's was a mural on the wall depicting a modern version of *The Last Supper*, a mural of typical Dubliners eating at a long refectory table. Alan loved this mural, a clever, post-modern, but delightfully accessible, work of art. It raised the cultural tone of the bistro, if it needed raising, which it didn't really, since it was also located next door to the house on Usher's Island where James Joyce's aunts had lived, and which he used as the setting for his most celebrated story, 'The Dead'. In short, of all the innumerable restaurants boasting literary associations in town, Gabriel's had the most irrefutable credentials. You simply could not eat in a more artistic place.

The funny thing about *The Last Supper* was that everyone was sitting at one side of the table, very conveniently, for painters and photographers. It was as if they had anticipated all the attention that would soon be coming their way. And Gabriel's had, in its clever, ironic way, set up one table in exactly the same manner, so that everyone seated at it faced in the same direction, getting a good view of the picture and also of the rest of the restaurant. It was great. Nobody was stuck facing the wall. You could see if anyone of any importance was among the clientele – and usually there were one or two stars, at least. You could see what they were wearing and what they were eating and drinking, although you had to guess what they were talking about, which made it even more interesting, in a funny sort of way. More interactive. It was like watching a silent movie without subtitles.

A problem with the arrangement was that people at one end of *The Last Supper* table had no chance at all of talking to those at the other end. But this, too, could be a distinct advantage, if the seating arrangements were intelligently handled. On this sort of outing, Alan always made sure that they were.

At the right end of the table he had placed his good old friends, Simon and Paul. (Joe had not come, as per usual. He was the real literary expert on the board, having won the Booker Prize, but he never attended meetings. Too full of himself. Still, they could use his name on the stationery.) Alan himself sat in the middle, where he could keep an eye on everyone. On his left-hand side were Mary, Jane and Pam. The women liked to stick together.

Alan, Simon and Paul ordered oysters and truffles and pâté de foie gras for starters. Mary, Jane and Pam ordered one soup of the day and two nothings. This was not owing to the gender division. Mary and Jane were long past caring about their figures, at least when out on a free lunch, and Pam was new and eager to try everything being a member of a board offered, even John Dory, which she had ordered for her main course. Their abstemiousness was due to the breakdown in communications caused by the seating arrangements. The ladies had believed that nobody was getting a starter, because Alan had muttered, 'I don't think I'll have a starter,' and then changed his mind and ordered the pâté de foie gras when they were chatting among themselves about a new production of *A Doll's House*, which was just showing at the Abbey. Mary had been to the opening, as she was careful to emphasise; she was giving it the thumbs down. Nora had been manic and the sound effects were appalling. The slam of the door that was supposed to reverberate down through a hundred years of drama couldn't even be heard in the second row of the stalls. That was the Abbey for you, of course. Such dreadful acoustics, the place has to be shut down. Pam and Jane nodded eagerly; Pam thought the

Abbey was quite nice but she knew if she admitted that in public, everyone would think she was a total loser who had probably failed her Leaving. Neither Pam nor Jane had seen *A Doll's House* but they had read a review by Fintan O'Toole, so they knew everything they needed to know. He hadn't liked the production, either, and had decided that the original play was not much good, anyway. *Farvel*, Ibsen!

In the middle of this conversation Pam's mobile phone began to play 'Waltzing Matilda' at volume level five. Alan gave her a reproving glance. If she had to leave her mobile phone on, she could at least have picked a tune by Shostakovich or Stravinsky. He himself had a few bars by a young Irish composer on his phone, ever mindful of his duty to the promotion of the national culture.

'Terribly sorry!' Pam slipped the phone into her bag, but not before she had glanced at the screen to find out who was calling. 'I forgot to switch it off.'

Which was rather odd, Mary thought, since Pam had placed the phone on the table, in front of her nose, the minute she had come into the restaurant. It had sat there under the water jug, looking like a tiny pistol in its little leather holster.

In the heel of the hunt, all this distraction meant that they neglected to eavesdrop on the men while they were placing their orders, so that they would get a rough idea of how extravagant they could be. How annoying it was now to see Simon slurping down his oysters, with lemon and black pepper, and Paul digging into his truffles, while they had nothing but *A Doll's House* and one soup of the day to amuse themselves with. And a glass of white wine. Paul, who was a great expert, had ordered that. A Sauvignon Blanc, the vineyard of Dubois Père et Fils, 2002.

'As nice a Sauvignon as I have tried in years,' he said, as he munched a truffle and sipped thoughtfully. 'Two thousand and two was a good year for everything in France, but this is exceptional.'

The ladies strained to hear what he was saying, much more interested in wine than drama. Mary, who had been so exercised a moment ago about Ibsen at the Abbey, seemed to have forgotten all about both. She was now taking notes, jotting down Paul's views. He was better, much better, than the people who do the columns in the paper, she commented excitedly as she scribbled. No commercial agenda – well, that they knew of. You never quite knew what anyone's agenda was, that was the trouble. Paul was apparently on the board because of his knowledge of books, and Simon, because of his knowledge of the legal world, and Joe, because he was famous. Mary, Jane and Pam were there because they were women. Mary was already on twenty boards and had had to call a halt, since her entire life was absorbed by meetings and lunches, receptions and launches. Luckily, she had married sensibly and did not have to work. Jane sat on ten boards and Pam had been nominated two months ago. This was her first lunch with any board, ever. She was a writer. Everyone wondered what somebody like her was doing here. It was generally agreed that she must know someone.

One person she knew was Francie Briody. He was also having lunch, in a coffee shop called the Breadbasket, a cold little kip of a place across the river. They served filled baguettes and sandwiches as well as coffee and he was lunching on a tuna submarine with corn and coleslaw. Francie was a writer, like Pam, although she wrote so-called literary women's fiction, chick lit for PhDs, and was successful. Francie wrote literary fiction for anybody who cared to read it, which was nobody. For as long as he could remember he had been a writer whom nobody read. And he was already fifty years of age. He had written three novels and about a hundred short stories, and other bits and bobs. Success of a kind had been his lot in life, but not of a kind to enable him to earn a decent living, or to eat anything other than tuna submarines, or to get him a seat on an arts organisation board. He had had one novel published, to mixed reviews; he had won a prize at Listowel Writers' Week for a short story fifteen years ago. Six of his short stories had been nominated for prizes – the Devon Cream Story Competition, the Blackstaff Young Authors, the William Carleton Omagh May Festival, among others – but he still had to work part-time in a public house, and he had failed to publish his last three books. Nobody was interested in a writer past the age of thirty.

It was all the young ones they wanted these days, and women, preferably young women with lots of shining hair and sweet photogenic faces. Pam. She wasn't that young any more, and not all that photogenic, but she'd got her foot in the door in time, when women and the Irish were all the rage, no matter what they looked like. Or wrote like.

He'd never been a woman – he had considered a pseudonym but he'd let that moment pass. And now he'd missed the boat. The love affair of the London houses and the German houses and the Italian and the Japanese with Irish literature was over. So everyone said. Once Seamus Heaney got the Nobel, the interest abated. Enough's enough. On to the next country. Bosnia or Latvia or God knows what. Slovenia.

Francie's latest novel, a heteroglossial, polyphonic, post-modern examination of post-modern Celtic Tiger

Ireland, with special insights into political corruption and globalisation, beautifully written in darkly masculinist ironic prose with shadows of *l'écriture féminine*, which was precisely and exactly what Fintan O'Toole swore that the Irish public and Irish literature was crying out for, had been rejected by every London house, big and small, that his agent could think of, and by the five Irish publishers who would dream of touching a literary novel as well, and also, Francie did not like to think of this, by the other thirty Irish publishers who believed chick lit was the modern Irish answer to James Joyce. Yes yes yes yes. The delicate chiffon scarf was flung over her auburn curls. Yes.

Yeah well.

He'd show the philistine fatso bastards. He pushed a bit of slippery yellow corn back into his sub. Extremely messy form of nourishment, it was astonishing that it had caught on, especially as the subs were slimy and slippery themselves.

Not like the home-made loaves served in Gabriel's on the south bank of the Liffey. Alan was nibbling a round of freshly baked, soft as silk, crispy as Paris on a fine winter's day, roll, to counteract the richness of the pâté, which was sitting slightly uneasily in his stomach.

'We did a good job,' he was saying to Pam, who liked to talk shop, being new.

'I'd always be so worried that we picked the wrong people,' she said in her charming, girlish voice.

She had nice blond hair but this did not make up for her idealism and her general lack of experience. Alan wished his main course would come quickly. Venison with lingonberry jus and basil mash.

'You'd be surprised but that very seldom happens,' he said.

'Judgements are so subjective vis-à-vis literature,' she said with a frown, remembering a bad review she'd received seven and a half years ago.

Alan suppressed a sigh. She was a real pain.

'There is almost always complete consensus on decisions,' he said. 'It's surprising, but the cream always rises. I ... we ... are never wrong.' His magical eyes twinkled.

Consensus? Pam frowned into her Sauvignon Blanc. A short discussion of the applicants for the bursaries, in which people nudged ambiguities around the table like footballers dribbling a ball, when all they want is the blessed trumpeting of the final whistle. They waited for Alan's pronouncement. If that was consensus, she was Emily Dickinson. As soon as Alan said, 'I think this is brilliant writing' or 'Rubbish, absolute rubbish', there was a scuffle of voices vying with each other to be the first to agree with the great man.

'Rubbish, absolute rubbish.' That was what he had said about Francie. 'He's persistent, I'll give him that.' Alan had allowed himself a smile, which he very occasionally permitted himself at the expense of minor writers.

The board guffawed loudly. Pam wouldn't tell Francie that. He would kill himself. He was at the end of his tether. But she would break the sad news over the phone in the loo, as she had promised. No bursary. Again.

'I don't know,' she persisted, ignoring Alan's brush-off. 'I feel so responsible somehow. All that effort and talent, and so little money to go around ...' Her voice trailed off. She could not find the words to finish the sentence, because she was drunk as an egg after two glasses. No breakfast, the meeting had started at nine.

Stupid bitch, thought Alan, although he smiled cheerily. Defiant. Questioning. Well, we know how to deal with them. Woman or no woman, she would never sit on another board. This was her first and her last supper. '*I feel so responsible somehow.*' Who did she think she was?

'This is a 2001 Bordeaux from a vineyard run by an Australian ex-pat just outside Bruges, that's the Bruges near Bordeaux of course, not Bruges-la-Morte in little Catholic Belgium.' Paul's voice had risen several decibels and Simon was getting a bit rambunctious.

They were well into the second bottle of the Sauvignon and had ordered two bottles of the Bordeaux, priced, Alan noticed, at €85 a pop. The lunch was going to cost about a thousand euro.

'Your venison, sir?' At last. He turned away from Pam and speared the juicy game. The grub of kings.

Francie made his king-size tuna submarine last a long time. It would have lasted, anyway, since the filling kept spilling out onto the table and it took ages to gather it up and replace it in the roll. He glanced at the plain round clock over the fridge. They'd been in there for two hours. How long would it be?

Fifteen years.

Since his first application.

Fifty.

His twelfth.

His twelfth time trying to get a bursary to write full-time.

It would be the makings of him. It would mean he could give up serving alcohol to fools for a whole year. He would write a new novel, the novel that would win the prizes and show the begrudgers. Impress Eileen Battersby. Impress Emer O'Kelly. Impress, maybe, Fintan fucking O'Toole. And the boost to his morale would be so fantastic … but once again that Alan King, who had been running literary

Ireland since he made his Confirmation probably, would shaft him. He knew.

Pam phoned him from the loo on her mobile. She had tried her best but there was no way. They had really loved his work, she said. There was just not enough money to go round. She was so sorry, so sorry ...

Yeah right.

Alan was the one who made the decisions. Pam had told him so herself. 'They do exactly what he says,' she said. 'It's amazing. I never knew how power worked. Nobody ever disagrees with him.'

Nobody who gets to sit on the same committees and eats the same lunches, anyway. As long as he was chair, Francie would not get a bursary. He would not get a travel grant. He would not get a production grant. He would not get a trip to China or Paris or even the University of Eastern Connecticut. He would not get a free trip to Drumshanbo in the County Leitrim for the Arsehole of Ireland Literature and Donkey Racing Weekend.

Alan King ruled the world.

The pen is stronger than the sword, Francie had learned in school. Was it Patrick Pearse who said that or some classical guy? Cicero or somebody. That's how old Francie was, they were still doing Patrick Pearse when he was in primary. He was pre-revisionism and he still hadn't got a bursary in literature, let alone got onto Aosdána, which gave some lousy writers like Pam a meal ticket for life. The pen is stronger. Good old Paddy Ó Piarsaigh. But he changed his mind, apparently. Francie looked at the Four Courts through the corner window of the Breadbasket. Who had been in that in 1916? He couldn't remember. Had anyone? Éamonn Ceannt or Seán Mac Diarmada or somebody nobody could remember. Burnt down the place in the end,

192

all the history of Ireland in it. IRA of their day. That was later, the Civil War. He had written about that, too. He had written about everything. Even about Alan. He had written a whole novel about him, and six short stories, but they were hardly going to find their mark if they never got published, and they were not going to get published if he did not get a bursary and some recognition from the establishment, and he was not going to get any recognition while Alan was running every literary and cultural organisation on the island ...

At last. The evening was falling in when the board members tripped and staggered out of Gabriel's, into the light and shade, the sparkle and darkness, that was Usher's Quay. Jane and Mary had of course left much earlier, anxious to get to the supermarkets before they closed.

But Pam, to the extreme annoyance of everyone, had lingered on, drinking the Bordeaux with the best of them. They had been irritated at first but had then passed into another stage. The sexual one. Inevitable as Australian Chardonnay at a book launch. They had stopped blathering on about wine and had begun to reminisce about encounters with ladies of the night in exotic locations. Paul claimed, in a high voice that had Alan looking around the restaurant in alarm, to have been seduced by a whore in a hotel in Moscow, who had bought him a vodka and insisted on accompanying him to his room, clad only in a coat of real wolfskin. Fantasy land. That eejit Pam was so shot herself she didn't seem to care what they said. Her mascara was slipping down her face and her blond hair was manky, as if she had sweated too much. It was high time she got a taxi. He'd shove her into one as soon as he got them out. He couldn't leave them here, they'd drink the board dry, and if they were unlucky, some journalist would happen upon them. He stopped for a second. Publicity was something they were always seeking and hardly ever got. But no, this would do them no good at all. There is such a thing as bad press, in spite of what he said at meetings. He paid the bill. There were long faces, of course. You'd think he was crucifying them, instead of having treated them to a lunch that had cost, including the large gratuity he was expected to fork out, €1,200 of Lottery money. Oh well, better than racehorses, he always said, looking at Gabriel's *Last Supper*. Was it Leonardo or Michelangelo had painted the original? He was so exhausted he couldn't remember. He took no nonsense from the boyos, though, and asked the waiter to put them into their coats no matter how they protested.

Pam had excused herself at the last minute, taking him aback.

'Don't wait for me,' she had said. She could still speak coherently. 'I'll be grand, I'll get a taxi. I'll put it on the account.'

She gave him a peck on the cheek – that's how drunk she was – and ran out the door, pulling her mobile out of her bag as she did so.

Not such a twit as all that. *'I'll put it on the account.'* He almost admired her for a second.

With the help of the waiter, he got the other pair of beauties bundled out to the pavement.

Their taxi had not yet arrived.

He deposited Simon and Paul on a bench placed outside for the benefit of smokers and moved to the kerb, the better to see.

Traffic moved freely along the quay. It was not as busy as usual. A quiet evening. The river was a blending delight of black and silver and mermaid green. Alan was not entirely without aesthetic sensibility. The sweet smell of hops floated along the water from the brewery. He'd always loved that, the heavy, cloying smell of it, like something you'd give a two-year-old to drink. Like hot jam tarts. In the distance he could just see the black trees of the Phoenix Park. Sunset. Peaches and molten gold, Dublin stretched against it. The north side could be lovely at times like this. When it was getting dark. The Wellington monument rose, a black silhouette, into the heavens, a lasting tribute to the power and glory of great men.

It was the last thing Alan saw.

He didn't even hear the shot explode like a backfiring lorry in the hum of the evening city.

Francie's aim was perfect. It was amazing that a writer who could not change a plug or bore a hole in a wall with a Black & Decker drill at point-blank range could shoot so straight across the expanse of the river. Well, he had trained. Practice makes perfect, they said, at the creative writing workshops. Be persistent, never lose your focus. He had not written a hundred short stories for nothing and a short story is an arrow in flight towards its target. They were always saying that. *Aim, write, fire.* And if there's a gun on the table in act one, it has to go off in act three, that's another thing they said.

But, laughed Francie, as he wrapped his pistol in a Tesco Bag for Life, in real life what eejit would put a gun on the table in act one? In real life a gun is kept well out of sight and it goes off in any act it likes. In real life there is no foreshadowing.

That's the difference, he thought, as he let the bag slide over the river wall. That's the difference between life and art. He watched the bag sink into the black lovely depths of

Anna Livia Plurabelle. Patrick Pearse gave up on the *peann* in the end. When push came to shove, he took to the *lámh láidir*.

He walked down towards O'Connell Bridge, taking out his mobile. Good old Pam. He owed her. 'For all men kill the thing they love,' he texted her, pleased to have remembered the line. 'By each let this be heard. Some do it with a bitter look, some with a flattering word. The coward does it with a kiss; the brave man with a gun.'

That wasn't right. *Word* didn't rhyme with *gun*.

'Some do it with a bitter look, some with a flattering pun.' Didn't really make sense. What rhymes with *gun*? Lots of words. *Fun, nun. Bun.* 'Some do it with a bitter pint, some with a sticky bun,' he texted in. 'Cheers! I'll buy you a bagel sometime.' He sent the message and tucked his phone into his pocket. Anger sharpened the wit, he had noticed that before. His best stories had always been inspired by the lust for revenge. He could feel a good one coming on … maybe he shouldn't have bothered killing Alan.

He was getting into a bad mood again. He stared disconsolately at the dancing river. The water was far from transparent, but presumably the murder investigation squad could find things in it. They knew it had layers and layers of meaning, just like the prose he wrote. Readers were too lazy to deconstruct properly but policeman were probably pretty assiduous when it came to interpreting and analysing the murky layers of the Liffey. Would that Bag for Life protect his fingerprints, DNA evidence? He didn't know. The modern writer has to do plenty of research. God is in the details. He did his best but he had a tendency to leave some books unread, some websites unvisited. Writing a story, or murdering a man, was such a complex task. You were bound to slip up somewhere.

Perfectionism is fatal, they said. Give yourself permission to err. Don't listen to the inner censor.

He had reached O'Connell Street and, hey, there was the 46A waiting for him. A good sign. They'd probably let him have a laptop in prison, he thought optimistically, as he hopped on the bus. They'd probably make him writer-in-residence. That's if they ever found the gun.

The Moon Shines Clear,
the Horseman's Here

The house is a holiday house, one of dozens dotting the landscape around here, each one perched in its own scrap of field, overlooking its own septic tank. Polly can see the chunks of thick white pipe sticking up from hers, her tank for the moment. The pipes are the main feature of the field, or garden, or patch of lawn, or whatever it might be called, which surrounds the house. The other feature is the well, a concrete block with black pipes emerging from it and snaking across the grass to a hole in the wall of the kitchen.

Polly had lived at home in this valley until she was almost eighteen. Her father was a teacher in the village school, and her mother a stay-at-home mother. She baked, milked cows, scrubbed the house, and was very particular about her religious duties, although not, thought Polly (not called Polly then, but Póilín), very seriously religious. Anyway, she made fun of the ladies who became *ex officio* keepers of the church, arranging the altar flowers and pandering to the priest and his every need, although she must have known that such women were found everywhere, were essential to the efficient running of the parish. Without them, there would certainly have been no flowers, no choirs, no special ceremonies on local feast days. Without them, the priest would have provided the bare necessities – Mass on Sunday, confession once a week, no frills. 'My New Curate', Polly's mother called the local women who provided all that decorative trimming of song and flowers and extra special prayers. However, she would never have missed Mass herself on Sunday; wearing a showy hat and white gloves, she and Polly sat with Polly's father in the first pew. This was the time when men and women sat on different sides of the church, but Polly's mother protested; she sat on the men's side. It was not a blow for gender equality but quite the opposite. She sat there to proclaim her superiority to all the other women, in their headscarves and dark old coats, or their trousers and anoraks. In the parish, she felt like royalty, and Mass was the appropriate context in which to give public expression to this attitude.

The family observed other essential religious formalities, some seemingly private in themselves but linked by invisible threads to the social and cultural web that enmeshed everybody. For instance, they said the Rosary every night after tea, praying for the souls of the departed dead and also for living souls to whom they were closely related or who had power and prestige. They prayed for their cousins, the Lynches and O'Sullivans in Cork and Tipperary, and for Eamon and Bean de Valera, and they prayed for the Taoiseach, and they prayed for the Archbishop of Dublin and the bishop of their diocese. They prayed for the Inspectors of Education, who would descend on the school once a year and ask the pupils insultingly silly questions, and for the county football team. It seemed to Polly that this praying strengthened their connections to these people; it seemed to her that she had some role when the county won the All-Ireland final in Croke Park. She might have been a cheerleader, not that she knew the word then. She was a silent supporter speeding her team to victory, and she had a hand, too, in the running of the country. Then sometime in the late sixties, the Rosary stopped. It seemed as if all Irish families reached some communal decision overnight, or as if someone in a position of authority had issued an edict and all the Catholics of Ireland obeyed it. Could there have been some telepathic referendum? Anyway, it stopped.

Polly's mother was different from the other mothers in the valley. Polly would have found it difficult to pinpoint in what this difference resided, but, if pushed to select one word, would have said 'old-fashioned'. Her mother did not like to wear make-up; indeed, she never even owned a lipstick. Her clothes were slightly out of date – excessively elegant white lace blouses and long skirts – when other, younger mothers had slacks with straps under the insteps and tight polo neck jumpers. She never wore trousers, even though a lot of her work was out of doors with the cattle and in her garden. At night she liked to do embroidery, executing tiny white flowers on white table runners, broderie anglaise, although she called it Mountmellick lace.

Polly's mother was snobbish. She was not a native of the valley, but of a big town, where her family had been leading lights in the Irish language movement. It was thanks to this that she had come to the valley to learn its dialect, and there met Polly's father. Now she lived in a simple way, but she still considered herself and her family a wide cut above most of her neighbours, and this sense of difference coloured every single aspect of her life. That was probably why she did not wear lipstick or mascara, or slacks, and it is definitely why she did not go to bingo on Thursdays with all the other women. Polly accepted her mother's self-assessment, and believed that she was more ladylike, more refined, more valuable, than other people's mothers, although she often felt more comfortable in those other people's kitchens than she did in her own.

The view is sublime. That's what Polly was told all the time she was growing up. That she lived in the most beautiful place in Ireland was drummed into her, along with tables and catechism and alphabet. She believed it as certainly as she believed that God made the world, or that Ireland ununited could never be at peace, or that Gaelic was the one true language of Ireland and eventually would be spoken by every Irish citizen. In fact, she probably believed in the beauty of the place more profoundly than in any of those other tenets of the local faith. It seemed verifiable. The crashing waves, the grey cliffs, the purple mountains; did these not, in their awesome wild grandeur, constitute perfect beauty? But even then she felt drawn to nature in its more intimate manifestations: a tern breaking the surface of the sea, a seal poking its shiny nose above the black water, hares boxing among the rushes at Easter. The little flowers that bloomed from May to November in a relentless routine of colours. Primroses, violets, orchids. Saxifrage, the colour of bloodshot eyes. Eyebright, selfheal. But she was not enjoined to admire such details. They were taken for granted, like the hidden natural resources, the still unpolluted wells, the little farms that kept the valley humming in tune with the seasons. Somehow, she deduced that all of this minor nature was commonplace, perhaps occurred in places that were not the most beautiful place in Ireland, perhaps in places not in Ireland at all.

There are no flowers in the fields now, because it is December. Rushes sprout like porcupines among the tussocks, and the rusty tendrils of montbretia spread themselves here and there in limp abandon. Otherwise nothing. What a month to choose for a dramatic return! Polly turns from the window and decides to light a fire, the traditional antidote to the gloom outside. When the briquettes are blazing in the grate and she is sitting in front of it, with a glass of red wine in her fist, she feels happier. Unlike its garden, the house is attractive, designed according to some international template for country cottages, with wooden roof beams, rough white walls, a slate floor. The fire makes it perfectly cosy.

When she was twelve, Polly went to secondary school in the nearby town, travelling by bus every morning and evening. The bus was a new idea; until recently, anyone who could afford to go to secondary school from this area would have had to board, and Polly's mother wanted her to go away, as she had, to a convent in the middle of Ireland, where she would learn to recognise how superior she was to her neighbours. But her father opposed this; he wished to encourage his pupils to avail themselves of the new educational opportunities. Polly had to set an example. She had to use the free bus. Her mother agreed reluctantly. If she had had the faintest idea of what went on in the bus, her resistance would have been stauncher. It was much more vulgar than a bingo hall. It was worse than the pub, to which her mother never went; it was as bad as the disco that was held in a hotel outside the town on Saturday nights.

Boys on the bus teased, cursed and swore. Girls huddled in the girls' section and either pretended not to pay any attention to the barrage of insults and mock endearments that was constantly fired at them from the boys' section, or they encouraged the boys, subtly, by glancing at them in a knowing, sly way, or overtly, by joining in and giving as good as they got. 'Give us a kiss.' 'Have you got your Aunt Fanny?' 'Fancy a carrot? Try this on for size.'

There were two kinds of girl on the bus: slags and swots. The slags wore thick beige make-up over their acne, and had long spiky eyelashes, a sort of badge of slagdom for all the world to see. Their hair was usually artificially coloured or streaked, or looked as if it was, although one might wonder why this should be, since they were aged between twelve and eighteen. But maybe they coloured their hair as they coloured their eyes, just to show the world who they were, just to show that they were defiantly, proudly sexual, just to show that they were not like the swots. The swots wore no make-up, and their hair was usually left alone and severely tied back from their faces with bands or ribbons. Or it was short, although that became more and more unusual as the sixties dragged to a close. The swots sat together at the front of the bus, quietly chatting among themselves about teachers and homework, and ignoring what was going on around them. The slags chewed gum ostentatiously, with the slow, long chews slags specialised in, and cast their sidelong, odalisque looks at the boys. The looks were also slow, slowness being one of the chief slag characteristics. What's the rush, their sauntering swagger seemed to say arrogantly. Time belonged to them and they had lots of it.

Sometimes a boy and a slag who were going together, tried to share a seat and hug and kiss en route, but this was not allowed by the bus driver. Girls and boys were not supposed to sit together. The bus driver, Micky the Bus, was a man aged about sixty who, though old, was sharp as a razor. He tolerated almost everything, except sitting together and canoodling. If he caught a couple breaking his one rule, he threw them off the bus. It was against the rules of the Department of Education, but that didn't bother Micky. He knew, quite rightly, that the Department would never find out what he had done. He knew that his word was law on this bus. This was before the days of litigation and before the days when children or teenagers were aware that they had any rights at all. Nobody would have dreamed of questioning Micky's absolute authority on his own bus, not even the beigest, blondest slag.

Once in town, boys and girls separated, going to their gender-specific schools – girls to the nuns and boys to the Christian Brothers. They never really understood what went on in the different schools, and this mystery about how the other half actually spent their day added spice to their lives. Polly, long before she was interested in any specific boy, felt it when they got out of the bus at the bank and the blue-clad boys all walked off in one direction, gaining dignity when revealed to their full height, their long, thin, blue and grey bodies moving purposefully up the hill to the grey castellated structure that looked like a fortress or a prison. She found them interesting then, and intriguing, as they disappeared into the secrets of their days.

There was a loneliness about going in the other direction, with the flock of girls in brown skirts and blazers, to a place as ordinary as a bowl of cornflakes. Polly felt that where she was going lacked importance, although, as soon as she got there, everything that transpired seemed important enough, and challenging. She was a good student.

A good student. She had to be, to satisfy her mother and

father. And it was not easy to keep it up. Not because she was not clever, or interested in her work, but because her friends did not approve of her academic achievement. Polly was in danger of going too far, which would have pleased her parents but outraged the girls in her class. So when she found herself speeding up – finding that she could enjoy reading history, or botany, derive a pleasure from learning and understanding, which was true satisfaction, not just the fulfilment of an urge to please some adult – she sensed some sort of danger. She held back. It was not so hard to do, and involved nothing more onerous than not reading as much as she was supposed to, half-doing her homework instead of doing it properly. Doing well was easy, it was a habit she could see her way into clearly, as if doing well were a clean, shining river, down which she could sail effortlessly once she had caught the wind. But not doing well was even easier. All she had to do was fail to hoist her sail, slide along under the work instead of gliding on top of it. She espoused the mediocrity that was what girls in that school, at that time, aspired to, even the best of them, her friends Katherine and Eileen, both of whom had been her closest friends since she was four years old and to whom she was bound by ties of eternal loyalty.

Polly has a week to spend in Ireland, and during that time she is going to face the devil. She has read somewhere that in everyone's life there are seven devils, and only when you meet them and overcome your fear of them can you find your guardian angel. (It was a novel about Chile, which she read in Danish: devils, angels, saints and sinners have lead roles in Chilean folk belief, according to this novel.) Her mother. That is one of her devils, the one she is going to meet and talk to, regale with the story of her life, Polly's version. Until Polly tells this story to her mother, she will be unfree, ununited, unwhole. She is not acting under psychiatric instructions. She does not need a psychiatrist to tell her this elemental truth. There is unfinished business between herself and her mother, between herself and this valley, and time is running out.

But there are distractions. She takes time settling in. She has to find her bearings. She has to find the shops. It is easy to fill the time with routine tasks when you are in a strange place, even if it was once a place called home. The first days she spends trying to heat the house and organise the water supply. The water is cloudy, white like lemon squash, full of clay or lime or something worse, and the central heating does not function. Men in caps come and mutter darkly in Irish to one another and hammer at the pipes, and Polly has to be at home to let them in.

Then it is desirable to explore her old haunts. She goes for a long walk to the hill at the back of the cottage. A road winding up past other bungalows, a few with grey smoke trailing up from their chimneys and most seeming empty, closed up like her house had been. After the last bungalow, a gate and then heather, sheep, sky for a mile, until you come on something surprising: a cobbled hilltop in the middle of nowhere. It is not the usual place for a school, exposed and far from where anyone lived. A film set, that is what it is, Polly remembers suddenly, a chink opening like a trapdoor in her head. There it is, something she has not thought about in thirty years: the commotion when the film had been made in the valley, the trucks trundling up the hill, the star-spotting, the jobs for extras. Everyone had been an extra. Katherine and Eileen had been schoolgirls in the classroom scenes. All the other people had been villagers, or men drinking beer from funny tin mugs in the pub, or country folk at the market. Even the animals got parts: Eileen's mother had hired out her hens for a pound apiece per day. But Polly had not participated. Her mother would not allow it, disapproving as she did of the film, which, although the word was not used, focused on a passionate adulterous affair, conducted in a range of scenic Irish settings. How Polly's mother discovered this was a mystery. Nobody else knew what the film was about. It was impossible for the extras to follow its plot, such being the nature of filming. But Polly's mother had her sources. And unlike most of her neighbours, she did not need whatever extra money she could lay her hands on. She did not need to prostitute herself or her daughter to Hollywood. The film had been a disappointing experience, an experience of total exclusion for Polly. No wonder she had forgotten all about it.

Polly kicks the film set cobbles with her walking boot and continues to the crest of the hill. The sun is shining, low and strong, but the joy has gone out of the day. She can feel night falling already, the afternoon is sinking into the silvery grey dusk although it is only four o'clock. The sheep bleat on the bare hillside. Polly feels a huge yearning for her home in Copenhagen; she longs to be there. In her old house, with the bustle of the city ten minutes away on the electric train, the opera at a moment's notice, a glass of wine in a warm pub, with the lovely Danish Christmas decorations up, the sense of a simple tradition of paper hearts and straw goats and tiny flickering candles everywhere, in every window, on every table. Copenhagen celebrates light in the deep midwinter, glows with optimism and hope.

Back in the house, she pulls the tweedy curtains to shut out the bleakness and throws a few sods of turf on the fire, then phones Lia, one of her friends, and tells her how she is feeling.

Lia says, 'Come home if you want to.' Which is what Polly knew she would say.

And Polly says, inevitably, 'I don't really want to. Not yet.'

'You don't have to do any of this if you don't feel like it, you know,' Lia goes on. 'And you are allowed to change your mind.'

'I know, I know. I will in a day or two if I decide that,' says Polly, laughing.

This is the sort of conversation she always has with Lia. Long, meandering sentences full of pauses, and words like 'feel' and 'decide' and 'maybe', phrases like 'well, wait and see' or 'it'll probably be OK'. They are so different from the conversations that Polly has with Karl, which are to the point, conducted in short, complete sentences, verging on the terse. He is practical and decisive, and it has taken him a long time to understand Polly's meandering, ever-changing mind.

Paddy Mullins sat with the rough element on the bus, smoking hand-rolled cigarettes and slagging people. A lot of the time these boys were laughing as they pushed one another and exchanged insults. 'Done your sums, Smelly?' 'Yes, Fat-arse, but I'm not showing them to you.' 'Surprised you had time. Seeing as how you were cleaning the pigsty again most of the night.' 'Shut up, Fat-arse, don't pick on him 'cos his daddy's a farmer.' 'Farmer? Tax dodger.' The language of the bus was English, although the language of home and of school was Irish, and some of the children, especially those from Polly's valley, did not know English very well. But they had to speak it anyway. English was trendy, the language of pop singers and films, the universal language of teenagers. Only the most prim, or the most childish, the most excluded, would persist with Irish in this context. The slags had a name for people like that: Ireeshians. Polly knew the rule of the bus and spoke English on it, but she was called an Ireeshian, anyway, because her father was a teacher and her mother was a snob and generally disliked.

She was also called 'Lick'. All teachers' children were called 'Lick-arse'; 'Lick' was its derivative, used by the girls, who eschewed strong language. Farmers' children were given the epithet 'Smelly'. Paddy was called 'Mackerel' because his father was a fisherman. He answered to the name, and gave as good as he got in these bouts of slagging, most of the time. But there were occasions when, for no discernible reason, he would fall out of the teasing loop. He would fall silent, and stare into space, thoughtful, enigmatic. Most of the boys did that. They had quiet moments, moments when they seemed to withdraw from the hullabaloo of a schoolboy's life and think deeply about something for five whole minutes at a time. What were they thinking when they did this? Polly did not know. But she would have liked to have found out, although as yet she had no inkling of how she could do this. Inside a boy's head was as impenetrable as inside a boys' school, somewhere she assumed she could simply never go.

Paddy would sit on his bus seat, gazing ahead of him, not necessarily out the window. Gazing at nothing. Then anyone could get a look at him. Not that he was anything special. Indeed, until this week Polly had considered that, whereas the girls on the bus all looked different, the boys all looked alike. There were smaller ones and taller ones, of course, with one unfortunate individual at either extreme.

And there were a few fair-haired ones, with pale complexions and gentle manners – they tended to be short-sighted and wore glasses – who were not rough boys but good boys, and who sat near the girls, consulting their books or, more often, chatting to girls. Their fair, feminine looks seemed to give them an advantage when it came to making friends with girls, as if they were less threatening in their less blatant masculinity. And of course they were not as aggressive as the bulk of the boys, that band of brown-haired barbarians who exuded maleness like a herd of bullocks and could not sit still. Dark, large-boned, stubble-chinned, too big for almost all the spaces they were obliged to inhabit, too big for the bus or the school, for the houses they lived in, these were boys whose true element was not a classroom or a school bus, but the high seas, or a meadow or a bog on the side of the mountain. A battlefield. Most of them were good footballers. Their school won the All-Ireland schools championship nearly every year.

Paddy was on the team but was the keeper, a position regarded with mockery by the girls and the fair-haired boys, although his teammates appeared to respect it well enough. Polly was accumulating information about him, almost without knowing what she was doing. He was a keeper, he was good at maths and chemistry, he was planning to be a scientist. He had once danced with a girl from the next parish for a whole summer but the relationship had fizzled out. He had been to Dublin many times with the team but never went on holiday anywhere. His father was a fisherman; they did not own even a small farm, just a house and a field, and he lived about ten miles from Polly's home – he had not gone to her primary school, and she did not know his family. They did not speak Irish in his house. There was some anomaly about his mother. Like Polly's, she was not from the district. Some people said she was English.

School finished at three thirty, and at four o'clock the bus collected pupils from both schools and ferried them home. So that meant almost half an hour in the town if you were very efficient about leaving your class. Usually this half hour was spent looking in the shops, or getting chips if you were lucky enough to have a shilling. People with a boyfriend or girlfriend found other ways to use the time – walking hand in hand on the pier, or chatting in the town park.

Paddy and Polly bumped into each other at the corner of the main street one day in May. This was about a month after she had begun to look at him. By now she knew the contours of his head, the line of his eyebrows, the set of his shoulders, better than she knew her own. But she did not know how he felt about her, although Eileen had said once, in her most serious tone, 'I think Paddy Mullins likes you.' So now Polly muttered hello, and averted her eyes, preparing to move quickly on. Even as she let his face slide from her view, to be replaced with a view of the pavement, she felt angry and frustrated, because she knew he would not have the same *savoir faire* to initiate any sort of conversation; one of the svelte, fair boys could do that, but not Paddy, one of the bullocks, the goalkeeper. He would not be able to talk, even if he wanted to as much as she did. Also, she knew in that second that he did want to. His surprise, his pleasure, when they met like that, told her everything she needed to know.

She was wrong about his *savoir faire*.

'Póilín,' he was saying. She stepped back and looked at him, astonished at her good luck, their good luck, that he was able to say the necessary words. 'I'm going down to look at the boats. Do you want to come?'

It was as if he had been doing this sort of thing all his life.

211

They got through the town as quickly as they could, and then strolled down the pier. The sea was choppy, but a choppy dark blue trimmed with snowy white, and the sun was shining on the fishing fleet, on the clustering red and blue and white boats: the *Star of the Sea* and the *Mary Elizabeth*, the *Ballyheigue Maiden* and the *Silver Mermaid*. The air was full of energy.

'That's the one I go out on.' He pointed at the *Silver Mermaid*. It was a large white fishing smack with lobster pots on deck, and heaps of green seine nets piled on the pier in front of it.

'Do you go out often?' She could not think of anything more original to say.

'Weekends when they're out and I don't have a match.' He smiled. His smile was stunning; it lit up the day and gave his face a sweet expression that it didn't normally have. Usually he looked rather worried, as if he were carrying some burden.

'Do you like it out there?' Polly realised that although she saw fishermen around every day, she hadn't a clue what they experienced, out in those boats in the middle of the night, hauling in fish, which disappeared into the new fish plant down the street. She could see it now, a grey block on the edge of the harbour and, in front, the bay with the low hills on the other side, and the blue bar in the middle distance, beyond the great ocean. 'What's it like?' Out there, she meant, on the sea.

'OK.' He looked out, then at the *Silver Mermaid*, then out again. He reflected and seemed to come to a decision to say more. Possibly he had never described the experience before. 'It's dark, and usually cold, and usually wet as well. We let down the nets over the side, five or six of us. Then we wait. That's the best part, waiting, gripping the net, wondering what happens next. Sometimes we talk or someone sings or we all sing. But usually we're just quiet. Standing there, waiting, in the night.'

He paused and Polly wondered if she should say something, contribute some question or comment. But she could not think of anything.

'When we haul in the nets, there are all kinds of fishes in them. Lots we have to throw back. Catfish, dogfish, cuttlefish. The cuttlefish are interesting. They have big brains, for fish. Once, I kept one in a jar.'

'For a pet?'

'No. To dissect in the lab.'

'Did you?'

'I didn't use enough alcohol and it rotted. It exploded. Very smelly!' He held his nose and laughed.

Polly laughed too, looking at the sea, trying to imagine the smell of exploded cuttlefish.

In a minute Paddy said, 'It's time to get the bus.'

It was a glorious May, as it often could be in that part of the world. Long, sunny days, some so warm you would feel like swimming, although the water would still be freezing. Swallows were flying high over the meadows, and larks twittered constantly, tiny dots so far away that they could have been daytime stars. Polly's mother was busy in her garden, one of the very few gardens in the valley. She raised bedding plants from seed in trays, which all through March and April had been placed under the windows of the house. Now she was raking beds, planting out nasturtiums and antirrhinums and sweet william, nicotiana, stocks. She was feeding her long rows of lettuce and onion, carrot and parsnip, her beds of herbs.

When Polly came home from school, at five o'clock, her mother would still be in the garden, her gardening apron over her summer dress, her red rubber gloves sticking out of the pocket. She would greet Polly with, 'You could get an hour in before tea!' Meaning, an hour of study. Then she could get three or four hours in after tea. Polly was doing the Leaving Cert in a month's time, in June, and her mother expected her to do well. What she meant by 'well' was quite specific. Polly would win a scholarship, a medal proclaiming her to be the best student in the county. At least that.

Polly had studied hard in secret for the last few months. To Eileen and Katherine she said, 'I'm hopeless. I'm way behind!' But at home she realised she was way ahead, and it astonished her that progress was actually possible, even now, even after her years of calculated dawdling: that by concentrated attention, careful effort, an improvement was discernible even to her, even without the endorsement of good marks or teachers' comments. She had never felt so in control of her work before.

The change in her relationship with Paddy did not alter this. After the walk on the pier, she knew something had happened to her. She had thought about Paddy quite a lot before, but in an idle, controlled way: she could daydream about him at will, when she had nothing better to do, almost as if he were a book she could open when her day's work was done, and close again as soon as more urgent considerations beckoned. Now she found herself filled with a glow of emotion no matter where she was or what she was doing; a pleasurable excitement shimmered not far under the surface of every single thing she was doing, bubbled in her veins, as if her blood had been injected with some lightening, fizzy substance, as if the air she breathed were transformed. *Light, bubble, crystal.* These were the words for what was happening to her. Walking on air, people said.

And she felt light as air, translucent as one of the new green leaves in the hedges. Since the whole of nature seemed to share in this lightness and newness, the fresh-looking waves and the new crop of grass, the tiny bright leaves on the brown fuchsia bushes, she felt that she was part of the world around her, the world of nature, as she had never felt before. She could have been a leaf, or a blade of grass, or even a calf or a bird or a lamb. Even a fish, swirling in the cold blue ocean.

She worked as hard as before. But sometimes she could not keep herself seated. Her physical energy got the better of her, rushed through her like an electric shock and forced her to abandon her sedentary ways and go for a long run along the lanes. Her mother watched these bouts with some foreboding, but said, 'I suppose you need some exercise.' Often she added, 'As long as it doesn't interfere too much.' Polly smiled. She smiled at everyone now, even her mother, and could not care less what anyone said to her. She transcended it all. She was superior, blessed, different, special, and none of the trivial irritants of life had the slightest influence on her.

The Leaving would be fine. She knew it. There was less than a month to go. If she did not open a book from now till the exam, she would probably still do very well.

Paddy and she met every day after school. They walked on the pier or they walked on the streets. Within days, the entire school population within a thirty-mile radius knew they were 'going together'. That meant it was a matter of a few more days till the adults got wind of it; some blabbing girl would be sure to mention it to her mother. But it did not mean that Polly's parents would find out, unless some malicious person, some mischief-maker, decided that they should. In this community, all normal adults would know that the last thing that Polly's parents wanted was that their daughter should be a having a relationship with a boy, especially a boy like Paddy. All normal parents would protect Polly and Paddy, and leave her parents, who were not popular, in the dark.

This is what happened.

After about a week of walking around in a state of increasing physical excitement, Paddy steered Polly to the town park, the known courting spot for schoolchildren. It was a walled park, secreted in the middle of the town, behind rows of houses and shops on all sides, and had a sheltered, enclosed atmosphere, very unusual in this place of exposed bare coasts, windy hills. Also, it was full of high trees, sycamores and elms and flowering cherries; the sheltering town allowed them to thrive here, whereas in the valley where Polly lived hardly a single tree would grow. They sat under an elm in the corner of the park and kissed, their first long kiss, so longed for that it stunned both of them. Paddy apparently had not kissed the girl he had been connected with the previous summer – Polly did not think he could have, because his experience of this seemed to match hers so exactly. That is, he was surprised by the powerfulness of the experience, by the delight it gave him, and at the same time it seemed the most natural thing in the world. He and she kissed as if they had never done anything else. You had to learn how to do almost everything else, even the most basic physical functions, but sex, apparently, you did not have to learn. Your body knew precisely what to do, without having a single lesson. At least, if you were like Polly and Paddy.

They had missed the school bus.

Every single child on that bus would know precisely why they had missed it.

Polly was OK. She had a phone in the house, and her

father had a car. She telephoned from the kiosk on the square; for once the old phone was not out of order. She told her father she had been delayed in the science lab, finishing an experiment, and he came to pick her up. Paddy had to set out on foot, hoping he would manage to hitch a lift.

From then on, they had to be careful about time.

The Leaving started. Polly sat in the school hall, at a brown desk, and read the pink examination papers. Nothing in them was a surprise; the traps they had been told to watch for had not been set, as far as she could see. The predictability of the whole examination had been the most surprising thing, and it was also vaguely disappointing. She had been given dire warnings. You must read the entire course. You never know what will come up. But when it came to the crunch, you did know. She felt cheated.

Paddy did not. In the boys' school, the examination technique was more refined. They knew exactly how much they had to do, and did not do a jot more. After every paper, Paddy was able to calculate exactly what marks he had got – A in Irish, C in English, A in chemistry. Polly breathed deeply, superstitious. How could he be so sure? Wasn't he tempting fate? The results were, according to her way of thinking, as mysterious and unforeseeable as any aspect of the future. That there was a direct link between the work she had done and the results, she was afraid to believe now, although she must have believed it when she was studying. She wanted the exam to be a lottery. That was the attitude of the girls in the girls' school, whereas the boys regarded it as something much less like a game of bingo and much more like a field to be ploughed. Such a sense of control was essential for schoolboys, whose main ambition and duty was to win football matches. Pretending the Leaving was some mystical rite of passage, a mysterious test of intellectual prowess, was a luxury they could not afford.

Polly never found out if Paddy's calculations were correct, but she won the lottery. Straight As. Three separate scholarships. Money flung at her from the county council, the Department of Education, the university. Her mother must have been so pleased. But no, she was not. She could not have cared less.

Her mother is sitting in front of the television watching a soap when Polly comes into the room. She has not bothered to get up, but the door is open. It is still safe to leave the door on the latch, then, in this place.

Polly walks in and says, 'Hello! Hello!'

There is no response whatsoever. Her mother continues to watch TV and does not even turn around.

She tries again. 'Hello,' Polly says. 'It's me, Polly.' She speaks Irish; although she has not spoken it in thirty years, as soon as she set foot in the valley it emerged from her mouth automatically. She repeats her greeting and calls herself Póilín, which does seem unnatural.

Nothing happens. So Polly goes and puts her hand on her mother's shoulder. Her mother turns. She does not seem at all surprised. Her poise has not deserted her. She smiles, so that her whole face lights up. She reaches towards Polly and Polly prepares for an embrace. But it does not come. Instead, her mother shakes her hand. She shakes hands and Polly feels a sudden giggle rising in her throat. The gesture seems so ridiculous. Her mother's hand, though, is very warm and Polly remembers that they were always like that; to feel those on your hand, on your forehead, had always been an intense comfort and a pleasure.

'Póilín!' she says. 'Póilín!'

She is deaf. Suddenly Polly realises this. She is deaf and apparently her sight is poor also; thick glasses occlude her eyes.

'I decided to come back,' Polly says slowly, looking closely at her mother. She has aged terribly. Of course. Her hair is white and sparse, she is wearing those horrible goggle-like glasses, her face is wrinkled with deep, shadowy ridges, the kind black-and-white photographers love, like the cracks of a river delta. But when she smiles, her face is still recognisably her face; whatever the essence of it was – its sweetness, its primness – has not changed. That same expression of polite surprise, the head tilted in a manner both coquettish and disapproving, the same poise. The same superiority.

The surroundings have not changed at all, in one sense, and in another, the house looks totally unfamiliar.

Polly had regarded their bungalow, which was the very first bungalow in this valley, as an extension of her mother, elegant and superior, better than any other house for miles around. But now she sees it is shoddy and lacks any vestige of style, as the old, derided houses do not. The floor is covered with green linoleum, with brown-grey patches in front of the range and near the door. The cupboards are painted cream; the table her mother is sitting at is red Formica. There is a kitchen cabinet, also cream, with red trimmings, against the wall. Nothing has been changed. Outside, the garden is overgrown with shrubs – ginger-coloured fuchsia and olearia block out the light in the kitchen. The grass is not knee high but it looks rough and unweeded. A solitary, crazy bramble taps against the windowpane.

'Your father is dead,' her mother says.

'I know.' Polly has to talk, although talk will mean nothing to her mother. Can she lip-read? Probably not, with those glasses. 'I heard.'

'And I'm deaf,' her mother says, without rancour. 'In case you didn't notice. I can't hear a thing you're saying. Are you speaking Irish? It's all the same to me what you speak.'

After the examinations, as June was drawing to a close, there was licence. Released from school, work, examinations, young people were given leeway to enjoy life. They were, for a while, expected to act their age, to explode with fun and vitality and youthfulness, by sharp contrast with what had been expected of them just weeks ago. The rules changed completely; studious, quiet types were out of fashion now and the correct thing to be was wild and exuberant. Polly's mother loosened the reins.

'Enjoy yourself!' she said. Her mother was weeding vegetable beds, hunting slugs from the lettuce, freeing the cabbage and parsley and onions from choking bindweed. 'Have a good time!'

It was, Polly knew, an order. Well, she would obey it, though not in the way her mother imagined.

An advantage of summer was that there was a bus twice a day, linking the valley to the town. In the new dispensation, Polly was able to take this bus every day, and could spend hours away from home. All her mother required to know was when she would return (on the last bus – there was not much choice about this). Occasionally, Polly mentioned that she was going swimming with her friends, and occasionally she was.

Most of the time she spent with Paddy. He was going to work in the fish factory, but had postponed this for two weeks. He was fishing at this time, for salmon, but usually the fishing expeditions took place during the night, leaving him free to be with Polly during the day.

They avoided the town as much as possible. There was still about their relationship a furtive air, since Polly had not told her parents about it, and as it progressed it seemed increasingly impossible to imagine confiding in them. It was no longer just her belief that her parents regarded all boys as out of bounds, indeed seemed to believe that any sort of relationship between the sexes was essentially wrong, and, what was worse, in extremely bad taste. It was not just that Paddy was everything her mother would abhor: English-speaking, poor, a fisherman, a member of a family which had turned its back on every value that she held dear. It was more that the nature of her relationship with Paddy had become, literally, unspeakable. Polly could not describe it in any words she knew, in any language, and her connection with her mother was, it seemed to her, only by means of words, the formulae Polly selected from her rich store of clichés to dish out, sparingly, to keep her mother at bay.

She got off the bus in the main street, outside the pub that served as a bus stop. Everyone got off there, and usually there were several neighbours to be nodded to, as well as some tourists – young people from Dublin or America, usually, backpackers with long, floating, hippy clothes, long curtains of hair, flowers in their hair. (Polly's dress was beginning to be modelled on what they wore, although she could not obtain the right things here, and in these hot days she wore a purple scarf tied over the top of her head and under her hair at the back.) She walked down towards the central part of town, just like everyone else, and usually bought some bread and cheese, and cans of minerals, at a small grocery before continuing to the end of town and turning up the road that led to the hills. This was a narrow road, winding between a few farmhouses and a few bungalows, then rising until it passed through the mountain range far above the town. The road was always busy with tourist cars passing, and that was why Paddy and Polly went there. When she met Paddy, they hitched a lift. All cars were going to the mountain pass. There was a carpark there, with a viewing point, where all visitors stopped and looked at the valley on the other side of the gap and took photographs. Local people hardly ever visited this place.

At the viewing park, Paddy and Polly said goodbye to whoever had given them the lift – a German woman travelling with her son, joking and eating chocolates; a lonely man from Boston who had come to Ireland to play golf – and said they were going for a walk. The visitors usually smiled indulgently and waved goodbye, and Polly could see that they did what she could not imagine anyone in the valley doing – they approved of her and Paddy; they were looking at them and thinking, this is a handsome young couple, authentic Irish folk, in love, how delightful. She knew these people from America and England and Germany viewed her and Paddy as components in the landscape, partly, like the sheep, and also as ambassadors from the universal land of youth, the land of love.

At the top of the hill, they turned and walked back in the direction of their own town, the direction from which they had just come. They turned off the road and down a turf track. Within seconds, the trail of cars vanished, and they were in a wilderness. Nothing but the rough heather, the clumps of bracken, sheep bleating all around them.

They lay in the heather and kissed and pressed their bodies together. 'With my body I thee worship,' Polly said to him, tracing the line of his profile with her finger. Where had she heard those lines? 'They are in the wedding service,' she said, because she had read this in a novel.

'Are they? I never heard them,' he said. He had not been

to many weddings and neither had she, and it was years later that she had discovered he was right, nobody said that, not in Catholic weddings. It was the English service, the Church of England, and when Polly realised that if you married in Ireland, which she never did, you did not mention anyone's body, she felt acutely let down, and bitter, and thought it was typical. How could she have imagined her mother uttering such a line? In Irish? Or in English or Latin? In the Catholic Church, as it happened, all you had to say at a wedding was 'I do'. The priest said everything else, speaking on your behalf.

She loved his body. The dark brown hair, thick and spiky – spiky with salt. The salty taste of his brown skin. His deep grey eyes, which reminded her of the sea as well, of the stillness, as she imagined it, the calm of the fish, although when Paddy encountered fish, they were anything but calm. She liked the dark hairs sprouting on his arms, thick like a bear's, and later she found those hairs on his legs and elsewhere. She loved his wide, generous mouth. It seemed she could not tire of exploring this body, even though it was one body, a tiny thing on the mountainside. It was a world, it was a continent, as John Donne said, in some poems she had found in the library. 'You are a continent,' she said, again tracing the line of his profile. Hill, rock, river. 'You are a map of the world.' He liked that better than the line from the wedding service.

They talked endlessly about themselves. She told him about her family, covering up the worst aspects but letting him understand that they would find him surprising when they finally had to meet him. He understood that, he was used to being disapproved of, especially by schoolteachers and people of that kind. The priest. His father was a native, a speaker of the language, but his mother was from a suburb of Dublin, not a very posh one, and that was the trouble. Not only did she speak English, she spoke it with a working-class Dublin accent. Paddy had a touch of this himself. She went to bingo religiously, and she went to the pub on Sundays with her husband, something that shocked even Polly. Her mother would have preferred to die, she was quite sure of that, than enter a public house.

'What does she look like? Your mother?'

He had difficulty describing her. 'Her name is Muriel. She has black hair.'

'Short or long?'

'Kind of shoulder length. And she's about five and a half feet. Thin'

'What sort of clothes does she wear?'

Paddy laughed. 'What is this? Is my mother wanted for some crime? Not speaking Irish?'

'No, sorry.' Polly kissed him and caressed his hair.

He said, in her arms, 'I don't know what sort of clothes she wears. Normal women's clothes. Jeans and jumpers mostly. She has shorts, actually, for this weather.'

Shorts. Polly imagined a short woman with dyed jet-black hair, red lips, skinny sticks of legs in red shorts. She imagined her with a cigarette dangling from her lips and with gold earrings, a sort of gypsy. She did not know where this picture came from.

The next time Polly comes, which is just the next day, she does not bother ringing the doorbell, but just walks into the kitchen, not making much noise. She wants to have a good look today before she lets her mother know she is here. She explores the parlour, goes back and has a look at the bedrooms. It is all like the kitchen: plain, 1970s style, nothing cute or old or cute and new, like the house Polly is staying in. It seems like her parents gave up on interior decorating, on their aim to be the best in the valley, a long, long time ago. A big photo of Polly is on the piano in the sitting room. Polly when she was twelve and making her Confirmation, in a pink tweed suit and a white straw-boater.

When she slips into the kitchen, her mother is in her chair in front of the television, talking. There is nobody else there, just herself, but she is engaged in a long monologue. Polly stands just inside the door and listens. It takes her a while to get accustomed to the flow of words, which seem to pour out of her mother's voice in a stream; not monotonous but unbroken, fluent as a river.

This is what she does all day.

She tells stories.

Today it is a story about a boy and a girl. The boy is called William, but the girl does not seem to have had a name, oddly enough.

> She was rich and beautiful, however, a landlord's daughter. Lots of rich young men came courting her, but she wouldn't have any of them. And one day a poor farmer's son came and wasn't he the one she fancied? She'd have nobody but him. Well now, her father was none too pleased about this turn of events, as you can well imagine, and what did he do but send his daughter away, away to her uncle's house, so that she would have no more to do with the poor young man.
>
> She went, and was far from happy with her fate. And while she was there, the poor young man, William, pined away and died. But she heard nothing, nobody bothered to let her know. And she stayed on at her uncle's for months. A year went by. And

a marriage was arranged for her with another young man, more suitable than William. And she was going to bed one night a few days before the wedding was to take place when a knock came at her window. And it was him, it was William. He was outside the window on horseback and he asked her to come with him. 'Let's go away somewhere where they won't bother us,' he said. She didn't need asking twice. Out she came through the window and onto the back of the horse and off they went, galloping across the fields. It was a bright night, the moon was shining, and she was as happy as could be.

Then her mother turns and catches sight of Polly.

'That's not the end, is it?' Polly asks.

'I forget how it ends,' says her mother. 'It's just old rubbish …' She is embarrassed at being caught out. 'I do it to pass the time. I used to hear those old things when I was a child and I thought I'd forgotten them.'

'I'd like to know how it ends,' says Polly.

'They were buried in my head somewhere, and when I told one, the others came back, one after the other. Funny, isn't it?' She stops talking and stares out the window. Then she adds, 'Usually I just watch the television. Most things are subtitled.'

Polly's picture of Paddy's mother was completely inaccurate, as she discovered just days later when she saw her. This was at Paddy's funeral. He was drowned at the beginning of August, while out fishing. The weather had not broken, there was no storm or sudden calamitous change to explain what had happened. But his boat had got into difficulties for no apparent reason. The rest of the crew were saved, but Paddy was not. 'He was knocked overboard by a freak wave,' was the explanation circulating in the community. 'He was swept against the Red Cliff.' Drownings occurred every few years in this area, and the Red Cliff was notoriously dangerous. 'His number was up,' a fisherman said, shrugging casually, in Polly's hearing. More people said, 'The good die young.' They had a proverb or cliché for every occasion, and dozens of them for the occasion of death.

The entire school population of the peninsula turned out at the funeral, which was attended by hundreds and hundreds of people. Polly's friends hugged her and squeezed her, trying to sympathise, horrified at the idea of what had happened to Paddy and to Polly but unable to grasp the enormity of it. Polly's parents were not at the funeral.

They knew about Paddy now. When he had died and become a celebrity, someone had revealed the secret. But they did not take it seriously.

'I believe you were friendly with the young man who drowned, Lord have mercy on him,' said her mother.

'Yes,' said Polly. She was paralysed. She could not believe that Paddy would not be there, at the spot where they met, if she took the bus and walked along the hill road. He was linked with the place, he could not move from it, in her imagination. She had seen his coffin, carried by six boys from the football team through a guard of honour, to the graveyard across the road. She had seen his coffin descend into the earth, and heard the clay fall on it. But she could not believe he was gone for good. How could he be, so quickly? This was four days after they had sat on the hillside discussing his mother's clothes. In that time he had changed from being a goalkeeper, a lover, a fisherman, to this: a corpse in the ground.

'It's a great tragedy for his family,' her mother then said, pursing her lips and tut-tutting. She turned her attention to the tablecloth she was embroidering with pink roses. Polly said nothing, but left the room.

She purses her lips again, in just that way, when Polly tries to tell her about her living arrangements; shows her photos of the house, of Karl. Her mother asks if she is married and Polly shakes her head. In Denmark there is no major legal disadvantage to this, and she and Karl have been together for twenty years. They do not think of themselves as unconnected or likely to part, and getting married is not something Karl believes in. 'I am an old fox,' he says. That's what they say in Denmark, 'fox' not 'dog'. You can't teach an old fox new tricks. He looks like a fox, though. Polly is reminded when he says this. He has reddish hair, still, and a sharp face. He's a schoolteacher, like her father, but the principal of a large secondary school in one of Copenhagen's best suburbs. They live in a house in the grounds, a privilege for the headmaster. Polly is telling her mother this – she can lip-read, a bit. She is trying to tell her something about Copenhagen, mentioning Tivoli, which is, as a rule, the one thing people have heard of. She talks about the fishing boats at Dragør, how she goes there sometimes to buy flatfish from the fishermen on the quay, how you can get huge flounders for a few crowns.

'They are still alive when you buy them,' Polly says. 'Huge flounders, fat halibut, dancing around in the basket.'

'They don't have the euro in Denmark,' her mother breaks in. She hasn't heard a thing. 'They have more sense, I suppose.'

When Polly found out that she was pregnant, just before

the Leaving results came out, she felt not as dismayed as she should have, although she knew it was in any practical sense a hopeless, insuperable tragedy. She had Paddy's baby. It was as if fate had awarded her some compensation for losing him. But it was not great compensation, in the circumstances.

'Tell your mother,' Eileen said. 'You'll have to. I mean, what are you going to do?'

'How can I tell her? She'll die,' said Polly.

Eileen shrugged. 'Sometimes things like that are easier than you think. When you do them.' This advice sounded good. Eileen saw the lift in Polly's expression and pressed her advantage. 'Things are usually easier than you think they'll be,' she reiterated. 'They're always easier, when they happen.'

She convinced Polly. Anyway, she had to tell her parents, as Eileen said. The best thing that could happen would be that they would understand, and help, although at that moment, Polly's mind could not wrap itself around the reality of what that help should consist of. A ménage of herself, her child and her parents was not imaginable, even as a dream.

She confronted her mother the next day in the kitchen. They had been to the beach together. Polly had swum in the breakers, finding the cold shock of water comforting; it demanded so much immediate attention that it diminished her problems. Her mother did not swim but sat, in her full cotton sundress, on a folding chair on the beach, reading the newspaper, *Inniu*. Afterwards, they had lunch together, salad and tea, and now Polly was smoking a cigarette, something her mother did not disapprove of, although she did not smoke herself. It seemed like a good moment to break the news.

Her reaction could not have been more surprising, but it was not surprising in the way Eileen had anticipated. Instead, it surprised, shocked, terrified Polly that her mother was capable of such anger. She screamed abuse and insults. She hit Polly with her fists and seemed to want to flog her in some ritualistic punishment of humiliation, degradation. But her father would have to administer this treatment, and fortunately for himself and Polly he was not available, having gone to the city for the day to buy new textbooks for school. Polly was to be locked in her room until he returned. She was to be starved. When all this was over, it was not clear what her mother's plans for her were, but they did not involve bringing up her grandchild in a normal family environment. *Homes, adoption, hiding,* were words that occurred, in a medley of Irish and English, a macaronic stream of abusive language that had never emanated from Polly's mother before. It seemed that one language did not contain enough invective to express the full depth and range of her anger. Clearly, this was the nadir of her existence. Nothing as tragic, as evil, as shameful, as her only child's pregnancy had ever befallen her.

Afterwards, Polly had simply left the house; as it happened, there were no locks on any of the room doors. She ran away without even a toothbrush, catching the afternoon bus to town and going on to Dublin on the train. She had some money; it was not so difficult. Her Leaving result she got from Eileen a month or so later. Eileen came to Dublin to visit her, to Polly's gratification and surprise, and tried to persuade Polly to go to college, as she had planned: she would have some money from her scholarships; if she padded it out, she would get by. Polly tried it, and her parents were unable, or did not bother, to prevent her. But she had Conor in April, just before the first-year examinations. She missed

230

them and no quarter was given, no special provision could be made. She lost her scholarship and left college. She got a job in a bank, lived in a bedsitter, and kept the baby, although Eileen tried to persuade her to be sensible and give him over for adoption. She could not part with him, although she soon found out that keeping him was quite astonishingly difficult, in every possible way. There was no money, there was no time, nobody even wanted to rent her a place to live; single mothers with babies were blacklisted by most landlords in Dublin. Everyone colluded in making her life as hard as it could be – her parents, the state, the system. Eileen, who was in Dublin herself, studying to be a nurse, continued to help, finding flats in her own name and installing Polly and Conor when the lease was signed.

When Conor was three, Polly got a chance to move to Copenhagen with the bank, and she took it. As she had hoped, nobody cared whether you were a single mother or not in Denmark. In fact, it seemed that most mothers were single, at least the ones she came across; it was almost something to brag about. They had grimly bobbed hair, dressed in corduroy pants and big green parkas, and smoked cigars. Some of them had jobs in the bank, but usually they were doing degrees in impractical subjects. Women's studies or ethnology or Greek and Roman civilisation. The state paid for their education, and paid them social welfare and child welfare while they were in college. All the talk was of feminism and women's rights and the country was packed with crèches and kindergartens, where children were looked after free, by students and nurses and women from Turkey, in what looked like luxurious surroundings. After a while, Polly left the bank and went to college at last, like all the other single mothers. She chose film studies, and eventually became a scriptwriter, writing soaps for the Danish television channel, then documentaries, which brought her all over the world: Faroes, Shetland, Greenland, Iceland. In Greenland she met Karl, who was hiking around the old Norse settlements, taking photos, and did not mind that she had Conor, although he had no intention of having any children himself, as Polly found out soon enough. By then Conor was twelve. He grew up, became a scientist, a marine biologist. After working for a few years in Denmark, he went on a round-the-world trip, and ended up in Australia, and got a visa and a temporary post at a university doing research on the breeding habits of pilot whales. He is still there.

Polly sits at her window, in her own bungalow, and listens to the fire whispering in the grate, to the wind whispering outside, whistling around the eaves. She has been here for longer than she had planned to stay and has decided to stay for one more week. She is going to begin work here, sketching the basis for a programme of some kind about the region: the Gaeltachts of Ireland, maybe, a topic she is well suited to covering but has always avoided. The house is warm and cosy, and now the valley seems to hold her, too. People she runs into in the shop nod to her and say hello, do not avoid her, as she thought they were doing initially. A few have recognised her and chatted to her about old times. Nobody mentions Paddy Mullins, or asks about the baby, but when Polly mentions that she has a grown-up son, they do not seem surprised. Eileen probably spilled the beans, or Katherine. It doesn't matter, they are interested in him, too, they want to hear about Australia and the whales. Lots of the local young people do round-the-world trips as a matter of course in their gap year; half the population of twenty-somethings seem to be in Thailand or New South Wales.

Nobody cares about what used to be called unmarried mothers now, either. There are heaps of them, even in the Gaeltacht. Still, nobody mentions Paddy Mullins. Maybe they forget he existed.

Polly tries to tell her mother about Conor, since she has told almost everyone else. 'I have a child,' she says.

Her mother cocks her head with a blank smile. Her ability to lip-read is most erratic.

'He's Paddy's child,' Polly continues. 'Paddy Mullins, the boy who drowned. Do you remember?'

'Would you like a cup of tea?' asks her mother. It is the first time she has offered Polly any refreshment. She gets up and walks across the kitchen to the range.

'I was in love with Paddy Mullins,' Polly says.

Her mother smiles and says, 'I was thinking of baking an apple tart.'

She finds the end of her mother's story.

> When they had gone a few miles, William said, 'I've a terrible headache, love.'
>
> 'Stop,' she said. 'Stop and have a rest. What hurry is on you?'
>
> 'I can't stop,' he said. 'There is a long journey ahead of us. I'm taking you home.'
>
> So all she could do was take out her handkerchief and she tied it around his forehead and she gave him a kiss. His head was as cold as ice and she felt frightened when she touched it. But she said nothing. And he galloped on until they were passing her own father's house. And she shouted and asked him to stop.
>
> 'Why would you want to stop?' William asked.

'The moon shines clear
The horseman's here.
Are you afraid, my darling?'
He said, and he spurred on the horse.

But the horse would not move an inch. The horse stopped at her father's gate and refused to move. He spurred and he whipped but it didn't matter. The horse had a mind of its own.

So, 'Go on inside,' he said, 'and sleep in your own bed tonight. And I'll be here waiting for you first thing in the morning. I'll sleep in the stable, myself and the horse.'

She kissed him goodnight and did as he told her.

And when she went inside, her father was there and he was surprised to see her. But she took courage and told him what had happened. She said William had come for her, and she could not live with anyone else.

Her father turned pale. 'William?' he said.

'Yes,' said she. 'He's outside, asleep in the stable.'

'That's impossible,' said her father. 'William died a year ago.'

She didn't believe him. How could she, the poor girl? So her father took her out. He had to do it. He took her to the graveyard and he took a shovel and he dug and dug. And there was William, in his coffin, dead and decayed. And around his poor head her handkerchief was tied, the handkerchief she'd tied around his forehead only the night before. Yes. And it was stained with blood. So she had to believe him then.

The story is in a collection of German ballads, which she finds in one of the bedrooms. So how did her mother learn

234

that? Had she read the book or were the stories flying around in the air like migratory birds, landing wherever they found suitable weather conditions, a good supply of food? What a gloomy story! Polly shivers and shuts the book firmly, feeling the dead hand of William like ice on her forehead.

That night Polly rings Conor and tells him she is here. She hopes he will say he will come over, but since he lives in Brisbane, he is not likely to come today or tomorrow. It is nice to talk to him, though, and to tell him what she is doing. She does not tell the truth, that her mother will not listen to her story. He listens, with appreciation, although it is early morning in Australia, and he has just woken up to a summer's day. He appreciates the drama of her news, Polly can tell that, and suggests that she go and visit Muriel, if she is still alive. Muriel, his paternal grandmother. Maybe Muriel is not deaf? Polly finds herself saying, yes, she will do that, and then she rings Karl to tell him she will stay on in Ireland for another week or perhaps two.

Something happens in the valley now, that takes Polly by surprise.

The Christmas lights go on.

All the little houses come alive.

Coloured lights fill every window, are strung along the edge of the roof, are draped in the hedges. Santa Clauses climb up fairy ladders to chimneys, reindeers glow in the bare gardens. Red and green and blue lights flash and twinkle in the deep dark winter valley; some of the bungalows seem to be jumping, they flash so much.

In the old days there was one candle, lit on Christmas Eve, in every house. When you walked through the valley to Midnight Mass, you saw these candles flickering in every window, the stars flickering overhead. Now the houses are flashing and jumping in myriad colours, glowing against the black sea and sky and mountain, brash and, it seems to Polly, beautiful. 'We're here!' the lights seem to proclaim. 'We've survived, we're not going away!'

She finds Muriel easily. She lives in the house she lived in thirty years ago, Paddy's house. It is, as Polly expected, decorated, though not as extravagantly as some of the other houses. There are coloured lights on a hedge by the gate, and another string around the door.

Muriel is watching TV when Polly calls. She's alone. Polly guesses, correctly, that Paddy's father is dead. It strikes her that the valley is full of widows. Muriel is wearing jeans and a jumper, and she is still small and thin. To Polly's surprise, she speaks Irish, but with a north Dublin accent.

'Of course I speak Irish,' she says. 'I've been here for fifty years. I'd have been out of the loop altogether if I hadn't learned it, wouldn't I?'

Her manner is chirpy, friendly, but with an underlying toughness, an urban edge that is different from anything you get around here. She offers tea and biscuits straight away; she turns down the TV but she does not turn it off. Polly opens her mouth and starts to explain why she is here. Muriel listens, half-smiling, her eyes thoughtful rather than sad. Then she takes Polly in her arms and holds her for a minute, against her woolly jumper, her thin body. Polly, of course, cries.

She cries and Muriel pats her hand and says, 'Yes, love, yes.'

They drink the tea.

Muriel talks about herself, about Paddy. He was a very quiet boy, but always good-humoured, she could talk to him more easily than she could ever talk to anyone, much more easily than she could talk to his father. His father is dead now, too. He – Paddy – had a depth of understanding.

236

He was more like a daughter than a son. On the night he drowned, he had kissed her goodbye, which was unusual, but she only remarked on it afterwards. It was a calm night, he had been out in much rougher weather and returned home unscathed. The truth about his death would not be known, but she had heard there had been a row on board, another young man had attacked Paddy; Paddy got thrown overboard and hit his head on a rock. The real story would never be told; the other man was the son of the owner of the boat; Paddy was dead, anyway, and the fishermen would never inform on one of their own. The whole story about going aground was made up, a sham. Fiction.

There are no tears from her. She tells the story calmly, pausing occasionally for dramatic effect or to let a shocking point sink in. It is a story she has told before, many times, in spite of her protestations that it is confidential, a secret. Probably, she told it to Paddy's father, and who else? Her best friends, her close relations? The story is polished. What is true is its terrible core, that Paddy, the son she could talk to, is dead. And even this no longer disturbs her. But of course it all happened so long ago. Paddy drowned thirty years ago. How could she cry? Tears do not last that long. Paddy has been transmogrified into a hero: a brave, strongly drawn character in a story that she has half-remembered, half-invented.

So Polly tells her story of Paddy, and for her it is a fresh story, it is the first time she has told it to anyone, and so her tale is not as polished, not as well paced, not as neatly composed as Muriel's. Still, it takes on a certain formality: Polly has to decide, as she sits on the fireside chair, keeping her eyes off the silent TV screen, where to start. The bus, the pier, the park? School? She decides, or memory decides, or Muriel, or the pressures of the moment, the pressure to relate, the pressure to sympathise, the pressure to attract compassion, the pressure to confess, the pressure to create, what to leave in, what to exclude.

The fact is, no matter what she decided, Muriel would be fascinated by this story of her son, which she had not heard before, not at all, although of course people had let her know of Polly's existence, had hinted at the reason for her sudden departure from the valley. But those were rumours, snippets of gossip, that had the power to disturb but not to enthral, console, nourish. So now she listens intently, her whole body still, concentrated on listening. For this story she is the perfect audience, and the story is shaped by her listening as much as by Polly's telling: Paddy's story belongs to the two of them. And why did Polly not understand that until Conor pointed it out?

When the story is finished, Muriel and Polly sit in silence. The coloured lights on the fuchsia bush twinkle against the black sea and the black mountain and the black sky. They sit in silence. They let the story settle. And for minutes it is as if he is here again, on this earth. Alive, seventeen. He is not on the pier or in the park or on the mountainside, but on the bus. He is sitting on the bus, silently staring out the window, motionless as a seagull on a rock, lost in a boy's dream.

Bikes I Have Lost

The Buildiners

My mother, whom my father calls the Tiger and we call Mammy, is marching purposefully into the Buildins. She's wearing her khaki raincoat, which has a military look to it, and her striped scarf, black and orange. She's on the warpath. Or, more accurately, on an intelligence mission: we are searching for my missing bike. It vanished from our road, where I was out playing this morning. I left it outside when I ran into the house to do a number one. (I told my mother I'd parked it at our garden gate but actually I'd left it standing on the middle of the road several doors down.) I'd spent the previous two hours cycling up and down, up and down, on my pride and joy, my blue Raleigh bike, my three-wheeler. I never called it a tricycle; I don't think that word was known on our road. My granny and granda, who gave me my most precious presents (my big plastic baby doll, Barbara, with the red and white frock, also plastic; my electric train), had given me this three-wheeler for my fourth birthday (they were put to the pin of their collar to pay for it, my mother said). It was by far the best bike on our road, and I was in no way shy about pointing this out to my pals – Annette, the smug owner of two dozen jigsaws; Janet, a frail only child whose mother took a nap in the afternoons (cue for half the neighbourhood, Janet's 'friends', to run wild in her house); Deirdre, whose claim to fame was that her mother was a Protestant; and Miriam May, with hair the colour of straw, curled into corkscrew ringlets, which framed her tiny, pale face like a judge's wig. I would give them a go on my bike in exchange for a favour I judged to be of exactly equivalent value. It might be a long session with the shiny, sweet-smelling, animal jigsaws in Annette's house up the lane, which itself had a provocative look, on account of having no windows on the street side. Or two goes on Miriam's yellow scooter. A 'lend' of one of Deirdre's Noddy books – she had half a dozen. Swapping, bartering, exchanging was a way of life with us. We were as good at calculating value and risk as any actuary by the time we were four.

The Buildins were the dark side of our absorbing world. In them lurked the enemy: the children who were rough. Mammy the Tiger kept us from them. Or tried to. The Buildiners wore raggedy clothes, and they were visibly dirty – at a time when none of us had a bath more than once a week and hair-washing was a laborious task that took half the day, and was avoided by everyone, washers and washees, as much as possible. The Buildiners, of course, were said to have nits in their hair, and they spoke a different version of Dublinese from ours, which sounded like a foreign language – but one we could understand all too well. You kept your ears open as you sneaked past the Buildins, stepping around sleeping dogs, black and slimy, who would bite you if you looked at them the wrong way, and carefully avoiding looking at the children, especially the older boys, who had pointy shoes, tight trousers, and flick knives. Looking was the big taboo. 'Hey, young wan,' a Buildiner might call, if she caught you engaging in that nefarious activity. All girls of whatever age were called young wan by them. I thought it was a bad word, like feck, and the sound of it scared me. 'What are ye gawkin' at, young wan?' they'd shout out, and I'd scurry on, scared to death. I didn't know what they would do to me, if they got me, but it would not be nice and would involve knives.

Buildiners usually kept off our cul-de-sac, apparently having as little wish to be in our territory as we had to be in theirs. And we weren't allowed go into the Buildins on our own, except on Saturday afternoons, when we crossed the main yard to Miss Fontane's flat. Miss Fontane was a dancing teacher and, puzzlingly, she was very nice, in spite of living in the Buildins. Her flat was spacious and attractive, a good deal cosier, with its thick red carpet and potted ferns, its walnut piano and oak gramophone, than our house. I didn't know how to reconcile Miss Fontane and her long, black hair, her red lipstick, and fluttering feet in their minute black 'poms', with the image I had of the Buildins in general. I didn't know how someone like her could live there, and how inside the grim brick walls so much comfort and warmth, so much music and cheer, could hide. I supposed she was the exception that proved the rule.

Which was: keep out.

But now we're in the enemy heartland because, naturally, the Buildiners were the prime suspects when the three-wheeler was found to be missing.

'God help us, Helen! They must've sneaked down the road when nobody was looking,' my mother said, in thoughtful dismay. 'You couldn't be up to them, the so-and-sos, could you?'

Now she's leading us across the main yard of the Buildins – a big concrete ground surrounded on three sides by the stern, red-brick faces of the flats. To call it an atrium or courtyard would give the wrong impression. It hasn't a trace of the greenery, the elegance, that those words suggest. Not a tree, a shrub or a blade of grass relieve its rawness. It's the colour of stainless-steel saucepans, or gun metal, and looks like the exercise yard of a very large prison, or some planet that is incapable of supporting organic life. The only living things in it are the Buildiners themselves and their skinny dogs; and the only inanimate thing that is not as bare and functional as a prison yard is a handball alley blocking off the sky. Even that has a penitential look. Nobody plays handball there, ever, although boys are always playing soccer down at that end of the yard. We can see them doing that right now, kicking a battered old ball and shouting as we cross the main yard, ears and eyes alert for ambushes. Good, the enemy is preoccupied. We make it across the first bastion.

But there's no sign of the bike.

On we go, round the corner, into the back lane of the Buildins. This is the very worst part, where the dogs are slimier and the children cheekier and the flick knives sharper than anywhere else. The lane is too narrow to admit any sunshine, and the gutters are so thick with litter you'd think rubbish was growing in them, like some sort of depraved, evil flowers. The entryways to the flats – which are open to the weather – give off a sour smell, the smell, we think, of profligacy, of wanton laziness. (Now, I know, the smell of poverty.) The windows on the ground floor at this side of the Buildins have iron bars on them.

And in there, in one of those dark, foul entries, we see my three-wheeler.

Two young fellas are with it, one sitting on the bike, the other just standing there. One is wearing a cap, pulled down tightly over his head almost to his eyes, even though it's quite a warm day. It's not a cap, actually, but a leather helmet, the kind Biggles wears. These helmets look tough and aggressive. Buildiner boys often have them; ordinary respectable boys wear school caps, made of soft cloth, blue or wine or bottle-green. Under their tough helmets these two boys have the hard faces that a lot of the boys in the Buildins have – they're cynical and weary, desperate, by the time they're seven. Already by then they know nobody is on their side – especially not the teachers, or the priests, or the mothers like my mother, who hate their guts. They are constantly on guard.

'Give me that bicycle,' says my mother, in a rough voice, roughened by anger and something else.

'I will not,' the boy on the bike says. He's about eight. There's a bead of green snot at the end of his nose and the skin all around it is red and raw, although otherwise he's very washy, even for a Buildiner.

'Indeed and you will,' says my mother. 'For two pins I'll put the guards on you and yez'll be off to Artane before you know what hit yez.'

'It's my bike,' he says, without conviction. He stays sitting on the saddle, clutching the handlebars. His knuckles are blue.

'Now, where would the like of you get a bike like that?' my mother says, smiling. She sees a funny side to it now.

The three-wheeler stands there, in the dark and filthy porch. With its royal-blue paint, its white mudguards, shining chrome handlebars, it gleams like a messenger from some other world. Not the world of our road, which is just a few steps up the social ladder from this one, but the world in the stories my mother reads to us at bedtime, that paradise where children roam carefree and pampered in snow-white socks and Mary Jane shoes, to experience great adventures or solve difficult mysteries, then return home to their lovely houses. It's a world to which she wants us to belong. These boys would not know such a world exists.

The boy with the Biggles helmet remains on the bike. The expression on his face changes slightly. His eyes lose that hard but dead look they had, and begin to sparkle with anger. His friend, too, stiffens, and scowls at us. He puts a hand in the pocket of his shorts.

I wait for my mother to react, to say something else. But her face has changed, too. It's rigid, with something that might be disbelief, or fear. She looks helpless.

We all stand there, as if we were turned to stone. We are like statues in the life-size crib at Christmas, gathered around the baby Jesus in the stable. Except we're in the Buildins, and we're gathered around my three-wheeler. I keep an eye on the hand in the pocket.

'Davy!' A loud Buildiner woman's voice shouts from somewhere upstairs.

All of us jump, startled out of our paralysis.

'Come up here, your tea's on the table!'

The voice is loud, but also soft and kind. It's not what you'd expect to hear in a place like this. Not at all what you'd expect.

'Come on up now, love, don't be lettin' it get cold on you.'

The two Buildiners exchange glances. The one who is standing with his hand in his pocket shrugs. The one with the helmet – Davy; he has a name, an ordinary name –

sighs deeply. He climbs down from the bike. He stands and looks at it for a minute, and then at my mother and me. Then, suddenly, he spits, not at us or even at the bike, but at the ground. And the spit comes slowly from his mouth, like dribbles from a leaky tap, rather than the angry liquid bullet you might expect. My mother looks surprised, but not annoyed. I look at the little puddle of spittle on the ground just beside the back wheel of the bike. The boy looks at it, too. It's the same colour as the snot at the end of his nose, with a dark red trace in it. He snuffles and takes a long look at the bike. His eyes aren't angry any more. He looks tired. The two of them turn and walk away, up the dark stone stairs to wherever they go when they're not out and about, breaking windows and robbing things.

'Well,' my mother says, taking hold of the bike. 'That's that.'

She looks tired, too. She starts to push my three-wheeler down the lane towards our own road. It doesn't occur to me to ride it, here in the Buildins. At this stage in my life and for a long time to come I'm only allowed to ride my bike on my own road, where it is safe to be.

Learning to ride

Riding a three-wheeler is child's play, in every sense of the word. The tricycle is rooted to the ground, by the force of gravity, like a bed or a table. It just happens to be on wheels. All you have to learn is how to turn the pedals and you're in motion.

A two-wheeler is obviously different, seeming to defy some physical law of nature. How do they do it? That is what I wondered, watching them: the older children, and grown-up cyclists.

The man next door, for instance. Tony. Every morning he went to work on a high black bike. He just swung his long leg over the bar and off he sped, light as a bird in the air. (My father had an old black bike, too, but it had lain unused in the garden shed ever since he got the car – an ancient Morris Eight. He used to go everywhere on his bike, and now he went everywhere in his car. He never walked, except inside the house.)

Imelda Fogarty, ten years old, had a two-wheeler. A lady's bike. It was a good bit smaller than Tony's and I could easily mount it. But when I tried to move, I fell off immediately. Why? Imelda laughed and said, 'It's cinchy!' But she couldn't tell me how to do it. 'It's easy-peasy,' she said. 'You just do it!' And up she'd hop and fly down the road. Even though she was silly, and had her ears pierced, she could perform this miracle. She could even cycle without putting her hands on the handlebar for several yards at a stretch.

It was very frustrating.

When I was seven, I woke up on Christmas morning at about 4 a.m.

At the end of the bed I shared with my sister was a biscuit-faced doll with blue eyes and yellow hair and a pale-yellow nylon dress with lace trimmings. There was a heap of other presents on the bed, and two grey socks hanging on the bedposts, lumpy and dumpy and stuffed to the gills with sweets and oranges and amazing little wind-up toys all the way from China.

And just inside the door, something light and elegant and perfect: a bicycle. A two-wheeler.

My heart leaped. I hadn't even asked for a two-wheeler, but Santy had brought me one, anyway! How clever of him!

We ran into our parents' bedroom to tell them the good news.

'No, no, Helen,' my mother said sleepily. 'The two-wheeler is for Orla.'

My sister.

Orla smiled smugly, although she didn't even want a two-wheeler.

The doll in the yellow frock was also hers.

I wondered if there was some mistake? It didn't make sense. And how did my mother know what Santy had intended?

She insisted that she did know, and enumerated the presents I'd got, which were many, but none of them was anything as desirable as the two-wheeler.

The bike was quite small – considerably smaller than Imelda Fogarty's Raleigh. It was a little small for me, in fact. But I wouldn't admit that, even to myself, and persisted in believing Santy had intended it for me, and that my mother was mistaken.

The bicycle didn't even look like a bicycle, but like a motorbike, the sort of motorbike a soldier might have, since it was painted the same grey-green colour as a jeep. Even though it was clearly second-hand, even though it didn't look like any bike I was familiar with, it was the most lovely thing I had ever seen.

I had three books, and two jigsaws, and a dress-up cardboard doll with dozens of paper dresses to be cut out and affixed to her flat body with tabs. Also, a small Irish colleen doll and a pair of leopard-skin gloves. All things I craved and had at some stage, coming up to Christmas, asked for. A good haul. But not half as good as Orla's, it seemed to me now.

There wasn't time to dwell on the problem, though, once

we all rose and the great day got under way. We had to get dressed up in our Christmas clothes and go to Mass, and then eat the big Christmas breakfast of grapefruit and sausages and rashers and pudding. Tony and his wife, Marcella, called in from next door and had a glass of sherry with my mother and father. Then there was the huge preparation for dinner, and then dinner itself, which lasted for hours.

The washing up.

At about five, when the day was slipping away, dismayingly, unbelievably fast, as it did every year, we retired to the dining room. Like everything else, this was part of our ritual. We would sit by the fire there and play one of the board games one of us had got from Santy. This year the game was Cluedo.

Cluedo was a very good game, which I enjoyed tremendously. The interesting characters, Miss Scarlett and Colonel Mustard, the locations – the Library, the Conservatory and the Ballroom – and, above all, the tiny, realistically-modelled weapons, elevated it to a different plane from other, less personable board games: it approached the condition of theatre, something we all adored. But after two games, my mother and father wanted to take a break – he fell asleep in his armchair and my mother played some baby game with our little brother who was getting cranky. Orla, who had tried out her bike before dinner and abandoned it in the front room, wanted to have a go of my paper doll. Reluctantly – because once you cut out the dresses, the joy of the paper doll is much diminished – I decided to let her. I instructed her not to cut out more than three outfits, leaving ten for me.

As soon as she started snipping, I slipped out.

There were fires in several rooms of the house for

Christmas Day – the dining room, the bedrooms. In the kitchen we always had the Aga. But the front room wasn't heated, nor was the hall. It was freezing out there. It felt colder than it would out of doors.

Never mind.

I got the bike out of the front room, wheeled it to the end of the hall, and sat on the saddle.

Down I fell, just the way I fell off Imelda Fogarty's bike.

But it was a small bike and there wasn't far to fall. Also, I fell on the linoleum of our hall, not the rough surface of the road outside.

I tried again immediately.

Again.

Again.

I'd no idea how you did it. And nobody had ever explained how. You just do it, they would say. You just do it.

You have to find out for yourself.

I tried, I tried, I kept falling off.

On what must have been the twentieth attempt, I leaned sideways and started moving. I stayed on for about four cycles of the wheels, for a few yards.

The hall was one of those narrow, long halls you get in the Victorian houses. (It seemed long to me, anyway.) It wasn't a bad place to learn to cycle; it looked like a shiny brown road, but it was indoors and had walls close by to grab onto, so that gave one confidence. I kept at it and after about an hour – it could have been five; it could have been weeks because I was in a zone where time stood still, even as I concentrated fiercely on learning to move – I could cycle the length of the hall.

At about eight o'clock, time for our Christmas tea, my mother came out, yawning, to go down to the kitchen and put the mince pies in the oven.

'What are you doing out here in the cold, alannah?' she said. She didn't give out to me for being on the bike.

'I can ride a two-wheeler!' I might have been declaring that I'd landed on the moon.

I gave a demonstration. By now I could go the full length of the hall, turn around and come back again. Actually, as I knew, I could go anywhere. I could cycle.

They all came out then, to see if it was true.

'It's not her bike,' Orla said. But she was tired and sated with Christmas, and she didn't really care. She preferred the doll to the bike, anyway.

My father had woken up. He laughed and said, 'She can do it, all right.' He seemed to appreciate my sense of triumph more than my mother or Orla did.

He asked me to demonstrate again, which I did, gladly. Then he opened the hall door.

Outside it was dark, but the street lamp on the other side of the road glowed, and there were lights in most of the windows. Janet's window was lit up magically by her Christmas tree, the only one on the street; they were just coming into fashion. Snow was falling. Big flakes drifted down through the black air like petals, and melted as they touched the ground.

My father jerked his head in a gesture that meant, have a go outside.

'She'll catch her death a' cold,' my mother said. She was still standing in the door of the dining room, catching a bit of the heat from the fire in there.

I went out before she could prevent me, not stopping to put on a coat. It wasn't much colder outside than in the hall, anyway. Up I hopped on the two-wheeler that was like a motorbike and down the road I sailed, like a seagull in the foam of the ocean, or an eagle in the sky on a summer's day, the soft white snow falling on my bare head and Christmas frock.

It's easy to ride a bike, everyone says. And that is true. It's a knack, like swimming – or like standing erect on your two legs and walking on the face of this earth. All a question of confidence, and trust. Trust in yourself, and trust in the way the physical world works. You have to know that you can keep your balance, and you have to be certain of that from the second you mount the bicycle and lean forward and start pedalling. He who hesitates falls off.

'Once you learn, you never forget,' my father said.

That's true, too.

My sister asked me how to do it. I couldn't explain.

'You just do it,' I said, as Imelda Fogarty had said to me. 'It's cinchy.'

She learned anyway, of course, but I never noticed when. Maybe you never do notice these milestones, which are among the more important in the greater scheme of life, except when you pass them yourself.

U-turns

As a reward for getting the Corporation scholarship (which wasn't all that hard to get if you were poor, because it was means tested), my mother bought me a real two-wheeler. It was not new. We bought it from our cousin Bernadette, who had used the bike to get from her bedsitter to the box factory in Rathmines, where she worked in the office, doing the books. Bernadette didn't need a bike any more because she'd just got married. Her husband was head foreman in the factory. 'She'll soon be driving her own car, wait and see,' my mother said. She was pleased, because she liked Bernadette and was glad she'd done well for herself. It was my mother the Tiger's ambition that all her younger relatives should end up richer and hence happier than all her older relatives. Her own mother had been a dairymaid who died of tuberculosis of the spine four years after her marriage. Her grandparents had been farm hands who could neither read nor write. My mother was planning that I and my sister should get the Leaving, and everything else, she believed, would follow on from that: new cars, semi-detached houses in the suburbs, pensions. Husbands, she didn't seem so interested in, but if they came with the prerequisite house and car, which Bernadette's did, they were to be welcomed.

The bike was pretty – red with white mudguards, a wicker basket in front, and, on the handlebar, a gleaming silver bell engraved with a schooner in full rig. The saddle was a padded white one, soft on the bum. I would need the basket, because I planned to cycle to school.

I was going to secondary in Ballsbridge, Marymount, an ordinary sort of school, whereas nearly everyone from my primary was going to St Bridget's, a famous all-Irish school on the north side of town. And why was I going to Marymount? Because it was nearer home, because the fees were lower, and because I had a half-scholarship there, as well as the Corporation scholarship, so we'd have a bit of money left over from that for extras, of which there were an enormous number. The uniform alone had cost a fortune, coming from Brown Thomas, a shop we'd never set foot in before. (We seldom even went down Grafton Street. Our shopping was done on Camden Street and South Great Georges Street, which were much less posh.) And then there were lots of little things. A divided skirt for gym, hockey boots, a hockey stick, a tennis racquet – all the things girls in those days needed for school, a long list of very expensive and mostly ugly things to wear and hit balls with.

Now I had the bike, I would save money on bus fares, I pointed out to my mother. Somehow she did not seem to understand what a great saving would be involved. But it was eight pence a day at least – thruppence to and from school, and tuppence for the return journey at lunch time, when the fare for schoolchildren going home for their lunch was a penny. 'That's more than half-a-crown a week we'll save,' I said. I chatted a lot to my mother, about everything. 'That's really quite good, isn't it?'

'Yes, alannah,' she said. She looked and sounded drained, and I knew that the whole secondary school project was becoming too much for her before I'd even started. Nobody had ever gone to secondary school in our family before. I mean, not in my immediate family, where I was the eldest, and naturally the first to go, but in the entire family going back to the beginnings of time. They'd all finished school at fourteen, the ones who went at all – which were, my grandparents, born around 1890, and their parents, born around 1865, but not their parents born around the time of the Famine, before there were any schools in Ireland. (You wonder what children actually did all day, when normal children go to school. Just played around until they were old enough to work. Hard to imagine.) Anyway, all this meant that going to secondary was a big step. A small step for me and a giant leap for my family, a jump into, as my mother would have hoped, a new socio-economic milieu. She wanted me to get a good job and be well-off, not like her, who had to scrimp and save all her life. Education was the way to riches. And that was the point of it. But the path to riches was proving too costly and impoverishing. And as with all investments, there was risk involved. She knew,

I guess, that interest rates could fall as well as rise, and that if the worst came to the worst, even her capital would go. (Though she must have known there wasn't much fear of that, given my general record as a studious and docile child.)

I didn't cycle to school the first day. Togged out in my stiff navy tunic and snowy blouse, my tie and blue blazer and matching beret, I took the number 18 bus from the stop under the chestnut trees around the corner from our road. I went up the stairs at the back of the bus, planning to sit at the very front, but there were three girls in the blue blazers and berets there already. Naturally, I sat as far away from them as I could, even though there was nothing I longed for more than their friendship. There was another girl, from the next road to ours, on the bus, too. I knew her by name and to see. Yvette.

Yvette was one of those girls who was so beautiful, even as a tiny child, that she had acquired a special status, not exactly a celebrity status, but the status of a precious object, maybe like an icon or a work of art, in the neighbourhood. Nobody expected anything of her. She didn't need to be well behaved, or clever, or to help around the house. (Though she was perfectly competent at all these things.) It was enough for her simply to exist. The only child of a widow, who had an office job, her hair was perfectly blond, at a time when 'fair' meant a sort of light brown. (Mine was black, which I did not appreciate one bit. Later, I got to referring to it as chestnut.) She had the face of a big china doll, the kind of doll that we all coveted before Sindy and Barbie came along. Usually, Yvette was dressed in pastel frocks, pink or mint or pale lemon, so it was a shock to see her in the navy tunic and blazer of a peculiar shade of blue, neither light nor dark. She looked lovely in it, of course. The stern design – pleated skirt, narrow waistband, baggy V-necked bodice designed to accommodate a bust in a state of gradual and inexorable expansion – looked chic on her. The beret nestled in her blond curls like a bluebird in a golden nest. Still, it was a shock to see her in the same uniform that I was wearing (hers fitted properly, which helped; it's not easy to look chic in a uniform that is four sizes too big, like mine and most people's). It was awe-inspiring to think that she was embarking on the self-same adventure. I wondered if I would actually get to know her. It would be like becoming acquainted with Shirley Temple.

But getting to know her wouldn't be easy, because the next day I didn't take the bus, but started going to school on my new bicycle.

My mother, it turned out, was worried about that. Her Tiger ambition deserted her. Faced with saying goodbye to me as I set off on my bike, she became an ordinary fussy pussycat of a mother.

'Be very careful now,' she said anxiously, as she did my plaits for me. I still couldn't do them properly myself. Her fingers flicked them into shape swiftly and expertly, the way they did everything. There was literally not a hair out of place when she snapped the elastic bands around the ends of the braids, and there wouldn't be, until she released them again next morning. In fact, I could have kept my hair in my mother's plaits for my whole life without bothering to redo them, so perfect and tight was her handiwork. 'Watch out at the traffic lights and when you're turning corners. Make sure to look over your shoulder.'

'Yeah, yeah, yeah, yeah,' I said, tossing my horsewhip hair into her face.

My mother had been fostered out as a child to an old aunt and uncle in Wexford. They were not even her blood relatives, but the brother and sister of her stepmother. Her mother had died when she was three, and after a few years, her father married again. Annie. Granny. My mother loved her. Granny had been a cook for a big house and could cook delicious puddings and bake a perfect apple pie, a rich fruit cake. In all her ways, she was ladylike and meticulous. We had her wedding photograph, a big one that had been doctored to resemble an oil painting, over our dining room table. But even though she loved her, Granny sent my mother down to Wexford to be company for these old people. Ben and Bea.

But my mother loved life there, too. They lived in a small cottage – maybe it was a council cottage – but there was plenty of room for the three of them. And also for hens and turkeys, a cow, a pig, a garden, where they grew potatoes and cabbage and onions and lettuce. Blackcurrants for jam, strawberries for cream, apple trees for tarts and pies. On Saturdays, Ben and Bea and my mother, whose name was Gretta, drove to the nearest town, in the pony and trap, for the messages. My mother – I imagined her with curls, which she had always had in my experience, though that was because her hair was permed, like all grown-up women's – sat up in front and drove, with Ben beside her and Bea in the back. That was on the way into town. On the way home, she sat in the back, too, on the leather side-seat, and ate biscuits. Strawberry Creams were her favourite, followed by Custard Creams, and she was given a pound of them in a brown paper bag every Saturday. The horse was called Brock, a big placid chestnut.

She went to the local school, where she was a success. It was a mile and a half away, along the tree-lined road, and when she was twelve, Bea bought her a bicycle. This was a proper lady's bike, black and big.

'That was the happiest day of my life,' my mother told me. 'I couldn't believe I was getting this bike. I'd never owned anything, to tell the God's truth, in me life till then.'

She kept that bike, the same one, until she got married.

The schoolteacher wanted her to go on to the secondary school. My mother was very good at arithmetic and history and English. Auntie Bea and Uncle Ben would have supported her. (She didn't mention a scholarship. Maybe she didn't apply for it – you had to fill in a form and sit a special examination at Easter to be in with a chance; they mightn't have known about that down there.) And she could have gone to school in town on her bike – it was six miles away, but she could have done that.

'I said no,' she said, without rancour or sentiment. 'I wanted to go home, to be with my father and brother. I didn't see the point.'

I wondered why she wanted to go home, if she was having such a good time in Wexford. And I sighed for her failure, her lack of ambition, and started a daydream about what her alternative life would have been. The life she would have had if she'd stayed with Ben and Bea, and gone to secondary, and moved on from there. She might have become a teacher, and learned to drive, and got her own car. A nice new house with a big window in a suburb, instead of the old brick house with narrow windows we had, near town, where nobody wanted to live any more. Maybe, if she'd gone to secondary, she wouldn't have married my father? Maybe she wouldn't have had me? Maybe I wouldn't exist?

What actually happened was that she got a job in a grocery shop and met her best friend, Teasy, there. They cycled all over Dublin, all over the county. On their day off they'd go out to Enniskerry and have tea in the tea shop there; they'd go to Sandymount, and Dún Laoghaire, and Blackrock. There is a photo of them, in their gabardine coats and headscarves, standing beside their black, practical-looking bikes, laughing. They were terrible gigglers.

'So what happened to your bike?' I asked.

'Och, alannah, I don't know what happened to it,' my mother said, with a certain air she had for moments like this, an air of nostalgia, sentimentality, which I found embarrassing. 'I suppose I left it in some shed after we were married.' She meant, in some shed at the back of the first house they lived in when they married, after she had met my father on the beach at Sandymount one scorching Sunday in July, where she and Teasy had cycled with some other pals for a picnic. He had got talking to Teasy's fiancé, Christy, who was of the party, playing rounders on the sand – they loved rounders. 'I didn't have much use for it after Daddy got the car.' She never learned to drive. Daddy drove her everywhere she wanted to go at weekends, and on weekdays she walked. We could walk most places we needed to get to from our house.

I could have walked to Marymount but it would have taken almost an hour – too long, in the morning. It was about two miles away. I could cycle it in less than twenty minutes. Down, down, I felt I was going – and the gradient was, subtly, downhill, since the school was nearer the coast then we were, though not on the coast. Down Charleston Road, down Appian Way, which was too narrow for all the traffic it had to support, even then, then down the wide, elegant Waterloo Road, and finally the best part – a quiet, perfect, traffic-free road, called by what seemed to be the elegant and lovely name of Marymount Road.

Charleston Road, Waterloo Road, and Marymount Road were lined all along their edges with trees. Great chestnut trees when I started school in the autumn. Once or twice a ripe chestnut got me on the head. Cycling along these roads was magical. I soared, as on wings. I tried tricks – after a while I could cycle for most of the way without putting my hands on the handlebars, and it gave me a great sense of achievement to do this. I wanted to show off, to boast about it at home, but (wisely) I didn't.

The school was fine. Although I knew nobody when I started, I got to know plenty of people soon enough. Those girls on the bus, the girl who sat beside me in class. Others. I didn't, though, make a best friend. Everyone seemed to have one already – most of them had arrived in the school with a best friend in tow, it was unusual to go to secondary school on your own. My old best friends were far away, living another life in St Bridget's. I hardly ever saw any of them.

Yvette, the only girl in the school from my immediate neighbourhood, was in another class.

The teaching in Marymount was excellent. I realised that when I was there, and even more so now. When I hear people saying they don't remember anything they learned at school, I have to admit, to myself, that I remember a good many things, and most of them I learned during that first year in Marymount. Big chunks of the Gospel according to Saint Luke, which we learned off by heart. Many passages from *The Merchant of Venice*, ditto, and also from *A Midsummer Night's Dream*, which the seniors put on at Easter. We first years were in the choir, singing 'Trip away; make no stay; Meet me all by break of day', and other songs. 'So we grew together, Like to a double cherry,' I can hear the girl from fifth year who played Helena saying – she was a tall, poignant-looking girl, and the play was so sad, the parting of the friends. 'Seeming parted, But yet an union in partition.' I was cycling every morning under the cherry blossom, quoting these lines, wishing I could play Helena.

The menu of subjects lived up to its promise. It was a Christmas stocking of Hector Grey novelties – Latin verbs and French pronunciation, Shakespeare plays and experiments in science. *Bully one, bully two, bully three* on the hockey pitch in Sandymount, fragrant with churned-up turf, cut grass.

But the lack of a best friend – which didn't worry me while I was there – was going to be a problem.

In March or so, I was invited to a birthday party, at the house of my best friend in primary, Deirdre. By now she was settled in and had new companions in St Bridget's, and I had to put up with that. They were at the party, but so were plenty of my old classmates. One of them, a small girl called Mandy, whom I knew from my very earliest days in primary, had changed. She used to be a teacher's pet, cherished because she was exceptionally small (the sort of girl who grows to be less than five foot as an adult – petite). As a little girl, she was doll-like, though she did not have the fairy tale good looks of, say, Yvette. She was famous for never missing a day – she got a prize for this on the last day of school, a silver cup – and for never turning up without her uniform on.

She had grown a bit taller, and was beginning to plump out. Something else had happened to her that happens to girls as they turn into women. She had learned to talk a lot.

Yakety-yak for the whole party.

Her subject was school. St Bridget's. (She called it Biddy's, without explaining what it was. Like people who talk too much, she took it for granted that everyone was familiar with the locations, the connections, the entire context of her life. Or maybe they just have so many stories to tell that they haven't time for boring explanations and trust the audience to fill in the gaps.)

Mandy was a brilliant storyteller. Half the party guests were at her feet, literally, gathered round her in a circle, riveted to her words. Her tales were character-based, and the characters were all teachers with names like Muggins and Bertie and Smutty and Pug. Muggins was an old nun who was crazy, just crazy, and Pug was the Irish teacher who gave the class Cadbury's chocolate every Friday if they did their homework and Pug was getting married in June and came to school one day with two odd shoes on, that was the day after her fiancé had proposed to her – can you imagine? – one shoe a brown moccasin teacher-kind of shoe and the other black patent with a little bow on it, we were in absolute stitches, we were breaking our sides, we just couldn't stop ...

It was this sort of stuff. Nothing much when you thought about it afterwards. But she created a vivid dramatic picture. And the picture was of a school that was not so much like the schools I read about in the Enid Blyton books, as a school that was even better than them. More full of life and laughs and fun. More replete with eccentric teachers. A school where the nuns and teachers were a constant source of amusement, like an ongoing circus, and where the girls never stopped breaking their sides laughing.

My Christmas exams went well. I was now considering becoming a scientist, like Marie Curie, whose biography I had read in a children's series. I imagined myself sitting under a pine tree, fondling the fragrant needles and discovering radiation. In English I was doing well, too. Our teacher, Miss Burns, had a contact in the radio station, and got us, the class, to put together a complete half hour programme. We wrote poems and essays and plays, and members of the class got to recite them, present them, on the radio. We did auditions. Presenting was what everyone wanted to do, to be 'on the radio'!

I didn't make the cut.

'I don't know what it is. Your voice is a little nasal,' said Miss Burns.

I didn't know what that meant, to have a voice that was nasal. I did not like my nose, the shape of it, and wondered if, apart from looking funny, it also affected my voice.

'But you can console yourself with the knowledge that you've written most of the programme,' she added.

It was true. I had surpassed myself. Poems, songs, funny anecdotes. A play. I'd written them all, in an orgy of writing. I liked Miss Burns and the topics she suggested, and when I heard the word 'radio', I took off. It didn't surprise me that I'd written most of the programme. I'd done more work than anyone else and I loved writing essays and anything else I was asked to write.

So I thought, if I don't become Marie Curie, I might like to become a writer. Like Frances Hodgson Burnett, whose books Miss Burns had recommended. Or G.K. Chesterton, whom I had discovered myself and liked.

The hockey, I liked too. And in spring we played tennis in Herbert Park.

I loved, above all, the cycling. Four times a day, I flew along those roads. Like a goddess.

*

I did not take to the headmistress.

I don't take to heads of institutions much – that's something I know now. Maybe they are often not very nice people. But it is more likely that I am afraid of them, for one thing, and for another, I resent anyone who has any power over me.

Sister Borromeo hadn't given me any cause to dislike her. She had given me a scholarship (but that put me in her power). She told me I was a good girl whenever she ran into me in the corridor. She commended me for wearing the full uniform. I didn't want to be commended. I wore the full uniform because I loved it. I loved the blazer and the tie, and even the beret, which you were supposed to despise. There was an ongoing battle in the school between Sister Borromeo and all the pupils about the wearing of this beret. She would make announcements over the loud-speaker system they had, the Tannoy – a little box in the middle of every ceiling.

Crackle, it would go, *crackle*. And then Sister Borromeo's voice would come through, like a voice on the radio.

'I want to remind you all that, according to the rules of Marymount, you are supposed to wear your full school uniform on the way to and from school. This includes the beret.'

This announcement would usually raise a laugh in the class. Even the teacher, whose work had been interrupted by the Tannoy, would allow herself a smile and a helpless shrug.

Hardly anybody wore the beret. (It flattened the hair, for one thing. This didn't bother me, since I still had my plaits. The hair on top was tightly pulled by my mother's efficient hands, and flat as a ballerina's.)

'Good girl, wearing your beret!' she said, beaming, one morning when she met me on the stairs.

I said nothing.

'Good girl, I said.' She sounded sharper and her smile was gone. 'It's so nice to see the beret on. It suits you so well.'

I smirked then and mumbled something. And as soon as she was out of sight, I whipped the beret off and stuffed it into my schoolbag, where it stayed for evermore.

The first week of term I had met Sister Borromeo in town.

I was traipsing around hunting for schoolbooks. The way they handled it was that you got lists of texts from the teachers during the first week of school – not one list, nothing as organised as that. Each teacher would write the titles of the books required for her class on the blackboard; the pupils transcribed the list in their jotters or copybooks. Then we'd go into town and go from bookshop to bookshop in search of the books. Every schoolchild in Dublin was doing the same thing for a week or two at the beginning of the first term. Long queues would form outside the bookshops as the children stood in line, waiting to get in. When you got to the counter, the tired and harassed assistants – students doing holiday jobs – would snatch your list and tell you what they had. 'Out of stock' was a phrase you learned quickly. 'Out of print' was another.

It was a tedious way of acquiring books, labour intensive, especially for the children. But it had its advantages: half-days for the first week, putting off the real start of school for at least that length of time. Standing in queues in the hot September sun wasn't all that diverting, but moving around the city, from Greene's on Clare Street to Fallon's on Talbot Street, stopping off at several shops in between, had a certain excitement to offer.

On my third day in school, I was making my way down

Talbot Street to Fallon's, and another shop, The Educational Company. I didn't like Talbot Street. It is very long and the shops on it are slightly seedy. The light on it is harsh, somehow, and it's altogether a disheartening, messy kind of street – stretching from too-busy O'Connell Street to the bleakness of Amiens Street Station, near the North Strand, which was bombed during the war and which still looked as if a bomb had hit it twenty-odd years later. By the time I had got to Talbot Street, having been up and down to Clare Street, which was lovely and green and mysterious, to the smart, encouraging shops on Dawson Street, and trudged across the Liffey to the north side, I was tired.

Sister Borromeo and another nun, Sister Assumption, were bobbing along up Talbot Street. There were a lot of religious shops on that street, selling holy statues, religious books, nun's habits, for all I know (they must have bought them somewhere).

'Hello, Helen,' said Sister Borromeo brightly.

Sister Assumption, who was good-humoured and mischievous, smiled and, unbelievably, winked.

'Hello, Sister,' I said. I still liked her at this stage.

That was all. They walked on.

This happened in September, just after school had started. The episode of the beret occurred months later, well into the second term, just before Easter, when we were deeply engrossed in rehearsing *A Midsummer Night's Dream*. The pretence of classwork had been dispensed with. We spent the entire schoolday in the hall, singing our songs, and waiting for our cues. By now we knew the play off by heart.

Some of the teachers expressed impatience.

Miss Burns was open about it. 'When are we supposed to get our work done?' she asked. She had got engaged to be married and wore her hair, which used to be any old way, a sort of limp bob, in a new style: up, with elaborate ringlets held by a clasp at the back of her head. She wore a white bouclé suit and patent shoes under her black gown. She looked imperious.

'It will soon be over,' we consoled her. She had become our ally, almost our equal, since the radio project.

'Oh well!' she smiled.

A few days after Deirdre's party, which was the day before the play was due to go on, Sister Borromeo called me to the office.

I was terrified. I could think of no reason for this call.

She was sitting behind a huge wooden desk, with a telephone on it and a few files. It was a type of desk I would see often again, in the future, but this was the first time I'd seen one. The desk of a managing director. Her room, too, the office, was spacious and polished, like an important director's. The only difference was that instead of some expensive-looking, inoffensive piece of art on the wall, she had a big statue of the Blessed Virgin in the corner.

'Sit down,' she said.

I sat down on a slippery leather chair.

'Your studies are going well,' she said. She seemed to have my school report opened in front of her. I wondered if this had something to do with the half-scholarship. 'But you are getting to be a little insolent,' she said. 'I have had some bad reports from a few of your teachers.'

This was a lie, I knew. I was never insolent.

'You do not wear your full uniform,' she went on.

This was also unfair. I didn't wear the beret. Now. But I was never without my tie, or anything else. I was more compliant than anyone else as far as the uniform was concerned.

'What I am really worried about is that you have mitched from school.' She stared at me from under her big wimple: the nuns in this school wore very wide wimples. They took the form of two big squares of the stiff white stuff, like plastic, that wimples are made from, on either side of their faces. They were like a sort of small tent with an open front – the kind of tent you see at farmers' markets. Her face was inside the tent, in the space where the stall would be, with its wares, the jars of pickles, the jams, the farm cheeses.

I was so startled I said something natural.

I said, 'What?'

Because I had never in my life mitched from school. For one thing, I didn't particularly want to. And for another, I didn't have the courage it takes to leave home in the morning, in your uniform and with your bag on your back, and head off to the beach, or into town, or wherever mitching kids go.

'I remember meeting you in town one day. Myself and Sister Assumption met you.'

'But that was during the school book week. We had a half-day,' I said.

'I don't think so,' she said firmly.

There was nothing to say to that. I moved into a zone of disbelief, a zone where I knew I was helpless to rescue myself. Because how can you help yourself if you are faced with a liar in a powerful place?

'Mitching is something we take very seriously in Marymount.' Her voice was precise and ladylike, like a little ivory paper knife with a sharp edge. 'You are a scholarship girl and we expect a certain standard of behaviour.'

I had stopped feeling startled, or frightened. I gained composure from my disbelief.

'We don't like to use the strap, Helen,' she said.

Now I was startled again, back into emotion. Strap?

'But we do if we are forced to,' she said.

I looked at her wimple-like-a-tent, and her black habit, and her black beads and the big black strap around her waist. The acre of polished desk, separating me from her. The slippery chair. The prinking statue of Our Lady. There were lilies in a silver vase in front of her, calla lilies, with their pointy yellow tongues sticking out of their wimple mouths. Like snakes' tongues.

She said she would let me off this time, but that I had better watch out.

She put it more elegantly, of course, but that was what she meant.

That night, I started my campaign to get out of Marymount.

I told my mother I really missed all my old friends. I told her I missed Irish, which was the language we had spoken in my primary school, and was the language of St Bridget's. I told her I had made no new pals, which was a lie, but I didn't have the sort of friend whom I could not betray, the sort of friend who would bind me to the school.

My mother didn't want me to move. It would mean buying a new uniform (which was no small expense). The fees in St Bridget's were higher, too (surprisingly, given its plebeian-sounding name). And there I would have no half-scholarship.

I kept at her.

Orla was going to start secondary in September, and she was going to St Bridget's – she was not like me, experimental. She knew where her friends were going and she was not going to make the mistake of going elsewhere.

Then something happened. Something that would go

down in Irish history and would incidentally change the course of my life. The Minister for Education, Donagh O'Malley, announced that he was introducing free education for secondary schools. From now on there would be no fees. That is, there would be no fees in schools that made the decision to opt in to the free scheme, but fees would continue in schools that decided to opt out, and preserve their exclusive, upper-class tone by keeping out poor children.

Both Marymount and St Bridget's opted into the scheme. Nobody would have to pay fees in those schools. Ever again.

'Well, I suppose it will just be the uniform,' said my mother. 'If you're really not content in that school, I'll see if you can change.' (Contented in that school, she would have said. Not content.)

So I did.

My mother wrote the necessary letters.

This all happened at the beginning of May.

The weather was glorious, as it often is in Dublin at that time of year. All along the roads on the way to school the cherry blossoms were in bloom. Morning and evening I cycled under the generous branches, flung like long arms out of the gardens over the road, spilling their benison of pink popcorn petals over the road, over me.

And suddenly, in the midst of all this miraculous flowering, I got what had been lacking all year. A special friend. One morning I whizzed around my corner and there was Yvette, turning from her cul-de-sac on to the main road. How like her to start now that the weather was warm and lovely, I thought. I supposed she hadn't wanted to cycle in the bad weather, not being made of such stern stuff as I. But

I did her an injustice. In fact, she had just been given the bicycle, for her birthday, a few days ago – she'd asked for it because she'd noticed me, cycling along, and thought it looked like so much fun.

Yvette had copy-catted me. Wonders would never cease.

Immediately, we became cycling companions. She waited for me at her corner in the mornings, and instead of zipping along alone, amusing myself by removing my hands from the bars, I cycled slowly, with Yvette beside me, chatting. It turned out that she wasn't stuck-up or precious or spoiled at all. That she looked exquisite didn't concern her in the least – she did not seem to even realise it, although she was fond of nice frocks (but then, so was I; so were almost all girls). Nor was she especially unusual, in spite of looking it. Our conversation was about teachers, and other girls, and what we had for homework, and where we would go for our holidays (she would go to Liverpool to visit her aunty; I would go to West Cork where my mother had rented a bungalow for a fortnight in August). We talked about sport. Yvette was very good at tennis, a game that suited her, of course, what with the white skirts and sunny courts, but she was even better at hockey, which isn't so glamorous.

After about a week of this cycling companionship, Yvette asked me to come around to her house for tea on Friday.

This was the first time any girl in the school had issued such an invitation.

So I got to see Yvette's house. It was the same type of house as my own, slightly smaller, with smaller gardens. And although it was pleasant enough, it was not as cosy or feminine or beautiful as I had anticipated. True, the favoured colour for floors was red, whereas my mother liked fawn or brown, and the wallpapers were white with red roses in the hall, blue cornflowers in the kitchen, which

270

created a cheerful effect. But when I visited, the hall floor was covered with newspapers, because her mother had just washed it, and a clotheshorse, hung with sheets and underwear, dominated the kitchen and gave off their warm, damp, rather embarrassing, smell. Work went on in Yvette's house, just as in mine, and it wasn't all that different in other respects. The food was chips and fried eggs, for instance, with tinned pears and condensed milk for sweet. Yvette and I watched television afterwards in their dining room, while her mother did the ironing down in the kitchen.

It was an ordinary enough visit. And yet it was momentous. I had got inside her house. She liked me enough to invite me in. We were, in short, en route to being best friends.

Too late. The letters were in the post. Within a week, everything was settled, and although I felt, if not regretful, certainly ambivalent, I was too cowardly to pull back and change my mind again.

So I left Marymount – nobody ever found out why – and I went across town to St Bridget's. It was not half as good a school as Marymount. The teachers were a mixed bunch, but they never used the strap there (or threatened to). And the headmistress was nice. A bit of a rebel – she advised me to go to Trinity College when the time came to leave, and then to come back and be a nun. This was at a time when there was a ban on Catholics in the archdiocese of Dublin going to Trinity. The headmistress of St Bridget's was the kind of person who would like to have a pupil flouting that ban. I couldn't imagine Sister Borromeo recommending anyone to ignore an episcopal regulation.

I couldn't cycle to St Bridget's, which was three miles away on the other side of the city. A long enough bus journey

– one that we did, all the same, four times a day, usually.

I did not entirely lose contact with Yvette. She lived just around the corner, after all. I invited her back to my house for tea just before school ended; that's when I told her I was changing schools. She was surprised but not devastated; she had plenty of friends. We saw each other from time to time afterwards, but of course our lives moved off in different directions. I was wearing a different uniform from hers now, and I wasn't cycling to school any more.

My bike lay in the garden shed – our garden was full of sheds. For a while after I changed school, I'd take it out and have a spin at weekends. I planned to go on long cycles, to the countryside, to the beach. Once or twice I did actually ride down to Sandymount, cycled along the seafront and then came back again. In my plans, I would go on a cycling holiday with girls from school. (I never made a very close friend in the new school – my old pals were in different classes from me and had regrouped by the time I got there. I had a few girls to whom I was close, but they lived far away and were not the type to cycle.) In my fantasy, we – me and this group of cheerful and enterprising girls – would cycle all over the country, camping in woodlands or fields at night, or staying in country inns. I would have pannier bags, and shorts, and a smile on my freckled face. The bee would suck in the cowslip's bell.

Of course, none of this happened.

I did use my bike again, though.

The year I did the Leaving I got a job in a bookshop. Greene's Bookshop. I was taken on in the summer to sell the schoolbooks, to be there in September when the school book rush was in full swing and they needed a lot of extra hands. It seemed like the perfect job. In practice it wasn't all that wonderful. It was a bit like being in the army during a big war, training and polishing your gun, waiting for the signal to launch an attack. For two months there was very little to do; boredom was the main problem for me and the other half-dozen students who had been taken on for the summer. Then came D-Day, the first of September. The school book rush. From then on, it was mayhem. There was not one second to draw a breath, from nine to five thirty, nine to one on Saturdays.

Greene's was not far from home. I took out my bike again and got the tyres changed with some of the money I was earning. I could fly down to the shop in the summer mornings in about ten minutes.

Usually, I parked it in the hall – they had a hall door that was not part of the shop proper, at the side. I'd drag it in there. I'd lost the key of the lock and for some reason hadn't bought a new one – I'd had to lash out on the tyres, I didn't feel like spending more money on my bike the minute I started working. I put it off till later. On my third Saturday, the door to the hall was locked, so I left the bike outside the shop at the side of one of the tables they had out there on the footpath, like *bouquinistes* in France. When I came out, the bike was gone.

You couldn't leave an unlocked bike unattended in Dublin in those days. It wasn't like Amsterdam or Copenhagen, those legendary cities, paradises for cyclists, where everyone is honest and most people ride a bike. In Dublin any unlocked bike was robbed while the saddle was still warm. So they said.

Chariot of fire

The day my red bicycle was stolen from Greene's Bookshop, I met my first great love.

He came into the shop looking for a copy of a novel and came to the schoolbook counter by mistake. (Later he told me that he had walked into the shop, looked to the left, where Eddie was sitting on his stool among the stands of paperbacks, and then to the right, where four beautiful girls were chatting together in front of a stack of textbooks. Naturally, he chose to turn right.) As always, when a customer came in and broke up our chattering, we all looked guilty (though there was nothing to do but chat, in these early weeks) and rushed to serve. I got there first.

The novel he wanted was *Nausea*. That's what he asked for. Just the title.

I was used to people just knowing the title – for the textbooks, of course, that was what you would need to know. Nobody knew or cared who wrote them. But I already knew that somebody could come looking for a novel called *The Sun Also Rises*, or *Wise Blood*, and say they'd forgotten the name of the author. Sometimes someone would not even know the title – they'd tell you what the book was about. It's about a girl whose sister has married a rich man and who isn't sure if she wants to get married herself or not. They're in London. It's got a bird on the cover.

It was a great thrill for us if we could identify the book for these customers.

'Oh yeah,' I smiled. 'Jean-Paul Sartre.'

He knew that, of course. He was just testing. Teasing.

'It might be over there in the paperback section,' I said. Then, because I could see that this looked like bad service, I added. 'Just hold on a second, I'll see if we have it.'

I went over to the other side of the shop and he followed. So I passed him on to Eddie (who had the Penguin edition).

'Eight hundred and fifty-five,' Andrea, one of my colleagues, said thoughtfully, as we watched him go out the door with his orange paper bag in one hand and his red and white helmet in the other.

The boys – all the summer staff were eighteen or nineteen – had a silly joke. They gave all young women who came into the shop marks out of a thousand for looks. Top marks were for Helen of Troy, the face that launched a thousand ships. Great-looking girls got nine hundred. They were capable of awarding fifteen, or two, to women they didn't like the look of. For a while we girls did the same thing for men. We did it for a few days and then stopped, bored with the exercise. Nobody had played the game for about two weeks at this stage, so Andrea had to add, 'Ships, featherhead,' before I copped on.

Seán was chunky, with curly brown hair, and a confident, cheeky smile. He hadn't struck me as especially attractive on the Helen of Troy scale. But he did seem like the kind of person I'd want to know. (Any man who bought *Nausea*, if he was reasonably attractive and friendly, would have seemed like the kind of person I'd want to know. I believed people who read serious books were bound to be interesting.)

Two days later Seán came back.

I recognised him immediately – he was carrying his helmet. Not many customers had them. His big motorbiker's leather jacket also made him distinctive.

He sauntered up to the counter – the schoolbook counter, my counter.

'Hi there,' he said. 'How are you?'

'Oh, hi!' I had no experience of courtship rituals. I'd never met a boy anywhere other than at a dance, and it did not occur to me that you could meet a potential date anywhere else. But, out of politeness, I batted the ball back to him. 'Are you enjoying *Nausea*?'

He smiled. 'I don't think anyone could possibly enjoy it.'

I must have looked snubbed. 'It's sort of bleak. Have you read it?'

I shook my head. 'I'm going to do philosophy next year,' I said. 'When I go to college.' I had no doubt but that I would get the Leaving, get the marks I needed for a grant, and go to college. Even though I hadn't worked very hard at some subjects, I was confident. But, knowing it was best to appear modest, I added, 'That's if I get the Leaving, of course.'

The next night we went out, to the cinema.

I met him under Clery's clock. We were to meet at half past seven and go to a film that started at eight, in the Carlton. *Love Story*. I'd dashed home at half past five – it took half an hour, now that I had no bike. Washed and changed into suitable clothes for a date – my first. And it turned out that I didn't have anything, not a single garment, that was right for the occasion. I pulled all the clothes out of my wardrobe and got panicky, trying on one thing, then the other, as the clock ticked inexorably onwards. In the end I wore a pale-green blouse and dark-green maxi skirt, which looked, I imagined, a bit like a riding habit, one that might have been worn by a nineteenth-century heroine, by Catherine Earnshaw perhaps. Or Lorna Doone (I hadn't read *Lorna Doone* but I loved her name). My aim was to look like a romantic, dreamy girl, but so far none of the clothes I had matched up to my image of what they should be, what I needed to achieve my vision. (My legs were too fat, and that is one reason why I liked the floaty, long, romantic skirts that were just coming into fashion, after the tyranny of the mini.)

By the time I reached Clery's I was nervous and drained after the ordeal of dressing. It was twenty-five to eight already and I worried that I had kept him waiting. Many people were standing around in the vicinity of the clock, and crowds of young people thronged the pavement, on their way to picture houses, or theatres, to other places of entertainment. But there was no sign of Seán. I waited for five minutes, at a slight distance from the clock, where I could see its big black hands jerkily making their way around its white moon face. I could also see Clery's windows and alternated glancing at the clock with examining the outfits on display. Miniskirts, tiny silk shifts in startling colours and patterns – orange and purple psychedelic blotches. Or black-and-white geometric patterns. So boring. There was nothing that I would want in the window. None of the clothes were designed for a girl who wanted to be called Lorna Doone and who was about to read *Nausea* and embark on a philosophy course in the autumn. Such clothes existed, and not only in my imagination. I saw the clothes I wanted sometimes, on girls who had spent the summer in Copenhagen or Paris or San Francisco. Indian smocks and gypsy skirts. Espadrilles, soft straw baskets. You could not get such things in Dublin then. You had to travel for them – which is what made them so desirable, and so sexy.

By a quarter to eight I had stopped worrying about espadrilles. I had other things on my mind. Where was Seán? It had never occurred to me that he wouldn't come and it still didn't. I had heard the term 'stood up', but usually from girls in my class, the advanced kind of girl who would not be doing philosophy in the autumn but probably doing a shorthand and typing course at a commercial college. Those girls, whose eyes above the school uniform were framed in thick black make-up, would talk about how they had stood a boy up. 'I had to stand him up,' they'd say. It didn't seem very important. They had to stand a boy up because they'd changed their mind about him, after making a date at a dance. Or because they had to wash their hair, or help a friend to manicure her nails. It was easier not to turn up than to phone and make an excuse, and not everyone had a phone, anyway. I'd never considered what it felt like to be that boy. To be waiting for a girl who just didn't show up. Our feeling was that the boy would just shrug and go home. We didn't attribute much sensitivity to them. We didn't believe they had feelings, not in the way we had.

At first, I didn't fear that Seán had stood me up, because why would he have bothered coming to the shop and asking to see me if he wasn't going to keep the date?

But as the hands on the big clock jerked on, I began to get anxious. How long should I wait? I played the game you play in these situations. I said to myself, I will wait for five more minutes and then I'll leave. And then when the five minutes had passed, I said that again.

Other people kept meeting one another, in the vicinity of the clock. Mainly couples. The person who had been waiting would see the other one coming and rush out of their niche to join the partner – they were like magnets, one would move out and the other would run in, and they'd join, kiss maybe, and then walk off hand in hand as often as not, laughing and talking.

Lucky, happy, people!

As eight o'clock drew nearer, I was almost the only person left under the clock, still waiting. The evening was growing colder. A big grey cloud scudded across the sun. The green double-deckers roared along the street, belching out grey fumes.

I was sure that everyone, on the buses, in the cars, was looking out the window at me, thinking, Look at your one, still waiting.

At eight o'clock he came.

He was not on his motorbike, and I hardly recognised him without his leather jacket and helmet under his arm.

'Listen, I'm really sorry ...'

He was pink and panting, wearing just a shirt, a pale-blue shirt, no tie. His hair was tousled and much more abundant than it had been before (on account of not being flattened by the helmet). He smelt mildly of a mixture of fresh sweat and flowery soap.

'It's OK,' I said, without giving the slightest indication that I'd been upset. And I didn't feel annoyed or angry, as I would have done if it had been anyone else who had kept me waiting. My main feeling was not even of relief, but of pleasure. All the waiting time was blotted out of my memory as if it had never existed.

We ran across the street, just where the pillar used to be, and up to the Carlton. There was a long queue, already moving, and we joined it.

'God, hope we get in now,' he said.

I didn't care. Already I was happy just to be with him, standing beside him in a queue. I wouldn't have said to myself that I was in love, but I had never really felt like this before. I had never felt happy just being with a person – always there had to be something else. Something to eat, something to do, something to talk about. Even being with my mother, when I was small, had not been like this. I needed to be with my mother to feel happy, but she was just a background against which my other desires would be fulfilled. She was like, say, the light that fills a room where you want to read, or play a game, or she was like the sunshine that is a background to the fun you have at the beach. Essential, but not by any means an end in herself.

I knew I'd enjoy this film (I loved most films I'd ever

seen, which had been precious few). But being with this person, the guy on the motorbike, was the main thing. (I did not think of him as a 'man', nor did I think of him as a 'boy'. He was just himself.) The film was going to be the background to the pleasure of being with him.

I wouldn't have formulated it like that then, or formulated it at all. All I knew, standing there, on the shadowy side of the street, was that I felt at ease, and pleased in a way I had not felt before in my life until then.

One Saturday, about three weeks after this, he collected me from the bookshop when we closed at one o'clock. This time he had the motorbike – it was parked just around the corner from the shop on Merrion Square.

He wondered if I'd like to go for a walk in the mountains. I would.

He looked at me thoughtfully. 'That's a very nice skirt,' he said. And after a few seconds, added, 'You look lovely.'

I was wearing a calf-length black skirt and a high-necked Victorian blouse that I'd bought the day before at lunch time, using more than half my pay packet for the week. The skirt had a very high waist.

'Hm,' Eddie in paperbacks had said when he saw it. He was admiring it. Everyone was. 'What would you call that? A cummerbund, I think, that's what it is.'

I didn't like the sound of the word 'cummerbund' much, but I was pleased that my outfit impressed people. I'd got it because it was a bit like one of the outfits Ali MacGraw wore in the movie.

For the pillion of a motorbike it was far from ideal.

'Slacks would be easier,' Seán said. 'But I hate slacks.'

I was glad I hadn't worn mine, although I had a new pair

of Levis, of which I had been inordinately proud until that moment. (Ali had worn jeans, once or twice, in the movie. But Seán had been less enthusiastic than I about the film. In fact, when I asked him if he'd enjoyed it, as we made our way to my bus stop, he had used a comment of a kind he had plenty of, as I would find out in due course: 'No comment!')

He insisted I wear his helmet.

I didn't think a helmet would suit me, and it didn't go with my high-necked lacy blouse. But I enjoyed putting it on all the same. It was like dressing up to play a game. I felt like an astronaut: an astronaut on top and Ali MacGraw underneath.

Driving – if it was driving – moving, whizzing, racing along the streets, then along the Bray Road and up the winding ways to the mountains, felt like flying. Cycling had felt like that, sometimes, but this was different. On a bicycle I had felt like a bird. Being on the Honda was more like being on a small plane. Faster and easier.

And there was the joy of being a pillion passenger.

There was a small strap in the middle of the saddle, which perhaps the passenger was supposed to hold on to. But on this model of bike you really had to grab the driver around the waist, to keep your balance. That's what I did. I put my two arms around Seán's waist, and held on tight, as we sped through Dublin and up into the mountains.

My skirt wasn't a problem. There was so much of it that it spread easily over the saddle and covered my legs. In fact, the blouse caused me more difficulty. Even though it was a very fine, sunny afternoon, I felt cold as we drove higher into the foothills and could have done with a jumper, if not a big anorak. Clinging to Seán became more and more necessary.

Somewhere past a pitch-and-putt course called Puck's Castle, we stopped.

In a carpark. There were just two cars in it, though, and it was a mountain carpark, with big evergreen trees embracing it and soft, spicy pine needles carpeting the ground. The air was glaucous – a lovely, delicate greyish-green.

You don't have to hop off a motorbike the second it stops, it's not like a bicycle. There's a stand to keep it steady on the ground. Seán put down the stand and climbed down first. I remained seated, not sure what to do. Truth to tell, I felt stiff and a bit winded from the ride. And I was freezing.

He took my hand and helped me down.

Then he removed the helmet, as if I were a child.

'Are you OK?' he asked. He looked very serious, stern almost, and very gentle at the same time.

I shook my head, ever so slightly.

The smell of the pines mixed with some other smell – the sweet, herby smell of clover. The trees whispered. Other than that, there was absolute silence.

The world was holding its breath.

He put his hand to my cheek and stroked it softly. 'You're cold,' he said. His voice trembled. 'You're cold.'

A bird sang, two notes, somewhere in the forest.

He put his arms around me then and we kissed.

The first time. But we went on and on for ages.

It's easier to learn to kiss than to learn to ride a bicycle, in some ways. But in some ways it's much harder to judge the moment correctly, to seize hold of your confidence, to take the plunge.

And falling in love is not like learning to ride a bicycle. It's more like falling off one.

As time goes on, though, you need to learn to turn into the wind and keep your balance.

That is what we could not do.

The summer was paradise. That's not an exaggeration. The motorbike, the trees in the forest, the salty walks on the beach, mixed together to create heaven on earth. Young love can fuse with nature if it gets a chance – it can become part of the fertile blend. Fish, flesh, fowl commended us all summer long, caught in the sensual music of the birds and the waves and the trees of our own endlessly fascinating story. A country for young men and women it was, especially if they had a means of transport, if they had a motorbike. Up the mountains and to the beaches and all over Dublin we went. We made love in woods and by the sea and on the banks of lakes and rivers – not made love properly, of course, we were far too timid and cautious and puritanical for that. We cuddled and pressed and kissed, for all we were worth, in the midst of nature.

Our examination results were very good when they came through. A further bond. I got an entrance scholarship, and he got a prize for coming first in his year. We felt like a special couple, lucky people, clever people. Obviously, we were made for one another.

Work kept us apart for half the time. We didn't question that limitation much, nor did we appreciate it. Seán would be at the shop door at half past five to collect me on the bike, and we would be together until midnight, or later, when he would leave me home.

When the summer jobs ended and college started, however, we were not constrained by the rigid timetables of jobs. We were not constrained by anything.

That should have been a huge excitement in itself. But it wasn't. That was the first problem. Seán had told me so much about what went on in college that I felt I had been there already. There was a sense of staleness about it, then, where there should have been novelty. And that was not the worst thing. The worst thing was that the most significant thing about the university was that Seán was in it.

My first day, for instance, focused on meeting Seán for lunch. So when I was walking up the avenue, finding my way around the warren of dark corridors, figuring out where Theatre R was, and the library, and greeting schoolfriends I had not seen since June, I was thinking, At half past twelve. Half past twelve. I'll meet him for lunch.

The canteen was thronged with thousands of students. Seán kept greeting people – girls and boys – he knew from last year.

He'd kept his head down in first year, studying obsessively, to earn the high honours he wanted to achieve. But he had got to know people all the same. And now they nodded to him, with a certain deference, because he had come top of the class.

We ate lunch and then Seán suggested we go into town. He needed to get some books.

The suggestion surprised me. It was my first day, I didn't want to leave. And I had a lecture after lunch.

'Go if you want to,' he said. 'But you'll be missing nothing if you don't. He's a terrible lecturer. Just read the text.'

I would have liked to go, anyway. After all, I had only been to two lectures in my life so far, and I did not think they were boring.

But.

'OK,' I said, looking around the canteen and the crowds of young people, talking and laughing. They looked carefree to me, like children playing a game, and I felt set apart, burdened with the heavy weight of my love.

I went into town with Seán, on the bike.

We walked around the bookshops and had coffee in Bewley's.

He told me about lecturers and professors I would have, and about the content of some of the courses. He spoke interestingly, vividly, of these things, as he was vivid and entertaining about everything. But I felt I was missing something. And I was not sharp enough, ruthless enough, to give a name to what that was.

Seán also talked about people in his own class, which was some special sub-group of high-powered students. Camilla and Olwyn and Rebecca – the girls had romantic, posh names, and even the sound of them sent pangs of jealousy pricking at my heart.

'Camilla is the most attractive girl in college,' he said then. This was when we were eating cherry buns. He went on to talk about some lecturer who fancied her and laughed. 'They're all smitten! They're gas!' he said.

I picked a cherry from the bun, then left the yellow cake on my plate.

I neglected about a third of my lectures in the first term, and half in the second and third.

Seán missed much more. By the final term, he wasn't attending anything. Caught in something – a sensual confusion, or some other sort of confusion for which we had no name – he neglected everything. It was as if he had said goodbye to his old life of study and concentration, and jumped off a cliff, bringing me with him.

Instead of studying or attending classes, we sat in the canteen, drinking coffee, or we walked around the campus, finding secret places where we could sit and kiss and press our bodies together. In the cold weather we found secret places indoors, too, even though that was taking a risk.

This was all appalling. But it happened gradually and, anyway, did not seem quite so appalling then. It was not very unusual for students to skip classes and lectures. With this observation, I tried to console myself. There were lots who did that, for no reason at all, and perhaps there still are. I had friends who didn't bother, quite often, going to class. They had no reason for that, no reason as compelling as mine (which was that Seán wanted me to stay with him). Not being an attender was one way of getting through college in those days. What was strange and discomfiting was that I didn't see myself as that type of student. I saw myself as the other kind, who was studious and careful, and who went to everything, and then to the library to work for hours. What were they doing there? Those students who sat for eight hours, reading, and taking notes? I couldn't even imagine what they were up to. That's how far I had gone. I had always loved reading but on the rare occasions when I managed to get to the library the words danced before my eyes.

A strange thing happens to students who don't attend lectures. They lose track of what is going on, at a superficial level and also at a deep level. The problem is not that they miss the content of what the lecturer is saying, which is often not all that important, anyway, at least not in arts. The problem is more that they lose the thread of the course. They lose the plot.

They lose their balance.

They tumble off the wheel and they get completely lost.

We got fed up of the life we were leading, naturally. But it affected us in different ways. Seán got fed up of me, while I clung more and more to him, in ever-increasing desperation. I was afraid if I lost my grip on him, I'd tumble into some even deeper abyss and be totally lost and destroyed. I feared this, although I hated the chaos we were in. (I was in love with him. That was the only thing I was sure of.)

At the end of the year, Seán failed his examinations and I scraped through mine. We struggled on through the summer – he was studying for repeats; I was back working in the bookshop. It rained all the time. I ate chocolate and missed Seán when I was at work. In the evenings and at weekends he was often busy – he had to study hard to cover the entire syllabus in two months, so that he would pass the repeats.

He passed, and we were both back in college in October.

But the relationship was over. During the summer he'd fallen in love with a girl in his class, one of those with the names. Not Camilla, the belle of Belfield. Rebecca. Rebecca hadn't failed her exams, but she'd been in college during the summer, anyway; she had some sort of summer job in the examinations office. (Also, wavy, fair hair, a small pert face, and a motherly demeanour. She wore a pale-blue blouse often, and a knee-length navy skirt, and had big round glasses. She looked like a cute little owl.)

I cut my hair and stopped wearing the flowing, hippy clothes Seán liked. Now I wore jeans and a denim jacket, or a miniskirt and high leather boots. I'd gone on a diet and lost a great deal of weight, so those clothes suited me now. People told me I looked great. Girls often told me they wished they had my figure, and boys, young-looking skinny boys, asked me on dates, which I sometimes accepted, though usually I did not enjoy them, since those boys could not measure up to Seán. Who could? I was very pleased with my new body, however – when I stopped menstruating, I wasn't worried in the slightest. No more mess.

Once, I got a shock. I became blind. I had walked from home to college, about half an hour's walk. When I came into the main hall, I felt my vision begin to fade from my eyes, slowly, like a light dimming. For a quarter of an hour I was in the dark. And then the sight returned, as slowly as it had disappeared, with bright spots and flashes and darts like lightning bolts. A bad headache. I guessed this temporary blindness was related to my dieting in some way, just like the loss of my periods was. But I told nobody about it. I thought they wouldn't believe me, anyway, and say it was my imagination. Nobody knew about anorexia in those days in Dublin. In that field I was a pioneer.

I didn't do well in my second-year examinations, either, even though I had attended everything. You can't really do well in exams if you're starving to death. I had realised that, after an academic year on my self-imposed fast, but the low marks I was getting on the weighing scales meant more to me than high marks on an examination transcript. One figure sank in tandem with the other. I was lucky to pass, just as I was lucky to be alive and healthy, to all intents and purposes. My brain and my body seemed to have a great capacity for survival. My heart was the trouble-spot. It was unreasonable and pathetic, but even after almost a whole year, I was still pining. I hardly knew why then, and I do not now. That sort of heartbreak is difficult to understand. If you're not enduring it, it seems ridiculous. It is ridiculous. But it's horrible, and real, and can be fatal.

When summer came around once more, I attempted to

find a cure for love in the time-honoured way: foreign travel. A change of scene might obliterate the memory, patch up my broken heart. Adventure, excitement, something more exotic than the bookshop was prescribed, by myself, as the most likely panacea for my woe.

The miracle cure was to be this: a job in a hotel on the Isle of Wight. I was to be a still room waitress. I didn't know what that was, but it sounded all right. Stillness was something I was fond of, and there is a touch of glamour to the word 'waitress'. The Isle of Wight, obviously, had a nice summery ring to it. I had always been a sucker for isles. And working in a hotel would force me to be sociable, bring me out of myself (which was where I'd spent nearly the whole year, deep inside that spot at the back of my eyes where I hid from the dangerous world outside). I'd meet people – the people who took their holidays in the Green Gables Boarding House in Sandown.

Finally, one definite advantage the Isle of Wight had over Dublin was that Seán and Rebecca were most unlikely to be there. Although I spent my days and nights longing to be with Seán, the very worst moments had been those when I had actually seen him, walking around arm in arm with Rebecca, or zipping through the campus on his motorbike, with her stuck to him like a human rucksack. In college I had developed elaborate ruses for avoiding encounters with them, hiding out in the ladies' reading room, for instance, where he wasn't allowed and where Rebecca would never come, either, since she was always glued to Seán. I had spent most of the year finding ways to make myself invisible, but somehow hoping that that would blot him out, too. But it hadn't. I am sure he didn't enjoy seeing me, but he didn't seem to make serious efforts to avoid that eventuality. He had Rebecca, after all, to cheer him up if the sight of the abandoned waif pricked his conscience.

I headed off to the Isle of Wight with Orla. Neither of us had ever been out of Ireland before and were delighted to be getting away from the place. The sound of the ship's siren when the anchor was lifted was a blast of some heavenly trumpet to my ears. The sound reverberated through me; it was a siren call heralding freedom, adventure, mysterious and unimaginable delights.

The Holyhead ferry was full of students from Dublin, going over to England, like us, for summer jobs – on building sites, in hotels and shops. A good few of them were going to pick fruit in Norfolk. 'For the jam factories,' as somebody explained, with some impatience, when I asked. 'That's where the money is. Doesn't every fool know that?'

Nobody else was going to the Isle of Wight.

It was a bright evening, post-exam-time, midsummer. The ferry bobbed out of the harbour, with seagulls screaming in great excitement around the stern. Up on deck I stayed, watching Ireland recede, delighted with the view of the coastline as we moved away across that mythical water, the Irish Sea. How different Dún Laoghaire looked from out here! Its stacked rooftops, its steeples rising into the peachy evening sky, the dusky purple hills behind all that, gave it a fairy tale appearance that it didn't have at all when you were in it. It seemed that the further away you got from Ireland, the more beautiful it became.

When it finally disappeared, I sighed with joy and went below deck, my sister with me.

The crossing to Wales lasts three and a half hours. You could hire a berth but it's not worth it, so we sat up in the plastic Pullman seats in a big lounge. A musician was playing folk songs in the adjoining pub, to the great pleasure of the hundreds of young people on board. He was a star at the time, and he was a good musician. There was plenty of singing, and drinking of beer, and a certain amount of vomiting over the gunwale or simply straight on to the deck.

We didn't drink alcohol then, and we weren't 'into' music (well, I wasn't into anything much), so we didn't join them. Just sat in our big chairs, reading. (I had a Margaret Drabble novel; I suppose you could say I was into her.) According to a well-considered plan, at eleven, halfway through the voyage, we treated ourselves to a snack. There was a canteen place at the end of the lounge, and I went there to get the tea and sandwiches. (When it came to the crunch, I just got one sandwich, for my sister. I could not bring myself to eat one. I didn't feel hungry. I never did.)

In the queue at the counter I met a girl who had been in my tutorial in first year. Iseult. I hadn't known her well – I knew no one well in first year because I was so busy with Seán.

'Hi!' She was a cheery girl with an electric mop of black hair, wiry glasses. A wide, generous smile. She looked like an American but she was from Clonskeagh or Stillorgan or somewhere like that.

She was going to Chester to work in an inn there as a barmaid. She would make a terrific barmaid.

'Hey,' she said, after we had exchanged information about our summer jobs. 'That was terrible, what happened to Seán Smyth.'

I turned to jelly. Whenever I heard his name, this happened to me – a mountain of panic and shame avalanched on top of me.

'What?' I could hardly squeeze the word out.

'Don't you know?' Concern darkened her lively face. 'You used to be friendly with him, I thought.'

Friendly.

'Well, I haven't seen him for a while,' I said. Even saying the pronoun 'him' was a struggle.

'OK.' She looked at me carefully.

Could it be that she did not know about me and Seán? Could it be that there were people in the world who did not know the whole sorry, shameful story?

'He was in an accident,' she said. 'Just a few days ago. It was in the paper.'

I must have reacted strongly because she put her hand on my elbow and guided me to a seat.

'Sorry,' she said. She held my hand. Hers was very hot and mine was very cold. 'I gave you a shock. I'm sorry, I thought everyone knew.' She paused again. Then, quietly, she told me he was dead. He came off his motorbike. 'Remember, he used to go everywhere on a Honda?'

I remembered.

My strength was beginning to return to me – the way my sight had returned that time I lost it last term, or the way the blood goes back to your head after you faint. Your balance is restored.

'I hadn't heard,' I said. I could hear that my voice was steadier and louder.

The holiday in England changed me again, body and soul. I stopped being anorexic. The work as a still room waitress – which means washing up, combined with making beds and chambermaiding – was so hard that you couldn't do it on the tiny rations I was accustomed to. I had to eat. And I got to like the food; the chef, who owned the hotel, was very good, and the menu of a seaside boarding house seemed tasty enough to me. Roast beef on Sunday, steak-and-kidney pie on Monday. Curried eggs on Friday – that was my favourite. Enormous salads with ham and grated cheddar cheese and beetroot, Everests of potato salad. I learned how to drink, too – lager and lime in pubs, and strawberry wine at barn dances. At one of those dances I met a chap from Liverpool, who looked like Ringo, with a long fringe of black hair, a black polo neck, jeans. Steve. He liked football and *Top of the Pops* and worked as a lifeguard on the beach at Sandown. And he had a car – a red sports car. In the evenings after work he would drive me around the island – to Cowes, Ventnor, Shanklin Chine. To the Downs. How I loved that name, the Downs! So summery, so English, so Isle of Wight!

I couldn't love Steve, though, and when we kissed in the car, I felt nothing much, but I went along with it. I knew he liked me more than I liked him, and I felt sorry for him because of that. But I assumed that was how it would be for me from now on. I wasn't all that sorry.

(That wasn't true, as it turned out. But it was never like the Seán summer again.)

Seán didn't break it off with me in the normal way. There is a normal way, even if it's not easy. Have a serious, sad talk. Write a note. Even make a phone call. But he didn't do any of these things. He never actually told me he had another girlfriend. I found out about Rebecca when I saw her on the back of his bike on the first day of my second year in college. The writing had been on the wall for months and I hadn't read it, but when I saw her, with his helmet on her long, fair hair, glued to him like a limpet, I knew I had lost him forever. I didn't need the confirmation I got all too soon of seeing them arm in arm, walking down the main concourse of Belfield.

But I wanted to hear him say something. I wanted to hear his voice.

On the second day of term I saw him – and Rebecca – eating lunch in the canteen. (I was still eating lunches then myself.) So, with my legs trembling, everything trembling, I approached him.

'Hi, can I talk to you?' I glanced at the girl and she looked at me distastefully, as if I were milk that had turned sour.

'No,' he said bluntly, and attended to his chips and burger.

I didn't say another word. I walked out of the crowded canteen. I ran away.

In my memory I replayed this scene very often during the year after he had left me. I relived the horror of it, and the embarrassment, both of which were acute. It was not, though, until about thirty years later that I rewrote my script. I realised then, suddenly, that I could have handled it in a different way. I could have made a scene. I could have shamed him, there, in front of Rebecca, in front of the whole college. 'What is the meaning of this?' I could have roared (or I could have asked in a calm, deadly voice – there was more than one version of the episode). 'You were kissing me in the mountains last week. Why haven't you contacted me since then?'

I wouldn't have got him back. But I could have made plenty of trouble for him. I could have made trouble for Rebecca and there might have been some satisfaction for me in that, some salvation of pride, some pleasure in revenge.

But it didn't occur to me that I could fight back, or ask for anything, even a word. The only thing I wanted to do was disappear, try to become invisible, and fade off the face of the earth.

When I got back to Dublin, I was tanned and filled out. Everyone said I looked wonderful, although I could read behind their eyes and see that some of them were thinking, My, hasn't she put on weight. (I hadn't put on much. A stone. I didn't care. I liked my brown skin and my short hair and my tanned legs, and I'd bought lots of sassy, dolly bird clothes in London on the way home, to show myself off.)

I asked my father to teach me to drive. He said yes, and on Sundays he brought me to the carpark in college – a place unofficially designated as a weekend driving school by the residents of the local suburbs – and gave me lessons in the car he had then, an Anglia, with a strange inverted back window, fourteen years old and rusting.

There was no question of putting me on his insurance policy. He would never have dreamed of sharing his car with anyone; he would as soon have shared his underpants or toothbrush. He didn't particularly relish me taking the wheel for the supervised lessons, either, but that sacrifice he was willing to make because he believed that everyone should have their own means of locomotion (he believed in private transport more than he believed in education, or perhaps in anything).

By Christmas I could drive from college to home and back again (uninsured, too). Then my mother, who was thrilled that I ate food again and had stopped moping about Seán – we never mentioned his death – had a bright idea. She went to a garage in town – it was over on the north side, a big Ford dealer – and bought a Cortina, huge and shiny, silver blue. It was not brand new, it had been a showroom model, but it was the newest and best car we'd ever had. She didn't tell my father about it until she'd paid for it. Then he had to go over there on the bus and drive it home; she didn't drive herself.

The Cortina was for him – and her, he continued to drive

her everywhere. (It was fine, it seemed, not to drive if you had a husband to chauffeur you around, but my father was preparing me for a single life, just in case.) I got the ancient Anglia as my Christmas present.

Hardly any students had their own cars then, especially if they were girls.

During second year, one of the things I did to try to get over Seán was join the drama society. I auditioned and got a part in a production of *Medea*. It wasn't a real part – it was in the chorus. I was so preoccupied with my problems that I hardly understood what was going on in the play, and I mimed many of the lines I was supposed to chant, with a large choir of women. (I think everyone who auditioned was given a part in the chorus, so it didn't matter that I wasn't pulling my weight.) Medea was played by a girl with an aquiline nose and black frizzy hair, and she was made up to look like a real witch. I had no sympathy with her, as she stood centre stage, ranting and screaming her head off in a stream of invective that I couldn't take in. If I'd listened more carefully, I might have gained something from the play, catharsis even, but I was too hungry to focus on it.

The only scene that impressed me was the most horrible scene in all of drama – where Medea sends the gift of the poisoned dress and crown to Creon's daughter, using her own two children as go-betweens, and Creon's daughter tries them on, prinking before the mirror, and then burns to death in agony. With her, I sympathised – who could not? I could feel the strange poisonous burning on my own skin.

We had no children in our production. We were all students – we had no access to children, or interest in having anything to do with them. (You would think, to hear us discuss the problem of the children, that we hardly knew what a child was.) The director of the play asked me to step out from the chorus and carry the gift from Medea to Creon's daughter – they had someone playing her part behind a muslin curtain. I was happy to do something that was so effortless. I glided out, like a wraith, and took the dress and crown from the black-haired Medea, and walked to the curtain where Creon's daughter waited, also thin as a wraith in a white nightdress. She had fair hair, softly curly, and was as dainty and translucent as a glass doll. (This scene is supposed to happen offstage. But our director, like many others, couldn't resist dramatising it.)

Creon's daughter has no name in the play, and no speaking part. But some sources say that she was called Glauce. That sounds ugly, but it has a nice meaning. Owl. The noun glaucoma, a disease of the eye, derives from it, I think, as does the adjective glaucous, which I always thought meant green, but means greyish-green, the colour of army tanks, and certain lichens.

The Coast of Wales

Opposite the flowerbed, which dazzles the eye with crimson primroses and tulips the precise pink of dentures, a woman in a yellow anorak is bent over a tap. As she fills her blue watering can, her small dog waits – he's a Yorkie or a Scottie, one of those shaggy little 'ie' dogs. He is silent, which is good because dogs aren't allowed in here. Patiently, he stares at the tap.

It's attached to a slim concrete post and is almost invisible against the background of stone and milky misty sky. That's why I never noticed it before. Now this woman with the black dog illuminates it with that yellow anorak of hers. There's something new to learn every time I come here. For instance, I've found out that the potted plants I place carefully on the clay dry up very quickly, even when it rains. You need to come and water them every few days. Some people know this and they've rigged up clever permanent contraptions: containers like stone window boxes, which they place on the concrete plinth, and fill with plants in season. It would be easier if you could sow something directly into the soil, but that's against the regulations.

The reason is that this is a lawn cemetery. That's another thing I've learned: the term 'lawn cemetery', and what it means, which is that grass grows on the graves. And that men from the county council cut this grass. They've been mowing regularly ever since spring got going, six weeks ago. These grass cutters also remove any unpermitted decorations – for example, teddy bears and plastic angels, Santa Clauses – from the graves, and throw them into the big skip by the gate. They also throw away withered flowers. You have to keep a close watch on your plants to make sure they don't decide to consign them to the skip before they're dead. All this cutting and throwing away, however, means the place is well kept. On sunny days it can look almost nice, at least after you get used to it.

I brought water in a bottle in my rucksack. And now I find out there's no need to carry water all the way from home. Water is heavier than it looks when it comes dancing out of the tap, light as stars.

This is what the graveyard looks like: an enormous housing estate, bisected by a thoroughfare. You can drive on this, and some people do, but I think that's inappropriate, like driving on a beach. Off this central artery are the cul-de-sacs, about twenty on each side. Hundreds of straight lines of graves, arranged symmetrically like boxy houses, with pocket handkerchief lawns in front of each one. True, there is a certain amount of variation in the headstones, as there is in houses on estates, but, as with them, diversity is limited by planning restrictions. The headstones must not be higher than four feet and so they all measure exactly four feet – naturally everyone goes for as much height as they can get. Apart from this, some choice is permitted, although all headstone designs and inscriptions have to be vetted by the authorities. They're obviously tolerant; there are some pretty unusual headstones around. You hesitate to use the words 'bad taste' in connection with death – another thing I've learned. Don't be judgemental about trivial things (and everything is trivial, by comparison with what's going on in this place). But I can't warm to the shiny slabs with gold inscriptions and smug angels on top. The white marble is nicer, even when it comes with expressions of profound sentiments in lines apparently plagiarised from country and western songs, or the 'Funny Stories' page of *Our Boys*.

His Life a Beautiful Memory, His Absence a Silent Grief.

Take care of Tom, Lord, as he Did Us, With Lots of Love and Little Fuss.

My favourites are the simple stones, plain grey, which have become more common, I'm pleased to report, over the past four or five years. (It's easy to date fashions in a graveyard.)

That's what I ordered for you. The style called 'boulder', the natural look that suits a man who wore tweed and spoke correct Irish, Welsh and Scots Gaelic. I thought it was a personal choice, but I've discovered that most of the poets and writers, teachers and academics are buried under similar stones. There's only one unique monument in the entire place: a wide slab of pinkish granite, thin as a butterfly's wing. Only a name and a date inscribed on it in tiny Times New Roman.

The architect who designed Belfield.

Of course.

To tell the truth, I wouldn't mind one of those. A high modernist headstone that looks as if it were imported, at great expense, from Finland or some other crucible of understated good taste. But you could copy it and the next thing IKEA would be supplying the same thing in a flat-pack at a fraction of the cost. They'd be all over the place.

I guess I'll stick with the country life look.

Unlike you, I know precisely how and where I will be buried (unless I am destroyed in a plane crash or murdered and chopped up into little bits and my body never found). I'll be under a homespun boulder on Row C, in the section called St Mark's, down near the wall and the old Church of Ireland. I thought when I was shown the spot that it was pretty, because it was in the shelter of the old church, with its bell tower and stone walls. The newer section of the graveyard, St Elizabeth's, didn't appeal to me one bit. It's a huge flat field that stretches despondently to the Irish Sea. The undertaker, who encouraged me to think very carefully before I made a decision, pointed out that as time went on St Elizabeth's would look 'less bleak'. 'The trees will grow,' he said, in his mild, and mildly ironic tone. He takes death in his stride, and thinks in the longer term.

But how much time have I got?

From St Mark's there is a fine view of the Dublin Mountains, today a rich eggy yellow, even in the milky haze. Easter egg time, almost everything in nature is yellow. Not only has it a fine view, always desirable in houses or graves, St Mark's also has the virtue of age, being in the oldest part of the graveyard, where unburnt corpses can no longer be buried – there's not enough room. For them, poor skeletons, no choice. It's St Elizabeth's; they'll have to grin and bear it, and wait for the trees to grow. But there's still space for little urns of ashes in the old section, just because not that many Dubliners choose cremation, and of those that do, many don't get a grave – their ashes are scattered in some scenic spot where they used to go on their holidays, or kept at home on the mantelpiece. Some of yours are at home too. I'm planning to scatter them on a nice headland near the place where we went on holiday on Anglesey where almost everyone speaks Welsh. But I rather like having them in the house so I'll probably hold on to some. That means your ashes will be in three different places. There's no rule against it; that's the beauty of ashes. You could never dismember a body and bury bits in various places – except in very exceptional circumstances, such as Daniel O'Connell's.

I'd have thought such ideas unhealthy, even disgusting. And terrifying. Before. Life is for the living, was my motto, not that I expressed it one way or the other. But now the dead are always on my mind and I'm quite an expert on graves and graveyards. I could set up an online advice centre and may do that when I get over your death. I have quite a lot of plans for that time, for the time when I get over it, when my energy returns and I start out on a new life as a person who has lost her husband but has survived. A widow, to use that word all widows I have met – they're all over the place – can't stand. People tell me that you'd want me to start a new life, to be happy. I suppose it is a safe bet that you wouldn't want me to be actively miserable. You didn't get a chance to express any preferences one way or the other, but others step into the breach: You should get a dog. Aren't you lucky it all happened so quickly? A massage would make you feel so much better. The sort of things we'd have a good laugh at, between ourselves, over dinner. I reckon we ate about 14,000 dinners together and so had at least 14,000 good laughs; 28,000? More. It would be so great to have just one more dinner so I could tell you about all that's been happening, relay all the comments: the sublime, the absurd, the in-between.

Quite a long dinner, we'd need, to tell the whole story.

They mean well.

St Mark's is not really as nice as I first thought. The church and the ivy-covered wall block the sun in the afternoon, so our grave is often in cold shade. Today, for once, I came in the morning, and the sun is shining on you. I take my plastic water bottle out of my rucksack and pour water on the purple flower, a senettia, and the white, a chrysanthemum. It's not the kind of flower you liked, or I like, but it was the only thing in the flower shop that looked healthy enough to survive in this graveyard for any length of time. And it has lasted and looks quite good here on the grave, which needs all the flowers it can get. The boulder hasn't come yet – they're waiting for a good block of granite. As if blocks of granite come rolling down the hill when they feel like it. You'd think they'd have a regular supplier. In the meantime all you have is a little wooden marker with your name on it, and dates. It has been a great help to me, especially at the beginning when I couldn't remember where the grave was. It took me a while to remember to turn left at Mary Byrne's grave, which is next to that of Enrico Cafolla, Professor of Music – easier to remember than Mary Byrne, beloved wife, Mum and Nana. (The word 'granny' never appears on headstones.) I never go astray now.

There isn't enough water in the bottle. The flowers are alive, but thirsty. The white petals of the chrysanthemum are turning to straw. The senettia is such a strong regal purple, a deep dyed purple, that its thin, blade-like petals could never turn brown, but they're getting limp. I decide to walk back to the tap and get more water. It'll take about ten minutes, to go there and back, but I have plenty of time now.

That is another thing. Before I had no time for anything. Now times seems to stretch endlessly in front of me, like the sea out there in front of the railway. But the sense of a wide expanse of ocean is an illusion. There is a coast that you can't see over the horizon. Wales. The land I love because it brought us such luck. After four years' waiting, we conceived a child there, on the first night of a holiday at Beaumaris. It's a mere sixty-six (nautical) miles away. Just because you can't see it doesn't mean it doesn't exist. And it's closer than, say, Ballinasloe.

As I go back towards the tap, I notice the woman I saw earlier. The woman in the yellow anorak. She's busy at a grave. No doubt she's a widow, like me, like most of the graveyard visitors, who spent their lives taking care of husbands and have no intention of stopping now, just because they're dead. So they keep coming to the graves to pull up the weeds, to water the flowers, to plant new things. The woman in the yellow anorak is touching her headstone with both hands and talking to it. As I pass, I hear what she's saying: 'Sandra came to dinner yesterday and we watched *Fair City*. I miss you so much, my dearest darling.'

The dog is nowhere to be seen.

The tap.

That's where the dog is, tied to the concrete post by his leash. He's a Scottie, I can see it now, I remember the difference. Black, with that long, sceptical, Scottish head.

'Hi, little dog,' I say. 'Excuse me while I fill this empty ginger ale bottle with water.'

I turn on the tap and squeeze the mouth of the bottle so it fits over the lip of the tap. This is not a good idea.

Just then, a hearse comes through the gate, followed by two black limousines; after them the straggle of ordinary cars. A few people stand at the corner, paying their respects as the hearse passes and swings quietly around the corner, making for St Elizabeth's.

I used to hate the sight of a hearse. My heart would sink if I met one on the road. But I no longer fear them now that I've met death face to face, tried to shoo it away, and lost the battle. Now I can cast a cold eye on every hearse that passes by, because I've driven behind yours.

Just as the hearse turns around the corner, this thing happens. The plastic bottle dislodges from the tap and a strong gush of water splashes on to the dog. Startled by the sudden cold shower, he breaks free. He can't have been tied very tightly. Off he dashes, in the direction of the woman in the yellow anorak.

And he runs right under the second big limousine, the one which probably contains the more distant relatives who are nevertheless too important to come in their own cars. I see him, all the funeral followers on the sidelines see him. The only person who does not see him is the driver of the limousine. He is such a tiny dog, the size of a well-fed rat. Dogs aren't allowed in the graveyard. The driver isn't expecting one to run out in front of him.

How ghastly. First your husband, then your dog.

This had occurred to me, in connection with dogs. And cats. Their mortality. If I get a dog, as so many people advise, it will die sometime. And by the time it dies, I will have grown to love it, even though a dog is no substitute for a husband. I'd be bereaved all over again in a different way. An easier way. But bereavement is never easy.

The hearse glides slowly along the road to Saint Elizabeth's. The first limousine turns the corner and follows it, and the second limousine turns too.

The driver still doesn't realise he has just run over a widow's dog.

But no.

No. It's OK. The dog is OK.

The car passed over him and just left him behind like a jellyfish on the beach when the tide goes out. Alive, with no more than an expression of mild surprise on his narrow face. He scampers off over the graves towards the spot where the woman he loves, who has seen none of this, is busily engaged in a conversation with someone she loves but who doesn't exist.

Animals don't know what we humans know.

All the people standing by the side of the road, including me, laugh, some more heartily than others.

'His lucky day,' someone says.

A short pause. We savour the exquisite taste of profound relief and consider the observation.

Trite but true like most of the clichés. There's quite a bit of luck involved, when it comes to the crunch, in matters of life and death.

I turn off the tap.

Then I kick the bottle and let the water spill over into the bed of crimson primroses, tulips the exact colour of dentures. I decide not to return to our grave. It's pointless. Unless the brash senettia, the weary chrysanthemum, get some rain and manage to soak it up, nothing I can do will keep them alive.

The mourners shake themselves, remember why they're here, and start to process sedately along the track that leads to St Elizabeth's, the railway line, and the Irish Sea. The haze has burnt off now and the water sparkles, blue as silk close to land, and a deep dark indigo, like a firm line of ink, on the horizon.

You still can't see Wales. But it is there, all right.

New Zealand Flax

The early purple orchids are plentiful this year. So plentiful that Frida wonders if they really are as special and rare as she has always believed. In her field they're as common as the other flowers of June, the clover, the buttercups. The yellow one, bird's-foot trefoil, sometimes called scrambled egg. Or, less meaningfully, bacon and eggs. Still, she swerves around any patch of grass graced by the chubby little orchids – turgid, phallic, episcopally purple – but mercilessly slices through buttercups and clover (the latter is the bees' favourite thing, and smells nicer than the orchids, when the sun shines.) Little islands of long grass with an orchid, or two or six, dot the 'lawn' – that's not the right name for it. The patch of field that she cuts, so it's like a pond of short grass in a forest of long rough stuff.

'Why don't you get someone to do it?' Her son is exasperated on the phone. Perhaps a tad guilty? He hasn't been down here in over a year, to cut grass or do anything else. It's time to paint the walls, and the windows, and he likes doing that. He says. 'You shouldn't be going all the way down there just to *cut the grass.*'

'I'll get somebody,' she says, 'before I leave.'

She has figured out, recently, that the best way of dealing with advice from him, or anyone, is to pretend to take it. Some people realise this when they're four years old, but better late than never.

The thing is, having to cut the grass provides her with a reason for coming down. That's why she doesn't get a boy or a man to do it. That, and the cost, although it would most likely cost less than the price of the petrol for the drive down and back. And then, a man or a boy on one of the lawnmowers that look like toy tractors would not avoid the early purple orchids, or the two little hydrangea bushes, or the clumps of New Zealand flax that she planted last year and that have survived the winter storms, the spring storms, and the early summer storms. *Barely* survived. The spikes of flax look like the soldiers who came home from the trenches, battered, their skin burnt, and minus a couple of limbs. A man or a boy speeding around the field on a big lawnmower would certainly cut them down. A man or a boy wouldn't even see them.

Well. There is only one other person on earth who would see those clumps of pathetic flax.

Did she think, *on earth*?

She wipes the wheels and puts the lawnmower back in the garage. Just come and take a look, would you? When the sun goes down.

The lawnmower feels wounded. It has been rattled – the grass was more than a foot high; no ordinary lawnmower should have to deal with such stuff; it was a job for a big lump of farm machinery, a combine harvester maybe.

The blade may have loosened. After two hours pushing against the gradient, the last thing Frida wants to do is examine the insides of the lawnmower. But she forces herself to take a look.

Yes. There is a screw loose on one of the wheels. Now, where does he keep the toolbox?

The grass was so long because she has been away for the month of May. You can't let the grass grow for the month of May and expect anything other than a hayfield. She's been in Finland; she's not sure why. Since this time last year she has travelled to all the countries Elk had ever lived in, or loved. Four or five. There have been various reasons for going to the different countries: a book launch, a sixtieth birthday party, a conference. A funeral. But there was always another reason under the surface, always exactly the same reason. Dreams have an overt narrative, which usually repeats random bits and pieces of your recent conscious experience, and a latent one, a broken record churning out the same old message for all of your life. Apparently her waking life is now operating on the same principle as her dream life.

This doesn't particularly surprise her.

Why travel? To get away from Elk, on the one hand, and to look for him, on the other. Why else go to his places, far-flung northern islands and archipelagos, rather than perfectly nice warm countries that might cheer her up? The only reason for the choice, which seemed not like a choice, was that he might be far away in the north, hidden in the deep evergreen forest, or sitting on the edge of a lake, fishing for pike? Or climbing the side of a volcano?

Maybe he's here, in the south of Ireland, in the cottage in Kerry, in the library, or sitting on the side of the ancient volcano at the back of the house, looking out at the Great Blasket?

The red toolbox is in the corner at the back, hidden

behind an old dustbin. She takes out a screwdriver and tightens the loose nut. When she is replacing the tool in the box, something catches her eye.

A bottle of wine.

Empty?

No. It's a Chablis. 2007.

They must have bought it one year – 2008? – on the way down from the farm shop in Nenagh where they often stopped for a coffee and to buy treats. Cheese from France, country butter from Tipperary. Mango chutney with caramelised onions that somebody in Cloughjordan makes. Mostly they drank the wine on the first night. But he must have tucked this one away in the garage for a special occasion and forgotten about it.

Or maybe she did that herself.

Once a year he wanted to drive to Brandon Creek; often on a Sunday afternoon when there was that Sunday-afternoon feeling, that mix of nostalgia (for what? For nothing you can put your finger on) and boredom. The sound of football commentaries, wildly excited, from car windows and cottage windows, which filled Frida with a strange ennui, a longing to escape to somewhere, she knew not where, even when she was eight years old. One of the great things about Elk was that he couldn't care less about football, didn't even know that that was an unusual gift, in a man.

But even so.

Let's go to Brandon Creek.

Cuas an Bhodaigh. St Brendan is supposed to have sailed from there, in a *naomhóg* and landed in America. Who knows? He could have landed in Iceland, like the monks from Teelin. But there is another tale associated with it, and that's what drew Elk to it. The story of the Big Bodach, a sea man who came sweeping in from the ocean and made love to a woman who was swimming there. Raped? But she fell in love with him; she went down to the water every day to meet him, so it was not rape, apparently. This woman had been married for seven years, but had no child. When the deed was done the water man walked back into the water and she never saw him again. But nine months later she gave birth to a son who was half human and half merman, as only she knew. The son had a problem: he could never sleep.

'The Devil's Son as Priest' it's called in the international index of tales. Although he's not a devil, just not human. Not someone you should be consorting with.

Reading it for the tenth time, it occurred to her that the man from the sea may be the father-in-law of the woman. The story may be about incest. She never noticed this aspect until now. You see something new every time you read a story, if it is any good.

One thing she often noticed: nobody went for a swim in Brandon Creek. It's a long narrow inlet, a fjordful of black water, fathoms deep, a ravine, a chasm, loomed over by Mount Brandon at the back and by black cliffs on each side. The creek crashes angrily down into the fjord, and the water slurps ominously into eerie crevices in the rock. There's no beach of any kind.

It's like an entrance to another world – and not a very nice one, if the gateway is anything to go by. You can understand that Brendan, obviously fond of high drama, would sail from here to the unknown, in mythology, and that a big *bodach* from beneath the wave, a merman, Neptune, would emerge here. Here, rather than some golden sandy cove or long stretch where children play in the frilly shallows and where any normal woman would go for her dip.

*

Frida parks the car high above the creek, in a sort of lay-by, and walks down a winding boreen to the water. A young couple are on the way up, the girl with long black hair, the boy a redhead. They are dancing up the road, laughing, waltzing and humming like bees in the sunshine. Or two butterflies. They don't see her at all, have eyes only for one another.

At the start of the pier, Kerry County Council has a warning: Do Not Enter This Pier if the Sea is High. DANGEROUS. The sea isn't high on this fine summer's evening. Down to the end of the pier she goes. There's a car parked on it. People drive the whole way down sometimes; it always amazes her. They hate walking so much, they'd rather risk drowning. A man in a navy blue jumper. Hello. A bit cheeky. Lovely day. She doesn't look at his face, but walks to the end and looks down into the water. It's not black when you're beside it. Transparent. Seaweed, and fishes, a flip-flop or something thrown away.

Behind her, she can sense the man in the blue jumper.

His eyes on her back.

She becomes conscious of how lonely it is here, at Cuas an Bhodaigh. She's alone at the end of a pier, with deep black water all around. This happens a lot. She's in a place she likes, on her own, and she suddenly feels, I shouldn't be here. Why am I here?

She turns and goes back along the pier and up the winding hill to her own car.

The man is at the back of his car as she approaches, doing something in the boot. She walks past, trying to look carefree.

'Here!' he hails her again.

She jumps out of her skin.

312

'Have you any use for crab claws?' He extends a plastic bag full of them. 'I've more than I need.'

'Thanks,' she takes the bag, and forces a smile. Elk loves crab claws, and so does she.

'A treat for your tea.'

'Thanks!' she repeats. 'We like them. Thanks.'

She walks slowly up the hill. The young couple have disappeared. Before she gets into her car she looks down at the inlet. The man in the blue jumper is reversing, down the slip, towards the water. She can hear it lapping and slapping against the stone, friendly, before it deepens and becomes a dark other world.

They'll have a nice dinner to celebrate the cutting of the grass and the survival of the New Zealand flax. She has the crab claws and the wine. New potatoes and salad and spinach. Lemon, oregano.

She peels the potatoes, puts them on. Slices spring onions and tomatoes; chops parsley. Spreads the white tablecloth, and sets it with the best cutlery she can find. Flowers. Buttercups, clover, and two of the orchids, which may be a protected species but since she has saved the lives of about fifty of them today her guilt is minimal. In the small glass jar they look lovely against the snow of the cloth. When it gets dark – which won't be till about half past ten – she will light the white candle.

She has Beethoven's 'Pastorale' beside the CD player for when dinner is ready. One of his favourites. One of everyone's favourites. Now she's listening to Kathleen Ferrier's hits although she shouldn't, because it opens with 'Blow the Wind Southerly', a song of longing for a sailor who won't come home, because he is drowned. Blow the

313

wind southerly, southerly, southerly. Blow, bonny breeze, my lover to me. And somewhere on the CD – it is towards the end – is Orfeo's lament for Euridice. What is life if thou art dead? The saddest song in the world. Tradition doesn't hold back on emotion and neither does opera, though few get as close to the bone as Gluck.

She travelled to get away, to look for something, to forget and to remember. But coming home all she wanted was to tell him about her travels. Coming home, she realised that the main point of them was to report them back. Actually, she usually realised that about two days in, but batted away the thought.

Which is why she has invited him to dinner tonight. There were so many aspects of them that only he would want to hear about. She wants to ask him about the loan words, how the Finns seemed to drop the 's' from some words they borrowed from Swedish. *Kuola* from *skole*, for instance. *Tie* instead of *stig*. And other words that are so strange. He would know why the Finns call a book *kirj*. You'd expect the word for book to come from Latin, or Greek, or Swedish, or even Russian. Where did they get *kirj* from?

Who cares about this sort of stuff?

Elk and Frida.

Into the thick goblets from the local pottery she pours the old wine. Sits down, and raises her goblet.

'*Kippis!*' she says, to the empty chair opposite her.

The Finnish for *sláinte*.

She sips the wine.

'It is very good,' she says. 'I can never sort out what the Finns did during the Second World War. Can you explain? So I get it straight?'

The sun is still high, in the south-west, over the island

they call the Dead Man. Frida prefers the other name, the Northern Island.

Euridice! *Eurid eeeeeeche.*

What is life without your love?

At last the sun starts to sink behind the Northern Island. Elk loved it when they showed that scene on RTÉ, back in the days when they played the national anthem at close of programming.

The blue of the night.

And when the sun slides down behind the Dead Man he comes out of the study and sits in his own place at the table.

'Will you have some wine?'

He looks at the bottle as if he has never seen one before. Puzzled, shakes his head.

He looks like himself. Not pale and thin as he was in the last year, or panic-stricken as on the last days in the hospital, with his horribly swollen stomach and tubes shoved down his throat. He's wearing his navy blue jumper, which is odd, because that's the jumper she keeps under her pillow at home in the city.

'Now you're here I don't know what to say to you.'

She leans over to take his hand. His long fingers, thin and agile from a lifetime of typing, like a pianist's. But he pulls it away, not unkindly.

'Well.' She says the first thing that comes to her head. And yet she knows the time is valuable, like the time you've got for a job interview. You've only got half an hour so don't waste it saying unimpressive things. 'I miss you.'

'Yes, my darling.' His voice is his voice. Soft, round, robust, male, like a mellow burgundy. Like a purple orchid. 'Well, I am glad to hear that, even if it is selfish.'

'I miss you a lot.'

No need to repeat yourself.

'Yes, yes. It's terrible.' He sighs. 'But spilt milk.'

'I went to Finland.'

'Good for you! *Puhutteko suomea?*'

'*Anteeksi! Minä en puhu suomea.*'

'Good woman!'

'That's all I learnt.'

'Did you have a sauna?'

'Nearly every day. You'd have loved that. We should have got one, for your back.'

He is blurred, like a photograph that is not in focus. Sometimes the photos are like that, on the computer, and then after a little while they swim into clarity.

'I was listening to that song, Euridice.'

'Maybe you could find something more cheerful?'

'I've got ABBA's *Greatest Hits* in the car.'

'*Ush!*'

'I cut the grass yesterday. I came down specially to do it. It was over a foot long.'

'My dear little darling.' Nobody ever calls her that any more. She's not even little. 'But you shouldn't come down here just to cut the grass. Why don't you get someone to do it?'

'I will,' she promises.

There is plenty to tell him. About the funeral. About the tributes, the obituaries – the solemn ones and the funny ones. That he has a new grandchild and that their other son is going to get married at the end of the summer. And especially that she has found out how much she loves him, that she always loved him and should have told him that more often. She should have told him that every minute. She needs to tell him these things, and to ask several more practical questions. Where is the article about 'The Dead Lover's Return'? The introduction to the book he was collaborating on with the guy in Galway? Is the bodach in that story the father-in-law of the woman? What used he do on Sundays, before they were married?

That's before she even gets to the big issue.

'I got a man to level the field.'

He looks out the window. The field is not actually very level. The man came with a digger or a bulldozer or something and dug it up, then put some grass seed in last August. It cost about a thousand euro but nobody has noticed that it is any different from before. Apart from Frida herself.

He walks to the window.

'It's very nice, my darling!'

He doesn't comment on the New Zealand flax. She points its spikes out to him, down by the septic tank. They look like nothing. Like a few rushes that the lawnmower missed.

'They're a bit scrawny but they'll get bigger and make a shelter belt and then I can grow other things.'

'That will be just lovely, won't it?'

He can be ironic and kind at the same time.

There is one thing she really has to tell him. She can't say it so she puts on the CD and the voice comes pouring into the dim room.

'What is life if thou art dead?'

He leans over, and his face is close to her, his woollen jumper.

'Dear darling. I miss you too.' He looks around the room, at the fireplace and the bookshelves and the pictures. 'I miss everything. And there is so much work I didn't get done.' For the first time his face is sad. 'But you don't want to come with me.'

'I do.'

It strikes her that this is the solution. It's simple.

'No, dear darling. You went to Finland. You cut the grass. And you've planted those … scraggy things!'

'New Zealand flax.'

He laughs.

'Yes, New Zealand flax! You've got to look after the New Zealand flax, and make sure it grows big and beautiful.'

Frida doesn't know why it has that name. It looks nothing like ordinary flax, that rare and beautiful blue corn from which linen is made. New Zealand flax is not blue, and its flowers look like withered prunes. It never flowers in this climate, and looks like a handful of green swords, rusty from the west wind, with pointed tips that cut you if you touch them. There's only one reason for planting it.

'It survived the winter!'

'Yes, my darling, it survived the winter.'

He gets up.

'Don't go.'

Please don't go.

'Yes, I must go. Before the sun rises. You know the rules!'

He walks towards the door.

'The sun won't rise for ages.'

'It has already risen in Finland.'

She runs after him.

'Will you come back?'

He turns.

'One of us had to go first. That's the way it is.'

They warn you. Till death do us part. You hear it but you don't take it in. You throw it away, into the bin, like the wrapping paper on a beautiful present.

He puts a hand towards her shoulder, but not on it. If only he could hold her in his arms for one second!

'Make the most of the time you have left. It will be over soon enough. There's plenty of work to do.' He winks. 'You can do mine, if you don't want to do your own.'

'Yes,' she says. 'I will.'

He always gives good advice.

Imagination is supposed to be a great thing. A gift. It can conjure up, it can invent. But its creations are as nothing, really, compared to the real thing.

The man on the pier didn't reverse into the water. He attached a rope, which was dangling from the back of his car, to a small boat in which he must have been out before she came, fishing or something. And he pulled it up after him, to dry land.

Little Red

A thing Fiona does is online dating.

Not dating exactly. She hardly ever goes on an actual date. But she writes quite a lot of messages to people on a site called Never Too Late. Sometimes the messages are one line long. Sometimes they are just those little smiley things: emojis. You can also send a 'wave' or a 'wink'. Fiona sends a lot of winks, because it's a new experience for her. She has never winked in real life, with her eye, even though her eye is perfectly capable of performing the action and nobody has ever told her not to. Winking. A male thing.

This is how all that started.

A year ago she was flying back to Dublin from a trade fair in Lisbon. It was May, but it had been unseasonably cold, so she was dressed in her winter work 'n' travel clothes. Black with a splash. Black jacket, black trousers. Black boots. (The splash is her bag, which is red.)

As Fiona was making her way to a free seat in the departure lounge, a woman doing the same thing dropped her glasses on the floor, and sighed. 'Feckit!' Fiona put down her stuff, picked up the glasses, and handed them to the woman. 'Thanks, pet!'

She was large, the woman who said feckit. Dressed in white trousers and pink flowery blouse.

'You're very good!'

Fiona nodded.

The woman sat down with a group of companions. Companions who were in good humour and expressed this at a high volume. Fiona sat as far away from them as she could and buried her head in her book – which was not a real book but an ebook. 'I only use it when travelling,' Fiona lied to people – colleagues in the book trade whose lives were passionately devoted to the preservation of the traditional book in the face of competition from non-traditional books and all the innumerable other post-Gutenberg ways of disseminating stories and information. Everyone she knew believed that a book printed on paper and bound in paper or cardboard (not to mention leather) was a precious and beautiful thing, a sacred thing. They all had Kindles but only for travelling (to book fairs and writers' festivals and, of course, ordinary holidays). Actually Fiona uses hers all the time. 'It's just so handy!' But it has disadvantages. It's hard to 'bury your head' in a Kindle, and it doesn't send out the signal at which a real book is adept: 'Do not disturb this reader, who is lost in another world, buried in her book.'

She wasn't lost. Far from it. Keeping her eyes on the screen she eavesdropped eagerly on the woman talking to her friends, regaling them with stories. Cushy Butterfield, Fiona named her, in the privacy of her own head. The name just popped in, from nowhere it seemed, although she knows perfectly well that all names, all images, all ideas, actually come from somewhere, somewhere in the thorny forest of your past, until out of the blue something hacks in and wakes them up.

Often in the departure lounge of an airport, waiting for the flight to Dublin, Fiona's heart sank when she heard the voices of her compatriots. The voices of the Others, the foreigners – their accents, their languages, always sounded beautiful to her ears, light and magical like fairy music. All those lovely words that she didn't understand. By comparison, the familiar flat accents of Dublin fell like heavy rain pounding on the roof on a dark November day. (Is she a snob?) For a while, for a while – until she got used to it again, until their humour, their slagging, cheered her up again, made her feel at home. She didn't feel like that now, not yet. And where did she feel at home? Where she had last felt at home was at home, in her house, with her husband. Unfortunately he was no longer at home. Not at the house they had called home together for twenty-five years. He had fallen deeply in love with someone he had met at a book fair in Slovenia five years ago. It was, he said, a love that couldn't be denied. So ridiculous, so bizarre, so unbelievable. The divorce, solid as lead, had come through earlier this year, five years after he moved to Trieste, where the other woman worked – she is Italian, her name is Lucia, she works in a bank. (So what was she doing at the book fair? 'She's a reader,' he replied. 'You know, Fiona. A human being who actually reads fiction even though she doesn't write it or criticise it or teach it.' Or sell it, like Fiona. He forgot that. Anyway the implication was that Lucia was an exceedingly rare type of human being, worth abandoning your wife of thirty years for.)

On the plane Fiona found herself sitting right beside Cushy Butterfield. What are the chances of that? Fiona had the aisle seat. Cushy Butterfield was in the middle, and a man – Cushy's husband, no doubt – was at the window. At least I'm not in the middle, thought Fiona. She nodded to Cushy, in the interests of politeness, then pulled out her Kindle and continued reading (Rachel Cusk, a sort of auto-fiction novel, the very latest fashion – the hybrid car of the written word). She observes the clichéd rule: don't engage in conversation with a fellow passenger until twenty minutes before landing, and usually not then either. She was aware that she missed many good biographical stories but she didn't want to pay the price of those, which could be hearing uninteresting stories for hours, and being expected to offer her own in exchange. Fiona couldn't do that. She possesses stories – who does not? – but it goes against her nature to confide in strangers, and most other people as well.

After about half an hour the crew came around with the food and drinks trolley. She was a little bit hungry. But she couldn't face the cheese and ham panini, the chicken-and-stuffing sandwich. She ordered instead a little bottle of wine and a Ritz cracker with Cheddar cheese – a bargain snack pack. After the food of Portugal – the little custard tarts, the fresh sardines, the wines of Douro and Alentejo – this would taste pathetic. But she needed a break from the book.

Cushy Butterfield got four little bottles of wine, two for herself and two for her husband.

Fiona had never seen anyone doing that before. Most fliers didn't buy the wine at all these days. They drank their own bottles of water. She felt a gush of empathy for Cushy. A woman who didn't mind passing the time on the plane with a drink, or being mildly outrageous.

'*Sláinte!*' Fiona raised her plastic glass to her.

'*Sláinte!*' Cushy raised hers.

The husband was asleep.

'I'm Molly,' Cushy said.

Fiona introduced herself.

'Were you on holidays?'

Do I look like it? Fiona told her she had been at a conference. Something to do with work. She never liked to tell people what her work was. And, like most people, Cushy was too polite to ask directly. She herself was a teacher, retired. She – Cushy-Molly – had been on a holiday with a group, the Grey Explorers. They had had a great time. She gave the name of the resort where they'd been based – not far from Lisbon. Fiona had been there, on an afternoon's outing, yesterday, with one of the organisers of the conference.

When Cushy moved on to the second bottle of wine, Fiona told her a bit about herself. (She had also finished her first bottle.) 'Get yourself another,' said Cushy. 'There isn't much in these little bottles.'

Fiona had never rung the bell in a plane before, for anything, even though she flies several times a year. But she rang it and got a second little bottle of red.

Cushy told her about a friend of hers who was a widow. (That's not the same thing, Fiona thought. Being divorced is worse.) But she'd met a member of the trouser brigade on one of the Grey Explorers' holidays last year. 'And now they're living together!'

Yeah, yeah, yeah.

'It's time for you to meet somebody,' she went on. 'That's if you're still interested in the trouser brigade.'

Fiona said, 'I'm sixty-four.'

'Never use the "a" word,' Cushy wagged her finger at her. A? Age. 'Forget it. You're a beautiful woman.'

Some lies are good to hear.

'And he's not going to come knocking on your door and ask you for a date.'

'What do you recommend?'

The Grey Explorers. Or … one of those online things.

The very next day, as soon as she got up and before she had unpacked, Fiona signed up for a dating agency. She provided a potted biography, answered a questionnaire about her job, hobbies, age, religion, what she was looking for in a relationship. Set up a standing order: twenty euro a month, for six months, after which you could cancel it at any time.

That was over three months ago.

She has talked to various men on the phone, and has gone out for a drink, for dinner and once to a film, with three of them. The one she felt she got on best with dropped her politely after two dates. She dropped another quite promising candidate after just one meeting and many phone calls. It's easy to let these relationships fizzle out – they even have a word for it, for dropping someone you meet online and never contacting them again. (The word is 'ghosting'.)

It did seem that most of those she met or talked to wanted more than she did. They wanted someone to replace the wife they had lost, mainly thanks to divorce, sometimes due to death. Someone to go to bed with. Without much delay. That they kissed – however chastely – on the first encounter alarmed her. (Not in a serious way; they weren't dangerous. She just wasn't used to hugging and kissing people she had known for about an hour and a half.)

She quickly figured out what she wanted. Less. Someone to meet for dinner from time to time. Someone to go to the movies with. Someone to go on holiday with. Bed? That would have to be part of the deal, obviously – although the thought of going to bed with anyone made her squirm. It's one thing when you're twenty or thirty. Forty. But sixty? Seventy? She thinks her body looks okay – although the varicose veins and the fungal toenails are best kept hidden from view, and generally are. But she can hardly have sex without taking her socks off. That's before she starts considering them. The grey-haired men with wrinkled faces and wide smiles. What does the elderly trouser brigade hide in its trousers? Does she want to find out?

Caucasian. Christian. Leaving Cert. 5' 9".

Likes: going to the cinema, music, walking.

Invariably what they are most grateful for is their families, and what they are most passionate about is sport. Mostly what they desire in a partner is warmth, affection and a good sense of humour.

Quite a few of them tick 'maybe in the future' beside the little pram symbol. This is surprising, given that they are, to a man, aged between 63 and 72 (the age group Fiona ticked when she registered).

The site gave them marks for suitability – good matches. The marks ranged from seventy upwards. Fiona thought eighty-five or so – an A when she did the Leaving – must be good, although it wasn't always clear why (Passionate about: rugby). Then she noticed a few that were graded at 125 or 130. Off the scale. Talk about grade inflation. (Where did it stop? 200? 1,000? But then, why should there be a limit? Who's setting the rules for the dating-site grades?)

A simple comparative analysis revealed that what the men with these Nobel Prize marks had in common with each other and with her was that they were atheists. So that was how the website was evaluating matches. Not on looks, interests, incomes, favourite foods. Smoking and drinking. Religion or lack of it was the key factor, the thing that would unite you with your soulmate. And, when you think about it, that made a certain amount of sense. Although souls, hers or theirs, were the last thing on their minds.

*

She is running away from a man who might be a policeman. He comes to her house, to arrest her, but she manages to escape. As fast as she can, she runs, and he gives chase. She twists and turns. There are houses, buildings, piles of rubble, bushes, convenient randomly placed pillars and posts to hide behind. (The scenario is based on one of the chase scenes in the detective dramas she is addicted to.) She feels a certain triumph, congratulating herself on her skill in eluding him. She crawls under a car and hides there. She can see his feet, passing, then stopping. He hauls her out and puts her in handcuffs.

In this dream she's not in a version of the house she lived in with her husband, or of the house she lived in with her parents, as in most dreams. She's in something that resembles her new house, the one where she lives now. After the divorce, the family house in Dublin was sold and they split the proceeds. Fiona put her furniture in storage and lived in a rented apartment for a year, which stretched to two years, while she decided where to settle down. During those years, the websites she spent hours on every evening were Daft and MyHome.ie, where you can see all the houses that are for sale in Ireland. She also spent many Saturday mornings driving around looking at houses and apartments open to view. Nothing was quite right. Then history and the personal intersected in the way it often does for people – financially. The economic recession ended. The cost of houses began to rise, slowly for a few months, then dramatically. Places doubled in price. The range of choices narrowed and it looked as if it would continue to do so if she didn't make her move rapidly. In year one of her divorce she had the option of a house or an apartment almost anywhere in Dublin. By year three, it was a small apartment on the northside or a house in a commuter town twenty or thirty miles out. She bought a bungalow by the sea, south of Wicklow town, which, her children told her, was sheer madness.

'I work from home,' she countered. 'There's a train from the town.'

'You'll be so isolated. And what about global warming? The sea will come and wash that house away in a few years.'

'I always wanted to live by the sea.'

Also, it was a nice place for the grandchildren to visit, at weekends. The sea, Brittas Bay, the Silver Strand. The sheep and the cows. (The grandchildren loved it. But they didn't visit as often as she had hoped they would.)

Here she dreams more than she used to in her old house. Something about the fresh air, it must be. Or the silence of the deep country night.

On a rainy morning she sent one of the atheists a message. *Let's meet for a coffee sometime.* Then the rain stopped and she went out to the garden to plant daffodil bulbs.

Now the wind has picked up. There's a storm brewing. She has come in and is sitting on her favourite chair, under the lamp, beside the fire, hugging a cup of coffee. The fire is not lit and neither is the lamp. Her laptop is plugged in but not on. She's staring out the window. Hardly even thinking. She finds she can sit and stare for quite long periods without being bored. It's a thing older people can do. You wouldn't call it mindfulness. Or laziness. She usen't to really understand when older people said, 'I don't have the same energy any more.' But she's beginning to get it. What is this life if, full of care, we have no time to stand and stare. No time to stand beneath the boughs and stare as long as sheep or cows. These lines have been in her head since she was about eight or nine. The poet is saying that the capacity to stare like a cow is a virtue. But is it? Really?

She is staring at something. The apple trees. The long grass – knapweed, montbretia, thistles, grass – that wild stuff. The roof of a house below. The sea. The horizon ... beyond, the coast of Wales, which you never see from here although it's not far away.

Sky ever changing, minute by minute it changes.

There's enough going on to keep her idle, sitting and staring, as long as a sheep or a cow.

And then.

A figure appears outside the patio door. He looks at her, and smiles.

Over the past ten or twenty years, everyone in Wicklow, like everyone everywhere, has got big patio doors, the better to see the view. This house is no exception. Now, from inside the house, you can see the whole shebang – fields and sea and sky and sheep and cows. But from outside the house, you can also see everything: the kitchen and living room, the sofa, the TV, the table. Fiona might as well be sitting in a shop window. She could be a plaster mannequin modelling the latest autumn fashions, as she sits there, staring at apple trees.

The man outside could be one of those men who comes to give an estimate on painting the windows, or fixing the TV, or cleaning out the septic tank. It's Sunday, so that is unlikely. But here in the country they can ignore city patterns, they can drop by when they have a minute, when they feel like it.

He is tall, with a long pointy face, a crest of grey hair springing back from his forehead, a sunburnt complexion. Neat clothes – jeans and a pale grey shirt, a grey anorak.

He knocks on the glass. There is no choice but to open the patio door.

Cushy Butterfield was not the first woman to tell Fiona that she should try to get a boyfriend – not that anyone else was as direct as Cushy. Of course there was no such suggestion for a year or two after the departure of her husband. But then she felt there were certain hints, mentions of how so-and-so – other divorcees, widows – had 'met someone'. Conversations about dating websites. It was as if the subtle competitiveness of the teenage years, then the race of the twenties to get a husband, was being replayed all over again, even though she'd passed that exam years before: got a husband, children, a house, all those things you used to have to get to prove you were a proper grown-up woman. Those misogynistic terms, 'on the shelf', 'old maid', had gone out of parlance. But had the attitudes that went with them really gone away? Is a woman alone regarded as deficient in some way? She had signed up to the dating agency because Cushy had been so persuasive. But she had stayed with it for more than one reason.

She opens the door.

Now the sun has come out. There are jokes about the weather, here as in many other places. We have the four seasons in one day. But it was especially changeable this autumn. You had the four seasons in half an hour.

'I'm Declan.'

Is that Declan the plumber or Declan the electrician or Declan the serial killer?

'I chatted to you on Never Too Late.'

'Oh yes.'

'You're probably wondering how I got your address?'

There were no addresses or even second names on the

website. Or phone numbers. Some members used false names, and didn't even put up a photo – although the advice, from the people who run the site, was that this limited your chances of finding a match.

'A little bit of detective work.' He has an attractive grin.

His accent is vaguely local. She doesn't remember sending a smile or a message to anyone who came from around here.

'Do tell.'

Without being invited, he has edged himself inside, just inside the glass door. She considers leaving it open. Even if she does, will she be able to make a successful dash for it if he tries anything? There are two houses nearby but nobody is in them at the moment. People come at the weekend, sometimes. Not this weekend.

Then she remembers the other door, which he possibly hasn't seen – the back door. She could go to the bathroom, out there at the back, and escape through that door. If she could somehow get the car key without him noticing she could be gone before he'd realise. That is if he hasn't blocked the gateway with his car – the men who come to fix things usually do that, never considering that she might want to drive somewhere while they are at work. It was a thing she'd noticed, and sometimes wondered about.

'Aren't you going to ask me to sit down?'

'We could almost sit outside.'

Easier to escape, if they are outside.

'Nah. Too windy.' He closes the door behind him and sits on the sofa.

'So, how *did* you find out where I live?'

'I googled you.'

'But that doesn't give my address.'

'I found you on Facebook.' The grin again. 'There are lots of photos of the landscape. And even of the house. The name of the house is on Facebook, on the photo of the gate.'

'Rosamund's Bower'. A ridiculous name Fiona had found in a biography of some Irish writer of fairy tales who lived in St John's Wood in the early nineteenth century. She happened to be reading it when she bought this house. One of the first things she did when she moved was order a nameplate from the hardware store and get her son to fasten it to the gatepost.

'Would you like something to drink? A cup of tea?'

'I'd like a glass of wine, if you have any.'

'Of course ... You're driving?'

'Maybe.'

The house is open plan. The kitchen is at the other side of the living room, separated only by a low island. He can see her every move. Unless she can manage to go to the bathroom, she can't get away from him – to phone someone, to text someone, to phone the police. The police! In the town, fifteen kilometres away.

She goes down to the kitchen and takes two wine glasses from a cupboard.

'Red or white?'

This is mad.

'Is there anything to eat?'

'Well, of course. Are you hungry?'

'I wouldn't say no to a sandwich.'

'All right. I was going to eat something myself now.'

She goes to the fridge and has a look. There's some cold ham, Cheddar cheese. The remains of a stuffed roast chicken. There's also bread which she baked three days ago.

'There isn't a lot.'

'You don't have company? Nobody visiting?'

'No.'

What a stupid answer!

'You like living alone?'

'Well … sometimes. I have a lot of friends in the neighbourhood. People are always dropping in.'

Nobody has ever dropped in the two years she's been here. As she tells the lie, she sees her mobile phone, lying on the countertop. For once her bad habit of leaving things in the wrong places has paid dividends. And luck is with her. He takes his eye off her for a second, goes to the window to look out, so she manages to grab the phone and stick it in the pocket of her jeans. He turns to look at her. She looks at her hands and sort of shakes them in the air.

'I should wash my hands before I start making sandwiches! I've been gardening – they're filthy.'

She'd normally wash them at the sink. There's a bar of soap, and a towel hanging beside the tea towels.

'Gardening in the rain?'

'Yes. That's the only time I can dig the soil in my field. The only time it's soft enough.'

That much was true.

'What did you sow?'

'Bulbs. Daffodils for the spring. And some crocuses.'

'Lovely.' He smiles. He is quite good-looking, for his age, which must be somewhere between 63 and 72, unless he lies about his age on Never Too Late (some of them do, she suspects). She has noticed, on the website, that she usually chooses men according to their looks, even if the website algorithm prioritises religion.

'I love the spring flowers.'

'The bathroom's just here. I won't be a minute.'

He doesn't try to stop her.

In the little hall, she quietly opens the back door – it is really the front door, the entrance door to this house, which has a rather peculiar design. Yes, his car is parked right in

333

front of the gateway, blocking her car in. If she left, she'd have to make a run for it. But she could do that. She could leave and make her way down to the nearest inhabited house, which is about a ten-minute walk. She could hide in the ditch when he came running, or driving, after her. The road is lined with thick bushes, brambles, fuchsia, Japanese knot.

'So you have a door here too?'

He's right behind her.

'Yes.' She is trembling now. Why hadn't she just bolted straight away? Instead of standing there thinking. Hesitating.

'This is actually the main door, even though it seems to be at the back.' She's gabbling on. 'There used to be a bell but it hasn't worked since I … for ages.'

'You could get a knocker.'

Actually, that's not a bad idea.

'I could put it on for you.'

'Could you?'

'Of course. It's easy. You get one next time you're in town and call me and I'll come and stick it on.'

'The light is gone too. That one.'

She points at the lamp attached to the wall.

'I'll take a look at that later. It may be just the bulb.'

Maybe he is not a serial killer?

She shuts the door and indicates the bathroom.

'I'll be out in a second.'

In the mirror, she sees herself. Her hair with grey streaks – she hasn't been to the hairdressers for a month, she has been considering letting it go grey, or white, or whatever colour it really is under its many coats of fading dye. She's wearing an old blue jumper over a T-shirt and jeans. No make-up.

When she went on dates with other men from the website, she dressed not too up, not too down. She made herself up carefully, and ensured her hair was properly coloured. She had experienced the nervous preparing – the washing, the painting, the selection of just the right outfit – that she used to experience when she was a girl, getting ready to go out on a date with someone she was madly in love with, whose admiration and approval, whose love and adoration, she longed for. In years and years of marriage she had forgotten that feeling. Not that she hadn't dressed up and done her hair and make-up, tried to look her best. But there was no nervousness involved, no excitement. Nothing at stake, unless you counted the admiration of friends, the eternal competition between the women in the looks department. 'She's looking great!' 'She's lost a bit of weight!' 'What a fabulous frock!' That was something you could take or leave; it was nice, but it was like a boring gift. Like a scented candle, or a bunch of chrysanthemums. Not like first-class honours or the lottery. So the excitement of the challenge she had felt before those few dates with unknown men had come as a real surprise. It was not unpleasant although it was very stressful. She doubted if she could ever fall in love with any of them. And yet, apparently, their endorsement, their approval, mattered.

She texts a friend. In Dublin. From the bathroom. 'I have had a visit from a strange man. He's probably okay. Ring me in an hour. If you don't get an answer, call the police.'

In an hour? By then she could be a corpse in the boot of his car (it's big, a four-wheel drive). Then she washes her hands, brushes her hair, and puts on foundation, lipstick and eyebrow pencil.

He is sitting on her chair, under the lamp, sipping his wine and gazing out at the sea, when she returns. She puts all the food on the table. The roast chicken and the cooked ham and the cheese. The bread and coleslaw and butter. The bottle of wine.

'Let's eat.'

'Thank you; it looks delicious! Maybe we can go for a walk afterwards, if the weather keeps up.'

'I'd like that,' she says.

Her grandchildren visited her here for a long weekend, with their parents of course, about a month ago. It had been ages since their last visit and Fiona was delighted that they had come. She did everything to make it a memorable adventure – got new toys, hid a leprechaun (plastic, hideous) in the long grass. Made good food and brought them on picnics. Told stories.

Since the eldest, Ellie, was six months old, Fiona has been telling her the story of Red Riding Hood, and many others. She told Red Riding Hood most often because Ellie had a lovely Red Riding Hood doll, that you could turn inside out and upside down, that could be a granny, or a wolf, or Red Riding Hood herself. Fiona always told the traditional story that ends with the wolf being slit open by the woodcutter, and the granny climbing out of his stomach.

But this time, Ellie wanted a different version. (She used the word 'version'.) 'Tell me the version that's not scary,' she said.

'What happens in that?' Fiona asked.

'The wolf doesn't eat the grandmother.'

So Fiona told her. At the end of the tale, the wolf and the grandmother and Red Riding Hood all sat down at the kitchen table and ate the stuff from the basket.

'Is that it?' Fiona asked, when she'd finished.

What was the point? Where was the story? And who had put such ideas into Ellie's head? That's what Fiona thought. It is not a proper story. No tension. No fear. No loss. No relief.

The key thing is missing.

But Ellie had nodded, apparently perfectly satisfied with what she had heard.